William Madison Randall Library

Donated in Loving Memory by Stephen K. and Jo Whalen

From the Collection of

James K. and Helen M. Whalen of Cuyahoga Falls, Ohio

2003

D1068728

THE BEST OF FRITZ LEIBER

The Best of Fritz Leiber

by FRITZ LEIBER

With a special introduction by
POUL ANDERSON

NELSON DOUBLEDAY, Inc.
Garden City, New York

COPYRIGHT © 1974 BY FRITZ LEIBER

All Rights Reserved

Published by arrangement with
Ballantine Books
Division of Random House, Inc.
201 East 50th Street
New York, NY 10022

Printed in the United States of America

PS
3523
.E 4583
B47
1974
c. 2

CONTENTS

The Wizard of Nehwon

WHEN I was first asked to write an introduction to a volume of Fritz
Leiber stories—the most important of such collections at that—my
reaction was inappropriately inelegant: "Huh?" I still think it had a
fundamental rightness. How can anybody properly comment on the
work of one who is not only his senior in the profession by a good
many years, but is universally acknowledged to be among its three or
four all-time titans?

Yet this was an honor I could not decline. It was like being in a
physics department back around 1935 and invited to introduce a
series of guest lectures by Einstein. A person in that position realizes
the audience hasn't come to hear, or read, him. But he'll try to avoid
boring platitudes. If he's lucky, he'll even convey a slight extra insight, which will help that audience appreciate the visitor and what
he'll say a little bit more than they might otherwise have done. Maybe
I'll luck out.

Let's first make a few remarks about the man himself, before going on to his writing. They will be only a few—despite the keyhole
school of criticism, the facts of a creator's life are not required for an
understanding of his or her work; or if they are, then that person has
to that extent failed as an artist. Fritz Leiber does employ a certain
amount of autobiography in his work, perhaps more than any other
maker of science fiction or fantasy. But he's far too skillful for you
to need to know what the personal element is. Besides, he lets you in

on some of it himself, for your pleasure, in his afterword to the present volume.

And I can't claim deep knowledge of him in any event. We have been friends for a long time, guests in each other's homes, and so on; but until recently, geographical separation prevented frequent encounters, and we never happened to strike up one of his extended correspondences which have delighted a number of people. Therefore, a mere scattering of reminiscences and data:

I first met Fritz Leiber at the 1949 world science fiction convention in Cincinnati. The author of such cornerstone tales as *Gather, Darkness!* and *Conjure Wife* seemed even more awe-inspiring in person, towering, classically handsome, altogether theatrical. The last of these qualities was not deliberate—rather, he was conventionally clad and soft-spoken—but he couldn't help it; personality will come through. He talked to me, a beginner with half a dozen stories in print, as graciously as he did to the biggest-name writer or editor present, or the humblest fan. Here "graciously" is used in an exact sense which is best defined by an example.

From time to time we are all afflicted with bores or boors. Some of us give them the brutal brush-off; most of us suffer them for a short while, then escape on a mumbled excuse. Fritz Leiber has repeatedly been seen to *listen* to such characters, *respond* to them, actively, sympathetically, and patiently enough that they never suspect the toleration. He cannot have an enemy in the world; instead, there is a worldful of people who all hope to be worthy of his friendship.

It is etymologically wrong but psychologically right to define a gentleman as one who is gentle, yet very much a man. Leiber has been a championship fencer and a chess player rated "expert." To see and hear him recite Chesterton's bravura "Lepanto" is an unforgettable experience. And, of course, in his writing he has stared down—or laughed down—death, horror, human absurdity, with guts worthy of a Jeffers, Kafka, or Cervantes.

Born in Chicago near the end of 1910, his father a famous Shakespearean actor for whom Fritz was named, he grew up in the atmosphere of the stage, which doubtless has a great deal to do with the highly visual and dramatic quality of his work. But he took his degree in psychology, which also shows. Variously a lay preacher, actor, college teacher of drama, and staff writer for an encyclopedia, he tried free-lancing sporadically. His first published story appeared in 1939, in that lustrous and mourned magazine *Unknown*. During World War II he reached a painful decision—that the struggle against fascism was more important than the pacifist convictions which he had long held, and still does—and he accepted a job in aircraft production. Afterward, he was on the staff of *Science Digest* for a dozen years. During all this time he acquired a wife and son and, between dry spells which readers regretted, wrote a lot of the best science fiction and fantasy in the business. Eventually he moved from Chicago to southern California and started writing full time. Since his wife's death (everybody who knew her misses Jonquil) he has lived in San Francisco.

So now Fritz Leiber is in his sixties, an age when most artists have either retired or are sterilely repeating themselves. The years show on him a bit—but not too much, and only physically. Inside, while possessing all the wisdom of a lifetime, he's younger than the average man of thirty. To give a small personal illustration: not long ago, in his rambles around his newly adopted city, he discovered a walking tour that will take you to every place where action occurs in Dashiell Hammett's *The Maltese Falcon*. Or . . . recently my wife gave an elaborate dinner to honor the memory of E. R. Eddison, upon the date of Lessingham's translation into Zimiamvia. Only those who would understand what that means were invited, and they were expected to come in costume. Fritz graced the party as the oldest, most sharply humorous, and best-dressed man present.

If anything, he keeps growing younger, more actively creative. His past unproductive periods seem to have been times during which, consciously or unconsciously, he was preparing himself to strike out in a different direction. The results were always surprising and consequential. Though ever aware of and sensitive to the great issues of the real world around him, he has never been a merely "relevant" writer. Instead, he has always been in the forefront in both themes and treatment. In these past several years we have been witnessing a new burst of pioneering, which looks as if it will continue while he lives. That makes especially appropriate the book, both retrospective and contemporary, which you are holding. And it brings up our real subject, Fritz Leiber's achievement.

I do not propose to offer you a critique. For one thing, while mildly disagreeing with a few of her judgments, I couldn't better the one by Judith Merril.* Besides, I lay no claim to being a critic, simply a working writer.

To be sure, that distinction is far from absolute. Thus Merril published excellent fiction in earlier days, while Leiber has done a certain amount of criticism. The question to consider is where the emphasis of a life—in this case Leiber's—has lain—or, at least, what an essayist is trying to do. I'll say little about the stories in this volume. They speak for themselves; moreover, you have the author's own notes. Rather, I'd like to consider in a very informal fashion, and from the viewpoint of a fellow practitioner, some of those items which are not on hand. You who already know them may enjoy a revival of memories. You who don't may get a better idea of Leiber's accomplishment and, I hope, will be led to read further.

It's too bad that we have no tale of Fafhrd and the Gray Mouser here. Not only did that charming pair of rogues—the tall Northern barbarian and the small city-bred trickster—launch the author's career; they are still going strong, to the joy of everybody who appreciates a rattling good fantasy adventure. But by no means are these stories conventional "sword and sorcery." The world of Nehwon is made real in wondrously imaginative detail, its human aspects as true as in any conscientious job of reporting. To visit the city of Lankhmar is to learn what decadence in fact means; to roam with our vulnerable vagabonds is to experience pity and terror as well as suspense, wry humor, and uproarious hilarity. Here Leiber in his way—like the late J. R. R. Tolkien in his, and not vastly different—has done, and is doing, for the heroic fantasy what Robert Louis Stevenson did for the pirate yarn: by originality and sheer writing genius, he revived an ossified genre and started it off on a fresh path.

I could likewise wish that this book held a sample or two of Leiber's horror stories. In my opinion, which Fritz modestly does not share, Lovecraft and Poe himself never dealt out comparable chills. The typical Leiber frightener gains tremendous power by its economy,

* In *The Magazine of Fantasy and Science Fiction* for July 1969, a special issue honoring Fritz Leiber. Previously, in November 1959, *Fantastic* had run an all-Leiber issue. These, and the awards voted him, indicate the esteem in which his work is held by those who know the field.

its evocative contemporary setting, and its bleak brilliance of concept—like "Smoke Ghost," to name a single tale, whose phantom is in and of the corrupted air pervading a modern industrial city.

And you would have enjoyed "The Sixty-Four-Square Madhouse" and/or "The Moriarty Gambit," both masterly chess stories, the latter also a grand Sherlock Holmes pastiche. Well, look them up. All the omissions I have mentioned are not the fault of author or editor, but merely due to lack of space. They would have crowded out equally vivid pieces that you do find here.

The novels were inevitably excluded. But any discussion of Leiber's work, or of science fantasy as a whole, must consider them. They are few in number, but each is unique and, with two exceptions, of major significance in the development of present-day imaginative literature.

The first exception is *Tarzan and the City of Gold,* "only" a delightful continuation of Burroughs. Come to think of it, though, a scholar of English letters would find it most interesting to trace out how Leiber managed to convey the flavor of his model while avoiding all its crudities, outdoing Burroughs in every way that counts, and throwing occasional philosophical and moral issues into the bargain. Does anybody need material for a master's thesis?

Doubtless many will argue with my assertion that *The Green Millennium* is not a landmark. It is, in the sense of being a fine book, highly recommended. But it carries further the world of "Coming Attraction" and "Poor Superman," both in the present collection, and thus does not break new ground—by Leiber's standards—however inventive and often astoundingly witty it is. All the rest of us, from Heinlein on down, would rank it among our own best, had we written it.

Heinlein offers a natural starting point for a few words about *Gather, Darkness!,* that prototype of the interplay of ideas which has always given vitality to science fiction. In 1940 appeared his serial *If This Goes On—,* wherein the United States has fallen under a totalitarian regime posing as the church of a new faith and using technological devices to work suitably impressive "miracles." A year later, under his pseudonym "Anson MacDonald," he brought forth *Sixth Column.* There, the United States has been invaded and occupied by a foreign power which allows the people freedom of religion but of nothing else. A small underground takes advantage of secret scientific knowledge—gathered just before the collapse, so that it was never brought to bear in the war—to give the priests of a stalking-horse faith similar capabilities.

Heinlein stopped with those two books, but Leiber saw that the theme was still full of potential. Suppose such a church came to power, then never stepped down again and never was overthrown for centuries. In *Gather, Darkness!* it has built a neo-medieval world of ignorant commoners dominated by a hierarchy that really can invoke "supernatural" sanctions in the name of its God. A liberation movement finally does start. But in this environment it calls itself "witchcraft" and claims to serve the Devil! There are many magnificently funny details (e.g., since the priesthood rides around in aircraft built to look like angels, the aircraft of the opposition are bat-winged and horned) but the story isn't simply a romp. Its account of brainwashing by chemical and electronic means is fast becoming a foul reality.

Gather, Darkness! was followed by a swarm of dull imitations. But surely, in due course, it partly inspired Philip José Farmer's seminal work *The Lovers*. That's what I mean by a landmark work.

I wonder how Women's Lib would react to a reissue of the fantasy novel from this period, *Conjure Wife*, with its assumption that all women are witches but they don't tell their men. Probably there'd be general pleasure. It was popular enough to get two filmed versions; and I know several ladies in the movement who still love the original story. As often elsewhere, Leiber doubled his strength by combining dazzling imagination with unsparing realism. The principal setting is a small college community, and I have since observed for myself how vicious the infighting can get in such a place. By the way, the hero, Norman Saylor, reappears in this collection. Leiber likes to interconnect tales whenever possible.

Likewise, several of Leiber's stories are part of a series incorporating the many-branched time-lines whose origins were described in the short novel *Destiny Times Three*. Ranging from a placid utopia through a cruel dictatorship to a freezing ruin of an Earth—and beyond—this novel is more than a fast-paced chase story; it is a vatic study of power over nature and over man, so easy to misuse and so nearly impossible to use rightly.

Similarly, Leiber wrote a number of stories in what has come to be known as the Change-War cycles—this series has rather overshadowed the one mentioned above. A couple of the Change-War stories are reprinted here. The heart of the cycle is in another novel, *The Big Time*. Few comparable tours de force exist anywhere in literature. The action takes place continuously in a single setting, a station outside the cosmos to which half-crazed soldiers from all time and space are sent for a little rest and recreation. Beneath the flamboyancies, tension racks up notch by notch toward a breaking-point climax followed by an ironic dénouement. It's fantastically good theater—literally. How I wish to see it staged!

Being such a virtuoso performance, *The Big Time* doesn't seem to have had any followers. I admit to keeping it in mind while writing my own *A Midsummer Tempest*, but cannot claim that that employs the dramatic unities as the former book did. Evidently nobody in our field can match Fritz Leiber here.

He went on to a different technique, the out-and-out satirical, in *The Silver Eggheads*. This account of an ultra-mechanized future lacks the misanthropy of a Swift but bites just as hard. I really think its blend of sardonicism, earthy (even slapstick) mirth, and underlying compassion is best likened to Aristophanes. For instance, consider what might be done with pseudo-female robots—

"Can you imagine, Flaxy, having it with a girl who is all velvet or plush, or who really goes all hot and cold, or who can softly sing you a full-orchestra symphony while you're doing it or maybe Ravel's *Bolero,* or who has slightly—not excessively —prehensile breasts or various refreshingly electric skin areas, or who has some of the features—not overdone, of course—of a cat or a vampire or an octopus, or who has hair like Medusa's or Shambleau's that lives and caresses you, or who has four arms like Siva, or a prehensile tail eight feet long, or . . . and at the same time is perfectly safe and can't bother or involve or infect or dominate you in any way?"

—consider this machinery, and when you are done laughing, consider the latest issue of *Playboy*.

A slightly similar minor motif occurs in *The Wanderer*. This novel concerns the effects on a large and varied cast of characters of a mobile planet coming near Earth. All kinds of things happen, all fascinating. But I have a reason for singling out the relationship, which eventually becomes erotic, between the human Paul and the highly evolved, feline-like Tigerishka. Leiber flinches no more from the fact that we are sexual beings than he does from the fact that we are limited, usually ridiculous, and ultimately mortal. This quotation will at least give you some extra words of his:

> After a space he came slowly floating up out of the infinite softness of that bottomless black bed, and there were the stars again, and Tigerishka lifted up a little above him so that very faintly, by starlight, he saw the violet of her petaled irises and the bronzy green of her cheeks and her mulberry lips parted, careless that she showed her whitely-glinting fangs, and she recited:
>
>> "Poor little ape, you're sick again tonight.
>> Has the shrill, fretful chatter fevered you?
>> Was it a dream-lion gave you such a fright?
>> And did the serpent Fear glide from the slough?
>> You cough, you moan, I hear your small teeth grate.
>> What are those words you mutter as you toss?
>> War, torture, guilt, revenge, crime, murder, hate?
>> I'll stroke your brow, poor little ape—you're cross.
>> Far wiser beings under far older stars
>> Have had your sickness, seen their hopes denied,
>> Sought God, fought Fate, pounded against the bars,
>> And like you, little ape, they some day died.
>> The bough swings in the wind, the night is deep.
>> Look at the stars, poor little ape, and sleep."
>
> "Tigerishka," Paul wondered with a sleepy puzzlement, "I started to write that sonnet years ago, but I could get only three lines. Did you—"
>
> "No," she said softly, "you finished it by yourself. I found it, lying there in the dark behind your eyes, tossed in a corner. Rest now, Paul. Rest. . . ."

To be thus aware of mortality, and of the ancient deeps within us while we live, is not morbid but mature. Leiber can even laugh with them—not at them, which is an evasion, but with them. He does so in

A Specter Is Haunting Texas. The satire there is more stark than in *The Silver Eggheads,* more reminiscent of Huxley or Heine though with a strong dash of . . . shall we say Buster Keaton? The hero, born and reared on the Moon, has in its low gravity grown up excessively tall and thin. Forced to visit Earth, he must wear a skeleton-like supportive framework which, with his black garb, makes him Death discarnate to the inhabitants of a crazy-quilt of nations formed after a nuclear war. One of his loves is equally a Death figure, the other Flesh itself. Needless to say, the author never puts it this crudely or obviously, and the overtones are infinite. Perhaps no other modern writers except James Branch Cabell and Vladimir Nabokov have gotten such fun out of the human tragicomedy; and they, for all their wit, have never had Leiber's uninhibited gusto.

Let us hope for much more from this man, in whatever vein he may next select. Meanwhile, the volume in your hands gives a good overview. If you are already familiar with Fritz Leiber, you know you have a treat in store. If it will be your first encounter with him, I envy you.

—POUL ANDERSON

THE BEST OF FRITZ LEIBER

Gonna Roll The Bones

SUDDENLY Joe Slattermill knew for sure he'd have to get out quick
or else blow his top and knock out with the shrapnel of his skull the
props and patches holding up his decaying home, that was like a
house of big wooden and plaster and wallpaper cards except for the
huge fireplace and ovens and chimney across the kitchen from him.

Those were stone-solid enough, though. The fireplace was chin-
high, at least twice that long, and filled from end to end with roaring
flames. Above were the square doors of the ovens in a row—his
Wife baked for part of their living. Above the ovens was the wall-
long mantelpiece, too high for his Mother to reach or Mr. Guts to
jump any more, set with all sorts of ancestral curios, but any of them
that weren't stone or glass or china had been so dried and darkened
by decades of heat that they looked like nothing but shrunken human
heads and black golf balls. At one end were clustered his Wife's
square gin bottles. Above the mantelpiece hung one old chromo, so
high and so darkened by soot and grease that you couldn't tell whether
the swirls and fat cigar shape were a whaleback steamer ploughing through a hurricane or a spaceship plunging through a storm of
light-driven dust motes.

As soon as Joe curled his toes inside his boots, his Mother knew
what he was up to. "Going bumming," she mumbled with conviction.
"Pants pockets full of cartwheels of house money, too, to spend on
sin." And she went back to munching the long shreds she stripped

fumblingly with her right hand off the turkey carcass set close to the terrible heat, her left hand ready to fend off Mr. Guts, who stared at her yellow-eyed, gaunt-flanked, with long mangy tail a-twitch. In her dirty dress, streaky as the turkey's sides, Joe's Mother looked like a bent brown bag and her fingers were lumpy twigs.

Joe's Wife knew as soon or sooner, for she smiled thin-eyed at him over her shoulder from where she towered at the centermost oven. Before she closed its door, Joe glimpsed that she was baking two long, flat, narrow, fluted loaves and one high, round-domed one. She was thin as death and disease in her violet wrapper. Without looking, she reached out a yard-long, skinny arm for the nearest gin bottle and downed a warm slug and smiled again. And without a word spoken, Joe knew she'd said, "You're going out and gamble and get drunk and lay a floozy and come home and beat me and go to jail for it," and he had a flash of the last time he'd been in the dark gritty cell and she'd come by moonlight, which showed the green and yellow lumps on her narrow skull where he'd hit her, to whisper to him through the tiny window in the back and slip him a half pint through the bars.

And Joe knew for certain that this time it would be that bad and worse, but just the same he heaved up himself and his heavy, muf-fledly clanking pockets and shuffled straight to the door, muttering, "Guess I'll roll the bones, up the pike a stretch and back," swinging his bent, knobbly-elbowed arms like paddlewheels to make a little joke about his words.

When he'd stepped outside, he held the door open a hand's breadth behind him for several seconds. When he finally closed it, a feeling of deep misery struck him. Earlier years, Mr. Guts would have come streaking along to seek fights and females on the roofs and fences, but now the big tom was content to stay home and hiss by the fire and snatch for turkey and dodge a broom, quarrelling and comforting with two house-bound women. Nothing had followed Joe to the door but his Mother's chomping and her gasping breaths and the clink of the gin bottle going back on the mantel and the creaking of the floor boards under his feet.

The night was up-side-down deep among the frosty stars. A few of them seemed to move, like the white-hot jets of spaceships. Down below it looked as if the whole town of Ironmine had blown or buttoned out the light and gone to sleep, leaving the streets and spaces to the equally unseen breezes and ghosts. But Joe was still in the hemisphere of the musty dry odour of the worm-eaten carpentry behind him, and as he felt and heard the dry grass of the lawn brush his calves, it occurred to him that something deep down inside him had for years been planning things so that he and the House and his Wife and Mother and Mr. Guts would all come to an end together. Why the kitchen heat hadn't touched off the tindery place ages ago was a physical miracle.

Hunching his shoulders, Joe stepped out, not up the pike, but down the dirt road that led past Cypress Hollow Cemetery to Night Town.

The breezes were gentle, but unusually restless and variable tonight, like leprechaun squalls. Beyond the drunken, whitewashed cemetery fence dim in the starlight, they rustled the scraggly trees of Cypress Hollow and made it seem they were stroking their beards of Spanish moss. Joe sensed that the ghosts were just as restless as the breezes, uncertain where and whom to haunt, or whether to take the night off, drifting together in sorrowfully lecherous companionship. While among the trees the red-green vampire lights pulsed faintly and irregularly, like sick fireflies or a plague-stricken space fleet. The feeling of deep misery stuck with Joe and deepened and he was tempted to turn aside and curl up in any convenient tomb or around some half-toppled head board and cheat his Wife and the other two behind him out of a shared doom. He thought: Gonna roll the bones, gonna roll 'em up and go to sleep. But while he was deciding, he got past the sagged-open gate and the rest of the delirious fence and Shantyville too.

At first Night Town seemed dead as the rest of Ironmine, but then he noticed a faint glow, sick as the vampire lights but more feverish, and with it a jumping music, tiny at first as a jazz for jitterbugging ants. He stepped along the springy sidewalk, wistfully remembering the days when the spring was all in his own legs and he'd bound into a fight like a bobcat or a Martian sand-spider. God, it had been years now since he had fought a real fight, or felt *the power*. Gradually the midget music got raucous as a bunny-hug for grizzly bears and loud as a polka for elephants, while the glow became a riot of gas flares and flambeaux and corpse-blue mercury tubes and jiggling pink neon ones that all jeered at the stars where the spaceships roved. Next thing, he was facing a three-storey false front flaring everywhere like a devil's elbow, with a pale blue topping of St. Elmo's fire. There were wide swinging doors in the center of it, spilling light above and below. Above the doorway, golden calcium light scrawled over and over again, with wild curlicues and flourishes, "The Boneyard," while a fiendish red kept printing out, "Gambling."

So the new place they'd all been talking about for so long had opened at last! For the first time that night, Joe Slattermill felt a stirring of real life in him and the faintest caress of excitement.

Gonna roll the bones, he thought.

He dusted off his blue-green work clothes with big, careless swipes and slapped his pockets to hear the clank. Then he threw back his shoulders and grinned his lips sneeringly and pushed through the swinging doors as if giving a foe the straight-armed heel of his palm.

Inside, The Boneyard seemed to cover the area of a township and the bar looked as long as the railroad tracks. Round pools of light on the green poker tables alternated with hourglass shapes of exciting gloom, through which drink girls and change-girls moved like white-legged witches. By the jazz-stand in the distance, belly dancers made *their* white hourglass shapes. The gamblers were thick and hunched down as mushrooms, all bald from agonizing over the fall of a card or a die or the dive of an ivory ball, while the Scarlet Women were like fields of poinsettia.

The calls of the croupiers and the slaps of dealt cards were as softly yet fatefully staccato as the rustle and beat of the jazz drums. Every tight-locked atom of the place was controlledly jumping. Even the dust motes jiggled tensely in the cones of light.

Joe's excitement climbed and he felt sift through him, like a breeze that heralds a gale, the faintest breath of a confidence which he knew could become a tornado. All thoughts of his House and Wife and Mother dropped out of his mind, while Mr. Guts remained only as a crazy young tom walking stiff-legged around the rim of his consciousness. Joe's own leg muscles twitched in sympathy and he felt them grow supplely strong.

He coolly and searchingly looked the place over, his hand going out like it didn't belong to him to separate a drink from a passing, gently bobbing tray. Finally his gaze settled on what he judged to be the Number One Crap Table. All the Big Mushrooms seemed to be there, bald as the rest but standing tall as toadstools. Then through a gap in them Joe saw on the other side of the table a figure still taller, but dressed in a long dark coat with collar turned up and a dark slouch hat pulled low, so that only a triangle of white face showed. A suspicion and a hope rose in Joe and he headed straight for the gap in the Big Mushrooms.

As he got nearer, the white-legged and shiny-topped drifters eddying out of his way, his suspicion received confirmation after confirmation and his hope budded and swelled. Back from one end of the table was the fattest man he'd ever seen, with a long cigar and a silver vest and a gold tie clasp at least eight inches wide that just said in thick script, "Mr. Bones." Back a little from the other end was the nakedest change-girl yet and the only one he'd seen whose tray, slung from her bare shoulders, and indenting her belly just below her breasts, was stacked with gold in gleaming little towers and with jet-black chips. While the dice-girl, skinnier and taller and longer armed than his Wife even, didn't seem to be wearing much but a pair of long white gloves. She was all right if you went for the type that isn't much more than pale skin over bones with breasts like china doorknobs.

Beside each gambler was a high round table for his chips. The one by the gap was empty. Snapping his fingers at the nearest silver change-girl, Joe traded all his greasy dollars for an equal number of pale chips and tweaked her left nipple for luck. She playfully snapped her teeth towards his fingers.

Not hurrying but not wasting any time, he advanced and carelessly dropped his modest stacks on the empty table and took his place in the gap. He noted that the second Big Mushroom on his right had the dice. His heart but no other part of him gave an extra jump. Then he steadily lifted his eyes and looked straight across the table.

The coat was a shimmering elegant pillar of black satin with jet buttons, the upturned collar of fine dull plush black as the darkest cellar, as was the slouch hat with down-turned brim and a band of only a thin braid of black horse-hair. The arms of the coat were long, lesser satin pillars, ending in slim, longfingered hands that moved swiftly when they did, but held each position of rest with a statue's poise.

Joe still couldn't see much of the face except for smooth lower forehead with never a bead or trickle of sweat—the eyebrows were like straight snippets of the hat's braid—and gaunt aristocratic cheeks and narrow but somewhat flat nose. The complexion of the face wasn't as white as Joe had first judged. There was a faint touch of brown in it, like ivory that's just begun to age, or Venusian soapstone. Another glance at the hands confirmed this.

Behind the man in black was a knot of just about the flashiest and nastiest customers, male or female, Joe had ever seen. He knew from one look that each bediamonded, pomaded bully had a belly gun beneath the flap of his flowered vest and a blackjack in his hip pocket, and each snake-eyed sporting girl a stiletto in her garter and a pearl-handled silver-plated derringer under the sequinned silk in the hollow between her jutting breasts.

Yet at the same time Joe knew they were just trimmings. It was the man in black, their master, who was the deadly one, the kind of man you knew at a glance you couldn't touch and live. If without asking you merely laid a finger on his sleeve, no matter how lightly and respectfully, an ivory hand would move faster than thought and you'd be stabbed or shot. Or maybe just the touch would kill you, as if every black article of his clothing were charged from his ivory skin outwards with a high-voltage, high-amperage ivory electricity. Joe looked at the shadowed face again and decided he wouldn't care to try it.

For it was the eyes that were the most impressive feature. All great gamblers have dark-shadowed deep-set eyes. But this one's eyes were sunk so deep you couldn't even be sure you were getting a gleam of them. They were inscrutability incarnate. They were unfathomable. They were like black holes.

But all this didn't disappoint Joe one bit, though it did terrify him considerably. On the contrary, it made him exult. His first suspicion was completely confirmed and his hope spread into full flower.

This must be one of those really big gamblers who hit Ironmine only once a decade at most, come from the Big City on one of the river boats that ranged the watery dark like luxurious comets, spouting long thick tails of sparks from their sequoia-tall stacks with top foliage of curvy-snipped sheet iron. Or like silver space-liners with dozens of jewel-flamed jets, their portholes atwinkle like ranks of marshalled asteroids.

For that matter, maybe some of those really big gamblers actually came from other planets where the nighttime pace was hotter and the sporting life a delirium of risk and delight.

Yes, this was the kind of man Joe had always yearned to pit his skill against. He felt *the power* begin to tingle in his rock-still fingers, just a little.

Joe lowered his gaze to the crap table. It was almost as wide as a man is tall, at least twice as long, unusually deep, and lined with black, not green, felt, so that it looked like a giant's coffin. There was something familiar about its shape which he couldn't place. Its bottom, though not its sides or ends, had a twinkling iridescence, as if it had been lightly sprinkled with very tiny diamonds. As Joe lowered his gaze all the way and looked directly down, his eyes barely over the table, he got the crazy notion that it went down all the way through the world, so that the diamonds were the stars on the other side, visible despite the sunlight there, just as Joe was always able to see the stars by day up the shaft of the mine he worked in, and so that if a cleaned-out gambler, dizzy with defeat, toppled forward into it, he'd fall forever, towards the bottom-most bottom, be it Hell or some black galaxy. Joe's thoughts swirled and he felt the cold, hard-fingered clutch of fear at his crotch. Someone was crooning beside him, "Come on, Big Dick."

Then the dice, which had meanwhile passed to the Big Mushroom immediately on his right, came to rest near the table's center, contradicting and wiping out Joe's vision. But instantly there was another oddity to absorb him. The Ivory dice were large and unusually round-cornered with dark red spots that gleamed like real rubies, but the spots were arranged in such a way that each face looked like a miniature skull. For instance, the seven thrown just now, by which the Big Mushroom to his right had lost his point, which had been ten, consisted of a two with the spots evenly spaced towards one side, like eyes, instead of towards opposite corners, and of a five with the same red eyespots but a central red nose and two spots close together below that to make teeth.

The long, skinny, white-gloved arm of the dice-girl snaked out like an albino cobra and scooped up the dice and whisked them on to the rim of the table right in front of Joe. He inhaled silently, picked up a single chip from his table and started to lay it beside the dice, then realized that wasn't the way things were done here, and put it back. He would have liked to examine the chip more closely, though. It was curiously lightweight and pale tan, about the colour of cream with a shot of coffee in it, and it had embossed on its surface a symbol he could feel, though not see. He didn't know what the symbol was, that would have taken more feeling. Yet its touch had been very good, setting the power tingling full blast in his shooting hand.

Joe looked casually yet swiftly at the faces around the table, not missing the Big Gambler across from him, and said quietly, "Roll a penny," meaning of course one pale chip, or a dollar.

There was a hiss of indignation from all the Big Mushrooms and the moonface of big-bellied Mr. Bones grew purple as he started forward to summon his bouncers.

The Big Gambler raised a black-satined forearm and sculptured hand, palm down. Instantly Mr. Bones froze and the hissing stopped faster than that of a meteor prick in self-sealing space steel. Then in a whispery, cultured voice, without the faintest hint of derision, the man in black said, "Get on him, gamblers."

Here, Joe thought, was a final confirmation of his suspicion, had it been needed. The really great gamblers were always perfect gentlemen and generous to the poor.

With only the tiny, respectful hint of a guffaw, one of the Big Mushrooms called to Joe, "You're faded."

Joe picked up the ruby-featured dice.

Now ever since he had first caught two eggs on one plate, won all the marbles in Ironmine, and juggled six alphabet blocks so they finally fell in a row on the rug spelling "Mother," Joe Slattermill had been almost incredibly deft at precision throwing. In the mine he could carom a rock off a wall of ore to crack a rat's skull fifty feet away in the dark and he sometimes amused himself by tossing little fragments of rock back into the holes from which they had fallen, so that they stuck there, perfectly fitted in, for at least a second. Sometimes, by fast tossing, he could fit seven or eight fragments into the hole from which they had fallen, like putting together a puzzle block.

If he could ever have got into space, Joe would undoubtedly have been able to pilot six Moon-skimmers at once and do figure eights through Saturn's rings blindfolded.

Now the only real difference between precision-tossing rocks or alphabet blocks and dice is that you have to bounce the latter off the end wall of a crap table, and that just made it a more interesting test of skill for Joe.

Rattling the dice now, he felt the power in his fingers and palm as never before.

He made a swift low roll, so that the bones ended up exactly in front of the white-gloved dice-girl. His natural seven was made up, as he'd intended, of a four and a three. In red-spot features they were like the five, except that both had only one tooth and the three no nose. Sort of baby-faced skulls. He had won a penny—that is, a dollar.

"Roll two cents," said Joe Slattermill.

This time, for variety, he made his natural with an eleven. The six was like the five, except it had three teeth, the bestlooking skull of the lot.

"Roll a nickel less one."

Two Big Mushrooms divided that bet with a covert smirk at each other.

Now Joe rolled a three and an ace. His point was four. The ace, with its single spot off center towards a side, still somehow looked like a skull—maybe of a Lilliputian Cyclops.

He took a while making his point, once absent-mindedly rolling three successive tens the hard way. He wanted to watch the dice-girl scoop up the cubes. Each time it seemed to him that her snake-swift fingers went under the dice while they were still flat on the felt. Finally he decided it couldn't be an illusion. Although the dice couldn't penetrate the felt, her white-gloved fingers somehow could, dipping in a flash through the black, diamond-sparkling material as if it weren't there.

Right away the thought of a crap-table-size hole through the earth came back to Joe. This would mean that the dice were rolling and lying on a perfectly transparent flat surface, impenetrable for them but nothing else. Or maybe it was only the dice-girl's hands that could penetrate the surface, which would turn into a mere fantasy Joe's earlier vision of a cleaned-out gambler taking the Big Dive down that dreadful shaft, which made the deepest mine a mere pin dent.

Joe decided he had to know which was true. Unless absolutely unavoidable, he didn't want to take the chance of being troubled by vertigo at some crucial stage of the game.

He made a few more meaningless throws, from time to time crooning for realism, "Come on, Little Joe." Finally he settled on his plan. When he did at last make his point—the hard way, with two twos— he caromed the dice off the far corner so that they landed exactly in front of him. Then, after a minimum pause for his throw to be seen by the table, he shot his left hand down under the cubes, just a flicker ahead of the dice-girl's strike, and snatched them up.

Wow! Joe had never had a harder time in his life making his face and manner conceal what his body felt, not even when the wasp had stung him on the neck just as he had been for the first time putting his hand under the skirt of his prudish, fickle, demanding Wife-to-be. His fingers and the back of his hand were in as much agony as if he'd stuck them into a blast furnace. No wonder the dice-girl wore white gloves. They must be asbestos. And a good thing he hadn't used his shooting hand, he thought as he ruefully watched the blisters rise.

He remembered he'd been taught in school what Twenty-Mile Mine also demonstrated: that the earth was fearfully hot under its crust. The crap-table-size hole must pipe up that heat, so that any gambler taking the Big Dive would fry before he'd fallen a furlong and come out less than a cinder in China.

As if his blistered hand weren't bad enough, the Big Mushrooms were all hissing at him again and Mr. Bones had purpled once more and was opening his melon-size mouth to shout for his bouncers.

Once again a lift of the Big Gambler's hand saved Joe. The whispery, gentle voice called, "Tell him, Mr. Bones."

The latter roared towards Joe, "No gambler may pick up the dice he or any other gambler has shot. Only my dice-girl may do that. Rule of the house!"

Joe snapped Mr. Bones the barest nod. He said coolly, "Rolling a dime less two," and when that still peewee bet was covered, he shot Phoebe for his point and then fooled around for quite a while, throwing anything but a five or a seven, until the throbbing in his left hand should fade and all his nerves feel rock-solid again. There had never been the slightest alteration in the power in his right hand; he felt that strong as ever, or stronger.

Midway of this interlude, the Big Gambler bowed slightly but respectfully towards Joe, hooding those unfathomable eye sockets, before turning around to take a long black cigarette from his prettiest and evilest-looking sporting girl. Courtesy in the smallest matters, Joe thought, another mark of the master devotee of games of chance. The Big Gambler sure had himself a flash crew, all right, though in idly looking them over again as he rolled, Joe noted one bummer towards the back who didn't fit in—a raggedly-elegant chap with the elflocked hair and staring eyes and TB-spotted cheeks of a poet.

As he watched the smoke trickling up from under the black slouch hat, he decided that either the lights across the table had dimmed or else the Big Gambler's complexion was yet a shade darker than he'd thought at first. Or it might even be—wild fantasy—that the Big Gambler's skin was slowly darkening tonight, like a meerschaum pipe being smoked a mile a second. That was almost funny to think of— there was enough heat in this place, all right, to darken meerschaum, as Joe knew from sad experience, but so far as he was aware it was all under the table.

None of Joe's thoughts, either familiar or admiring, about the Big Gambler decreased in the slightest degree his certainty of the supreme menace of the man in black and his conviction that it would be death to touch him. And if any doubts had stirred in Joe's mind, they would have been squelched by the chilling incident which next occurred.

The Big Gambler had just taken into his arms his prettiest-evilest sporting girl and was running an aristocratic hand across her haunch with perfect gentility, when the poet chap, green-eyed from jealousy and lovesickness, came leaping forward like a wildcat and aimed a long gleaming dagger at the black satin back.

Joe couldn't see how the blow could miss, but without taking his genteel right hand off the sporting girl's plush rear end, the Big Gambler shot out his left arm like a steel spring straightening. Joe couldn't tell whether he stabbed the poet chap in the throat, or judo-chopped him there, or gave him the Martian double-finger, or just touched him, but anyhow the fellow stopped as dead as if he'd been shot by a silent elephant gun or an invisible ray pistol and he slammed down on the floor. A couple of darkies came running up to drag off the body and nobody paid the least attention, such episodes apparently being taken for granted at The Boneyard.

It gave Joe quite a turn and he almost shot Phoebe before he intended to.

But by now the waves of pain had stopped running up his left arm and his nerves were like metal-wrapped new guitar strings, so three rolls later he shot a five, making his point, and set in to clean out the table.

He rolled nine successive naturals, seven sevens and two elevens, pyramiding his first wager of a single chip to a stake of over four thousand dollars. None of the Big Mushrooms had dropped out yet, but some of them were beginning to look worried and a couple were sweating. The Big Gambler still hadn't covered any part of Joe's bets, but he seemed to be following the play with interest from the cavernous depths of his eye sockets.

Then Joe got a devilish thought. Nobody could beat him tonight, he knew, but if he held on to the dice until the table was cleaned out, he'd never get a chance to see the Big Gambler exercise *his* skill, and he was truly curious about that. Besides, he thought, he ought to return courtesy for courtesy and have a crack at being a gentleman himself.

"Pulling out forty-one dollars less a nickel," he announced. "Rolling a penny."

This time there wasn't any hissing and Mr. Bones's moonface didn't cloud over. But Joe was conscious that the Big Gambler was staring at him disappointedly, or sorrowfully, or maybe just speculatively.

Joe immediately crapped out by throwing boxcars, rather pleased to see the two best-looking tiny skulls grinning rubytoothed side by side, and the dice passed to the Big Mushroom on his left.

"Knew when his streak was over," he heard another Big Mushroom mutter with grudging admiration.

The play worked rather rapidly around the table, nobody getting very hot and the stakes never more than medium high. "Shoot a fin." "Rolling a sawbuck." "An Andrew Jackson." "Rolling thirty bucks." Now and then Joe covered part of a bet, winning more than he lost. He had over seven thousand dollars, real money, before the bones got around to the Big Gambler.

That one held the dice for a long moment on his statue-steady palm while he looked at them reflectively, though not the hint of a furrow appeared in his almost brownish forehead down which never a bead of sweat trickled. He murmured, "Rolling a double sawbuck," and when he had been faded, he closed his fingers, lightly rattled the cubes—the sound was like big seeds inside a small gourd only half dry—and negligently cast the dice towards the end of the table.

It was a throw like none Joe had ever seen before at any crap table. The dice travelled flat through the air without turning over, struck the exact juncture of the table's end and bottom, and stopped there dead, showing a natural seven.

Joe was distinctly disappointed. On one of his own throws he was used to calculating something like, "Launch three-up, five north, two and a half rolls in the air, hit on the six-five-three corner, three-quarter roll and a one-quarter side-twist right, hit end on the one-two edge, one-half reverse roll and three-quarter side-twist left, land on five face, roll over twice, come up two," and that would be for just one of the dice, and a really commonplace throw, without extra bounces.

By comparison, the technique of the Big Gambler had been ridiculously, abysmally, horrifyingly simple. Joe could have duplicated it with the greatest ease, of course. It was no more than an elementary form of his old pastime of throwing fallen rocks back into their holes. But Joe had never once thought of pulling such a babyish trick at the crap table. It would make the whole thing too easy and destroy the beauty of the game.

Another reason Joe had never used the trick was that he'd never dreamed he'd be able to get away with it. By all the rules he'd ever heard of, it was a most questionable throw. There was the possibility that one or the other die hadn't completely reached the end of the table, or lay a wee bit cocked against the end. Besides, he reminded himself, weren't both dice supposed to rebound off the end, if only for a fraction of an inch?

However, as far as Joe's very sharp eyes could see, both dice lay perfectly flat and sprang up against the end wall. Moreover, everyone else at the table seemed to accept the throw, the dice-girl had scooped up the cubes, and the Big Mushrooms who had faded the man in black were paying off. As far as the rebound business went, well, The Boneyard appeared to put a slightly different interpretation on that rule, and Joe believed in never questioning House Rules except in dire extremity—both his Mother and Wife had long since taught him it was the least troublesome way.

Besides, there hadn't been any of his own money riding on that roll.

In a voice like wind through Cypress Hollow or on Mars, the Big Gambler announced, "Roll a century." It was the biggest bet yet tonight, ten thousand dollars, and the way the Big Gambler said it made it seem something more than that. A hush fell on The Boneyard, they put the mutes on the jazz horns, the croupiers' calls became more confidential, the cards fell softlier, even the roulette balls seemed to be trying to make less noise as they rattled into their cells. The crowd around the Number One Crap Table quietly thickened. The Big Gambler's flash boys and girls formed a double semicircle around him, ensuring him lots of elbow room.

That century bet, Joe realized, was thirty bucks more than his own entire pile. Three or four of the Big Mushrooms had to signal each other before they'd agreed how to fade it.

The Big Gambler shot another natural seven with exactly the same flat, stop-dead throw.

He bet another century and did it again.

And again.

And again.

Joe was getting mighty concerned and pretty indignant too. It seemed unjust that the Big Gambler should be winning such huge bets with such machinelike, utterly unromantic rolls. Why, you couldn't even call them rolls, the dice never turned over an iota, in the air or after. It was the sort of thing you'd expect from a robot, and a very dully programmed robot at that. Joe hadn't risked any of his own chips fading the Big Gambler, of course, but if things went on like this he'd have to. Two of the Big Mushrooms had already retired sweatingly from the table, confessing defeat, and no one had taken their places. Pretty soon there'd be a bet the remaining Big Mushrooms couldn't entirely cover between them, and then he'd have to risk some of his own chips or else pull out of the game himself—and he couldn't do that, not with the power surging in his right hand like chained lightning.

Joe waited and waited for someone else to question one of the Big Gambler's shots, but no one did. He realized that, despite his efforts to look imperturbable, his face was slowly reddening.

With a little lift of his left hand, the Big Gambler stopped the dice-girl as she was about to snatch at the cubes. The eyes that were like black wells directed themselves at Joe, who forced himself to look back into them steadily. He still couldn't catch the faintest gleam in them. All at once he felt the lightest touch-on-neck of a dreadful suspicion.

With the utmost civility and amiability, the Big Gambler whispered, "I believe that the fine shooter across from me has doubts about the validity of my last throw, though he is too much of a gentleman to voice them. Lottie, the card test."

The wraith-tall, ivory dice-girl plucked a playing card from below the table and with a venomous flash of her little white teeth spun it low across the table through the air at Joe. He caught the whirling pasteboard and examined it briefly. It was the thinnest, stiffest, flattest, shiniest playing card Joe had ever handled. It was also the Joker, if that meant anything. He spun it back lazily into her hand and she slid it very gently, letting it descend by its own weight, down the end wall against which the two dice lay. It came to rest in the tiny hollow their rounded edges made against the black felt. She deftly moved it about without force, demonstrating that there was no space between either of the cubes and the table's end at any point.

"Satisfied?" the Big Gambler asked. Rather against his will Joe nodded. The Big Gambler bowed to him. The dice-girl smirked her short, thin lips and drew herself up, flaunting her white-china-doorknob breasts at Joe.

Casually, almost with an air of boredom, the Big Gambler returned to his routine of shooting a century and making a natural seven. The Big Mushrooms wilted fast and one by one tottered away from the table. A particularly pink-faced Toadstool was brought extra cash by a gasping runner, but it was no help, he only lost the additional centuries. While the stacks of pale and black chips beside the Big Gambler grew skyscraper-tall.

Joe got more and more furious and frightened. He watched like a hawk or spy satellite the dice nesting against the end wall, but never could spot justification for calling for another card test, or nerve himself to question the House Rules at this late date. It was maddening, in fact insanitizing, to know that if only he could get the cubes once more he could shoot circles around that black pillar of sporting aristocracy. He damned himself a googelplex of ways for the idiotic, conceited, suicidal impulse that had led him to let go of the bones when he'd had them.

To make matters worse, the Big Gambler had taken to gazing steadily at Joe with those eyes like coal mines. Now he made three rolls running without even glancing at the dice or the end wall, as far as Joe could tell. Why, he was getting as bad as Joe's Wife or Mother—watching, watching, watching Joe.

But the constant staring of those eyes that were not eyes was mostly throwing a terrific scare into him. Supernatural terror added itself to his certainty of the deadliness of the Big Gambler. Just who, Joe kept asking himself, had he got into a game with tonight? There was curiosity and there was dread—a dreadful curiosity as strong as his desire to get the bones and win. His hair rose and he was all over goose bumps, though the power was still pulsing in his hand like a braked locomotive or a rocket wanting to lift from the pad.

At the same time the Big Gambler stayed just that—a black satin-coated, slouch-hatted elegance, suave, courtly, lethal. In fact, almost the worst thing about the spot Joe found himself in was that, after admiring the Big Gambler's perfect sportsmanship all night, he must now be disenchanted by his machinelike throwing and try to catch him out on any technicality he could.

The remorseless mowing down of the Big Mushrooms went on. The empty spaces outnumbered the Toadstools. Soon there were only three left.

The Boneyard had grown still as Cypress Hollow or the Moon. The jazz had stopped and the gay laughter and the shuffle of feet and the squeak of goosed girls and the clink of drinks and coins. Everybody seemed to be gathered around the Number One Crap Table, rank on silent rank.

Joe was racked by watchfulness, sense of injustice, selfcontempt, wild hopes, curiosity and dread. Especially the last two.

The complexion of the Big Gambler, as much as you could see of it, continued to darken. For one wild moment Joe found himself wondering if he'd got into a game with a nigger, maybe a witch-craft-drenched Voodoo Man whose white make-up was wearing off.

Pretty soon there came a century wager which the two remaining Big Mushrooms couldn't fade between them. Joe had to make up a sawbuck from his miserably tiny pile or get out of the game. After a moment's agonizing hesitation, he did the former.

And lost his ten.

The two Big Mushrooms reeled back into the hushed crowd.

Pit-black eyes bored into Joe. A whisper: "Rolling your pile."

Joe felt well up in him the shameful impulse to confess himself licked and run home. At least his six thousand dollars would make a hit with his Wife and Ma.

But he just couldn't bear to think of the crowd's laughter, or the thought of living with himself knowing that he'd had a final chance, however slim, to challenge the Big Gambler and passed it up.

He nodded.

The Big Gambler shot. Joe leaned out over and down the table, forgetting his vertigo, as he followed the throw with eagle or space-telescope eyes.

"Satisfied?"

Joe knew he ought to say, "Yes," and slink off with head held as high as he could manage. It was the gentlemanly thing to do. But then he reminded himself that he wasn't a gentleman, but just a dirty, working-stiff miner with a talent for precision hurling.

He also knew that it was probably very dangerous for him to say anything but, "Yes," surrounded as he was by enemies and strangers. But then he asked himself what right had he, a miserable, mortal, homebound failure, to worry about danger.

Besides, one of the ruby-grinning dice looked just the tiniest hair out of line with the other.

It was the biggest effort yet of Joe's life, but he swallowed and managed to say, "No. Lottie, the card test."

The dice-girl fairly snarled and reared up and back as if she were going to spit in his eyes, and Joe had a feeling her spit was cobra venom. But the Big Gambler lifted a finger at her in reproof and she skimmed the card at Joe, yet so low and viciously that it disappeared under the black felt for an instant before flying up into Joe's hand.

It was hot to the touch and singed a pale brown all over, though otherwise unimpaired. Joe gulped and spun it back high.

Sneering poisoned daggers at him, Lottie let it glide down the end wall . . . and after a moment's hesitation, it slithered behind the die Joe had suspected.

A bow and then the whisper: "You have sharp eyes, sir. Undoubtedly that die failed to reach the wall. My sincerest apologies and . . . your dice, sir."

Seeing the cubes sitting on the black rim in front of him almost gave Joe apoplexy. All the feelings racking him, including his curiosity, rose to an almost unbelievable pitch of intensity, and when he'd said, "Rolling my pile," and the Big Gambler had replied, "You're faded," he yielded to an uncontrollable impulse and cast the two dice straight at the Big Gambler's ungleaming, midnight eyes.

They went right through into the Big Gambler's skull and bounced around inside there, rattling like big seeds in a big gourd not quite yet dry.

Throwing out a hand, palm back, to either side, to indicate that none of his boys or girls or anyone else must make a reprisal on Joe, the Big Gambler dryly gargled the two cubical bones, then spat them out so that they landed in the center of the table, the one die flat, the other leaning against it.

"Cocked dice, sir," he whispered as graciously as if no indignity whatever had been done him. "Roll again."

Joe shook the dice reflectively, getting over the shock. After a little bit he decided that though he could now guess the Big Gambler's real name, he'd still give him a run for his money.

A little corner of Joe's mind wondered how a live skeleton hung together. Did the bones still have gristle and thews, were they wired, was it done with force-fields, or was each bone a calcium magnet clinging to the next?—this tying in somehow with the generation of the deadly ivory electricity.

In the great hush of The Boneyard, someone cleared his throat, a Scarlet Woman tittered hysterically, a coin fell from the nakedest change-girl's tray with a golden clink and rolled musically across the floor.

"Silence," the Big Gambler commanded and in a movement almost too fast to follow whipped a hand inside the bosom of his coat and out to the crap table's rim in front of him. A short-barrelled silver revolver lay softly gleaming there. "Next creature, from the humblest nigger night-girl to you, Mr. Bones, who utters a sound while my worthy opponent rolls, gets a bullet in the head."

Joe gave him a courtly bow back, it felt funny, and then decided to start his run with a natural seven made up of an ace and a six. He rolled and this time the Big Gambler, judging from the movements of his skull, closely followed the course of the cubes with his eyes that weren't there.

The dice landed, rolled over, and lay still. Incredulously, Joe realized that for the first time in his crap-shooting life he'd made a mistake. Or else there was a power in the Big Gambler's gaze greater than that in his own right hand. The six cube had come down okay, but the ace had taken an extra half roll and come down six too.

"End of the game," Mr. Bones boomed sepulchrally.

The Big Gambler raised a brown skeletal hand. "Not necessarily," he whispered. His black eyepits aimed themselves at Joe like the mouths of siege guns. "Joe Slattermill, you still have something of value to wager, if you wish. Your life."

At that a giggling and a hysterical tittering and a guffawing and a braying and a shrieking burst uncontrollably out of the whole Boneyard. Mr. Bones summed up the sentiments when he bellowed over the rest of the racket. "Now what use or value is there in the life of a bummer like Joe Slattermill? Not two cents, ordinary money."

The Big Gambler laid a hand on the revolver gleaming before him and all the laughter died.

"I have a use for it," the Big Gambler whispered. "Joe Slattermill, on my part I will venture all my winnings of tonight, and throw in the world and everything in it for a side bet. You will wager your life, and on the side your soul. You to roll the dice. What's your pleasure?"

Joe Slattermill quailed, but then the drama of the situation took hold of him. He thought it over and realized he certainly wasn't going to give up being stage center in a spectacle like this to go home broke to his Wife and Mother and decaying House and the dispirited Mr. Guts. Maybe, he told himself encouragingly, there wasn't a power in the Big Gambler's gaze, maybe Joe had just made his one and only crap-shooting error. Besides, he was more inclined to accept Mr. Bones's assessment of the value of his life than the Big Gambler's.

"It's a bet," he said.

"Lottie, give him the dice."

Joe concentrated his mind as never before, the power tingled triumphantly in his hand, and he made his throw.

The dice never hit the felt. They went swooping down, then up, in a crazy curve far out over the end of the table, and then came streaking back like tiny red-glinting meteors towards the face of the Big Gambler, where they suddenly nested and hung in his black eye sockets, each with the single red gleam of an ace showing.

Snake eyes.

The whisper, as those red-glinting dice-eyes stared mockingly at him: "Joe Slattermill, you've crapped out."

Using thumb and middle finger—or bone rather—of either hand, the Big Gambler removed the dice from his eye sockets and dropped them in Lottie's white-gloved hand.

"Yes, you've crapped out, Joe Slattermill," he went on tranquilly. "And now you can shoot yourself"—he touched the silver gun—"or cut your throat"—he whipped a gold-handled bowie knife out of his coat and laid it beside the revolver—"or poison yourself"—the two weapons were joined by a small black bottle with white skull and crossbones on it—"or Miss Flossie here can kiss you to death." He drew forward beside him his prettiest, evilest-looking sporting girl. She preened herself and flounced her short violet skirt and gave Joe a provocative, hungry look, lifting her carmine upper lip to show her long white canines.

"Or else," the Big Gambler added, nodding significantly towards the black-bottomed crap table, "you can take the Big Dive."

Joe said evenly, "I'll take the Big Dive."

He put his right foot on his empty chip table, his left on the black rim, fell forward . . . and suddenly kicking off from the rim, launched himself in a tiger spring straight across the crap table at the Big Gambler's throat, solacing himself with the thought that certainly the poet chap hadn't seemed to suffer long.

As he flashed across the exact center of the table he got an instant photograph of what really lay below, but his brain had no time to develop that snapshot, for the next instant he was ploughing into the Big Gambler.

Stiffened brown palm edge caught him in the temple with a lightning-like judo chop . . . and the brown fingers or bones flew all apart like puff paste. Joe's left hand went through the Big Gambler's chest as if there were nothing there but black satin coat, while his right hand, straight-armedly clawing at the slouch-hatted skull, crunched it to pieces. Next instant Joe was sprawled on the floor with some black clothes and brown fragments.

He was on his feet in a flash and snatching at the Big Gambler's tall stacks. He had time for one left-handed grab. He couldn't see any gold or silver or any black chips, so he stuffed his left pants pocket with a handful of the pale chips and ran.

Then the whole population of The Boneyard was on him and af- ter him. Teeth, knives and brass knuckles flashed. He was punched, clawed, kicked, tripped and stamped on with spike heels. A gold- plated trumpet with a bloodshot-eyed black face behind it bopped him on the head. He got a white flash of the golden dice-girl and made a grab for her, but she got away. Someone tried to mash a lighted cigar in his eye. Lottie, writhing and flailing like a white boa constrictor, almost got a simultaneous strangle hold and scissors on him. From a squat wide-mouth bottle Flossie, snarling like a feline fiend, threw what smelt like acid past his face. Mr. Bones peppered shots around him from the silver revolver. He was stabbed at, gouged, rabbit-punched, scragmauled, slugged, kneed, bitten, bear- hugged, butted, beaten and had his toes trampled.

But somehow none of the blows or grabs had much real force. It was like fighting ghosts. In the end it turned out that the whole popu- lation of The Boneyard, working together, had just a little more strength than Joe. He felt himself being lifted by a multitude of hands and pitched out through the swinging doors so that he thudded down on his rear end on the board sidewalk. Even that didn't hurt much. It was more like a kick of encouragement.

He took a deep breath and felt himself over and worked his bones. He didn't seem to have suffered any serious damage. He stood up and looked around. The Boneyard was dark and silent as the grave, or the planet Pluto, or all the rest of Ironmine. As his eyes got ac- customed to the starlight and occasional roving spaceship-gleam, he saw a padlocked sheet-iron door where the swinging ones had been.

He found he was chewing on something crusty that he'd somehow carried in his right hand all the way through the final fracas. Mighty tasty, like the bread his Wife baked for best customers. At that instant his brain developed the photograph it had taken when he had glanced down as he flashed across the center of the crap table. It was a thin wall of flames moving sideways across the table and just beyond the flames the faces of his Wife, Mother, and Mr. Guts, all looking very surprised. He realized that what he was chewing was a fragment of the Big Gambler's skull, and he remembered the shape of the three loaves his Wife had started to bake when he left the House. And he understood the magic she'd made to let him get a little ways away and feel half a man, and then come diving home with his fingers burned.

He spat out what was in his mouth and pegged the rest of the bit of giant-popover skull across the street.

He fished in his left pocket. Most of the pale poker chips had been mashed in the fight, but he found a whole one and explored its surface with his fingertips. The symbol embossed on it was a cross. He lifted it to his lips and took a bite. It tasted delicate, but delicious. He ate it and felt his strength revive. He patted his bulging left pocket. At least he'd started out well provisioned.

Then he turned and headed straight for home, but he took the long way, around the world.

Sanity

"COME IN, Phy, and make yourself comfortable."

The mellow voice—and the suddenly dilating doorway—caught the general secretary of the World playing with a blob of greenish gasoid, squeezing it in his fist and watching it ooze between his fingers in spatulate tendrils that did not dissipate. Slowly, crookedly, he turned his head. World Manager Carrsbury became aware of a gaze that was at once oafish, sly, vacuous. Abruptly the expression was replaced by a nervous smile. The thin man straightened himself, as much as his habitually drooping shoulders would permit, hastily entered, and sat down on the extreme edge of a pneumatically form-fitting chair.

He embarrassedly fumbled the blob of gasoid, looking around for a convenient disposal vent or a crevice in the upholstery. Finding none, he stuffed it hurriedly into his pocket. Then he repressed his fidgetings by clasping his hands resolutely together, and sat with downcast eyes.

"How are you feeling, old man?" Carrsbury asked in a voice that was warm with a benign friendliness.

The general secretary did not look up.

"Anything bothering you, Phy?" Carrsbury continued solicitously. "Do you feel a bit unhappy, or dissatisfied, about your . . . er . . . transfer, now that the moment has arrived?"

Still the general secretary did not respond. Carrsbury leaned forward across the dully silver, semicircular desk and, in his most winning tones, urged, "Come on, old fellow, tell me all about it."

The general secretary did not lift his head, but he rolled up his strange, distant eyes until they were fixed directly on Carrsbury. He shivered a little, his body seemed to contract, and his bloodless hands tightened their interlocking grip.

"I know," he said in a low, effortful voice. "You think I'm insane."

Carrsbury sat back, forcing his brows to assume a baffled frown under the mane of silvery hair.

"Oh, you needn't pretend to be puzzled," Phy continued, swiftly now that he had broken the ice. "You know what that word means as well as I do. Better—even though we both had to do historical research to find out."

"Insane," he repeated dreamily, his gaze wavering. "Significant departure from the norm. Inability to conform to basic conventions underlying all human conduct."

"Nonsense!" said Carrsbury, rallying and putting on his warmest and most compelling smile. "I haven't the slightest idea of what you're talking about. That you're a little tired, a little strained, a little distraught—that's quite understandable, considering the burden you've been carrying, and a little rest will be just the thing to fix you up, a nice long vacation away from all this. But as for your being . . . why, ridiculous!"

"No," said Phy, his gaze pinning Carrsbury. "You think I'm insane. You think all my colleagues in the World Management Service are insane. That's why you're having us replaced with those men you've been training for ten years in your Institute of Political Leadership—ever since, with my help and connivance, you became World manager."

Carrsbury retreated before the finality of the statement. For the first time his smile became a bit uncertain. He started to say something, then hesitated and looked at Phy, as if half hoping he would go on.

But that individual was once again staring rigidly at the floor.

Carrsbury leaned back, thinking. When he spoke it was in a more natural voice, much less consciously soothing and fatherly.

"Well, all right, Phy. But look here, tell me something, honestly. Won't you—and the others—be a lot happier when you've been relieved of all your responsibilities?"

Phy nodded somberly. "Yes," he said, "we will . . . but"—his face became strained—"you see—"

"But—?" Carrsbury prompted.

Phy swallowed hard. He seemed unable to go on. He had gradually slumped toward one side of the chair, and the pressure had caused the green gasoid to ooze from his pocket. His long fingers crept over and kneaded it fretfully.

Carrsbury stood up and came around the desk. His sympathetic frown, from which perplexity had ebbed, was not quite genuine.

"I don't see why I shouldn't tell you all about it now, Phy," he said simply. "In a queer sort of way I owe it all to you. And there isn't any point now in keeping it a secret . . . there isn't any danger—"

"Yes," Phy agreed with a quick bitter smile, "you haven't been in any danger of a *coup d'état* for some years now. If ever we should have revolted, there'd have been"—his gaze shifted to a point in the opposite wall where a faint vertical crease indicated the presence of a doorway—"your secret police."

Carrsbury started. He hadn't thought Phy had known. Disturbingly, there loomed in his mind a phrase *The cunning of the insane.* But only for a moment. Friendly complacency flooded back. He went behind Phy's chair and rested his hands on the sloping shoulders.

"You know, I've always had a special feeling toward you, Phy," he said, "and not only because your whims made it a lot easier for me to become World manager. I've always felt that you were different from the others, that there were times when—" He hesitated.

Phy squirmed a little under the friendly hands. "When I had my moments of sanity?" he finished flatly.

"Like now," said Carrsbury softly, after a nod the other could not see. "I've always felt that sometimes, in a kind of twisted, unrealistic way, you *understood*. And that has meant a lot to me. I've been alone, Phy, dreadfully alone, for ten whole years. No companionship anywhere, not even among the men I've been training in the Institute of Political Leadership—for I've had to play a part with them too, keep them in ignorance of certain facts, for fear they would try to seize power over my head before they were sufficiently prepared. No companionship anywhere, except for my hopes—and for occasional moments with you. Now that it's over and a new regime is beginning for us both, I can tell you that. And I'm glad."

There was a silence. Then—Phy did not look around, but one lean hand crept up and touched Carrsbury's. Carrsbury cleared his throat. Strange, he thought, that there could be even a momentary rapport like this between the sane and the insane. But it was so.

He disengaged his hands, strode rapidly back to his desk, turned.

"I'm a throwback, Phy," he began in a new, unused, eager voice. "A throwback to a time when human mentality was far sounder. Whether my case was due chiefly to heredity, or to certain unusual accidents of environment, or to both, is unimportant. The point is that a person had been born who was in a position to criticize the present state of mankind in the light of the past, to diagnose its condition, and to begin its cure. For a long time I refused to face the facts, but finally my researches—especially those in the literature of the twentieth century—left me no alternative. The mentality of mankind had become—aberrant. Only certain technological advances, which had resulted in making the business of living infinitely easier and simpler, and the fact that war had been ended with the creation of the present world state, were staving off the inevitable breakdown of civilization. But only staving it off—delaying it. The great masses of mankind had become what would once have been called hopelessly neurotic. Their leaders had become . . . you said it first, Phy . . . insane. Incidentally, this latter phenomenon—the drift of psychological aberrants toward leadership—has been noted in all ages."

He paused. Was he mistaken, or was Phy following his words with indications of a greater mental clarity than he had ever noted before, even in the relatively non-violent World secretary? Perhaps—he had often dreamed wistfully of the possibility—there was still a chance of saving Phy. Perhaps, if he just explained to him clearly and calmly—

"In my historical studies," he continued, "I soon came to the conclusion that the crucial period was that of the Final Amnesty, concurrent with the founding of the present world state. We are taught that at that time there were released from confinement millions of political prisoners—and millions of others. Just who were those others? To this question, our present histories gave only vague and platitudinous answers. The semantic difficulties I encountered were exceedingly obstinate. But I kept hammering away. Why, I asked myself, have such words as insanity, lunacy, madness, psychosis, disappeared from our vocabulary—and the concepts behind them from our thought? Why has the subject 'abnormal psychology' disappeared from the curricula of our schools? Of greater significance, why is our modern psychology strikingly similar to the field of abnormal psychology as taught in the twentieth century, and to that field alone? Why are there no longer, as there were in the twentieth century, any institutions for the confinement and care of the psychologically aberrant?"

Phy's head jerked up. He smiled twistedly. "Because," he whispered slyly, "everyone's insane now."

The cunning of the insane. Again that phrase loomed warningly in Carrsbury's mind. But only for a moment. He nodded.

"At first I refused to make that deduction. But gradually I reasoned out the why and wherefore of what had happened. It wasn't only that a highly technological civilization had subjected mankind to a wider and more swiftly-tempoed range of stimulations, conflicting suggestions, mental strains, emotional wrenchings. In the literature of twentieth century psychiatry there are observations on a kind of psychosis that results from success. An unbalanced individual keeps going so long as he is fighting something, struggling toward a goal. He reaches his goal—and goes to pieces. His repressed confusions come to the surface, he realizes that he doesn't know what he wants at all, his energies hitherto engaged in combatting something outside himself are turned against himself, he is destroyed. Well, when war was finally outlawed, when the whole world became one unified state, when social inequality was abolished . . . you see what I'm driving at?"

Phy nodded slowly. "That," he said in a curious, distant voice, "is a very interesting deduction."

"Having reluctantly accepted my main premise," Carrsbury went on, "everything became clear. The cyclic six-months' fluctuations in world credit—I realized at once that Morganstern of Finance must be a manic-depressive with a six-months' phase, or else a dual personality with one aspect a spendthrift, the other a miser. It turned out to be the former. Why was the Department of Cultural Advancement stagnating? Because Manager Hobart was markedly catatonic. Why the boom in Extraterrestrial Research? Because McElvy was a euphoric."

Phy looked at him wonderingly. "But naturally," he said, spreading his lean hands, from one of which the gasoid dropped like a curl of green smoke.

Carrsbury glanced at him sharply. He replied. "Yes, I know that you and several of the others have a certain warped awareness of the differences between your . . . personalities, though none whatsoever of the basic aberration involved in them all. But to get on. As soon as I realized the situation, my course was marked out. As a sane man, capable of entertaining fixed realistic purposes, and surrounded by individuals of whose inconsistencies and delusions it was easy to make use, I was in a position to attain, with time and tact, any goal at which I might aim. I was already in the Managerial Service. In three years I became World manager. Once there, my range of influence was vastly enhanced. Like the man in Archimedes' epigram, I had a place to stand from which I could move the world. I was able, in various guises and on various pretexts, to promulgate regulations the actual purpose of which was to soothe the great neurotic masses by curtailing upsetting stimulations and introducing a more regimented and orderly program of living. I was able, by humoring my fellow executives and making the fullest use of my greater capacity for work, to keep world affairs staggering along fairly safely—at least stave off the worst. At the same time I was able to begin my Ten Years' Plan—the training, in comparative isolation, first in small numbers, then in larger, as those instructed could in turn become instructors, of a group of prospective leaders carefully selected on the basis of their relative freedom from neurotic tendencies."

"But that—" Phy began rather excitedly, starting up.

"But what?" Carrsbury inquired quickly.

"Nothing," muttered Phy dejectedly, sinking back.

"That about covers it," Carrsbury concluded, his voice suddenly grown a little duller. "Except for one secondary matter. I couldn't afford to let myself go ahead without any protection. Too much depended on me. There was always the risk of being wiped out by some ill-co-ordinated but none the less effective spasm of violence, momentarily uncontrollable by tact, on the part of my fellow executives. So, only because I could see no alternative, I took a dangerous step.

I created"—his glance strayed toward the faint crease in the side wall—"my secret police. There is a type of insanity known as paranoia, an exaggerated suspiciousness involving delusions of persecution. By means of the late twentieth century Rand technique of hypnotism, I inculcated a number of these unfortunate individuals with the fixed idea that their lives depended on me and that I was threatened from all sides and must be protected at all costs. A distasteful expedient, even though it served its purpose. I shall be glad, very glad to see it discontinued. You can understand, can't you, why I had to take that step?"

He looked questioningly at Phy—and became aware with a shock that that individual was grinning at him vacuously and holding up the gasoid between two fingers.

"I cut a hole in my couch and a lot of this stuff came out," Phy explained in a thick naive voice. "Ropes of it got all over my office. I kept tripping." His fingers patted at it deftly, sculpturing it into the form of a hideous transparent green head, which he proceeded to squeeze out of existence. "Queer stuff," he rambled on. "Rarefied liquid. Gas of fixed volume. And all over my office floor, tangled up with the furniture."

Carrsbury leaned back and shut his eyes. His shoulders slumped. He felt suddenly a little weary, a little eager for his day of triumph to be done. He knew he shouldn't be despondent because he had failed with Phy. After all, the main victory was won. Phy was the merest of side issues. He had always known that, except for flashes, Phy was hopeless as the rest. Still—

"You don't need to worry about your office floor, Phy," he said with a listless kindliness. "Never any more. Your successor will have to see about cleaning it up. Already, you know, to all intents and purposes, you have been replaced."

"That's just it!" Carrsbury started at Phy's explosive loudness. The World secretary jumped up and strode toward him, pointing an excited hand. "That's what I came to see you about! That's what I've been trying to tell you! I can't be replaced like that! None of the others can, either! It won't work! You can't do it!"

With a swiftness born of long practice, Carrsbury slipped behind his desk. He forced his features into that expression of calm, smiling benevolence of which he had grown unutterably weary.

"Now, now, Phy," he said brightly, soothingly, "if I can't do it, of course I can't do it. But don't you think you ought to tell me why? Don't you think it would be very nice to sit down and talk it all over and you tell me why?"

Phy halted and hung his head, abashed.

"Yes, I guess it would," he said slowly, abruptly falling back into the low, effortful tones. "I guess I'll have to. I guess there just isn't any other way. I had hoped, though, not to have to tell you everything." The last sentence was half question. He looked up wheedlingly at Carrsbury. The latter shook his head, continuing to smile. Phy went back and sat down.

"Well," he finally began, gloomily kneading the gasoid, "it all began when you first wanted to be World manager. You weren't the usual type, but I thought it would be kind of fun—yes, and kind of helpful." He looked up at Carrsbury. "You've really done the world a lot of good in quite a lot of ways, always remember that," he assured him. "Of course," he added, again focusing the tortured gasoid, "they weren't exactly the ways you thought."

"No?" Carrsbury prompted automatically. *Humor him. Humor him.* The wornout refrain droned in his mind.

Phy sadly shook his head. "Take those regulations you promulgated to soothe people—"

"Yes?"

"—they kind of got changed on the way. For instance, your prohibition, regarding reading tapes, of all exciting literature . . . oh, we tried a little of the soothing stuff you suggested at first. Everyone got a great kick out of it. They laughed and laughed. But afterwards, well, as I said, it kind of got changed—in this case to a prohibition of all *unexciting* literature."

Carrsbury's smile broadened. For a moment the edge of his mind had toyed with a fear, but Phy's last remark had banished it.

"Every day I coast past several reading stands," Carrsbury said gently. "The fiction tapes offered for sale are always in the most chastely and simply colored containers. None of those wild and lurid pictures that one used to see everywhere."

"But did you ever buy one and listen to it? Or project the visual text?" Phy questioned apologetically.

"For ten years I've been a very busy man," Carrsbury answered. "Of course I've read the official reports regarding such matters, and at times glanced through sample resumes of taped fiction."

"Oh, sure, that sort of official stuff," agreed Phy, glancing up at the wall of tape files beyond the desk. "What we did, you see, was to keep the monochrome containers but go back to the old kind of contents. The contrast kind of tickled people. Remember, as I said before, a lot of your regulations have done good. Cut out a lot of unnecessary noise and inefficient foolishness, for one thing."

That sort of official stuff. The phrase lingered unpleasantly in Carrsbury's ears. There was a trace of irrepressible suspicion in his quick over-the-shoulder glance at the tiered tape files.

"Oh, yes," Phy went on, "and that prohibition against yielding to unusual or indecent impulses, with a long listing of specific categories. It went into effect all right, but with a little rider attached: 'unless you really want to.' That seemed absolutely necessary, you know." His fingers worked furiously with the gasoid. "As for the prohibition of various stimulating beverages—well, in this locality they're still served under other names, and an interesting custom has grown up of behaving very soberly while imbibing them. Now when we come to that matter of the eight-hour working day—"

Almost involuntarily, Carrsbury had got up and walked over to the outer wall. With a flip of his hand through an invisible U-shaped beam, he switched on the window. It was as if the outer wall had disappeared. Through its near-perfect transparency, he peered down with fierce curiosity past the sleekly gleaming facades to the terraces and parkways below.

The modest throngs seemed quiet and orderly enough. But then there was a scurry of confusion—a band of people, at this angle all tiny heads with arms and legs, came out from a shop far below and began to pelt another group with what looked like foodstuffs. While, on a side parkway, two small ovoid vehicles, seamless drops of silver because their vision panels were invisible from the outside, butted each other playfully. Someone started to run.

Carrsbury hurriedly switched off the window and turned around.

Those were just off-chance occurrences, he told himself angrily. Of no real statistical significance whatever. For ten years mankind had steadily been trending toward sanity despite occasional relapses. He'd seen it with his own eyes, seen the day-by-day progress—at least enough to know. He'd been a fool to let Phy's ramblings effect him —only tired nerves had made that possible.

He glanced at his timepiece.

"Excuse me," he said curtly, striding past Phy's chair, "I'd like to continue this conversation, but I have to get along to the first meeting of the new Central Managerial Staff."

"Oh but you can't!" Instantly Phy was up and dragging at his arm. "You just can't do it, you know! It's impossible!"

The pleading voice rose toward a scream. Impatiently Carrsbury tried to shake loose. The seam in the side wall widened, became a doorway. Instantly both of them stopped struggling.

In the doorway stood a cadaverous giant of a man with a stubby dark weapon in his hand. Straggly black beard shaded into gaunt cheeks. His face was a cruel blend of suspicion and fanatical devotion, the first directed along with the weapon at Phy, the second— and the somnambulistic eyes—at Carrsbury.

"He was threatening you?" the bearded man asked in a harsh voice, moving the weapon suggestively.

For a moment an angry, vindictive light glinted in Carrsbury's eyes. Then it flicked out. What could he have been thinking, he asked himself. This poor lunatic World secretary was no one to hate.

"Not at all, Hartman," he remarked calmly. "We were discussing something and we became excited and allowed our voices to rise. Everything is quite all right."

"Very well," said the bearded man doubtfully, after a pause. Reluctantly he returned his weapon to its holster, but he kept his hand on it and remained standing in the doorway.

"And now," said Carrsbury, disengaging himself, "I must go."

He had stepped on to the corridor slidewalk and had coasted halfway to the elevator before he realized that Phy had followed him and was plucking timidly at his sleeve.

"You can't go off like this," Phy pleaded urgently, with an apprehensive backward glance. Carrsbury noted that Hartman had also followed—an ominous pylon two paces to the rear. "You must give me a chance to explain, to tell you why, just like you asked me."

Humor him. Carrsbury's mind was deadly tired of the drone, but mere weariness prompted him to dance to it a little longer. "You can talk to me in the elevator," he conceded, stepping off the slidewalk. His finger flipped through a U-beam and a serpentine movement of light across the wall traced the elevator's obedient rise.

"You see, it wasn't just that matter of prohibitory regulations," Phy launched out hurriedly. "There were lots of other things that never did work out like your official reports indicated. Departmental budgets for instance. The reports showed, I know, that appropriations for Extraterrestrial Research were being regularly slashed. Actually, in your ten years of office, they increased tenfold. Of course, there was no way for you to know that. You couldn't be all over the world at once and see each separate launching of supra-stratospheric rockets."

The moving light became stationary. A seam dilated. Carrsbury stepped into the elevator. He debated sending Hartman back. Poor babbling Phy was no menace. Still—*the cunning of the insane.* He decided against it, reached out and flipped the control beam at the sector which would bring them to the hundredth and top floor. The door snipped softly shut. The cage became a surging darkness in which floor numerals winked softly. Twenty-one. Twenty-two. Twenty-three.

"And then there was the Military Service. You had it sharply curtailed."

"Of course I did." Sheer weariness stung Carrsbury into talk. "There's only one country in the world. Obviously, the only military requirement is an adequate police force. To say nothing of the risks involved in putting weapons into the hands of the present world population."

"I know," Phy's answer came guiltily from the darkness. "Still, what's happened is that, unknown to you, the Military Service has been increased in size, and recently four rocket squadrons have been added."

Fifty-seven. Fifty-eight. *Humor him.* "Why?"

"Well, you see we've found out that Earth is being reconnoitered.

Maybe from Mars. Maybe hostile. Have to be prepared. We didn't tell you . . . well, because we were afraid it might excite you."

The voice trailed off. Carrsbury shut his eyes. How long, he asked himself, how long? He realized with dull surprise that in the last hour people like Phy, endured for ten years, had become unutterably weary to him. For the moment even the thought of the conference over which he would soon be presiding, the conference that was to usher in a sane world, failed to stir him. Reaction to success? To the end of a ten years' tension?

"Do you know how many floors there are in this building?"

Carrsbury was not immediately conscious of the new note in Phy's voice, but he reacted to it.

"One hundred," he replied promptly.

"Then," asked Phy, "just where are we?"

Carrsbury opened his eyes to the darkness. One hundred twenty-seven, blinked the floor numeral. One hundred twenty-eight. One hundred twenty-nine.

Something cold dragged at Carrsbury's stomach, pulled at his brain. He felt as if his mind were being slowly and irresistibly twisted. He thought of hidden dimensions, of unsuspected holes in space. Something remembered from elementary physics danced through his thoughts: If it were possible for an elevator to keep moving upward with uniform acceleration, no one inside an elevator could determine whether the effects they were experiencing were due to acceleration or to gravity—whether the elevator were standing motionless on some planet or shooting up at everincreasing velocity through free space.

One hundred forty-one. One hundred forty-two.

"Or as if you were rising through consciousness into an unsuspected realm of mentality lying above," suggested Phy in his new voice, with its hint of gentle laughter.

One hundred forty-six. One hundred forty-seven. It was slowing now. One hundred forty-nine. One hundred fifty. It had stopped.

This was some trick. The thought was like cold water in Carrsbury's face. Some cunning childish trick of Phy's. An easy thing to hocus the numerals. Carrsbury groped irascibly about in the darkness, encountered the slick surface of a holster, Hartman's gaunt frame.

"Get ready for a surprise," Phy warned from close at his elbow.

As Carrsbury turned and grabbed, bright sunlight drenched him, followed by a griping, heartstopping spasm of vertigo.

He, Hartman, and Phy, along with a few insubstantial bits of furnishings and controls, were standing in the air fifty stories above the hundred-story summit of World Managerial Center.

For a moment he grabbed frantically at nothing. Then he realized they were not falling and his eyes began to trace the hint of walls and ceiling and floor and, immediately below them, the ghost of a shaft.

Phy nodded. "That's all there is to it," he assured Carrsbury casually. "Just another of those charmingly odd modern notions against which you have legislated so persistently—like our incomplete staircases and roads to nowhere. The Buildings and Grounds Committee decided to extend the range of the elevator for sightseeing purposes. The shaft was made air-transparent to avoid spoiling the form of the original building and to improve the view. This was achieved so satisfactorily that an electronic warning system had to be installed for the safety of passing airjets and other craft. Treating the surfaces of the cage like windows was an obvious detail."

He paused and looked quizzically at Carrsbury. "All very simple," he observed, "but don't you find a kind of symbolism in it? For ten years now you've been spending most of your life in that building below. Every day you've used this elevator. But not once have you dreamed of these fifty extra stories. Don't you think that something of the same sort may be true of your observations of other aspects of contemporary social life?"

Carrsbury gaped at him stupidly.

Phy turned to watch the growing speck of an approaching aircraft. "You might look at it too," he remarked to Carrsbury, "for it's going to transport you to a far happier, more restful life."

Carrsbury parted his lips, wet them. "But—" he said, unsteadily. "But—"

Phy smiled. "That's right, I didn't finish my explanation. Well, you might have gone on being World manager all your life, in the isolation of your office and your miles of taped official reports and your occasional confabs with me and the others. Except for your Institute of Political Leadership and your Ten-Year-Plan. That upset things. Of course, we were as much interested in it as we were in you. It had definite possibilities. We hoped it would work out. We would have been glad to retire from office if it had. But, most fortunately, it didn't. And that sort of ended the whole experiment."

He caught the downward direction of Carrsbury's gaze.

"No," he said, "I'm afraid your pupils aren't waiting for you in the conference chamber on the hundredth story. I'm afraid they're still in the Institute." His voice became gently sympathetic. "And I'm afraid that it's become . . . well . . . a somewhat different sort of institute."

Carrsbury stood very still, swaying a little. Gradually his thoughts and his will power were emerging from the waking nightmare that had paralyzed them. *The cunning of the insane*—he had neglected that trenchant warning. In the very moment of victory—

No! He had forgotten Hartman! This was the very emergency for which that counterstroke had been prepared.

He glanced sideways at the chief member of his secret police. The black giant, unconcerned by their strange position, was glaring fixedly at Phy as if at some evil magician from whom any malign impossibility could be expected.

Now Hartman became aware of Carrsbury's gaze. He divined his thought.

He drew his dark weapon from its holster, pointed it unwaveringly at Phy.

His black-bearded lips curled. From them came a hissing sound. Then, in a loud voice, he cried, "You're dead, Phy! I disintegrated you."

Phy reached over and took the weapon from his hand.

"That's another respect in which you completely miscalculated the modern temperament," he remarked to Carrsbury, a shade argumentatively. "All of us have certain subjects on which we're a trifle unrealistic. That's only human nature. Hartman's was his suspiciousness—a weakness for ideas involving plots and persecutions. You gave him the worst sort of job—one that catered to and encouraged his weaknesses. In a very short time he became hopelessly unrealistic. Why for years he's never realized that he's been carrying a dummy pistol."

He passed it to Carrsbury for inspection.

"But," he added, "give him the proper job and he'd function well enough—say something in creation or exploration. Fitting the man to the job is an art with infinite possibilities. That's why we had Morgenstern in Finance—to keep credit fluctuating in a safe, predictable rhythm. That's why a euphoric is made manager of Extraterrestial Research—to keep it booming. Why a catatonic is given Cultural Advancement—to keep it from tripping on its face in its haste to get ahead."

He turned away. Dully, Carrsbury observed that the aircraft was hovering close to the cage and sidling slowly in.

"But in that case why—" he began stupidly.

"Why were you made World manager?" Phy finished easily. "Isn't that fairly obvious? Haven't I told you several times that you did a lot of good, indirectly? You interested us, don't you see? In fact, you were practically unique. As you know, it's our cardinal principle to let every individual express himself as he wants to. In your case, that involved letting you become World manager. Taken all in all it worked out very well. Everyone had a good time, a number of constructive regulations were promulgated, we learned a lot—oh, we didn't get everything we hoped for, but one never does. Unfortunately, in the end, we were forced to discontinue the experiment."

The aircraft had made contact.

"You understand, of course, why that was necessary?" Phy continued hurriedly, as he urged Carrsbury toward the opening port. "I'm sure you must. It all comes down to a question of sanity. What is sanity—now, in the twentieth century, any time? Adherence to a norm. Conformity to certain basic conventions underlying all human conduct. In our age, departure from the norm has become the norm. Inability to conform has become the standard of conformity. That's quite clear, isn't it? And it enables you to understand, doesn't it, your own case and that of your proteges? Over a long period of years you persisted in adhering to a norm, in conforming to certain basic conventions. You were completely unable to adapt yourself to the society around you. You could only pretend—and your proteges wouldn't have been able to do even that. Despite your many engaging personal characteristics, there was obviously only one course of action open to us."

In the port Carrsbury turned. He had found his voice at last. It was hoarse, ragged. "You mean that all these years you've just been *humoring* me?"

The port was closing. Phy did not answer the question.

As the aircraft edged out, he waved farewell with the blob of green gasoid.

"It'll be very pleasant where you're going," he shouted encouragingly. "Comfortable quarters, adequate facilities for exercise, and a complete library of twentieth century literature to while away your time."

He watched Carrsbury's rigid face, staring whitely from the vision port, until the aircraft had diminished to a speck.

Then he turned away, looked at his hands, noticed the gasoid, tossed it out the open door of the cage, studied its flight for a few moments, then flicked the downbeam.

"I'm glad to see the last of that fellow," he muttered, more to himself than to Hartman, as they plummeted toward the roof. "He was beginning to have a very disturbing influence on me. In fact, I was beginning to fear for my"—his expression became suddenly vacuous —"sanity."

Wanted—An Enemy

THE bright stars of Mars made a glittering roof for a fantastic tableau. A being equipped with retinal vision would have seen an Earthman dressed in the familiar coat and trousers of the twentieth century standing on a boulder that put him a few feet above the rusty sand. His face was bony and puritanic. His eyes gleamed wildly from deep sockets. Occasionally his long hair flopped across them. His lips worked vociferously, showing big yellowed teeth, and there was a cloud of blown spittle in front of them, for he was making a speech —in the English language. He so closely resembled an old-style soap-box orator that one looked around for the lamp-post, the dull-faced listeners overflowing the curb, and the strolling cop.

But the puzzling globe of soft radiance surrounding Mr. Whitlow struck highlights from enamel-black shells and jointed legs a little resembling those of an ant under a microscope. Each individual in the crowd consisted of a yard-long oval body lacking a separate head or any sensory or other orifices in its gleaming black surface except for a small mouth that worked like a sliding door and kept opening and closing at regular intervals. To this body were attached eight of the jointed legs, the inner pairs showing highly manipulative end-organs.

These creatures were ranged in a circle around Mr. Whitlow's boulder. Facing him was one who crouched a little apart from the rest, on a smaller boulder. Flanking this one, were two whose faintly silvered shells suggested weathering and, therefore, age.

Beyond them—black desert to a horizon defined only by the blotting out of the star fields.

Low in the heavens gleamed sky-blue Earth, now Mars' evening star, riding close to the meager crescent of Phobos.

To the Martian coleopteroids this scene presented itself in a very different fashion, since they depended on perception rather than any elaborate sensory set-up. Their internal brains were directly conscious of everything within a radius of about fifty yards. For them the blue earthshine was a diffuse photonic cloud just above the threshold of perception, similar to but distinct from the photonic clouds of the starlight and faint moonshine; they could perceive no image of Earth unless they used lenses to create such an image within their perceptive range. They were conscious of the ground beneath them as a sandy hemisphere tunneled through by various wrigglers and the centipedelike burrowers. They were conscious of each other's armored, neatly-compartmented bodies, and each other's thoughts. But chiefly their attention was focused on that squidgy, uninsulated, wasteful jumble of organs that thought of itself as Mr. Whitlow—an astounding moist suppet of life on dry, miserly Mars.

The physiology of the coleopteroids was typical of a depleted-planet economy. Their shells were double; the space between could be evacuated at night to conserve heat, and flooded by day to absorb it. Their lungs were really oxygen accumulators. They inhaled the rarefied atmosphere about one hundred times for every exhalation, the double-valve mouth permitting the building up of high internal pressure. They had one hundred percent utilization of inhaled oxygen, and exhaled pure carbon dioxide freighted with other respiratory excretions. Occasional whiffs of this exceedingly bad breath made Mr. Whitlow wrinkle his flaring nostrils.

Just what permitted Mr. Whitlow to go on functioning, even speechifying, in the chill oxygen dearth was by no means so obvious. It constituted as puzzling a question as the source of the soft glow that bathed him.

Communication between him and his audience was purely telepathic. He was speaking vocally at the request of the coleopteroids, because like most nontelepaths he could best organize and clarify his thoughts while talking. His voice died out abruptly in the thin air. It sounded like a phonograph needle scratching along without amplification, and intensified the eerie ludicrousness of his violent gestures and facial contortions.

"And so," Whitlow concluded wheezily, brushing the long hair from his forehead, "I come back to my original proposal: Will you attack Earth?"

"And we, Mr. Whitlow," thought the Chief Coleopteroid, "come back to our original question, which you still have not answered: Why should we?"

Mr. Whitlow made a grimace of frayed patience. "As I have told you several times, I cannot make a fuller explanation. But I assure you of my good faith. I will do my best to provide transportation for you, and facilitate the thing in every way. Understand, it need only be a token invasion. After a short time you can retire to Mars with your spoils. Surely you cannot afford to pass up this opportunity."

"Mr. Whitlow," replied the Chief Coleopteroid with a humor as poisonously dry as his planet, "I cannot read your thoughts unless you vocalize them. They are too confused. But I can sense your biases. You are laboring under a serious misconception as to our psychology. Evidently it is customary in your world to think of alien intelligent beings as evil monsters, whose only desire is to ravage, destroy, tyrannize, and inflict unspeakable cruelties on creatures less advanced than themselves. Nothing could be farther from the truth. We are an ancient and unemotional race. We have outgrown the passions and vanities—even the ambitions—of our youth. We undertake no projects except for sound and sufficient reason."

"But if that's the case, surely you can see the practical advantages of my proposal. At little or no risk to yourselves, you will acquire valuable loot."

The Chief Coleopteroid settled back on his boulder, and his thoughts did the same. "Mr. Whitlow, let me remind you that we have never gone to war lightly. During the whole course of our history, our only intelligent enemies have been the molluscoids of the tideless seas of Venus. In the springtide of their culture they came conquesting in their water-filled spaceships, and we fought several long and bitter wars. But eventually they attained racial maturity and a certain dispassionate wisdom, though not equivalent to our own. A perpetual truce was declared, on condition that each party stick to its own planet and attempt no more forays. For ages we have abided by that truce, living in mutual isolation. So you can see, Mr. Whitlow, that we would be anything but inclined to accept such a rash and mysterious proposal as yours."

"May I make a suggestion?" interjected the Senior Coleopteroid on the Chief's right. His thoughts flicked out subtly toward Whitlow. "You seem, Earthling, to possess powers that are perhaps even in excess of our own. Your arrival on Mars without any perceptible means of transport and your ability to endure its rigors without any obvious insulation, are sufficient proofs. From what you tell us, the other inhabitants of your planet possess no such powers. Why don't you attack them by yourself, like the solitary armored poison-worm? Why do you need our aid?"

"My friend," said Mr. Whitlow solemnly, bending forward and fixing his gaze on the silvery-shelled elder, "I abhor war as the foulest evil, and active participation in it as the greatest crime. Nonetheless, I would sacrifice myself as you suggest, could I attain my ends that way. Unfortunately I cannot. It would not have the psychological effect I desire. Moreover"—he paused embarrassedly—"I might as well confess that I am not wholly master of my powers. I don't understand them. The workings of an inscrutable providence have put into my hands a device that is probably the handiwork of creatures vastly more intelligent than any in this solar system, perhaps even this cosmos. It enables me to cross space and time. It protects me from danger. It provides me with warmth and illumination. It concentrates your Martian atmosphere in a sphere around me, so that I can breathe normally. But as for using it in any larger way—I'd be mortally afraid of its getting out of control. My one small experiment was disastrous. I wouldn't dare."

The Senior Coleopteroid shot a guarded aside to the Chief. "Shall I try to hypnotize his disordered mind and get this device from him?"

"Do so."

"Very well, though I'm afraid the device will protect his mind as well as his body. Still, it's worth the chance."

"Mr. Whitlow," thought the Chief abruptly, "it is time we got down to cases. Every word you say makes your proposal sound more irrational, and your own motives more unintelligible. If you expect us to take any serious interest, you must give us a clear answer to one question: Why do you want us to attack Earth?"

Whitlow twisted. "But that's the one question I don't want to answer."

"Well, put it this way then," continued the Chief patiently. "What personal advantage do you expect to gain from our attack?"

Whitlow drew himself up and tucked in his necktie. "None! None whatsoever! I seek nothing for myself!"

"Do you want to rule Earth?" the Chief persisted.

"No! No! I detest all tyranny."

"Revenge, then? Has Earth hurt you and are you trying to hurt it back?"

"Absolutely not! I would never stoop to such barbaric behavior. I hate no one. The desire to see anyone injured is furthest from my thoughts."

"Come, come, Mr. Whitlow! You've just begged us to attack Earth. How can you square that with your sentiments?"

Whitlow gnawed his lip baffledly.

The Chief slipped in a quick question to the Senior Coleopteroid. "What progress?"

"None whatsoever. His mind is extraordinarily difficult to grasp. And as I anticipated, there is a shield."

Whitlow rocked uneasily on his shoulder, his eyes fixed on the star-edged horizon.

"I'll tell you this much," he said. "It's solely because I love Earth and mankind so much that I want you to attack her."

"You choose a strange way of showing your affection," the Chief observed.

"Yes," continued Whitlow, warming a bit, his eyes still lost. "I want you to do it in order to end war."

"This gets more and more mysterious. Start war to stop it? That is a paradox which demands explanation. Take care, Mr. Whitlow, or I will fall into your error of looking on alien beings as evil and demented monsters."

Whitlow lowered his gaze until it was fixed on the Chief. He sighed windily. "I guess I'd better tell you," he muttered. "You'd have probably found out in the end. Though it would have been simpler the other way—"

He pushed back the rebellious hair and massaged his forehead, a little wearily. When he spoke again it was in a less oratorical style.

"I am a pacifist. My life is dedicated to the task of preventing war. I love my fellow men. But they are steeped in error and sin. They are victims of their baser passions. Instead of marching on, hand in hand, trustingly, toward the glorious fulfillment of all their dreams, they insist on engaging in constant conflict, in vile war."

"Perhaps there is a reason for that," suggested the Chief mildly. "Some inequalities that require leveling or—"

"Please," said the pacifist reprovingly. "These wars have grown increasingly more violent and terrible. I, and others, have sought to reason with the majority, but in vain. They persist in their delusions. I have racked my brain to find a solution. I have considered every conceivable remedy. Since I came into the possession of . . . er . . . the device, I have sought throughout the cosmos and even in other time-streams, for the secret of preventing war. With no success. Such intelligent races as I encountered were either engaged in war, which ruled them out, or had never known war—these were very obliging but obviously could volunteer no helpful information—or else had outgrown war by the painful and horrible process of fighting until there was nothing more to fight about."

"As we have," the Chief thought, in an undertone.

The pacifist spread his hands, palms toward the stars. "So, once more, I was thrown on my own resources. I studied mankind from every angle. Gradually I became convinced that its worst trait—and the one most responsible for war—was its overgrown sense of self-importance. On my planet man is the lord of creation. All the other animals are merely one among many—no species is pre-eminent. The flesh-eaters have their flesh-eating rivals. Each browser or grazer competes with other types for the grass and herbage. Even the fish in the seas and the myriad parasites that swarm in bloodstreams are divided into species of roughly equal ability and competence. This makes for humility and a sense of perspective. No species is inclined to fight among itself when it realizes that by so doing it will merely clear the way for other species to take over. Man alone has no serious rivals. As a result, he has developed delusions of grandeur—and of persecution and hate. Lacking the restraint that rivalry would provide, he fouls his planetary nest with constant civil war.

"I mulled this idea for some time. I thought wistfully of how different mankind's development might have been had he been compelled to share his planet with some equally intelligent species, say a mechanically-minded sea dweller. I considered, how, when great natural catastrophes occur, such as fires and floods and earthquakes and plagues, men temporarily quit squabbling and work hand in hand—rich and poor, friend and enemy alike. Unfortunately such cooperation only lasts until man once more asserts his mastery over his environment. It does not provide a constant sobering threat. And then . . . I had an inspiration."

Mr. Whitlow's gaze swept the black-shelled forms—a jumble of satiny crescent highlights ringing the sphere of light enveloping him. Similarly his mind swept their cryptically armored thoughts.

"I remembered an incident from my childhood. A radio broadcast —we make use of high velocity vibrations to transmit sound—had given an impishly realistic fictional report of an invasion of Earth by beings from Mars, beings of that evil and destructive nature which, as you say, we tend to attribute to alien life. Many believed the report. There were brief scares and panics. It occurred to me how, at the first breath of an actual invasion of that sort, warring peoples would forget their differences and join staunchly together to meet the invader. They would realize that the things they were fighting about were really trifling matters, phantoms of moodiness and fear. Their sense of perspective would be restored. They would see that the all-important fact was that they were men alike, facing a common enemy, and they would rise magnificently to the challenge. Ah my friends, when that vision occurred to me, of warring mankind at one stroke united, and united forever, I stood trembling and speechless. I—"

Even on Mars, emotion choked him.

"Very interesting," thought the Senior Coleopteroid blandly, "but wouldn't the method you propose be a contradiction of that higher morality to which I can perceive you subscribe?"

The pacifist bowed his head. "My friend, you are quite right—in the large and ultimate sense. And let me assure you"—the fire crept back into his hoarse voice—"that when that day comes, when the question of interplanetary relations arises, I will be in the vanguard of the interspecieists, demanding full equality for coleopteroid and man alike. But"—his feverish eyes peered up again through the hair that had once more fallen across his forehead—"that is a matter for the future. The immediate question is: How to stop war on Earth. As I said before, your invasion need only be a token one, and of course the more bloodless, the better. It would only take one taste of an outside menace, one convincing proof that he has equals and even superiors in the cosmos, to restore man's normalcy of outlook, to weld him into a mutually-protective brotherhood, to establish peace forever!"

He threw his hands wide and his head back. His hair flipped into its proper place, but his tie popped out again.

"Mr. Whitlow," thought the Chief, with a cold sardonic merriment, "if you have any notion that we are going to invade another planet for the sake of improving the psychology of its inhabitants, disabuse yourself of it at once. Earthlings mean nothing to us. Their rise is such a recent matter that we hardly had taken note of it until you called it to our attention. Let them go on warring, if they want to. Let them kill themselves off. It is no concern of ours."

Whitlow blinked. "Why—" he started angrily. Then he caught himself. "But I wasn't asking you to do it for humanitarian reasons. I pointed out that there would be loot—"

"I very much doubt if your Earthlings have anything that would tempt us."

Whitlow almost backed off his boulder. He started to splutter something, but again abruptly changed his tack. There was a flicker of shrewdness in his expression. "Is it possible you're holding back because you're afraid the Venusian molluscoids will attack you if you violate the perpetual truce by making a foray against another planet?"

"By no means," thought the Chief harshly, revealing for the first time a certain haughtiness and racial pride bred of dry eons of tradition. "As I told you before, the molluscoids are a distinctly inferior race. Mere waterlings. We have seen nothing of them for ages. For all we know they've died out. Certainly we wouldn't be bound by any outworn agreements with them, if there were a sound and profitable

reason for breaking them. And we are in no sense—no sense whatever—afraid of them."

Whitlow's thoughts fumbled confusedly, his spatulate-fingered
hands making unconsciously appropriate gestures. Driven back to his
former argument, he faltered lamely. "But surely then there must be
some loot that would make it worth your while to invade Earth. After
all, Earth is a planet rich in oxygen and water and minerals and
life forms, whereas Mars has to contend with a dearth of all these
things."

"Precisely," thought the Chief. "And we have developed a style
of life that fits in perfectly with that dearth. By harvesting the interplanetary dust in the neighborhood of Mars, and by a judicious use
of transmutation and other techniques, we are assured of a sufficient
supply of all necessary raw materials. Earth's bloated abundance
would be an embarrassment to us, upsetting our system. An increased oxygen supply would force us to learn a new rhythm of breathing to avoid oxygen-drowning, besides making any invasion of Earth
uncomfortable and dangerous. Similar hazards might attend an over-
supply of other elements and compounds. And as for Earth's obnox-
iously teeming life forms, none of them would be any use to us on
Mars—except for the unlucky chance of one of them finding har-
borage in our bodies and starting an epidemic."

Whitlow winced. Whether he knew it or not, his planetary vanity
had been touched. "But you're overlooking the most important
things," he argued, "the products of man's industry and ingenuity.
He has changed the face of his planet much more fully than you have
yours. He has covered it with roads. He does not huddle savagely in
the open as you do. He has built vast cities. He has constructed all
manner of vehicles. Surely among such a wealth of things you would
find many to covet."

"Most unlikely," retorted the Chief. "I cannot see envisaged in
your mind any that would awaken even our passing interest. We are
adapted to our environment. We have no need of garments and housing and all the other artificialities which your ill-adjusted Earthlings
require. Our mastery of our planet is greater than yours, but we do
not advertise it so obtrusively. From your picture I can see that your
Earthlings are given to a worship of bigness and a crude type of ex-
hibitionism."

"But then there are our machines," Whitlow insisted, seething inwardly, plucking at his collar. "Machines of tremendous complexity, for every purpose. Machines that would be as useful to another species as to us."

"Yes, I can imagine them," commented the Chief cuttingly. "Huge, clumsy, jumbles of wheels and levers, wires and grids. In any case, ours are better."

He shot a swift question to the Senior. "Is his anger making his mind any more vulnerable?"

"Not yet."

Whitlow made one last effort, with great difficulty holding his indignation in check. "Besides all that, there's our art. Cultural treasures of incalculable value. The work of a species more richly creative than your own. Books, music, paintings, sculpture. Surely—"

"Mr. Whitlow, you are becoming ridiculous," said the Chief. "Art is meaningless apart from its cultural environment. What interest could we be expected to take in the fumbling self-expression of an immature species? Moreover, none of the art forms you mention would be adapted to our style of perception, save sculpture—and in that field our efforts are incomparably superior, since we have a direct consciousness of solidity. Your mind is only a shadow-mind, limited to flimsy two-dimensional patterns."

Whitlow drew himself up and folded his arms across his chest. "Very well!" he grated out. "I see I cannot persuade you. But"—he shook his finger at the Chief—"let me tell you something! You're contemptuous of man. You call him crude and childish. You pour scorn on his industry, his science, his art. You refuse to help him in his need. You think you can afford to disregard him. All right. Go ahead. That's my advice to you. Go ahead—and see what happens!" A vindictive light grew in his eyes. "I know my fellow man. From years of study I know him. War has made him a tyrant and exploiter. He has enslaved the beasts of field and forest. He has enslaved his own kind, when he could, and when he couldn't he has bound them with the subtler chains of economic necessity and the awe of prestige. He's wrong-headed, brutal, a tool of his baser impulses—and also he's clever, doggedly persistent, driven by a boundless ambition! He already has atomic power and rocket transport. In a few decades he'll have spaceships and subatomic weapons. Go ahead and wait!

Constant warfare will cause him to develop those weapons to un-dreamed of heights of efficient destructiveness. Wait for that too! Wait until he arrives on Mars in force. Wait until he makes your acquaintance and realizes what marvelous workers you'd be with your armored adaptability to all sorts of environments. Wait until he picks a quarrel with you and defeats you and enslaves you and ships you off, packed in evil-smelling hulls, to labor in Earth's mines and on her ocean bottoms, in her stratosphere and on the planetoids that man will be desirous of exploiting. Yes, go ahead and wait!"

Whitlow broke off, his chest heaving. For a moment he was con-scious only of his vicious satisfaction at having told off these exas-perating beetle-creatures. Then he looked around.

The coleopteroids had drawn in. The forms of the foremost were defined with a hatefully spiderish distinctness, almost invading his sphere of light. Similarly their thoughts had drawn in, to form a menacing wall blacker than the encircling Martian night. Gone were the supercilious amusement and dispassionate withdrawal that had so irked him. Incredulously he realized that he had somehow broken through their armor and touched them on a vulnerable spot.

He caught one rapid thought, from the Senior to the Chief: "And if the rest of them are anything like this one, they'll behave just as he says. It is an added confirmation."

He looked slowly around, his hair-curtained forehead bent for-ward, searching for a clue to the coleopteroids' sudden change in attitude. His baffled gaze ended on the Chief.

"We've changed our minds, Mr. Whitlow," the Chief volunteered grimly. "I told you at the beginning that we never hesitate about undertaking projects when given a sound and sufficient reason. What your silly arguments about humanitarianism and loot failed to pro-vide, your recent outburst has furnished us. It is as you say. The Earth-lings will eventually attack us, and with some hope of success, if we wait. So, logically we must take preventive action, the sooner the better. We will reconnoiter Earth, and if conditions there are as you assert, we will invade her."

From the depths of a confused despondency Whitlow was in an instant catapulted to the heights of feverish joy. His fanatical face beamed. His lanky frame seemed to expand. His hair flipped back.

"Marvelous!" he chortled, and then rattled on excitedly, "Of course, I'll do everything I can to help. I'll provide transport—"

"That will not be necessary," the Chief interrupted flatly. "We have no more trust in your larger powers than you have yourself. We have our own spaceships, quite adequate to any undertaking. We do not make an ostentatious display of them, any more than we make a display of the other mechanical aspects of our culture. We do not use them, as your Earthlings would, to go purposely skittering about. Nevertheless, we have them, stored away in the event of need."

But not even this contemptuous rebuff could spoil Whitlow's exultation. His face was radiant. Halfformed tears made him blink his hectic eyes. His Adam's apple bobbed chokingly.

"Ah my friends . . . my good, good friends! If only I could express to you . . . what this moment means to me! If I could only tell you how happy I am when I envisage the greater moment that is coming! When men will look up from their trenches and foxholes, from their bombers and fighters, from their observation posts and headquarters, from their factories and homes, to see this new menace in the skies. When all their petty differences of opinion will drop away from them like a soiled and tattered garment. When they will cut the barbed-wire entanglements of an illusory hate, and join together, hand in hand, true brothers at last, to meet the common foe. When, in the accomplishment of a common task, they will at last achieve perfect and enduring peace!"

He paused for breath. His glazed eyes were lovingly fixed on the blue star of Earth, now just topping the horizon.

"Yes," faintly came the Chief's dry thought. "To one of your emotional temperament, it will probably be a very satisfying and touching scene—for a little while."

Whitlow glanced down blankly. It was as if the Chief's last thought had lightly scratched him—a feathery flick from a huge poisoned claw. He did not understand it, but he was conscious of upwelling fear.

"What—" he faltered. "What . . . do you mean?"

"I mean," thought the Chief, "that in our invasion of Earth it probably won't be necessary for us to use the divide-and-rule tactics that would normally be indicated in such a case—you know, joining with one faction on Earth to help defeat the other—warring beings never care who their allies are—and then fomenting further disunities, and so on. No, with our superiority in armament, we can probably do a straight cleanup job and avoid bothersome machinations. So you'll probably have that glimpse of Earthlings united that you set so much store by."

Whitlow stared at him from a face white with dawning horror. He licked his lips. "What did you mean by—'for a little while'?" he whispered huskily. "What did you mean by 'glimpse'?"

"Surely that should be obvious to you, Mr. Whitlow," replied the Chief with offensive good humor. "You don't for one minute suppose we'd make some footling little invasion and, after overawing the Earthlings, retire? That would be the one way to absolutely assure their eventual counterinvasion of Mars. Indeed, it would probably hasten it—and they'd come as already hostile destroyers intent on wiping out a menace. No, Mr. Whitlow, when we invade Earth, it will be to protect ourselves from a potential future danger. Our purpose will be total and complete extermination, accomplished as swiftly and efficiently as possible. Our present military superiority makes our success certain."

Whitlow goggled at the Chief blankly, like a dirty and somewhat yellowed plaster statue of himself. He opened his mouth—and shut it without saying anything.

"You never believed, did you, Mr. Whitlow," continued the Chief kindly, "that we'd ever do anything for your sake? Or for anyone's—except us coleopteroids?"

Whitlow stared at the horrible, black, eight-legged eggs crowding ever closer—living embodiments of the poisonous blackness of their planet.

All he could think to mumble was: "But . . . but I thought you said . . . it was a misconception to think of alien beings as evil monsters intent only on ravaging . . . and destroying—"

"Perhaps I did, Mr. Whitlow. Perhaps I did," was the Chief's only reply.

In that instant Mr. Whitlow realized what an alien being really was.

As in a suffocating nightmare, he watched the coleopteroids edge closer. He heard the Chief's contemptuously unguarded aside to the Senior, "Haven't you got hold of his mind yet?" and the Senior's "No," and the Chief's swift order to the others.

Black eggs invaded his lightsphere, cruel armored claws opening to grab—those were Mr. Whitlow's last impressions of Mars.

Instants later—for the device provided him with instantaneous transportation across any spatial expanse—Mr. Whitlow found himself inside a bubble that miraculously maintained normal atmospheric pressure deep under the tideless Venusian seas. The reverse of a fish in a tank, he peered out at the gently waving luminescent vegetation and the huge mud-girt buildings it half masked. Gleaming ships and tentacled creatures darted about.

The Chief Molluscoid regarded the trespasser on his private gardens with a haughty disfavor that even surprise could not shake.

"What are you?" he thought coldly.

"I . . . I've come to inform you of a threatened breach in an age-long truce."

Five eyes on longish stalks regarded him with a coldness equal to that of the repeated thought: "But what are you?"

A sudden surge of woeful honesty compelled Mr. Whitlow to reply, "I suppose . . . I suppose you'd call me a warmonger."

The Man Who Never Grew Young

MAOT is becoming restless. Often toward evening she trudges to where the black earth meets the yellow sand and stands looking across the desert until the wind starts.

But I sit with my back to the reed screen and watch the Nile.

It isn't just that she's growing young. She is wearying of the fields. She leaves their tilling to me and lavishes her attentions on the flock. Every day she takes the sheep and goats farther to pasture.

I have seen it coming for a long time. For generations the fields have been growing scantier and less diligently irrigated. There seems to be more rain. The houses have become simpler—mere walled tents. And every year some family gathers its flocks and wanders off west.

Why should I cling so tenaciously to these poor relics of civilization—I, who have seen king Cheops' men take down the Great Pyramid block by block and return it to the hills?

I often wonder why I never grow young. It is still as much a mystery to me as to the brown farmers who kneel in awe when I walk past.

I envy those who grow young. I yearn for the sloughing of wisdom and responsibility, the plunge into a period of lovemaking and breathless excitement, the carefree years before the end.

But I remain a bearded man of thirty-odd, wearing the goatskin as I once wore the doublet or the toga, always on the brink of that plunge yet never making it.

It seems to me that I have always been this way. Why, I cannot even remember my own disinterment, and everyone remembers that.

Maot is subtle. She does not ask for what she wants, but when she comes home at evening she sits far back from the fire and murmurs disturbing fragments of song and rubs her eyelids with green pigment to make herself desirable to me and tries in every way to infect me with her restlessness. She tempts me from the hot work at midday and points out how hardy our sheep and goat are becoming.

There are no young men among us any more. All of them start for the desert with the approach of youth, or before. Even toothless, scrawny patriarchs uncurl from their grave-holes, and hardly pausing to refresh themselves with the food and drink dug up with them, collect their flocks and wives and hobble off into the west.

I remember the first disinterment I witnessed. It was in a country of smoke and machines and constant news. But what I am about to relate occurred in a backwater where there were still small farms and narrow roads and simple ways.

There were two old women named Flora and Helen. It could not have been more than a few years since their own disinterments, but those I cannot remember. I think I was some sort of nephew, but I cannot be sure.

They began to visit an old grave in the cemetery a half mile outside town. I remember the little bouquets of flowers they would bring back with them. Their prim, placid faces became troubled. I could see that grief was entering their lives.

The years passed. Their visits to the cemetery became more frequent. Accompanying them once, I noted that the worn inscription on the headstone was growing clearer and sharper, just as was happening to their own features. "John, loving husband of Flora. . . ."

Often Flora would sob through half the night, and Helen went about with a set look on her face. Relatives came and spoke comforting words, but these seemed only to intensify their grief.

Finally the headstone grew brand-new and the grass became tender green shoots which disappeared into the raw brown earth. As if these were the signs their obscure instincts had been awaiting, Flora and Helen mastered their grief and visited the minister and the mortician and the doctor and made certain arrangements.

On a cold autumn day, when the brown curled leaves were whirling up into the trees, the procession set out—the empty hearse, the dark silent automobiles. At the cemetery we found a couple of men with shovels turning away unobstrusively from the newly opened grave. Then, while Flora and Helen wept bitterly and the minister spoke solemn words, a long narrow box was lifted from the grave and carried to the hearse.

At home the lid of the box was unscrewed and slid back, and we saw John, a waxen old man with a long life before him.

Next day, in obedience to what seemed an age-old ritual, they took him from the box, and the mortician undressed him and drew a pungent liquid from his veins and injected the red blood. Then they took him and laid him in bed. After a few hours of stoney-eyed waiting, the blood began to work. He stirred and his first breath rattled in his throat. Flora sat down on the bed and strained him to her in a fearful embrace.

But he was very sick and in need of rest, so the doctor waved her from the room. I remember the look on her face as she closed the door.

I should have been happy too, but I seem to recall that I felt there was something unwholesome about the whole episode. Perhaps our first experiences of the great crises of life always affect us in some such fashion.

I love Maot. The hundreds I have loved before her in my wanderings down the world do not take away from the sincerity of my affection. I did not enter her life, or theirs, as lovers ordinarily do—from the grave or in the passion of some terrible quarrel. I am always the drifter.

Maot knows there is something strange about me. But she does not let that interfere with her efforts to make me do the thing she wants.

I love Maot and eventually I will accede to her desire. But first I will linger a while by the Nile and the mighty pageantry conjured up by its passage.

My first memories are always the most difficult and I struggle the hardest to interpret them. I have the feeling that if I could get back a little beyond them, a terrifying understanding would come to me. But I never seem able to make the necessary effort.

They begin without antecedent in cloud and turmoil, darkness and fear. I am a citizen of a great country far away, beardless and wearing ugly confining clothing, but no different in age and appearance from today. The country is a hundred times bigger than Egypt, yet it is only one of many. All the peoples of the world are known to each other, and the world is round, not flat, and it floats in an endless immensity dotted with islands of suns, not confined under a star-speckled bowl.

Machines are everywhere, and news goes round the world like a shout, and desires are many. There are undreamed-of abundance, unrivaled opportunities. Yet men are not happy. They live in fear. The fear, if I recall rightly, is of a war that will engulf and perhaps destroy us all. It overhangs us like the dark.

The weapons they have ready for that war are terrible. Great engines that sail pilotless, not through the water but the air, halfway around the world to destroy some enemy city. Others that dart up beyond the air itself, to come in attacking from the stars. Poisoned clouds. Deadly motes of luminous dust.

But worst of all are the weapons that are only rumored.

For months that seem eternities we wait on the brink of that war. We know that the mistakes have been made, the irrevocable steps taken, the last chances lost. We only await the event.

It would seem that there must have been some special reason for the extremity of our hopelessness and horror. As if there had been previous worldwide wars and we had struggled back from each desperately promising ourselves that it would be the last. But of any such, I can remember nothing. I and the world might well have been created under the shadow of that catastrophe, in a universal disinterment.

The months wear on. Then, miraculously, unbelievably, the war begins to recede. The tension relaxes. The clouds lift. There is great activity, conferences and plans. Hopes for lasting peace ride high.

This does not last. In sudden holocaust, there arises an oppressor named Hitler. Odd, how that name should come back to me after these millennia. His armies fan out across the globe.

But their success is short-lived. They are driven back, and Hitler trails off into oblivion. In the end he is an obscure agitator, almost forgotten.

Another peace then, but neither does it last. Another war, less fierce than the preceding, and it too trails off into a quieter era.

And so on.

I sometimes think (I must hold on to this) that time once flowed in the opposite direction, and that, in revulsion from the ultimate war, it turned back upon itself and began to retrace its former course. That our present lives are only a return and an unwinding. A great retreat.

In that case time may turn again. We may have another chance to scale the barrier.

But no . . .

The thought has vanished in the rippling Nile.

Another family is leaving the valley today. All morning they have toiled up the sandy gorge. And now, returning perhaps for a last glimpse, to the verge of the yellow cliffs, they are outlined against the morning sky—upright specks for men, flat specks for animals.

Maot watches beside me. But she makes no comment. She is sure of me.

The cliff is bare again. Soon they will have forgotten the Nile and its disturbing ghosts of memories.

All our life is a forgetting and a closing in. As the child is absorbed by its mother, so great thoughts are swallowed up in the mind of genius. At first they are everywhere. They environ us like the air. Then there is a narrowing in. Not all men know them. Then there comes one great man, and he takes them to himself, and they are a secret. There only remains the disturbing conviction that something worthy has vanished.

I have seen Shakespeare unwrite the great plays. I have watched Socrates unthink the great thoughts. I have heard Jesus unsay the great words.

There is an inscription in stone, and it seems eternal. Coming back centuries later I find it the same, only a little less worn, and I think that it, at least, may endure. But some day a scribe comes and laboriously fills in the grooves until there is only blank stone.

Then only he knows what was written there. And as he grows young, that knowledge dies forever.

It is the same in all we do. Our houses grow new and we dismantle them and stow the materials inconspicuously away, in mine and quarry, forest and field. Our clothes grow new and we put them off. And we grow new and forget and blindly seek a mother.

All the people are gone now. Only I and Maot linger.

I had not realized it would come so soon. Now that we are near the end, Nature seems to hurry.

I suppose that there are other stragglers here and there along the Nile, but I like to think that we are the last to see the vanishing fields, the last to look upon the river with some knowledge of what it once symbolized, before oblivion closes in.

Ours is a world in which lost causes conquer. After the second war of which I spoke, there was a long period of peace in my native country across the sea. There were among us at that time a primitive people called Indians, neglected and imposed upon and forced to live apart in unwanted areas. We gave no thought to these people. We would have laughed at anyone who told us they had power to hurt us.

But from somewhere a spark of rebellion appeared among them. They formed bands, armed themselves with bows and inferior guns, took the warpath against us.

We fought them in little unimportant wars that were never quite conclusive. They persisted, always returning to the fight, laying ambushes for our men and wagons, harrying us continually, eventually making sizable inroads.

Yet we still considered them of such trifling importance that we found time to engage in a civil war among ourselves.

The issue of this war was sad. A dusky portion of our citizenry were enslaved and made to toil for us in house and field.

The Indians grew formidable. Step by step they drove us back across the wide midwestern rivers and plains, through the wooded mountains to eastward.

On the eastern coast we held for a while, chiefly by leaguing with a transoceanic island nation, to whom we surrendered our independence.

There was an enheartening occurrence. The enslaved Negroes were gathered together and crowded in ships and taken to the southern shores of this continent, and there liberated or given into the hands of warlike tribes who eventually released them.

But the pressure of the Indians, sporadically aided by foreign allies, increased. City by city, town by town, settlement by settlement, we pulled up our stakes and took ship ourselves across the sea. Toward the end the Indians became strangely pacific, so that the last boatloads seemed to flee not so much in physical fear as in supernatural terror of the green silent forests that had swallowed up their homes.

To the south the Aztecs took up their glass knives and flint-edged swords and drove out the . . . I think they were called Spaniards.

In another century the whole western continent was forgotten, save for dim, haunting recollections.

Growing tyranny and ignorance, a constant contraction of frontiers, rebellions of the downtrodden, who in turn became oppressors—these constituted the next epoch of history.

Once I thought the tide had turned. A strong and orderly people, the Romans, arose and put most of the diminished world under their sway.

But this stability proved transitory. Once again the governed rose against the governors. The Romans were driven back—from England, from Egypt, from Gaul, from Asia, from Greece. Rising from barren fields came Carthage to contest successfully Rome's preeminence. The Romans took refuge in Rome, became unimportant, dwindled, were lost in a maze of migrations.

Their energizing thoughts flamed up for one glorious century in Athens, then ceased to carry weight.

After that, the decline continued at a steady pace. Never again was I deceived into thinking the trend had changed.

Except this one last time.

Because she was stony and sun-drenched and dry, full of temples and tombs, given to custom and calm, I thought Egypt would endure. The passage of almost changeless centuries encouraged me in this belief. I thought that if we had not reached the turning point, we had at least come to rest.

But the rains have come, the temples and tombs fill the scars in the cliffs, and the custom and calm have given way to the restless urges of the nomad.

If there is a turning point, it will not come until man is one with the beasts.

And Egypt must vanish like the rest.

Tomorrow Maot and I set out. Our flock is gathered. Our tent is rolled.

Maot is afire with youth. She is very loving.

It will be strange in the desert. All too soon we will exchange our last and sweetest kiss and she will prattle to me childishly and I will look after her until we find her mother.

Or perhaps some day I will abandon her in the desert, and her mother will find her.

And I will go on.

The Ship Sails At Midnight

THIS IS the story of a beautiful woman.

And of a monster.

It is also the story of four silly, selfish, culture-bound inhabitants of the planet Earth. Es, who was something of an artist. Gene, who studied atoms—and fought the world and himself. Louis, who philosophized. And Larry—that's my name—who tried to write books.

It was an eerie, stifling August when we met Helen. The date is fixed in my mind because our little city had just had its mid-western sluggishness ruffled by a series of those scares that either give rise to oddity items in the newspapers, or else are caused by them—it's sometimes hard to tell which. People had seen flying disks and heard noises in the sky—someone from the college geology department tried unsuccessfully to track down a meteorite. A farmer this side of the old coal pits got all excited about something "big and shapeless" that disturbed his poultry and frightened his wife, and for a couple of days men tracked around fruitlessly with shotguns—just another of those "rural monster" scares.

Even the townfolk hadn't been left out. For their imaginative enrichment they had a "Hypnotism Burglar," an apparently mild enough chap who blinked soft lights in people's faces and droned some siren-song outside their houses at night. For a week high-school girls squealed twice as loud after dark, men squared their shoulders adventurously at strangers, and women peered uneasily out of their bedroom windows after turning out the lights.

Louis and Es and I had picked up Gene at the college library and wanted a bite to eat before we turned in. Although by now they had almost petered out, we were talking about our local scares—a chilly hint of the supernatural makes good conversational fare in a month too hot for any real thinking. We slouched into the one decent open-all-night restaurant our dismal burg possesses (it wouldn't have that if it weren't for the "wild" college folk) and found that Benny had a new waitress.

She was really very beautiful, much too exotically beautiful for Benny's. Masses of pale gold ringlets piled high on her head. An aristocratic bone structure (from Es's greedy look I could tell she was instantly thinking sculpture). And a pair of the dreamiest, calmest eyes in the world.

She came over to our table and silently waited for our orders. Probably because her beauty flustered us, we put on an elaborate version of our act of "intellectuals precisely and patiently explaining their desires to a pig-headed member of the proletariat." She listened, nodded, and presently returned with our orders.

Louis had asked for just a cup of black coffee.

She brought him a half cantaloup also.

He sat looking at it for a moment. Then he chuckled incredulously. "You know, I actually wanted that," he said. "But I didn't know I wanted it. You must have read my subconscious mind."

"What's that?" she asked in a low, lovely voice with intonations rather like Benny's.

Digging into his cantaloup, Louis sketched an explanation suitable for fifth-graders.

She disregarded the explanation. "What do you use it for?" she asked.

Louis, who is something of a wit, said, "I don't use it. It uses me."

"That the way it should be?" she commented.

None of us knew the answer to that one, so since I was the Gang's specialist in dealing with the lower orders, I remarked brilliantly, "What's your name?"

"Helen," she told me.

"How long have you been here?"

"Couple days," she said, starting back toward the counter.

"Where did you come from?"

She spread her hands. "Oh—places."

Whereupon Gene, whose humor inclines toward the fantastic, asked, "Did you arrive on a flying disk?"

She glanced back at him and said, "Wise guy."

But all the same she hung around our table, filling sugar basins and what not. We made our conversation especially erudite, each of us merrily spinning his favorite web of half understood intellectual jargon and half-baked private opinion. We were conscious of her presence, all right.

Just as we were leaving, the thing happened. At the doorway something made us all look back. Helen was behind the counter. She was looking at us. Her eyes weren't dreamy at all, but focused, intent, radiant. She was smiling.

My elbow was touching Es's naked arm—we were rather crowded in the doorway—and I felt her shiver. Then she gave a tiny jerk and I sensed that Gene, who was holding her other arm (they were more or less sweethearts), had tightened his grip on it.

For perhaps three seconds it stayed just like that, the four of us looking at the one of her. Then Helen shyly dropped her gaze and began to mop the counter with a rag.

We were all very quiet going home.

Next night we went back to Benny's again, rather earlier. Helen was still there, and quite as beautiful as we remembered her. We exchanged with her a few more of those brief, teasing remarks—her voice no longer sounded so much like Benny's—and staged some more intellectual pyrotechnics for her benefit. Just before we left, Es went up to her at the counter and talked to her privately for perhaps a minute, at the end of which Helen nodded.

"Ask her to pose for you?" I asked Es when we got outside.

She nodded. "That girl has the most magnificent figure in the world," she proclaimed fervently.

"Or out of it," Gene confirmed grudgingly.

"And an incredibly exciting skull," Es finished.

It was characteristic of us that Es should have been the one to really break the ice with Helen. Like most intellectuals, we were rather timid, always setting up barriers against other people. We clung to adolescence and the college, although all of us but Gene had been graduated from it. Instead of getting out into the real world, we lived by sponging off our parents and doing academic odd jobs for the professors (Es had a few private students). Here in our home city we had status, you see. We were looked upon as being frightfully clever and sophisticated, the local "bohemian set" (though Lord knows we were anything but that). Whereas out in the real world we'd have been greenhorns.

We were scared of the world, you see. Scared that it would find out that all our vaunted abilities and projects didn't amount to much—and that as for solid achievements, there just hadn't been any. Es was only a mediocre artist; she was afraid to learn from the great, especially the living great, for fear her own affected little individuality would be engulfed. Louis was no philosopher; he merely cultivated a series of intellectual enthusiasms, living in a state of feverish private—and fruitless—excitement over the thoughts of other men. My own defense against reality consisted of knowingness and a cynical attitude; I had a remarkable packrat accumulation of information; I had a line on everything—and also always knew why it wasn't worth bothering with. As for Gene, he was the best of us and also the worst. A bit younger, he still applied himself to his studies, and showed promise in nuclear physics and math. But something, perhaps his small size and puritanical farm background, had made him moody and contrary, and given him an inclination toward physical violence that threatened some day to get him into real trouble. As it was, he'd had his license taken away for reckless driving. And several times we'd had to intervene—once unsuccessfully—to keep him from getting beaten up in bars.

We talked a great deal about our "work." Actually we spent much more time reading magazines and detective stories, lazing around, getting drunk, and conducting our endless intellectual palavers.

If we had one real virtue, it was our loyalty to each other, though it wouldn't take a cynic to point out that we desperately needed each other for an audience. Still, there was some genuine feeling there.

In short, like many people on a planet where mind is wakening and has barely become aware of the eon-old fetters and blindfolds oppressing it, and has had just the faintest glimpse of its tremendous possible future destiny, we were badly cowed—frightened, frustrated, self-centered, slothful, vain, pretentious.

Considering how set we were getting in those attitudes, it is all the more amazing that Helen had the tremendous effect on us that she did. For within a month of meeting her, our attitude toward the whole world had sweetened, we had become genuinely interested in people instead of being frightened of them, and we were beginning to do real creative work. An astonishing achievement for an unknown little waitress!

It wasn't that she took us in hand or set us an example, or anything like that. Quite the opposite. I don't think that Helen was responsible for a half dozen positive statements (and only one really impulsive act) during the whole time we knew her. Rather, she was like a Great Books discussion leader, who never voices an opinion of his own, but only leads other people to voice theirs—playing the part of an intellectual midwife.

Louis and Gene and I would drop over to Es's, say, and find Helen getting dressed behind the screen or taking a cup of tea after a session of posing. We'd start a discussion and for a while Helen would listen dreamily, just another shadow in the high old shadowy room. But then those startling little questions of hers would begin to come, each one opening a new vista of thought. By the time the discussion was finished—which might be at the Blue Moon bar or under the campus maples or watching the water ripple in the old coal pits— we'd have got somewhere. Instead of ending in weary shoulder-shrugging or cynical grousing at the world or getting drunk out of sheer frustration, we'd finish up with a plan—some facts to check, something to write or shape or try.

And then, people! How would we ever have got close to people without Helen? Without Helen, Old Gus would have stayed an ancient and bleary-eyed dishwasher at Benny's. But with Helen, Gus became for us what he really was—a figure of romance who had sailed the Seven Seas, who had hunted for gold on the Orinoco with twenty female Indians for porters (because the males were too lazy and proud to hire out to do anything) and who had marched at the head of his Amazon band carrying a newborn baby of one of the women in his generous arms (because the women assured him that a man-child was the only burden a man might carry without dishonor).

Even Gene was softened in his attitudes. I remember once when two handsome truckdrivers tried to pick up Helen at the Blue Moon. Instantly Gene's jaw muscles bulged and his eyes went blank and he began to wag his right shoulder—and I got ready for a scene. But Helen said a word here and there, threw in a soft laugh, and began to ask the truckdrivers her questions. In ten minutes we were all at ease and the four of us found out things we'd never dreamed about dark highways and diesels and their proud, dark-souled pilots (so like Gene in their temperaments).

But it was on us as individuals that Helen's influence showed up the biggest. Es's sculptures acquired an altogether new scope. She dropped her pet mannerisms without a tear and began to take into her work whatever was sound and good. She rapidly developed a style that was classical and yet had in it something that was wholly of the future. Es is getting recognition now and her work is still good, but there was a magic about her "Helenic Period" which she can't recapture. The magic still lives in the pieces she did at that time—particularly in a nude of Helen that has all the serenity and purpose of the best ancient Egyptian work, and something much more. As we watched that piece take form, as we watched the clay grow into Helen under Es's hands, we dimly sensed that in some indescribable way Helen was growing into Es at the same time, and Es into Helen. It was such a beautiful, subtle relationship that even Gene couldn't be jealous.

At the same time Louis gave over his fickle philosophical flirtations and found the field of inquiry for which he'd always been looking—a blend of semantics and introspective psychology designed to chart the chaotic inner world of human experience. Although his present intellectual tactics lack the brilliance they had when Helen was nudging his mind, he still keeps doggedly at the project, which promises to add a whole new range of words to the vocabulary of psychology and perhaps of the English language.

Gene wasn't ripe for creative work, but from being a merely promising student he became a brilliant and very industrious one, rather to the surprise of his professors. Even with the cloud that now overhangs his life and darkens his reputation, he has managed to find worthwhile employment on one of the big nuclear projects.

As for myself, I really began to write. Enough said.

We sometimes used to speculate as to the secret of Helen's effect on us, though we didn't by any means give her all the credit in those days. We had some sort of theory that Helen was a completely "natural" person, a "noble savage" (from the kitchen), a bridge to the world of proletarian reality. Es once said that Helen couldn't have had a Freudian childhood, whatever she meant by that. Louis spoke of Helen's unthinking social courage and Gene of the catalytic effect of beauty.

Oddly, in these discussions we never referred to that strange, electric experience we'd all had when we first met Helen—that tearing moment when we'd looked back from the doorway. We were always strangely reticent there. And none of us ever voiced the conviction that I'm sure all of us had at times: that our social and psychoanalytic theories weren't worth a hoot when it came to explaining Helen, that she possessed powers of feeling and mind (mostly concealed) that set her utterly apart from every other inhabitant of the planet Earth, that she was like a being from another, far saner and lovelier world.

That conviction isn't unusual, come to think of it. It's the one every man has about the girl he loves. Which brings me to my own secret explanation of Helen's effect on me (though not on the others).

It was simply this. I loved Helen and I knew Helen loved me. And that was quite enough.

It happened scarcely a month after we'd met. We were staging a little party at Es's. Since I was the one with the car, I was assigned to pick up Helen at Benny's when she got through. On the short drive I passed a house that held unpleasant memories for me. A girl had lived there whom I'd been crazy about and who had turned me down. (No, let's be honest, I turned her down, though I very much wanted her, because of some tragic cowardice, the memory of which always sears me like a hot iron.)

Helen must have guessed something from my expression, for she said softly, "What's the matter, Larry?" and then, when I ignored the question, "Something about a girl?"

She was so sympathetic about it that I broke down and told her the whole story, sitting in the parked and lightless car in front of Es's. I let myself go and lived through the whole thing again, with all its biting shame. When I was finished I looked up from the steering wheel. The streetlight made a pale aureole around Helen's head and a paler one where the white angora sweater covered her shoulders. The upper part of her face was in darkness, but a bit of light touched her full lips and narrow, almost fennec- or fox-like chin.

"You poor kid," she said softly, and the next moment we were kissing each other, and a feeling of utter relief and courage and power was budding deep inside me.

A bit later she said to me something that even at the time I realized was very wise.

"Let's keep this between you and me, Larry," she said. "Let's not mention it to the others. Let's not even hint." She paused, and then added, a trifle unhappily, "I'm afraid they wouldn't appreciate it. Sometime, I hope—but not quite yet."

I knew what she meant. That Gene and Louis and even Es were only human—that is, irrational—in their jealousies, and that the knowledge that Helen was my girl would have put a damper on the exciting but almost childlike relationship of the five of us. (As the fact of Es's and Gene's love would never have done. Es was a rather cold, awkward girl, and Louis and I seldom grudged poor, angry Gene her affection.)

So when Helen and I dashed in and found the others berating Benny for making Helen work overtime, we agreed that he was an unshaven and heartless louse, and in a little while the party was going strong and we were laughing and talking unconstrainedly. No one could possibly have guessed that a new and very lovely factor had been added to the situation.

After that evening everything was different for me. I had a girl. Helen was (why not say the trite things, they're true) my goddess, my worshipper, my slave, my ruler, my inspiration, my comfort, my refuge—oh, I could write books about what she meant to me.

I guess all my life I will be writing books about that.

I could write pages describing just one of the beautiful moments we had together. I could drown myself in the bitter ghosts of sensations. Rush of sunlight through her hair. Click of her heels on a brick sidewalk. Light of her presence brightening a mean room. Chase of unearthly expressions across her sleeping face.

Yet it was on my mind that Helen's love had the greatest effect. It unfettered my thoughts, gave them passage into a far vaster cosmos.

One minute I'd be beside Helen, our hands touching lightly in the dark, a shaft of moonlight from the dusty window silvering her hair. The next, my mind would be a billion miles up, hovering like an iridescent insect over the million bright worlds of existence.

Or I'd be surmounting walls inside my mind—craggy, dire ramparts that have been there since the days of the cave man.

Or the universe would become a miraculous web, with Time the spider. I couldn't see all of it—no creature could see a trillionth of it in all eternity—but I would have a sense of it all.

Sometimes the icy beauty of those moments would become too great, and I'd feel a sudden chill of terror. Then the scene around me would become a nightmare and I'd half expect Helen's eyes to show a catlike gleam and slit, or her hair to come rustlingly alive, or her arms to writhe bonelessly, or her splendid skin to slough away, revealing some black and antlike form of dread.

Then the moment would pass and everything would be sheer loveliness again, richer for the fleeting terror.

My mind is hobbled once more now, but I still know the taste of the inward freedom that Helen's love brought.

You might think from this that Helen and I had a lot of times alone together. We hadn't—we couldn't have, with the Gang. But we had enough. Helen was clever at arranging things. They never suspected us.

Lord knows there were times I yearned to let the Gang in on our secret. But then I would remember Helen's warning and see the truth of it.

Let's face it. We're all of us a pretty vain and possessive people. As individuals, we cry for attention. We jockey for admiration. We swim or sink according to whether we feel we're being worshipped or merely liked. We demand too much of the person we love. We want them to be a neverfailing prop to our ego.

And then if we're lonely and happen to see someone else loved, the greedy child wakes, the savage stirs, the frustrated Puritan clenches his teeth. We seethe, we resent, we hate.

No, I saw that I couldn't tell the others about Helen and myself. Not Louis. Not even Es. And as for Gene, I'm afraid that with his narrow-minded upbringing, he'd have been deeply shocked by what he'd have deduced about our relationship. We were supposed, you know, to be "wild" young people, "bohemians." Actually we were quite straitlaced—Gene especially, the rest of us almost as much.

I knew how I would have felt if Helen had happened to become Louis's or Gene's girl. That says it.

To tell the truth, I felt a great deal of admiration for the Gang, because they could do alone what I was only doing with Helen's love. They were enlarging their minds, becoming creative, working and playing hard—and doing it without my reward. Frankly, I don't know how I could have managed it myself without Helen's love. My admiration for Louis, Es, and Gene was touched with a kind of awe.

And we really were getting places. We had created a new mind-spot on the world, a sprouting-place for thought that wasn't vain or self-conscious, but concerned wholly with its work and its delights. The Gang was forming itself into a kind of lens for viewing the world, outside and in.

Any group of people can make themselves into that sort of lens, if they really want to. But somehow they seldom get started. They don't have the right inspiration.

We had Helen.

Always, but mostly in unspoken thoughts, we'd come back to the mystery of how she had managed it. She was mysterious, all right. We'd known her some six months now, and we were as much in the dark about her background as when we first met her. She wouldn't tell anything even to me. She'd come from "places." She was a "drifter." She liked "people." She told us all sorts of fascinating incidents, but whether she'd been mixed up in them herself or just heard them at Benny's (she could have made a Trappist jabber) was uncertain.

We sometimes tried to get her to talk about her past. But she dodged our questions easily and we didn't like to press them.

You don't cross-examine Beauty.

You don't demand that a Great Books discussion leader state his convictions.

You don't probe a goddess about her past.

Yet this vagueness about Helen's past caused us a certain uneasiness. She'd drifted to us. She might drift away.

If we hadn't been so involved in our thought-sprouting, we'd have been worried. And if I hadn't been so happy, and everything so smoothly perfect, I'd have done more than occasionally ask Helen to marry me and hear her answer, "Not now, Larry."

Yes, she was mysterious.

And she had her eccentricities.

For one thing, she insisted on working at Benny's although she could have had a dozen better jobs. Benny's was her window on the main street of life, she said.

For another, she'd go off on long hikes in the country, even in the snowiest weather. I met her coming back from one and was worried, tried to be angry. But she only smiled.

Yet, when spring came round again and burgeoned into summer, she would never go swimming with us in our favorite coal pit.

The coal pits are a place where they once strip-mined for the stuff where it came to the surface. Long ago the huge holes were left to fill with water and their edges to grow green with grass and trees. They're swell for swimming.

But Helen would never go to our favorite, which was one of the biggest and yet the least visited—and this year the water was unusually high. We changed to suit her, of course, but because the one she didn't like happened to be near the farmhouse of last August's "rural monster" scare, Louis joshed her.

"Maybe a monster haunts the pool," he said. "Maybe it's a being come from another world on a flying disk."

He happened to say that on a lazy afternoon when we'd been swimming at the new coal pit and were drying on the edge, having cigarettes. Louis' remark started us speculating about creatures from another world coming secretly to visit Earth—their problems, especially how they'd disguise themselves.

"Maybe they'd watch from a distance," Gene said. "Television, supersensitive microphones."

"Or clairvoyance, clairaudience," Es chimed, being rather keen on para-psychology.

"But to really mingle with people . . ." Helen murmured. She was stretched on her back in white bra and trunks, looking deep into the ranks of marching clouds. Her olive skin tanned to an odd hue that went bewitchingly with her hair. With a sudden and frightening poignancy I was aware of the catlike perfection of her slim body.

"The creature might have some sort of elaborate plastic disguise," Gene began doubtfully.

"It might have a human form to begin with," I ventured. "You know, the idea that Earth folk are decayed interstellar colonists."

"It might take possession of some person here," Louis cut in. "Insinuate its mind or even itself into the human being."

"Or it might grow itself a new body," Helen murmured sleepily. That was one of the half dozen positive statements she ever made.

Then we got to talking about the motives of such an alien being. Whether it would try to destroy men, or look on us as cattle, or study us, or amuse itself with us, or what not.

Here Helen joined in again, distant-eyed but smiling. "I know you've all laughed at the comic-book idea of some Martian monster lusting after beautiful white women. But has it ever occurred to you that a creature from outside might simply and honestly fall in love with you?"

That was another of Helen's rare positive statements.

The idea was engaging and we tried to get Helen to expand it, but she wouldn't. In fact, she was rather silent the rest of that day.

As the summer began to mount toward its crests of heat and growth, the mystery of Helen began to possess us more often—that, and a certain anxiety about her.

There was a feeling in the air, the sort of uneasiness that cats and dogs get when they are about to lose their owner.

Without exactly knowing it, without a definite word being said, we were afraid we might lose Helen.

Partly it was Helen's own behavior. For once she showed a kind of restlessness, or rather preoccupation. At Benny's she no longer took such an interest in "people."

She seemed to be trying to solve some difficult personal problem, nerve herself to make some big decision.

Once she looked at us and said, "You know, I like you kids terribly." Said it the way a person says it when he knows he may have to lose what he likes.

And then there was the business of the Stranger.

Helen had been talking quite a bit with a strange man, not at

Benny's, but walking in the streets, which was unusual. We didn't know who the Stranger was. We hadn't actually seen him face to face. Just heard about him from Benny and glimpsed him once or twice. Yet he worried us.

Understand, our happiness went on, yet faintly veiling it was this new and ominous mist.

Then one night the mist took definite shape. It happened on an occasion of celebration. After a few days during which we'd sensed they'd been quarreling, Es and Gene had suddenly announced that they were getting married. On an immediate impulse we'd all gone to the Blue Moon.

We were having the third round of drinks, and kidding Es because she didn't seem very enthusiastic, almost a bit grumpy—when he came in.

Even before he looked our way, before he drifted up to our table, we knew that this was the Stranger.

He was a rather slender man, fair haired like Helen. Otherwise he didn't look like her, yet there was a sense of kinship. Perhaps it lay in his poise, his wholly casual manner.

As he came up, I could feel myself and the others getting tense, like dogs at the approach of the unknown.

The Stranger stopped by our table and stood looking at Helen as if he knew her. The four of us realized more than ever that we wanted Helen to be ours alone (and especially mine), that we hated to think of her having close ties with anyone else.

What got especially under my skin was the suggestion that there was some kinship between the Stranger and Helen, that behind his proud, remote-eyed face, he was talking to her with his mind.

Gene apparently took the Stranger for one of those unpleasant fellows who strut around bars looking for trouble—and proceeded to act as if he were one of those same fellows himself. He screwed his delicate features into a cheap frown and stood up as tall as he could, which wasn't much. Such tough-guy behavior, always a symptom of frustration and doubts of masculinity, had been foreign to Gene for some months. I felt a pulse of sadness—and almost winced when Gene opened the side of his mouth and began, "Now look here, Joe—"

But Helen laid her hand on his arm. She looked calmly at the

Stranger for a few more moments and then she said, "I won't talk to you that way. You must speak English."

If the Stranger was surprised, he didn't show it. He smiled and said softly, with a faint foreign accent, "The ship sails at midnight, Helen."

I got a queer feeling, for our city is two hundred miles from anything you'd call navigable waters.

For a moment I felt what you might call supernatural fear. The bar so tawdry and dim, the line of hunched neurotic shoulders, the plump dice-girl at one end and the tiny writhing television screen at the other. And against that background, Helen and the Stranger, light-haired, olive-skinned, with proud feline features, facing each other like duelists, on guard, opposed, yet sharing some secret knowledge. Like two aristocrats come to a dive to settle a quarrel—like that, and something more. As I say, it frightened me.

"Are you coming, Helen?" the Stranger asked.

And now I was really frightened. It was as if I'd realized for the first time just how terribly much Helen meant to all of us, and to me especially. Not just the loss of her, but the loss of things in me that only she could call into being. I could see the same fear in the faces of the others. A lost look in Gene's eyes behind the fake gangster frown. Louis' fingers relaxing from his glass and his chunky head turning toward the Stranger, slowly, with empty gaze, like the turret-guns of a battleship. Es starting to stub out her cigarette and then hesitating, her eyes on Helen—although in Es's case I felt there was another emotion besides fear.

"Coming?" Helen echoed, like someone in a dream.

The Stranger waited. Helen's reply had twisted the tension tighter. Now Es did stub out her cigarette with awkward haste, then quickly drew back her hand. I felt suddenly that this had been bound to happen, that Helen must have had her life, her real life, before we had known her, and that the Stranger was part of it; that she had come to us mysteriously and now would leave us as mysteriously. Yes, I felt all of that, although in view of what had happened between Helen and me, I knew I shouldn't have.

"Have you considered everything?" the Stranger asked finally.

"Yes," Helen replied.

"You know that after tonight there'll be no going back," he continued as softly as ever. "You know that you'll be marooned here forever, that you'll have to spend the rest of your life among . . ." (he looked around at us as if searching for a word) ". . . among barbarians."

Again Helen laid her hand on Gene's arm, although her glance never left the Stranger's face.

"What is the attraction, Helen?" the Stranger went on. "Have you really tried to analyze it? I know it might be fun for a month, or a year, or even five years. A kind of game, a renewal of youth. But when it's over and you're tired of the game, when you realize that you're alone, completely alone, and that there's no going back ever— Have you thought of that?"

"Yes, I have thought of all that," Helen said, as quietly as the Stranger, but with a tremendous finality. "I won't try to explain it to you, because with all your wisdom and cleverness I don't think you'd quite understand. And I know I'm breaking promises—and more than promises. But I'm not going back. I'm here with my friends, my true and equal friends, and I'm not going back."

And then it came, and I could tell it came to all of us—a great big lift, like a surge of silent music or a glow of invisible light. Helen had at last declared herself. After the faint equivocations and reservations of the spring and summer, she had put herself squarely on our side. We each of us knew that what she had said she meant wholly and forever. She was ours, ours more completely than ever before. Our quasi-goddess, our inspiration, our key to a widening future; the one who always understood, who could open doors in our imaginations and feelings that would otherwise have remained forever shut. She was our Helen now, ours and (as my mind persisted in adding exultingly) especially mine.

And we? We were the Gang again, happy, poised, wise as Heaven and clever as Hell, out to celebrate, having fun with whatever came along.

The whole scene had changed. The frightening aura around the Stranger had vanished completely. He was just another of those hundreds of odd people whom we met when we were with Helen.

He acted almost as if he were conscious of it. He smiled and said quickly, "Very well. I had a feeling you'd decide this way." He started to move off. Then, "Oh, by the way, Helen—"

"Yes?"

"The others wanted me to say goodby to you for them."

"Tell them the same and the best of luck."

The Stranger nodded and again started to turn away, when Helen added, "And you?"

The Stranger looked back.

"I'll be seeing you once more before midnight," he said lightly, and almost the next moment, it seemed, was out the door.

We all chuckled. I don't know why. Partly from relief, I suppose, and partly—God help us!—in triumph over the Stranger. One thing I'm sure of: three (and maybe even four) of us felt for a moment happier and more secure in our relationship to Helen than we ever had before. It was the peak. We were together. The Stranger had been vanquished, and all the queer unspoken threats he had brought with him. Helen had declared herself. The future stood open before us, full of creation and achievement, with Helen ready to lead us into it. For a moment everything was perfect. We were mankind, vibrantly alive, triumphantly progressing.

It was, as I say, perfect.

And only human beings know how to wreck perfection.

Only human beings are so vain, so greedy, each wanting everything for himself alone.

It was Gene who did it. Gene who couldn't stand so much happiness and who had to destroy it, from what self-fear, what Puritanical self-torment, what death-wish I don't know.

It was Gene, but it might have been any of us.

His face was flushed. He was smiling, grinning rather, in what I now realize was an oafish and over-bearing complacency. He put his hand on Helen's arm in a way none of us had ever touched Helen before, and said, "That was great, dear."

It wasn't so much what he said as the naked possessiveness of the gesture. It was surely that gesture of ownership that made Es explode, that started her talking in a voice terribly bitter, but so low it was some moments before the rest of us realized what she was getting at.

When we did we were thunderstruck.

She was accusing Helen of having stolen Gene's love.

It's hard to make anyone understand the shock we felt. As if some-one had accused a goddess of abominations.

Es lit another cigarette with shaking fingers, and finished up.

"I don't want your pity, Helen. I don't want Gene married off to me for the sake of appearances, like some half-discarded mistress. I like you, Helen, but not enough to let you take Gene away from me and then toss him back—or half toss him back. No, I draw the line at that."

And she stopped as if her emotions had choked her.

As I said, the rest of us were thunderstruck. But not Gene. His face got redder still. He slugged down the rest of his drink and looked around at us, obviously getting ready to explode in turn.

Helen had listened to Es with a half smile and an unhappy half frown, shaking her head from time to time. Now she shot Gene a warning, imploring glance, but he disregarded it.

"No, Helen," he said, "Es is right. I'm glad she spoke. It was a mistake for us ever to hide our feelings. It would have been a ten times worse mistake if I'd kept that crazy promise I made you to marry Es. You go too much by pity, Helen, and pity's no use in man-aging an affair like this. I don't want to hurt Es, but she'd better know right now that it's another marriage we're announcing tonight."

I sat there speechless. I just couldn't realize that that drunken, red-faced poppinjay was claiming that Helen was his girl, his wife to be.

Es didn't look at him. "You cheap little beast," she whispered.

Gene went white at that, but he kept on smiling.

"Es may not forgive me for this," he said harshly, "but I don't think it's me she's jealous of. What gets under her skin is not so much losing me to Helen as losing Helen to me."

Then I could find words.

But Louis was ahead of me.

He put his hand firmly on Gene's shoulder.

"You're drunk, Gene," he said, "and you're talking like a drunken fool. Helen's my girl."

They started up, both of them, Louis's hand still on Gene's shoulder.

Then, instead of hitting each other, they looked at me.

Because I had risen too.

"But . . ." I began, and faltered.

Without my saying it, they knew.

Louis's hand dropped away from Gene.

All of us looked at Helen. A cold, terribly hurt, horribly disgusted look.

Helen blushed and looked down. Only much later did I realize it was related to the look she'd given the four of us that first night at Benny's.

". . . but I fell in love with all of you," she said softly.

Then we did speak, or rather Gene spoke for us. I hate to admit it, but at the time I felt a hot throb of pleasure at all the unforgivable things he called Helen. I wanted to see the lash laid on, the stones thud.

Finally he called her some names that were a little worse.

Then Helen did the only impulsive thing I ever knew her to do.

She slapped Gene's face. Once. Hard.

There are only two courses a person can take when he's been rebuked by a goddess, even a fallen goddess. He can grovel and beg forgiveness. Or he can turn apostate and devil-worshipper.

Gene did the latter.

He walked out of the Blue Moon, blundering like a blind drunk.

That broke up the party, and Gus and the other bartender, who'd been about to interfere, returned relievedly to their jobs.

Louis went off to the bar. Es followed him. I went to the far end myself, under the writhing television screen, and ordered a double scotch.

Beyond the dozen intervening pairs of shoulders, I could see that Es was trying to act shameless. She was whispering things to Louis. At the same time, and even more awkwardly, she was flirting with one of the other men. Every once in a while she would laugh shrilly, mirthlessly.

Helen didn't move. She just sat at the table, looking down, the half smile fixed on her lips. Once Gus approached her, but she shook her head.

I ordered another double scotch. Suddenly my mind began to work furiously on three levels.

On the first I was loathing Helen. I was seeing that all she'd done for us, all the mind-spot, all the house of creativity we'd raised together, had been based on a lie. Helen was unutterably cheap, common.

Mostly, on that level, I was grieving for the terrible wrong I felt she'd done me.

The second level was entirely different. There an icy spider had entered my mind from realms undreamt. There sheer supernatural terror reigned. For there I was adding up all the little hints of strangeness we'd had about Helen. The Stranger's words had touched it off and now a thousand details began to drop into place: the coincidence of her arrival with the flying disk, rural monster, and hypnotism scare; her interest in people, like that of a student from a far land; the impression she gave of possessing concealed powers; her pains never to say anything definite, as if she were on guard against imparting some forbidden knowledge; her long hikes into the country; her aversion for the big and yet seldom-visited coal pit (big and deep enough to float a liner or hide a submarine); above all, that impression of unearthliness she'd at times given us all, even when we were most under her spell.

And now this matter of a ship sailing at midnight. From the Great Plains.

What sort of ship?

On that level my mind shrank from facing the obvious result of its labor. It was too frighteningly incredible, too far from the world of the Blue Moon and Benny's and cheap little waitresses.

The third level was far mistier, but it was there. At least I tell myself it was there. On this third level I was beginning to see Helen in a better light and the rest of us in a worse. I was beginning to see the lovelessness behind our idea of love—and the faithfulness, to the best in us, behind Helen's faithlessness. I was beginning to see how hateful, how like spoiled children, we'd been acting.

Of course, maybe there wasn't any third level in my mind at all. Maybe that only came afterwards. Maybe I'm just trying to flatter myself that I was a little more discerning, a little "bigger" than the others.

Yet I like to think that I turned away from the bar and took a couple of steps toward Helen, that it was only those "second level"

fears that slowed me so that I'd only taken those two faltering steps
(if I took them) before—

Before Gene walked in.

I remember the clock said eleven thirty.

Gene's face was dead white, and knobby with tension.

His hand was in his pocket.

He never looked at anyone but Helen. They might have been
alone. He wavered—or trembled. Then a terrible spasm of energy
stiffened him. He started toward the table.

Helen got up and walked toward him, her arms outstretched. In
her half smile were all the compassion and fatalism—and love—I can
imagine there being in the universe.

Gene pulled a gun out of his pocket and shot Helen six times. Four
times in the body, twice in the head.

She hung for a moment, then pitched forward into the blue smoke.
It puffed away from her to either side and we saw her lying on her
face, one of her outstretched hands touching Gene's shoe.

Then, before a woman could scream, before Gus and the other
chap could jump the bar, the outside door of the Blue Moon opened
and the Stranger came in. After that none of us could have moved
or spoken. We cringed from his eyes like guilty dogs.

It wasn't that he looked anger at us, or hate, or even contempt.
That would have been much easier to bear.

No, even as the Stranger passed Gene—Gene, pistol dangling from
two fingers, looking down in dumb horror, edging his toe back by
terrified inches from Helen's dead hand—even as the Stranger sent
Gene a glance, it was the glance a man might give a bull that has
gored a child, a pet ape that has torn up his mistress in some inscrutable and pettish animal rage.

And as, without a word, the Stranger picked Helen up in his arms,
and carried her silently through the thinning blue smoke into the
street, his face bore that same look of tragic regret, of serene ac-
ceptance.

That's almost all there is to my story. Gene was arrested, of course,
but it's not easy to convict a man of murder of a woman without real
identity.

For Helen's body was never found. Neither was the Stranger.

Eventually Gene was released and, as I've said, is making a life for himself, despite the cloud over his reputation.

We see him now and then, and try to console him, tell him it might as easily have been Es or Louis or I, that we were all blind, selfish fools together.

And we've each of us got back to our work. The sculptures, the word-studies, the novels, the nuclear notions are not nearly as brilliant as when Helen was with us. But we keep turning them out. We tell ourselves Helen would like that.

And our minds all work now at the third level—but only by fits and starts, fighting the jungle blindness and selfishness that are closing in again. Still, at our best, we understand Helen and what Helen was trying to do, what she was trying to bring the world even if the world wasn't ready for it. We glimpse that strange passion that made her sacrifice all the stars for four miserable blind-worms.

But mostly we grieve for Helen, together and alone. We know there won't be another Helen for a hundred thousand years, if then. We know that she's gone a lot farther than the dozens or thousands of light-years her body's been taken for burial. We look at Es's statue of Helen, we read one or two of my poems to her. We remember, our minds come half alive and are tortured by the thought of what they might have become if we'd kept Helen. We picture her again sitting in the shadows of Es's studio, or sunning herself on the grassy banks after a swim, or smiling at us at Benny's. And we grieve.

For we know you get only one chance at someone like Helen.

We know that because, half an hour after the Stranger carried Helen's body from the Blue Moon, a great meteor went flaming and roaring across the countryside (some say up from the countryside and out toward the stars) and the next day it was discovered that the waters of the coal pit Helen wouldn't swim in, had been splashed, as if by the downward blow of a giant's fist, across the fields for a thousand yards.

The Enchanted Forest

THE DARKNESS was fusty as Formalhautian Aa leaves, acrid as a Rigelian brush fire, and it still shook faintly, like one of the dancing houses of the Wild Ones. It was filled with a petulant, low humming, so like that of a wounded Earth-wasp.

Machinery whirred limpingly, briefly. An oval door opened in the darkness. Soft green light filtered in—and the unique scent, aromatic in this case yet with a grassy sourness, of a new planet.

The green was imparted to the light by the thorny boughs or creepers crisscrossing the doorway. To eyes dreary from deep sub-space the oval of interlaced, wrist-thick tendrils was a throat-lumping sight.

A human hand moved delicately from the darkness toward the green barrier. The finger-long, translucent thorns quivered, curved back ever so slowly, then struck—a hairbreadth short, for the hand had stopped.

The hand did not withdraw, but lingered just in range, caressing danger. A sharp gay laugh etched itself against the woundedly-humming dark.

Have to dust those devilish little green daggers to get out of the wreck, Elven thought. *Lucky they were here though. The thorn forest's cushioning-effect may have been the straw that saved the spaceboat's back—or at least mine.*

Then Elven stiffened. The humming behind him shaped itself into faint English speech altered by centuries of slurring, but still essentially the same.

"You fly fast, Elven."

"Faster than any of your hunters," Elven agreed softly without looking around, and added, "FTL—meaning Faster Than Light."

"You fly far, Elven. Tens of lightyears," the wounded voice continued.

"Scores," Elven corrected.

"Yet I speak to you, Elven."

"But you don't know where I am. I came on a blind reach through deep sub-space. And your FTL radio can take no fix. You are shouting at infinity, Fedris."

"And fly you ever so fast and far, Elven," the wounded voice persisted, "you must finally go to ground, and then we will search you out."

Again Elven laughed gayly. His eyes were still on the green doorway. "You will search me out! Where will you search me out, Fedris? On which side of the million planets of the sos? On which of the hundred million planets not of the sos?"

The wounded voice grew weaker. "Your home planet is dead, Elven. Of all the Wild Ones, only you slipped through our cordon."

This time Elven did not comment vocally. He felt at his throat and carefully took from a gleaming locket there a tiny white sphere no bigger than a lady beetle. Holding it treasuringly in his cupped palm, he studied it with a brooding mockery. Then, still handling it as if it were an awesome object, he replaced it in the locket.

The wounded voice had sunk to a ghostly whisper.

"You are alone, Elven. Alone with the mystery and terror of the universe. The unknown will find you, Elven, even before we do. Time and space and fate will all conspire against you. Chance itself will—"

The spectral FTL-radio voice died as the residual power in the wrecked machinery exhausted itself utterly. Silence filled the broken gut of the spaceboat.

Silence that was gayly shattered when Elven laughed a last time. Fedris the Psychologist! Fedris the Fool! Did Fedris think to sap his nerve with witch-doctor threats and the power of suggestion? As if a man—or woman—of the Wild Ones could ever be brought to believe in the supernatural!

Not that there wasn't an unearthliness loose in the universe, Elven reminded himself somberly—an unearthly beauty born of danger and ultimate self-expression. But only the Wild Ones knew *that* unearthliness. It could never be known to the poor tame hordes of the sos, who would always revere safety and timidity as most members of the human sos—or society—have revered them—and hate all lovers of beauty and danger.

Just as they had hated the Wild Ones and so destroyed them.

All save one.

One, had Fedris said? Elven smiled cryptically, touched the locket at his neck, and leaped lightly to his feet.

A short time later he had what he needed from the wreck.

"And now, Fedris," he murmured, "I have a work of creation to perform." He smiled. "Or should I say recreation?"

He directed at the green doorway the blunt muzzle of a dustgun. There was no sound or flash, but the green boughs shook, blackened —the thorns vanishing—and turned to a drifting powder fine and dark as the ashes carpeting Earth's Moon. Elven sprang to the doorway and for a moment he was poised there, yellow-haired, cool-lipped, laughing-eyed, handsome as a young god—or adolescent devil—in his black tunic embroidered with platinum. Then he leaned out and directed the dustgun's ultrasonic beam downward until he had cleared a patch of ground in the thorn forest. When this moment's work was over, he dropped lightly down, the fine dust puffing up to his knees at the impact.

Elven snapped off his dustgun, flirted sweat from his face, laughed at his growing exasperation, and looked around at the thorn forest. It had not changed an iota in the miles he'd made. Just the glassy thorns and the lance-shaped leaves and the boughs rising from the bare, reddish earth. Not another planet to be seen. Nor had he caught the tiniest glimpse of moving life, large or small—save the thorns themselves, which "noticed" him whenever he came too close. As an experiment he'd let a baby one prick him and it had stung abominably.

Such an environment! What did it suggest, anyhow? Cultivation? Or a plant that permeated its environs with poison, as Earth's redwood its woody body. He grinned at the chill that flashed along his spine.

And, if there were no animal life, what the devil were the thorns for?

A ridiculous forest! In its simplicity suggesting the enchanted forests of ancient Earthly fairy tales. That idea should please witch doctor Fedris!

If only he had some notion of the general location of the planet he was on, he might be able to make better guesses about its other life forms. Life spores did drift about in space, so that solar systems and even star regions tended to have biological similarities. But he'd come too fast and too curiously, too fast even to see stars, in the Wild Ones' fastest and most curious boat, to know where he was.

Or for Fedris to know where he was, he reminded himself.

Or for any deep-space approach-warning system, if there were one on this planet, to have spotted his arrival. For that matter he hadn't foreseen his arrival himself. There had been just the dip up from sub-space, the sinister black confetti of the meteorite swarm, the collision, the wrecked spaceboat's desperate fall, clutching at the nearest planet.

He should be able to judge his location when night came and he could see the stars. That is, if night ever came on this planet. Or if that high fog ever dispersed.

He consulted his compass. The needle of the primitive but useful instrument held true. At least this planet had magnetic poles.

And it probably had night and day, to support vegetable life and such a balmy temperature.

Once he got out of this forest, he'd be able to plan. Just give him cities! One city!

He tucked the compass in his tunic, patting the locket at his neck in a strangely affectionate, almost reverent way.

He looked at the laced boughs ahead. Yes, it was exactly like those fairy forests that cost fairy-book knights so much hackwork with their two-handed swords.

Easier with a dustgun—and he had scores of miles of cleared path in his store of ultrasonic refills.

He glanced back at the slightly curving tunnel he'd made.

Through the slaty ashes on its floor, wicked green shoots were already rising.

He snapped on the duster.

The boughs were so thick at its edge that the clearing took Elven by surprise. One moment he was watching a tangled green mat blacken under the duster's invisible beam. The next, he had stepped out—not into fairyland, but into the sort of place where fairy tales were first told.

The clearing was about a half mile in diameter. Round it the thorn forest made a circle. A little stream bubbled out of the poisonous greenery a hundred paces to his right and crossed the clearing through a shallow valley. Beyond the stream rose a small hill.

On the hillside was a ragged cluster of gray buildings. From one of them rose a pencil of smoke. Outside were a couple of carts and some primitive agricultural implements.

Save for the space occupied by the buildings, the valley was under intensive cultivation. The hill was planted at regular intervals with small trees bearing clusters of red and yellow fruit. Elsewhere were rows of bushy plants and fields of grain rippling in the breeze. All vegetation, however, seemed to stop about a yard from the thorn forest.

There was a mournful lowing. Around the hillside came a half dozen cattle. A man in a plain tunic was leisurely driving them toward the buildings. A tiny animal, perhaps a cat, came out of the building with the smoke and walked with the cattle, rubbing against their legs. A young woman came to the door after the cat and stood watching with folded arms.

Elven drank in the atmosphere of peace and rich earth, feeling like a man in an ancient room. Such idyllic scenes as this must have been Earth's in olden times. He felt his taut muscles relaxing.

A second young woman stepped out of a copse of trees just ahead and stood facing him, wide-eyed. She was dressed in a greenish tunic of softened, spun, and woven vegetable fibers. Elven sensed in her a certain charm, half sophisticated, half primitive. She was like one of the girls of the Wild Ones in a rustic play suit. But her face was that of an awestruck child.

He walked toward her through the rustling grain. She dropped to her knees.

"You . . . you—" she murmured with difficulty. Then, more swiftly, in perfect English speech, "Do not harm me, lord. Accept my reverence."

"I will not harm you, if you answer my questions well," Elven replied, accepting the advantage in status he seemed to have been given. "What place is this?"

"It is the Place," she replied simply.

"Yes, but what place?"

"It is the Place," she repeated quakingly. "There are no others."

"Then where did I come from?" he asked.

Her eyes widened a little with terror. "I do not know." She was redhaired and really quite beautiful.

Elven frowned. "What planet is this?"

She looked at him doubtfully. "What is a planet?"

Perhaps there were going to be language difficulties after all, Elven thought. "What sun?" he asked.

"What is sun?"

He pointed upward impatiently. "Doesn't that stuff ever go away?"

"You mean," she faltered fearfully, "does the sky ever go away?"

"The sky is always the same?"

"Sometimes it brightens. Now comes night."

"How far to the end of the thorn forest?"

"I do not understand." Then her gaze slipped beyond him, to the ragged doorway made by his duster. Her look of awe was intensified, became touched with horror. "You have conquered the poison needles," she whispered. Then she abased herself until her loose, red hair touched the russet shoots of the grain. "Do not hurt me, all-powerful one," she gasped.

"I cannot promise that," Elven told her curtly. "What is your name?"

"Sefora," she whispered.

"Very well, Sefora. Lead me to your people."

She sprang up and fled like a doe back to the farm buildings.

When Elven reached the roof from which the smoke rose, taking the leisurely pace befitting his dignity as god or overlord or whatever the girl had taken him for, the welcoming committee had already formed. Two young men bent their knees to him, and the young woman he had seen standing at the doorway held out to him a platter of orange and purple fruit. The Conqueror of the Poison Needles sampled this refreshment, then waved it aside with a curt nod of approval, although he found it delicious.

When he entered the rude farmhouse he was met by a blushing Sefora who carried cloths and a steaming bowl. She timidly indicated his boots. He showed her the trick of the fastenings and in a few moments he was sprawled on a couch of hides stuffed with aromatic leaves, while she reverently washed his feet.

She was about twenty, he discovered talking to her idly, not worrying about important information for the moment. Her life was one of farm work and rustic play. One of the young men—Alfors—had recently become her mate.

Outside the gray sky was swiftly darkening. The other young man, whom Elven had first seen driving the cattle and who answered to the name of Kors, now brought armfuls of knotty wood, which he fed to the meager fire, so that it crackled up in rich yellows and reds. While Tulya—Kors' girl—busied herself nearby with work that involved mouthwatering odors.

The atmosphere was homey, though somewhat stiff. After all, Elven reminded himself, one doesn't have a god to dinner every night. But after a meal of meat stew, fresh-baked bread, fruit conserves, and a thin wine, he smiled his approval and the atmosphere quickly became more celebratory, in fact quite gay. Alfors took a harp strung with gut and sang simple praises of nature, while later Sefora and Tulya danced. Kors kept the fire roaring and Elven's wine cup full, though once he disappeared for some time, evidently to care for the animals.

Elven brightened. These rustic folk faintly resembled his own Wild Ones. They seemed to have a touch of that reckless, ecstatic spirit so hated by the tame folk of the sos. (Though after a while the resemblance grew too painfully strong, and with an imperious gesture he moderated their gaiety.)

Meanwhile, by observation and question, he was swiftly learning, though what he learned was astonishing rather than helpful. These four young people were the sole inhabitants of their community. They knew nothing of any culture other than their own.

They had never seen the sun or the stars. Evidently this was a planet whose axes of rotation and of revolution around its sun were the same, so that the climate was always unvarying at each latitude, the present locality being under a cloud belt. Later he might check this, he told himself, by determining if the days and nights were always of equal length.

Strangest of all, the two couples had never been beyond the clearing. The thorn forest, which they conceived of as extending to infinity, was a barrier beyond their power to break. Fires, they told him, sizzled out against it. It swiftly dulled their sharpest axes. And they had a healthy awe of its diabolically sentient thorns.

All this suggested an obvious line of questioning.

"Where are your parents?" Elven asked Kors.

"Parents?" Kors' brow wrinkled.

"You mean the shining ones?" Tulya broke in. She looked sad. "They are gone."

"Shining ones?" Elven quizzed. "People like yourselves?"

"Oh no. Beings of metal with wheels for feet and long, clever arms that bent anywhere."

"I have always wished I were made of lovely, bright metal," Sefora commented wistfully, "with wheels instead of ugly feet, and a sweet voice that never changed, and a mind that knew everything and never lost its temper."

Tulya continued, "They told us when they went why they must go. So that we could live by our own powers alone, as all beings should. But we loved them and have always been sorry."

There was no getting away from it, Elven decided after making some casual use of his special mind-searching powers to test the veracity of their answers. These four people had actually been reared by robots of some sort. But why? A dozen fantastic, unprovable possibilities occurred to him. He remembered what Fedris had said about the mystery of the universe, and smiled wryly.

Then it was his turn to answer questions, hesitant and awestricken ones. He replied simply, "I am a black angel from above. When God created his universe he decided it would be a pretty dull place if there weren't a few souls in it willing to take all risks and dare all dangers. So here and there among his infinite flocks of tame angels, sparingly, he introduced a wild strain, so that there would always be a few souls who would kick up their heels and jump any fences. Yes, and break the fences down too, exposing the tame flocks to night with its unknown beauties and dangers." He smiled around impishly, the firelight making odd highlights on his lips and cheeks. "Just as I've broken down your thorn fence."

It had been pitch black outside for some time. The wine jar was almost empty. Elven yawned. Immediately preparations were made for his rest. The cat got up from the hearth and came and rubbed Elven's legs.

The first pale glow of dawn aroused Elven and he slipped out of bed so quietly that he wakened no one, not even the cat. For a moment he hesitated in the gray room heavy with the smell of embers and the lees of wine. It occurred to him that it would be rather pleasant to live out his life here as a sylvan god adored by nymphs and rustics.

But then his hand touched his throat and he shook his head. This was no place for him to accomplish his mission—for one thing, there weren't enough people. He needed cities. With a last look at his blanket-huddled hostesses and hosts—Sefora's hair had just begun to turn ruddy in the increasing light—he went out.

As he had expected, the thorn forest had long ago repaired the break he had made near the stream. He turned in the opposite direction and skirted the hill until he reached the green wall beyond. There, consulting his compass, he set his course away from the wrecked spaceboat. Then he began to dust.

By early afternoon—judging time from the changing intensity of the light—he had made a dozen miles and was thinking that perhaps he should have stayed at the wreck long enough to try to patch up a levitator. If only he could get up a hundred feet to see what—if anything—was going to happen to this ridiculous forest!

For it still fronted him unchangingly, like some wizard growth from a book of fairy tales. The glassy thorns still curved back and struck whenever he swayed too close. And behind him the green shoots still pushed up through the slaty powder.

He thought, what a transition—from ultraphotonic flight in a spaceboat, to this worm's-crawl. Enough to bore a Wild One to desperation, to make him think twice of the simple delights of a life spent as a sylvan god.

But then he unfastened the locket at his throat and took out the tiny white sphere. His smile became an inspired one as he gazed at it gleaming on his palm.

Only one of the Wild Ones had escaped from their beleaguered planet, Fedris had said.

What did Fedris know!

He knew that before Elven reached his spaceboat, he had escaped in disguise through the tremendous cordons of the sos. That in the course of that escape he had twice been searched so thoroughly that it would have been a miracle if he could have concealed more than this one tiny tablet.

But this one tiny tablet was enough.

In it were all the Wild Ones.

Early humans had often been fascinated by the idea of an invisible man. Yet it hadn't occurred to them that the invisible man has always existed, that each one of us begins as an invisible man—the single cell from which each human grows.

Here in this white tablet were the genetic elements of all the Wild Ones, the chromosomes and genes of each individual. Here were fire-eyed Vlana, swashbuckling Nar, softlaughing Forten—they, and a billion others! The identical twins of each last person destroyed with the planet of the Wild Ones, waiting only encasement in suitable denucleated growth cells and nurture in some suitable mother. All rolling about prettily in Elven's palm.

So much for the physical inheritance.

And as for the social inheritance, there was Elven.

Then it could all begin again. Once more the Wild Ones could dream their cosmos-storming dreams and face their beautiful dangers. Once more they could seek to create, if they chose, those giant atoms, seeds of new universes, because of which the sos had destroyed them. Back in the Dawn Age physicists had envisioned the single giant atom from which the whole universe had grown, and now it was time to see if more such atoms could be created from energy drawn from sub-space. And who were Fedris and Elven and the sos to say whether or not the new universes might—or should—destroy the old? What matter how the tame herds feared those beautiful, sub-microscopic eggs of creation?

It *must* all begin again, Elven resolved.

Yet it was as much the feel of the thorn shoots rising under his feet, as his mighty resolve, that drove him on.

An hour later his duster disintegrated a tangle of boughs that had only sky behind it. He stepped into a clearing a half mile in diameter. Just ahead a bubbling stream went through a little valley, where russet grain rippled. Beyond the valley was a small, orchard-covered hill. On its hither side, low gray buildings clustered raggedly. From one rose a thread of smoke. A man came around the hill, driving cattle.

Elven's second thought was that something must have gone wrong with his compass, some force must have been deflecting it steadily, to draw him back in a circle.

His first thought, which he had repressed quickly, had been that here was the mystery Fedris had promised him, something super-natural from the ancient fairy-book world.

And as if time too had been drawn back in a circle—he repressed this notion even more quickly—he saw Sefora standing by the familiar copse of trees just ahead.

Elven called her name and hurried toward her, a little surprised at his pleasure in seeing her again.

She saw him, brought up her hand and swiftly tossed something to him. He started to catch it against his chest, thinking it a gleaming fruit.

He jerked aside barely in time.

It was a gleaming and wickedly heavy-bladed knife.

"Sefora!" he shouted.

The red-haired nymph turned and fled like a doe, screaming, "Alfors! Kors! Tulya!" Elven raced after her.

It was just beyond the first out-building that he ran into the am-bush, which seemed to have been organized impromptu in an ancient carpenter's shop. Alfors and Kors came roaring at him from the barn, the one swinging a heavy mallet, the other a long saw. While from the kitchen door, nearer by, Tulya rushed with a cleaver.

Elven caught her wrist and the two of them reeled with the force of her swing. Reluctantly then—hating his action and only obeying necessity—he snatched out his duster for a snap-shot at the nearest of the others.

Kors staggered, lifted his hand to his eyes and brushed away dust. Now Alfors was the closest. Elven could see the inch-long teeth on the twanging, singing saw-blade. Then its gleaming lower length dissolved along with Alfors' hand, while its upper half went screeching past his head.

Kors came on, screaming in pain, swinging the mallet blindly. Elven sent him sprawling with a full-intensity shot that made his chest a small volcano of dust, swung round and cut down Alfors, ducked just in time as the cleaver, transferred to Tulya's other hand, swiped at his neck. They went down together in a heap, the duster at Tulya's throat.

Brushing the fine gray ashes frantically from his face, Elven looked up to see Sefora racing toward him. Her flaming red hair and livid face were preceded by the three gleaming tines of a pitchfork.

"Sefora!" he cried and tried to get up, but Alfors had fallen across his legs. "Sefora!" he cried again imploringly, but she didn't seem to hear him and her face looked only hate, so he snapped on the duster, and tines and face and hair went up in a gray cloud. Her headless body pitched across him with a curious little vault as the blunted pitchfork buried its end in the ground. She hit and rolled over twice. Then everything was very still, until a cow lowed restlessly.

Elven dragged himself from under what remained of Alfors and stood up shakily. He coughed a little, then with a somewhat horrified distaste raced out of the settling gray cloud. As soon as he was in clean air he emptied his lungs several times, shuddered a bit, smiled ruefully at the four motionless forms on which the dust was settling, and set himself to figure things out.

Evidently some magnetic force had deflected his compass needle, causing him to travel in a circle. Perhaps one of the magnetic poles of this planet was in the immediate locality. Of course this was no ordinary polar climate or day-night cycle; still, there was no reason why a planet's axes of magnetism and rotation mightn't be far removed from each other.

The behavior of his last evening's hosts and hostesses was a knottier problem. It seemed incredible that his mere disappearance, even granting they thought him a god, had offended them so that they had become murderous. Ancient Earth-peoples had killed gods and god-symbols, of course, yet that had been a matter of deliberate ritual, not sudden blood-frenzy.

For a moment he found himself wondering if Fedris had somehow poisoned their minds against him, if Fedris possessed some FTL agency that had rendered the whole universe allergic to Elven. But that, he knew, was the merest morbid fancy, a kind of soured humor.

Perhaps his charming rustics had been subject to some kind of cyclic insanity.

He shrugged, then resolutely went into the house and prepared himself a meal. By the time it was ready the sky had darkened. He built a big fire and put in some time constructing out of materials in his pack, a small gyrocompass. He worked with an absent-minded mastery, as one whittles a toy for a child. He noticed the cat watching him from the doorway, but it fled whenever he called to it, and it refused to be lured by the food he set on the hearth. He looked up at the wine jars dangling from the rafters, but did not reach them down.

After a while he disposed himself on the couch Kors and Tulya had occupied the night before. The room grew dim as the fire died down. He succeeded in keeping his thoughts away from what lay outside, except that once or twice his mind pictured the odd little vault Sefora's body had made in pitching over him. In the doorway the cat's eyes gleamed.

When he woke it was full day. He quickly got his things together, adding a little fruit to his pack. The cat shot aside as he went out the door. He did not look at the scene of yesterday's battle. He could hear flies buzzing there. He went over the hill to where he had entered the thorn forest last morning. The thorn trees, with their ridiculous fairy-book persistence, had long ago repaired the opening he'd made. There was no sign of it. He turned on the tiny motor of the gyrocompass, leveled his gun at the green wall, and started dusting.

It was as monotonous a work as ever, but he went about it with a new and almost unsmiling grimness. At regular intervals he consulted the gyrocompass and sighted back carefully along the arrow-straight, shoot-green corridor that narrowed with more than perspective. Odd, the speed with which those thorns grew!

In his mind he rehearsed his long-range course of action. He could count, he must hope, on a generation's freedom from Fedris and the forces of the sos. In that time he must find a large culture, preferably urban, or one with a large number of the right sort of domestic animals, and make himself absolute master of it, probably by establishing a new religion. Then the proper facilities for breeding must be arranged. Next the seeds of the Wild Ones pelleted in the locket at his throat must be separated—as many as there were facilities for—and placed in their living or nonliving mothers. Probably living. And probably not human—that might present too many sociological difficulties.

It amused him to think of the Wild Ones reborn from sheep or goats, or perhaps some wholly alien rooter or browser, and his mind conjured up a diverting picture of himself leading his strange flocks over hilly pastures, piping like ancient Pan—until he realized that his mind had pictured Sefora and Tulya dancing along beside him, and he snapped off the mental picture with a frown.

Then would come the matter of the rearing and education of the Wild Ones. His hypothetical community of underlings would take care of the former; the latter must all proceed from his own brain— supplemented by the library of educational micro-tapes in the wrecked spaceboat. Robots of some sort would be an absolute necessity. He remembered the conversation of the night before last, which had indicated that there were or had been robots on this planet, and lost himself in tenuous speculation—though not forgetting his gyrocompass observations.

So the day wore on for Elven, walking hour after hour behind a dustgun into a dustcloud, until he was almost hypnotized in spite of his self-watchfulness and a host of disquieting memories fitfully thronged his mind: the darkness of sub-space; the cat's eyes at the doorway, the feel of its fur against his ankle; dust billowing from Tulya's throat; the little vault Sefora's body had given in pitching over him, almost as if it rode an invisible wave in the air; an imaginary vision of the blasted planet of the Wild Ones, its dark side aglow with radioactives visible even in deep space; the wasplike humming in the wrecked spaceboat; Fedris' ghostly whisper, "The unknown will find you, Elven—"

The break in the thorn forest took him by surprise.

He stepped into a clearing half a mile in diameter. Just ahead a stream bubbled through a little valley rippling with russet grain. Beyond was a small, orchard-covered hill against whose side low, gray buildings clustered raggedly. From one rose a ribbon of smoke.

He hardly felt the thorns sting him as he backed into them, though the stimulus they provided was enough to send him forward again a few steps. But such trifles had no effect on the furious working of his mind. He must, he told himself, be up against a force that distorted a gyrocompass as much as a magnet, that even distorted the visual lines of space.

Or else he really was in a fairy-book world where no matter how hard you tried to escape through an enchanted forest, you were always led back at evening to—

He fancied he could see a black cloud of flies hovering near the low gray buildings.

And then he heard a rustling in the copse of trees just ahead and heard a horribly familiar voice call excitedly, "Tulya! Come quickly!"

He began to shake. Then his hair-triggered muscles, obeying some random stimulus, hurled him forward aimlessly, jerked him to a stop as suddenly. Thigh-deep in the grain, he stared around wildly. Then his gaze fixed on a movement in the twilit grain—two trails of movement, shaking the grain but showing nothing more. Two trails of movement working their way from the copse to him.

And then suddenly Sefora and Tulya were upon him, springing from their concealment like mischievous children, their eyes gleaming, their mouths smiling with a wicked delight. Tulya's throat, that he had yesterday seen billow into dust, bulged with laughter. Sefora's red hair, that he had watched puff into a gray cloud, rippled in the breeze.

He tried to run back into the forest but they cut him off and caught him with gales of laughter. At the touch of their hands all strength went out of him, and it seemed to him that his bones were turning to an icy mush as they dragged him along stumblingly through the grain.

"We won't hurt you," Tulya assured him between peals of wicked laughter.

"Oh, Tulya, but he's shy!"

"Something's made him unhappy, Sefora."

"He needs loving, Tulya!" And Elven felt Sefora's cold arms go round his neck and her wet lips press his. Gasping, he tried to push away, and the lips bubbled more laughter. He closed his eyes tight and began to sob.

When next he opened them, he was standing near the gray buildings, and someone had put wreaths of flowers around his neck and smeared fruit on his chin, and Alfors and Kors had come, and all four of them were dancing around him wildly in the twilight, hand in hand, laughing, laughing.

Then Elven laughed too, louder and louder, and their gleaming eyes encouraged him, and he began to spin round and round inside their spinning circle, and they grimaced their joy at his comradeship. And then he raised his dustgun and snapped it on and kept on spinning until the circle of other laughers was only an expanding dust ring. Then, still laughing, he ran over the hill, a cat scampering in swift rushes at his side, until he came to a thorny wall. After his hands and face were puffing with stings, he remembered to lift something he'd been holding in his hand and touch a button on it. Then he marched into a dust cloud, singing.

All night he marched and sang, pausing only to reload the gun with a gleeful automatism, or to take from his pack another flash-globe of cold light, which revealed the small world of green thorns and dust motes around him. Mostly he sang an old Centaurian *lied* that went:

> We'll fall through the stars, my Deborah,
> We'll fall through the skeins of light,
> We'll fall out of the Galaxy
> And I'll kiss you again in the night.

Only sometimes he sang "Sefora" instead of "Deborah" and "kill" instead of "kiss." At times it seemed to him that he was followed by prancing goats and sheep and strange monsters that were really his brothers and sisters. And at other times there danced along beside him two nymphs, one red-haired. They sang with him in high sweet voices and smiled at him wickedly. Toward morning he grew tired and unstrapped the pack from his back and threw it away, and later he ripped something from his throat and threw that away, too.

As the sky paled through the boughs, the nymphs and beasts vanished and he remembered that he was someone dangerous and important, and that something quite impossible had truly happened to him. But that if he could really manage to think things through—

The thorn forest ended. He stepped into a clearing a half mile in diameter. Just ahead a stream gurgled through a small valley. Beyond was an orchard-covered hill. Russet grain rippled in the valley. On the hillside low gray buildings clustered raggedly. From one rose a thin streamer of smoke.

And toward him, striding lithely through the grain, came Sefora. Elven screamed horribly and pointed the dustgun. But the range was too great. Only a ribbon of grain stretching halfway to her went up in dust. She turned and raced toward the buildings. He followed her, gun still pointed and snapped on at full power, running furiously along the dust path, taking wild leaps through the gray clouds.

The dust path drew closer and closer to Sefora, until it almost lapped her heels. She darted between two buildings.

Then something tightened like a snake around Elven's knees, and as he pitched forward something else tightened around his upper body, jerking his elbows against his sides. The dustgun flew from his hand as he smashed against the ground.

Then he was lying on his back gasping, and through the thinning dust cloud Alfors and Kors were looking down at him as they wound their lassos tighter and tighter around him, trussing him up. He heard Alfors say, "Are you all right, Sefora?" and a voice reply, "Yes. Let me see him." And then Sefora's face appeared through the dust cloud and looked down into his with cold curiosity, and her red hair touched his cheek, and Elven closed his eyes and screamed many times.

"It was all very simple and there was, of course, absolutely nothing of the supernatural," the Director of Human Research assured Fedris, taking a sip of mellow Magellanic wine from the cup at his elbow. "Elven merely walked in a straight line."

Fedris frowned. He was a small man with a worried look that the most thoroughgoing psychoanalysis had been unable to eradicate. "Of course the Galaxy is tremendously grateful to you for capturing Elven. We never dreamed he'd got as far as the Magellanics. Can't say what horrors we may have escaped—"

"I deserve no credit," the director told him. "It was all sheer accident, and the matter of Elven's nerve cracking. Of course you'd prepared the ground there by hinting to him that the supernatural might take a hand."

"That was the merest empty threat, born of desperation," Fedris interrupted, reddening a bit.

"Still, it prepared the ground. And then Elven had the devilish misfortune of landing right in the middle of our project on Magellanic 47. And that, I admit, might be enough to startle anyone." The director grinned.

Fedris looked up. "Just what is your project? All I know is that it's rather hush-hush."

The director settled back in his easy-chair. "The scientific understanding of human behavior has always presented extraordinary difficulties. Ever since the Dawn Age men have wanted to analyze their social problems in the same way they analyze the problems of physics and chemistry. They've wanted to know exactly what causes produce exactly what results. But one great obstacle has always licked them."

Fedris nodded. "Lack of controls."

"Exactly," the director agreed. "With rats, say, it would be easy. You can have two—or a hundred—families of rats, each family with identical heredity, each in an identical environment. Then you can vary one factor in one family and watch the results. And when you get results you can trust them, because the other family is your control, showing what happens when you don't vary the factor."

Fedris looked at him wonderingly. "Do you mean to say—?"

The director nodded. "On Magellanic 47 we're carrying on that same sort of work, not with rats, but with human beings. The cages are half-mile clearings with identical weather, terrain, plants, animals —everything identical down to the tiniest detail. The bars of the cages are the thorn trees, which our botanists developed specially for the purpose. The inmates of the cages—the human experimental animals—are identical twins—though centuplets would be closer to the right word. Identical upbringings are assured for each group by the use of robot nurses and mentors, set to perform always the same unvarying routine. These robots are removed when the members of the group are sufficiently mature for our purposes. All our observations are, of course, competely secret—and also intermittent, which had the unfortunate result of letting Elven do some serious damage before he was caught.

"Do you see the setup now? In the thorn forest in which Elven was wrecked there were approximately one hundred identical clearings set at identical intervals. Each clearing looked exactly like the other, and each contained one Sefora, one Tulya, one Alfors, and one Kors. Elven thought he was going in a circle, but actually he was going in a straight line. Each evening it was a different clearing he came to. Each night he met a new Sefora.

"Each group he encountered was identical except for one factor—the factor we were varying—and that had the effect of making it a bit more grisly for him. You see, in those groups we happened to be running an experiment to determine the causes of human behavior patterns toward strangers. We'd made slight variations in their environment and robot-education, with the result that the first group he met was submissive toward strangers; the second was violently hostile; the third as violently friendly; the fourth highly suspicious. Too bad he didn't meet the fourth group first—though, of course, they'd have been unable to manage him except that he was half mad with supernatural terror."

The director finished his wine and smiled at Fedris. "So you see it all *was* the sheerest accident. No one was more surprised than I when, in taking a routine observation, I found that my 'animals' had this gibbering and trussed-up intruder. And you could have knocked me over with a molecule when I found out it was Elven."

Fedris whistled his wonder. "I can sympathize with the poor devil," he said, "and I can understand, too, why your project is hush-hush."

The director nodded. "Yes, experimenting with human beings is a rather hard notion for most people to take. Still it's better than running all mankind as one big experiment without controls. And we're extremely kind to our 'animals'. As soon as our experiment with each is finished, it's our policy to graduate them, with suitable re-education, into the sos."

"Still—" said Fedris doubtfully.

"You think it's a bit like some of the ideas of the Wild Ones?"

"A bit," Fedris admitted.

"Sometimes I think so too," the director admitted with a smile, and poured his guest more wine.

While deep in the thorn forest on Magellanic 47, green shoots and tendrils closed round a locket containing a white tablet, encapsulating all the Wild Ones save Elven in a green and tiny tomb.

Coming Attraction

THE COUPE with the fishhooks welded to the fender shouldered up over the curb like the nose of a nightmare. The girl in its path stood frozen, her face probably stiff with fright under her mask. For once my reflexes weren't shy. I took a fast step toward her, grabbed her elbow, yanked her back. Her black skirt swirled out.

The big coupe shot by, its turbine humming. I glimpsed three faces. Something ripped. I felt the hot exhaust on my ankles as the big coupe swerved back into the street. A thick cloud like a black flower blossomed from its jouncing rear end, while from the fishhooks flew a black shimmering rag.

"Did they get you?" I asked the girl.

She had twisted around to look where the side of her skirt was torn away. She was wearing nylon tights.

"The hooks didn't touch me," she said shakily. "I guess I'm lucky."

I heard voices around us:

"Those kids! What'll they think up next?"

"They're a menace. They ought to be arrested."

Sirens screamed at a rising pitch as two motor-police, their rocket-assist jets full on, came whizzing toward us after the coupe. But the black flower had become an inky fog obscuring the whole street. The motor-police switched from rocket assists to rocket brakes and swerved to a stop near the smoke cloud.

"Are you English?" the girl asked me. "You have an English accent."

Her voice came shudderingly from behind the sleek black satin mask. I fancied her teeth must be chattering. Eyes that were perhaps blue searched my face from behind the black gauze covering the eyeholes of the mask. I told her she'd guessed right. She stood close to me. "Will you come to my place tonight?" she asked rapidly. "I can't thank you now. And there's something else you can help me about."

My arm, still lightly circling her waist, felt her body trembling. I was answering the plea in that as much as in her voice when I said, "Certainly." She gave me an address south of Inferno, an apartment number and a time. She asked me my name and I told her.

"Hey, you!"

I turned obediently to the policeman's shout. He shooed away the small clucking crowd of masked women and barefaced men. Coughing from the smoke that the black coupe had thrown out, he asked for my papers. I handed him the essential ones.

He looked at them and then at me. "British Barter? How long will you be in New York?"

Suppressing the urge to say, "For as short a time as possible," I told him I'd be here for a week or so.

"May need you as a witness," he explained. "Those kids can't use smoke on us. When they do that, we pull them in."

He seemed to think the smoke was the bad thing. "They tried to kill the lady," I pointed out.

He shook his head wisely. "They always pretend they're going to, but actually they just want to snag skirts. I've picked up rippers with as many as fifty skirt-snags tacked up in their rooms. Of course, sometimes they come a little too close."

I explained that if I hadn't yanked her out of the way, she'd have been hit by more than hooks. But he interrupted, "If she'd thought it was a real murder attempt, she'd have stayed here."

I looked around. It was true. She was gone.

"She was fearfully frightened," I told him.

"Who wouldn't be? Those kids would have scared old Stalin himself."

"I mean frightened of more than 'kids.' They didn't look like 'kids.' "

"What did they look like?"

I tried without much success to describe the three faces. A vague impression of viciousness and effeminacy doesn't mean much.

"Well, I could be wrong," he said finally. "Do you know the girl? Where she lives?"

"No," I half lied.

The other policeman hung up his radiophone and ambled toward us, kicking at the tendrils of dissipating smoke. The black cloud no longer hid the dingy façades with their five-year-old radiation flashburns, and I could begin to make out the distant stump of the Empire State Building, thrusting up out of Inferno like a mangled finger.

"They haven't been picked up so far," the approaching policeman grumbled. "Left smoke for five blocks, from what Ryan says."

The first policeman shook his head. "That's bad," he observed solemnly.

I was feeling a bit uneasy and ashamed. An Englishman shouldn't lie, at least not on impulse.

"They sound like nasty customers," the first policeman continued in the same grim tone. "We'll need witnesses. Looks as if you may have to stay in New York longer than you expect."

I got the point. I said, "I forgot to show you all my papers," and handed him a few others, making sure there was a five dollar bill in among them.

When he handed them back a bit later, his voice was no longer ominous. My feelings of guilt vanished. To cement our relationship, I chatted with the two of them about their job.

"I suppose the masks give you some trouble," I observed. "Over in England we've been reading about your new crop of masked female bandits."

"Those things get exaggerated," the first policeman assured me. "It's the men masking as women that really mix us up. But, brother, when we nab them, we jump on them with both feet."

"And you get so you can spot women almost as well as if they had naked faces," the second policeman volunteered. "You know, hands and all that."

"Especially all that," the first agreed with a chuckle. "Say, is it true that some girls don't mask over in England?"

"A number of them have picked up the fashion," I told him. "Only a few, though—the ones who always adopt the latest style, however extreme."

"They're usually masked in the British newscasts."

"I imagine it's arranged that way out of deference to American taste," I confessed. "Actually, not very many do mask."

The second policeman considered that. "Girls going down the street bare from the neck up." It was not clear whether he viewed the prospect with relish or moral distaste. Likely both.

"A few members keep trying to persuade Parliament to enact a law forbidding all masking," I continued, talking perhaps a bit too much.

The second policeman shook his head. "What an idea. You know, masks are a pretty good thing, brother. Couple of years more and I'm going to make my wife wear hers around the house."

The first policeman shrugged. "If women were to stop wearing masks, in six weeks you wouldn't know the difference. You get used to anything, if enough people do or don't do it."

I agreed, rather regretfully, and left them. I turned north on Broadway (old Tenth Avenue, I believe) and walked rapidly until I was beyond Inferno. Passing such an area of undecontaminated radio-activity always makes a person queasy. I thanked God there weren't any such in England, as yet.

The street was almost empty, though I was accosted by a couple of beggars with faces tunnelled by H-bomb scars, whether real or of makeup putty, I couldn't tell. A fat woman held out a baby with webbed fingers and toes. I told myself it would have been deformed anyway and that she was only capitalizing on our fear of bomb-induced mutations. Still, I gave her a seven-and-a-half-cent piece. Her mask made me feel I was paying tribute to an African fetish.

"May all your children be blessed with one head and two eyes, sir."

"Thanks," I said, shuddering, and hurried past her.

". . . There's only trash behind the mask, so turn your head, stick to your task: Stay away, stay away—from—the—girls!"

This last was the end of an anti-sex song being sung by some religionists half a block from the circle-and-cross insignia of a femalist temple. They reminded me only faintly of our small tribe of British monastics. Above their heads was a jumble of billboards advertising predigested foods, wrestling instruction, radio handies and the like.

I stared at the hysterical slogans with disagreeable fascination. Since the female face and form have been banned on American signs, the very letters of the advertiser's alphabet have begun to crawl with sex—the fat-bellied, big-breasted capital B, the lascivious double O. However, I reminded myself, it is chiefly the mask that so strangely accents sex in America.

A British anthropologist has pointed out, that, while it took more than 5,000 years to shift the chief point of sexual interest from the hips to the breasts, the next transition to the face has taken less than 50 years. Comparing the American style with Moslem tradition is not valid; Moslem women are compelled to wear veils, the purpose of which is to make a husband's property private, while American women have only the compulsion of fashion and use masks to create mystery.

Theory aside, the actual origins of the trend are to be found in the anti-radiation clothing of World War III, which led to masked wrestling, now a fantastically popular sport, and that in turn led to the current female fashion. Only a wild style at first, masks quickly became as necessary as brassières and lipsticks had been earlier in the century.

I finally realized that I was not speculating about masks in general, but about what lay behind one in particular. That's the devil of the things; you're never sure whether a girl is heightening loveliness or hiding ugliness. I pictured a cool, pretty face in which fear showed only in widened eyes. Then I remembered her blonde hair, rich against the blackness of the satin mask. She'd told me to come at the twenty-second hour—10 P.M.

I climbed to my apartment near the British Consulate; the elevator shaft had been shoved out of plumb by an old blast, a nuisance in these tall New York buildings. Before it occurred to me that I would be going out again, I automatically tore a tab from the film strip under my shirt. I developed it just to be sure. It showed that the total radiation I'd taken that day was still within the safety limit. I'm not phobic about it, as so many people are these days, but there's no point in taking chances.

I flopped down on the day bed and stared at the silent speaker and the dark screen of the video set. As always, they made me think, somewhat bitterly, of the two great nations of the world. Mutilated by each other, yet still strong, they were crippled giants poisoning the planet with their respective dreams of an impossible equality and an impossible success.

I fretfully switched on the speaker. By luck the newscaster was talking excitedly of the prospects of a bumper wheat crop, sown by planes across a dust bowl moistened by seeded rains. I listened carefully to the rest of the program (it was remarkably clear of Russian telejamming) but there was no further news of interest to me. And, of course, no mention of the Moon, though everyone knows that America and Russia are racing to develop their primary bases into fortresses capable of mutual assault and the launching of alphabet-bombs toward Earth. I myself knew perfectly well that the British electronic equipment I was helping trade for American wheat was destined for use in spaceships.

I switched off the newscast. It was growing dark and once again I pictured a tender, frightened face behind a mask. I hadn't had a date since England. It's exceedingly difficult to become acquainted with a girl in America, where as little as a smile, often, can set one of them yelping for the police—to say nothing of the increasingly puritanical morality and the roving gangs that keep most women indoors after dark. And naturally, the masks which are definitely not, as the Soviets claim, a last invention of capitalist degeneracy, but a sign of great psychological insecurity. The Russians have no masks, but they have their own signs of stress.

I went to the window and impatiently watched the darkness gather. I was getting very restless. After a while a ghostly violet cloud appeared to the south. My hair rose. Then I laughed. I had momentarily fancied it a radiation from the crater of the Hell-bomb, though I should instantly have known it was only the radio-induced glow in the sky over the amusement and residential area south of Inferno.

Promptly at twenty-two hours I stood before the door of my un-known girl-friend's apartment. The electronic say-who-please said just that. I answered clearly, "Wysten Turner," wondering if she'd given my name to the mechanism. She evidently had, for the door opened. I walked into a small empty living-room, my heart pounding a bit.

The room was expensively furnished with the latest pneumatic hassocks and sprawlers. There were some midgie books on the table. The one I picked up was the standard hard-boiled detective story in which two female murderers go gunning for each other.

The television was on. A masked girl in green was crooning a love song. Her right hand held something that blurred off into the foreground. I saw the set had a handie, which we haven't in England as yet, and curiously thrust my hand into the handie orifice beside the screen. Contrary to my expectations, it was not like slipping into a pulsing rubber glove, but rather as if the girl on the screen actually held my hand.

A door opened behind me. I jerked out my hand with as guilty a reaction as if I'd been caught peering through a keyhole.

She stood in the bedroom doorway. I think she was trembling. She was wearing a grey fur coat, white speckled, and a grey velvet evening mask with shirred grey lace around the eyes and mouth. Her fingernails twinkled like silver.

It hadn't occurred to me that she'd expect us to go out.

"I should have told you," she said softly. Her mask veered nerv-ously toward the books and the screen and the room's dark corners. "But I can't possibly talk to you here."

I said doubtfully, "There's a place near the Consulate . . ."

"I know where we can be together and talk," she said rapidly. "If you don't mind."

As we entered the elevator I said, "I'm afraid I dismissed the cab."

But the cab driver hadn't gone for some reason of his own. He jumped out and smirkingly held the front door open for us. I told him we preferred to sit in back. He sulkily opened the rear door, slammed it after us, jumped in front and slammed the door behind him.

My companion leaned forward. "Heaven," she said.

The driver switched on the turbine and televisor.

"Why did you ask if I were a British subject?" I said, to start the conversation.

She leaned away from me, tilting her mask close to the window. "See the Moon," she said in a quick, dreamy voice.

"But why, really?" I pressed, conscious of an irritation that had nothing to do with her.

"It's edging up into the purple of the sky."

"And what's your name?"

"The purple makes it look yellower."

Just then I became aware of the source of my irritation. It lay in the square of writhing light in the front of the cab beside the driver.

I don't object to ordinary wrestling matches, though they bore me, but I simply detest watching a man wrestle a woman. The fact that the bouts are generally "on the level," with the man greatly outclassed in weight and reach and the masked females young and personable, only makes them seem worse to me.

"Please turn off the screen," I requested the driver.

He shook his head without looking around. "Uh-uh, man," he said. "They've been grooming that babe for weeks for this bout with Little Zirk."

Infuriated, I reached forward, but my companion caught my arm. "Please," she whispered frightenedly, shaking her head.

I settled back, frustrated. She was closer to me now, but silent and for a few moments I watched the heaves and contortions of the powerful masked girl and her wiry masked opponent on the screen. His frantic scrambling at her reminded me of a male spider.

I jerked around, facing my companion. "Why did those three men want to kill you?" I asked sharply.

The eyeholes of her mask faced the screen. "Because they're jealous of me," she whispered.

"Why are they jealous?"

She still didn't look at me. "Because of him."

"Who?"

She didn't answer.

I put my arm around her shoulders. "Are you afraid to tell me?" I asked. "What *is* the matter?"

She still didn't look my way. She smelled nice.

"See here," I said laughingly, changing my tactics, "you really should tell me something about yourself, I don't even know what you look like."

I half playfully lifted my hand to the band of her neck. She gave it an astonishingly swift slap. I pulled it away in sudden pain. There were four tiny indentations on the back. From one of them a tiny bead of blood welled out as I watched. I looked at her fingernails and saw they were actually delicate and pointed metal caps.

"I'm dreadfully sorry," I heard her say, "but you frightened me. I thought for a moment you were going to . . ."

At last she turned to me. Her coat had fallen open. Her evening dress was Cretan Revival, a bodice of lace beneath and supporting the breasts without covering them.

"Don't be angry," she said, putting her arms around my neck. "You were wonderful this afternoon."

The soft grey velvet of her mask, moulding itself to her cheek, pressed mine. Through the mask's lace the wet warm tip of her tongue touched my chin.

"I'm not angry," I said. "Just puzzled and anxious to help."

The cab stopped. To either side were black windows bordered by spears of broken glass. The sickly purple light showed a few ragged figures slowly moving toward us.

The driver muttered, "It's the turbine, man. We're grounded." He sat there hunched and motionless. "Wish it had happened somewhere else."

My companion whispered, "Five dollars is the usual amount."

She looked out so shudderingly at the congregating figures that I suppressed my indignation and did as she suggested. The driver took the bill without a word. As he started up, he put his hand out the window and I heard a few coins clink on the pavement.

My companion came back into my arms, but her mask faced the television screen, where the tall girl had just pinned the convulsively kicking Little Zirk.

"I'm so frightened," she breathed.

Heaven turned out to be an equally ruinous neighborhood, but it had a club with an awning and a huge doorman uniformed like a spaceman, but in gaudy colors. In my sensuous daze I rather liked it all. We stepped out of the cab just as a drunken old woman came down the sidewalk, her mask awry. A couple ahead of us turned their heads from the half revealed face, as if from an ugly body at the beach. As we followed them in I heard the doorman say, "Get along, grandma, and cover yourself."

Inside, everything was dimness and blue glows. She had said we could talk here, but I didn't see how. Besides the inevitable chorus of sneezes and coughs (they say America is fifty per cent allergic these days), there was a band going full blast in the latest robop style, in which an electronic composing machine selects an arbitrary sequence of tones into which the musicians weave their raucous little individualities.

Most of the people were in booths. The band was behind the bar. On a small platform beside them, a girl was dancing, stripped to her mask. The little cluster of men at the shadowy far end of the bar weren't looking at her.

We inspected the menu in gold script on the wall and pushed the buttons for breast of chicken, fried shrimps and two scotches. Moments later, the serving bell tinkled. I opened the gleaming panel and took out our drinks.

The cluster of men at the bar filed off toward the door, but first they stared around the room. My companion had just thrown back her coat. Their look lingered on our booth. I noticed that there were three of them.

The band chased off the dancing girl with growls. I handed my companion a straw and we sipped our drinks.

"You wanted me to help you about something," I said. "Incidentally, I think you're lovely."

She nodded quick thanks, looked around, leaned forward. "Would it be hard for me to get to England?"

"No," I replied, a bit taken aback. "Provided you have an American passport."

"Are they difficult to get?"

"Rather," I said, surprised at her lack of information. "Your country doesn't like its nationals to travel, though it isn't quite as stringent as Russia."

"Could the British Consulate help me get a passport?"

"It's hardly their . . ."

"Could you?"

I realized we were being inspected. A man and two girls had paused opposite our table. The girls were tall and wolfish-looking, with spangled masks. The man stood jauntily between them like a fox on its hind legs.

My companion didn't glance at them, but she sat back. I noticed that one of the girls had a big yellow bruise on her forearm. After a moment they walked to a booth in the deep shadows.

"Know them?" I asked. She didn't reply. I finished my drink. "I'm not sure you'd like England," I said. "The austerity's altogether different from your American brand of misery."

She leaned forward again. "But I must get away," she whispered.

"Why?" I was getting impatient.

"Because I'm so frightened."

There were chimes. I opened the panel and handed her the fried shrimps. The sauce on my breast of chicken was a delicious steaming compound of almonds, soy and ginger. But something must have been wrong with the radionic oven that had thawed and heated it, for at the first bite I crunched a kernel of ice in the meat. These delicate mechanisms need constant repair and there aren't enough mechanics.

I put down my fork. "What are you really scared of?" I asked her.

For once her mask didn't waver away from my face. As I waited I could feel the fears gathering without her naming them, tiny dark shapes swarming through the curved night outside, converging on the radioactive pest spot of New York, dipping into the margins of the purple. I felt a sudden rush of sympathy, a desire to protect the girl opposite me. The warm feeling added itself to the infatuation engendered in the cab.

"Everything," she said finally.

I nodded and touched her hand.

"I'm afraid of the Moon," she began, her voice going dreamy and brittle as it had in the cab. "You can't look at it and not think of guided bombs."

"It's the same Moon over England," I reminded her.

"But it's not England's Moon any more. It's ours and Russia's. You're not responsible.

"Oh, and then," she said with a tilt of her mask, "I'm afraid of the cars and the gangs and the loneliness and Inferno. I'm afraid of the lust that undresses your face. And—" her voice hushed— "I'm afraid of the wrestlers."

"Yes?" I prompted softly after a moment.

Her mask came forward. "Do you know something about the wrestlers?" she asked rapidly. "The ones that wrestle women, I mean. They often lose, you know. And then they have to have a girl to take their frustration out on. A girl who's soft and weak and terribly frightened. They need that, to keep them men. Other men don't want them to have a girl. Other men want them just to fight women and be heroes. But they must have a girl. It's horrible for her."

I squeezed her fingers tighter, as if courage could be transmitted— granting I had any. "I think I can get you to England," I said.

Shadows crawled onto the table and stayed there. I looked up at the three men who had been at the end of the bar. They were the men I had seen in the big coupe. They wore black sweaters and close-fitting black trousers. Their faces were as expressionless as dopers. Two of them stood about me. The other loomed over the girl.

"Drift off, man," I was told. I heard the other inform the girl: "We'll wrestle a fall, sister. What shall it be? Judo, slapsie or kill-who-can?"

I stood up. There are times when an Englishman simply must be maltreated. But just then the foxlike man came gliding in like the star of a ballet. The reaction of the other three startled me. They were acutely embarrassed.

He smiled at them thinly. "You won't win my favour by tricks like this," he said.

"Don't get the wrong idea, Zirk," one of them pleaded.

"I will if it's right," he said. "She told me what you tried to do this afternoon. That won't endear you to me, either. Drift."

They backed off awkwardly. "Let's get out of here," one of them said loudly, as they turned. "I know a place where they fight naked with knives."

Little Zirk laughed musically and slipped into the seat beside my companion. She shrank from him, just a little. I pushed my feet back, leaned forward.

"Who's your friend, baby?" he asked, not looking at her.

She passed the question to me with a little gesture. I told him.

"British," he observed. "She's been asking you about getting out of the country? About passports?" He smiled pleasantly. "She likes to start running away. Don't you, baby?" His small hand began to stroke her wrist, the fingers bent a little, the tendons ridged, as if he were about to grab and twist.

"Look here," I said sharply. "I have to be grateful to you for ordering off those bullies, but—"

"Think nothing of it," he told me. "They're no harm except when they're behind steering wheels. A well-trained fourteen-year-old girl could cripple any one of them. Why even Theda here, if she went in for that sort of thing . . ." He turned to her, shifting his hand from her wrist to her hair. He stroked it, letting the strands slip slowly through his fingers. "You know I lost tonight, baby, don't you?" he said softly.

I stood up. "Come along," I said to her. "Let's leave."

She just sat there, I couldn't even tell if she was trembling. I tried to read a message in her eyes through the mask.

"I'll take you away," I said to her. "I can do it. I really will."

He smiled at me. "She'd like to go with you," he said. "Wouldn't you, baby?"

"Will you or won't you?" I said to her. She still just sat there.

He slowly knotted his fingers in her hair.

"Listen, you little vermin," I snapped at him. "Take your hands off her."

He came up from the seat like a snake. I'm no fighter. I just know that the more scared I am, the harder and straighter I hit. This time I was lucky. But as he crumpled back, I felt a slap and four stabs of pain in my cheek. I clapped my hand to it. I could feel the four gashes made by her dagger finger caps, and the warm blood oozing out from them.

She didn't look at me. She was bending over Little Zirk and cuddling her mask to his cheek and crooning: "There, there, don't feel bad, you'll be able to hurt me afterward."

There were sounds around us, but they didn't come close. I leaned forward and ripped the mask from her face.

I really don't know why I should have expected her face to be anything else. It was very pale, of course, and there weren't any cosmetics. I suppose there's no point in wearing any under a mask.

The eyebrows were untidy and the lips chapped. But as for the general expression, as for the feelings crawling and wriggling across it—

Have you ever lifted a rock from damp soil? Have you ever watched the slimy white grubs?

I looked down at her, she up at me. "Yes, you're so frightened, aren't you?" I said sarcastically. "You dread this little nightly drama, don't you? You're scared to death."

And I walked right out into the purple night, still holding my hand to my bleeding cheek. No one stopped me, not even the girl wrestlers. I wished I could tear a tab from under my shirt, and test it then and there, and find I'd taken too much radiation, and so be able to ask to cross the Hudson and go down New Jersey, past the lingering radiance of the Narrows Bomb, and so on to Sandy Hook to wait for the rusty ship that would take me back over the seas to England.

Poor Superman

THE FIRST angry rays of the sun—which, startlingly enough, still rose in the east at twenty-four-hour intervals—pierced the lacy tops of Atlantic combers and touched thousands of sleeping Americans with unconscious fear, because of their unpleasant similarity to the rays from World War III's atomic bombs.

They turned to blood the witch circle of rusty steel skeletons around Inferno in Manhattan. Without comment, they pointed a cosmic finger at the tarnished brass plaque commemorating the martyrdom of the three physicists after the dropping of the Hell Bomb. They tenderly touched the rosy skin and strawberry bruises on the naked shoulders of a girl sleeping off a drunk on the furry and radiantly heated floor of a nearby roof garden. They struck green magic from the glassy blot that was Old Washington. Twelve hours before, they had revealed things as eerily beautiful, and more ravaged, in Asia and Russia. They pinked the white walls of the colonial dwelling of Morton Opperly near the Institute for Advanced Studies; upstairs they slanted impartially across the Pharaohlike and open-eyed face of the elderly physicist and the ugly, sleep-surly one of young Willard Farquar in the next room. And in nearby New Washington they made of the spire of the Thinkers' Foundation a blue and optimistic glory that outshone White House, Jr.

It was America approaching the end of the twentieth century. America of juke-box burlesque and your local radiation hospital.

America of the mask fad for women and Mystic Christianity. America of the off-the-bosom dress and the New Blue Laws. America of the Endless War and the loyalty detector. America of marvelous Maizie and the monthly rocket to Mars. America of the Thinkers and (a few remembered) the institute. "Knock on titanium," "Whadya do for blackouts?" "Please, lover, don't think when I'm around" America, as combat-shocked and crippled as the rest of the bomb-shattered planet.

Not one impudent photon of the sunlight penetrated the triple-paned, polarizing windows of Jorj Helmuth's bedroom in the Thinkers' Foundation, yet the clock in his brain awakened him to the minute, or almost. Switching off the Educational Sandman in the midst of the phrase, ". . . applying tensor calculus to the nucleus," he took a deep, even breath and cast his mind to the limits of the world and his knowledge. It was a somewhat shadowy vision, but, he noted with impartial approval, definitely less shadowy than yesterday morning.

Employing a rapid mental scanning technique, he next cleared his memory chains of false associations, including those acquired while asleep. These chores completed, he held his finger on a bedside button, which rotated the polarizing windowpanes until the room slowly filled with a muted daylight. Then, still flat on his back, he turned his head until he could look at the remarkably beautiful blond girl asleep beside him.

Remembering last night, he felt a pang of exasperation, which he instantly quelled by taking his mind to a higher and dispassionate level from which he could look down on the girl and even himself as quaint, clumsy animals. Still, he grumbled silently, Caddy might have had enough consideration to clear out before he awoke. He wondered if he shouldn't have used his hypnotic control on the girl to smooth their relationship last night, and for a moment the word that would send her into deep trance trembled on the tip of his tongue. But no, that special power of his over her was reserved for far more important purposes.

Pumping dynamic tension into his twenty-year-old muscles and confidence into his sixty-year-old mind, the forty-year-old Thinker rose from bed. No covers had to be thrown off; nuclear central heating made them unnecessary. He stepped into his clothing—the

severe tunic, tights, and sockassins of the modern businessman.
Next he glanced at the message tape beside his phone, washing down
with ginger ale a vita-amino-enzyme tablet, and walked to the window.
There, gazing along the rows of newly planted mutant oaks lining
Decontamination Avenue, his smooth face broke into a smile.

It had come to him, the next big move in the intricate game making up his life—and mankind's. Come to him during sleep, as so many
of his best decisions did, because he regularly employed the time-
saving technique of somno-thought, which could function at the same
time as somno-learning.

He set his who?-where? robot for "Rocket Physicist" and "Genius
Class." While it worked, he dictated to his steno-robot the following
brief message:

Dear Fellow Scientist:
    *A project is contemplated that will have a crucial bearing on
man's future in deep space. Ample non-military government
funds are available. There was a time when professional men
scoffed at the Thinkers. Then there was a time when the Thinkers perforce neglected the professional men. Now both times
are past. May they never return! I would like to consult you this
afternoon, three o'clock sharp, Thinkers' Foundation I.*

Jorj Helmuth

Meanwhile the who?-where? had tossed out a dozen cards. He
glanced through them, hesitated at the name "Willard Farquar,"
looked at the sleeping girl, then quickly tossed them all into the
addresso-robot and plugged in the steno-robot.

The buzz light blinked green and he switched the phone to audio.

"The President is waiting to see Maizie, sir," a clear feminine voice
announced. "He has the general staff with him."

"Martian peace to him," Jorj Helmuth said. "Tell him I'll be down
in a few minutes."

Huge as a primitive nuclear reactor, the great electronic brain
loomed above the knot of hush-voiced men. It almost filled a two-
story room in the Thinkers' Foundation. Its front was an orderly

expanse of controls, indicators, telltales, and terminals, the upper ones reached by a chair on a boom.

Although, as far as anyone knew, it could sense only the information and questions fed into it on a tape, the human visitors could not resist the impulse to talk in whispers and glance uneasily at the great cryptic cube. After all, it had lately taken to moving some of its own controls—the permissible ones—and could doubtless improvise a hearing apparatus if it wanted to.

For this was the thinking machine beside which the Marks and Eniacs and Maniacs and Maddidas and Minervas and Mimirs were less than morons. This was the machine with a million times as many synapses as the human brain, the machine that remembered by cutting delicate notches in the rims of molecules (instead of kindergarten paper punching or the Coney Island shimmying of columns of mercury). This was the machine that had given instructions on building the last three quarters of itself. This was the goal, perhaps, toward which fallible human reasoning and biased human judgment and feeble human ambition had evolved.

This was the machine that really thought—a million-plus!

This was the machine that the timid cyberneticists and stuffy professional scientists had said could not be built. Yet this was the machine that the Thinkers, with characteristic Yankee push, *had* built. And nicknamed, with characteristic Yankee irreverence and girl-fondness, "Maizie."

Gazing up at it, the President of the United States felt a chord plucked within him that hadn't been sounded for decades, the dark and shivery organ chord of his Baptist childhood. Here, in a strange sense, although his reason rejected it, he felt he stood face to face with the living God: infinitely stern with the sternness of reality, yet infinitely just. No tiniest error or willful misstep could ever escape the scrutiny of this vast mentality. He shivered.

The grizzled general—there was also one who was gray—was thinking that this was a very odd link in the chain of command. Some shadowy and usually well-controlled memories from World War II faintly stirred his ire. Here he was giving orders to a being immeasurably more intelligent than himself. And always orders of the "Tell me how to kill that man" rather than the "Kill that man" sort. The distinction bothered him obscurely. It relieved him to know that Maizie had built-in controls which made her always the servant of humanity, or of humanity's right-minded leaders—even the Thinkers weren't certain which.

The gray general was thinking uneasily, and, like the President, at a more turbid level, of the resemblance between Papal infallibility and the dictates of the machine. Suddenly his bony wrists began to tremble. He asked himself: Was this the Second Coming? Mightn't an incarnation be in metal rather than flesh?

The austere Secretary of State was remembering what he'd taken such pains to make everyone forget: his youthful flirtation at Lake Success with Buddhism. Sitting before his guru, his teacher, feeling the Occidental's awe at the wisdom of the East, or its pretense, he had felt a little like this.

The burly Secretary of Space, who had come up through United Rockets, was thanking his stars that at any rate the professional scientists weren't responsible for this job. Like the grizzled general, he'd always felt suspicious of men who kept telling you how to do things, rather than doing them themselves. In World War III he'd had his fill of the professional physicists, with their eternal taint of a misty sort of radicalism and free-thinking. The Thinkers were better—more disciplined, more human. They'd called their brain machine Maizie, which helped take the curse off her. Somewhat.

The President's secretary, a paunchy veteran of party caucuses, was also glad that it was the Thinkers who had created the machine, though he trembled at the power that it gave them over the Administration. Still, you could do business with the Thinkers. And nobody (not even the Thinkers) could do business (that sort of business) with Maizie!

Before that great square face with its thousands of tiny metal features only Jorj Helmuth seemed at ease, busily entering on the tape the complex Questions of the Day that the high officials had handed him: logistics for the Endless War in Pakistan, optimum size for next year's sugar-corn crop, current thought trends in average Soviet minds—profound questions, yet many of them phrased with surprising simplicity. For figures, technical jargon, and layman's language were alike to Maizie; there was no need to translate into mathematical shorthand, as with the lesser brain machines.

The click of the taper went on until the Secretary of State had twice nervously fired a cigarette with his ultrasonic lighter and twice quickly put it away. No one spoke.

Jorj looked up at the Secretary of Space. "Section Five, Question Four—whom would that come from?"

The burly man frowned. "That would be the physics boys, Opperly's group. Is anything wrong?"

Jorj did not answer. A bit later he quit taping and began to adjust controls, going up on the boom chair to reach some of them. Eventually he came down and touched a few more, then stood waiting.

From the great cube came a profound, steady purring. Involuntarily the six officials backed off a bit. Somehow it was impossible for a man to get used to the sound of Maizie starting to think.

Jorj turned, smiling. "And now, gentlemen, while we wait for Maizie to cerebrate, there should be just enough time for us to watch the take-off of the Mars rocket."

He switched on a giant television screen. The others made a quarter turn, and there before them glowed the rich ochers and blues of a New Mexico sunrise and, in the middle distance, a silvery spindle.

Like the generals, the Secretary of Space suppressed a scowl. Here was something that ought to be spang in the center of his official territory, and the Thinkers had locked him completely out of it. That rocket there—just an ordinary Earth satellite vehicle commandeered from the Army, but equipped by the Thinkers with Maizie-designed nuclear motors capable of the Mars journey and more. The first spaceship—and the Secretary of Space was not in on it!

Still, he told himself, Maizie had decreed it that way. And when he remembered what the Thinkers had done for him in rescuing him from breakdown with their mental science, in rescuing the whole Administration from collapse, he realized he had to be satisfied. And that was without taking into consideration the amazing additional mental discoveries that the Thinkers were bringing down from Mars.

"Lord!" the President said to Jorj, as if voicing the Secretary's feeling, "I wish you people could bring a couple of those wise little devils back with you this trip. Be a good thing for the country."

Jorj looked at him a bit coldly. "It's quite unthinkable," he said. "The telepathic abilities of the Martians make them extremely sensitive. The conflicts of ordinary Earth minds would impinge on them psychotically, even fatally. As you know, the Thinkers were able to contact them only because of our degree of learned mental poise and errorless memory chains. So for the present it must be our task alone to glean from the Martians their astounding mental skills. Of course, some day in the future, when we have discovered how to armor the minds of the Martians—"

"Sure, I know," the President said hastily. "Shouldn't have mentioned it, Jorj."

Conversation ceased. They waited with growing tension for the great violet flames to bloom from the base of the silvery shaft.

Meanwhile the question tape, like a New Year's streamer tossed out a high window into the night, sped on its dark way along spinning rollers. Curling with an intricate aimlessness curiously like that of such a streamer, it tantalized the silvery fingers of a thousand relays, saucily evaded the glances of ten thousand electric eyes, impishly darted down a narrow black alleyway of memory banks, and, reaching the center of the cube, suddenly emerged into a small room where a suave fat man in shorts sat drinking beer.

He flipped the tape over to him with practiced finger, eyeing it as a stockbroker might have studied a ticker tape. He read the first question, closed his eyes and frowned for five seconds. Then with the staccato self-confidence of a hack writer, he began to tape out the answer.

For many minutes the only sounds were the rustle of the paper ribbon and the click of the taper, except for the seconds the fat man took to close his eyes, or to drink beer. Once, too, he lifted a phone, asked a concise question, waited half a minute, listened to an answer, then went back to the grind.

Until he came to Section Five, Question Four. That time he did his thinking with his eyes open.

The question was: "Does Maizie stand for Maelzel?"

He sat for a while slowly scratching his thigh. His loose, persuasive lips tightened, without closing, into the shape of a snarl.

Suddenly he began to tape again.

"Maizie does not stand for Maelzel. Maizie stands for amazing, humorously given the form of a girl's name. Section Six, Answer

One: The mid-term election viewcasts should be spaced as follows . . ."

But his lips didn't lose the shape of a snarl.

Five hundred miles above the ionosphere, the Mars rocket cut off its fuel and slumped gratefully into an orbit that would carry it effortlessly around the world at that altitude. The pilot unstrapped himself and stretched, but he didn't look out the viewport at the dried-mud disk that was Earth, cloaked in its haze of blue sky. He knew he had two maddening months ahead of him in which to do little more than that. Instead, he unstrapped Sappho.

Used to free fall from two previous experiences, and loving it, the fluffy little cat was soon bounding about the cabin in curves and gyrations that would have made her the envy of all back-alley and parlor felines on the planet below. A miracle cat in the dream world of free fall. For a long time she played with a string that the man would toss out lazily. Sometimes she caught the string on the fly, sometimes she swam for it frantically.

After a while the man grew bored with the game. He unlocked a drawer and began to study the details of the wisdom he would discover on Mars this trip—priceless spiritual insights that would be balm to a war-battered mankind.

The cat carefully selected a spot three feet off the floor, curled up on the air, and went to sleep.

Jorj Helmuth snipped the emerging answer tape into sections and handed each to the appropriate man. Most of them carefully tucked theirs away with little more than a glance, but the Secretary of Space puzzled over his.

"Who the devil would Maelzel be?" he asked.

A remote look came into the eyes of the Secretary of Space. "Edgar Allan Poe," he said frowningly, with eyes half closed.

The grizzled general snapped his fingers. "Sure! Maelzel's chess player. Read it when I was a kid. About an automaton that played chess. Poe proved it had a man inside it."

The Secretary of Space frowned. "Now what's the point in a fool question like that?"

"You said it came from Opperly's group?" Jorj asked sharply.

The Secretary of Space nodded. The others looked at the two men puzzledly.

"Who would that be?" Jorj pressed. "The group, I mean."

The Secretary of Space shrugged. "Oh, the usual little bunch over at the institute. Hindeman, Gregory, Opperly himself. Oh yes, and young Farquar."

"Sounds like Opperly's getting senile," Jorj commented coldly. "I'd investigate."

The Secretary of Space nodded. He suddenly looked tough. "I will. Right away."

Sunlight striking through french windows spotlighted a ballet of dust motes untroubled by air-conditioning. Morton Opperly's living room was well kept but worn and quite behind the times. Instead of reading tapes there were books; instead of steno-robots, pen and ink; while in place of a four-by-six TV screen, a Picasso hung on the wall. Only Opperly knew that the painting was still faintly radioactive, that it had been riskily so when he'd smuggled it out of his bomb-singed apartment in New York City.

The two physicists fronted each other across a coffee table. The face of the elder was cadaverous, large-eyed, and tender—fined down by a long life of abstract thought. That of the younger was forceful, sensuous, bulky as his body, and exceptionally ugly. He looked rather like a bear.

Opperly was saying, "So when he asked who was responsible for the Maelzel question, I said I didn't remember." He smiled. "They still allow me my absent-mindedness, since it nourishes their contempt. Almost my sole remaining privilege." The smile faded. "Why do you keep on teasing the zoo animals, Willard?" he asked without rancor. "I've maintained many times that we shouldn't truckle to them by yielding to their demand that we ask Maizie questions. You and the rest have overruled me. But then to use those questions to convey veiled insults isn't reasonable. Apparently the Secretary of Space was bothered enough about this last one to pay me a 'copter call within twenty minutes of this morning's meeting at the foundation. Why do you do it, Willard?"

The features of the other convulsed unpleasantly. "Because the Thinkers are charlatans who must be exposed," he rapped out. "We know their Maizie is no more than a tea-leaf-reading fake. We've traced their Mars rockets and found they go nowhere. We know their Martian mental science is bunk."

"But we've already exposed the Thinkers very thoroughly," Opperly interposed quietly. "You know the good it did."

Farquar hunched his Japanese-wrestler shoulders. "Then it's got to be done until it takes."

Opperly studied the bowl of lilies-of-the-valley by the coffeepot. "I think you just want to tease the animals, for some personal reason of which you probably aren't aware."

Farquar scowled. "We're the ones in the cages."

Opperly continued his inspection of the flowers' bells. "All the more reason not to poke sticks through the bars at the lions and tigers strolling outside. No, Willard, I'm not counseling appeasement. But consider the age in which we live. It wants magicians." His voice grew especially tranquil. "A scientist tells people the truth. When times are good—that is, when the truth offers no threat—people don't mind. But when times are very, very bad—" A shadow darkened his eyes. "Well, we all know what happened to—" And he mentioned three names that had been household words in the middle of the century. They were the names on the brass plaque dedicated to the three martyred physicists.

He went on, "A magician, on the other hand, tells people what they wish were true—that perpetual motion works, that cancer can be cured by colored lights, that a psychosis is no worse than a head cold, that they'll live forever. In good times magicians are laughed at. They're a luxury of the spoiled wealthy few. But in bad times people sell their souls for magic cures and buy perpetual-motion machines to power their war rockets."

Farquar clenched his fist. "All the more reason to keep chipping away at the Thinkers. Are we supposed to beg off from a job because it's difficult and dangerous?"

Opperly shook his head. "We're to keep clear of the infection of violence. In my day, Willard, I was one of the Frightened Men. Later I was one of the Angry Men and then one of the Minds of Despair. Now I'm convinced that all my posturings were futile."

"Exactly!" Farquar agreed harshly. "You postured. You didn't act. If you men who discovered atomic energy had only formed a secret league, if you'd only had the foresight and the guts to use your tremendous bargaining position to demand the power to shape mankind's future—"

"By the time you were born, Willard," Opperly interrupted dreamily, "Hitler was merely a name in the history books. We scientists weren't the stuff out of which cloak-and-dagger men are made. Can you imagine Oppenheimer wearing a mask or Einstein sneaking into the Old White House with a bomb in his brief case?" He smiled. "Besides, that's not the way power is seized. New ideas aren't useful to the man bargaining for power—his weapons are established facts, or lies."

"Just the same, it would have been a good thing if you'd had a little violence in you."

"No," Opperly said.

"I've got violence in me," Farquar announced, shoving himself to his feet.

Opperly looked up from the flowers. "I think you have," he agreed.

"But what are we to do?" Farquar demanded. "Surrender the world to charlatans without a struggle?"

Opperly mused for a while. "I don't know what the world needs now. Everyone knows Newton as the great scientist. Few remember that he spent half his life muddling with alchemy, looking for the philosopher's stone. That was the pebble by the seashore he really wanted to find."

"Now you are justifying the Thinkers!"

"No, I leave that to history."

"And history consists of the actions of men," Farquar concluded. "I intend to act. The Thinkers are vulnerable, their power fantastically precarious. What's it based on? A few lucky guesses. Faithhealing. Some science hocus-pocus, on the level of those juke-box burlesque acts between the strips. Dubious mental comfort given to a few nerve-torn neurotics in the Inner Cabinet—and their wives. The fact that the Thinkers' clever stage-managing won the President a doubtful election. The erroneous belief that the Soviets pulled out of Iraq and Iran because of the Thinkers' Mind Bomb threat. A brain machine that's just a cover for Jan Tregarron's guesswork. Oh yes, and that hogwash of 'Martian Wisdom.' All of it mere bluff! A few pushes at the right times and points are all that are needed—and the Thinkers know it! I'll bet they're terrified already, and will be more so when they find that we're gunning for them. Eventually they'll be making overtures to us, turning to us for help. You wait and see."

"I am thinking again of Hitler," Opperly interposed quietly. "On his first half-dozen big steps, he had nothing but bluff. His generals were against him. They knew they were in a cardboard fort. Yet he won every battle, until the last. Moreover," he pressed on, cutting Farquar short, "the power of the Thinkers isn't based on what they've got, but on what the world hasn't got—peace, honor, a good conscience—"

The front-door knocker clanked. Farquar answered it. A skinny old man with a radiation scar twisting across his temple handed him a tiny cylinder. "Radiogram for you, Willard." He grinned across the hall at Opperly. "When are you going to get a phone put in, Mr. Opperly?"

The physicist waved to him. "Next year, perhaps, Mr. Berry."

The old man snorted with good-humored incredulity and trudged off.

"What did I tell you about the Thinkers making overtures?" Farquar chortled suddenly. "It's come sooner than I expected. Look at this."

He held out the radiogram, but the older man didn't take it. Instead he asked, "Who's it from? Tregarron?"

"No, from Helmuth. There's a lot of sugar corn about man's future in deep space, but the real reason is clear. They know that they're going to have to produce an actual nuclear rocket pretty soon, and for that they'll need our help."

"An invitation?"

Farquar nodded. "For this afternoon." He noticed Opperly's anxious though distant frown. "What's the matter?" he asked. "Are you bothered about my going? Are you thinking it might be a trap—that after the Maelzel question they may figure I'm better rubbed out?"

The older man shook his head. "I'm not afraid for your life, Willard. That's yours to risk as you choose. No, I'm worried about other things they might do to you."

"What do you mean?" Farquar asked.

Opperly looked at him with a gentle appraisal. "You're a strong and vital man, Willard, with a strong man's prides and desires." His voice trailed off for a bit. Then, "Excuse me, Willard, but wasn't there a girl once? A Miss Arkady—"

Farquar's ungainly figure froze. He nodded curtly, face averted.

"And didn't she go off with a Thinker?"

"If girls find me ugly, that's their business," Farquar said harshly, still not looking at Opperly. "What's that got to do with this invitation?"

Opperly didn't answer the question. His eyes got more distant. Finally he said, "In my day we had it a lot easier. A scientist was an academician, cushioned by tradition."

Willard snorted. "Science had already entered the era of the police inspectors, with laboratory directors and political appointees stifling enterprise."

"Perhaps," Opperly agreed. "Still, the scientist lived the safe, restricted, highly respectable life of a university man. He wasn't exposed to the temptations of the world."

Farquar turned on him. "Are you implying that the Thinkers will somehow be able to buy me off?"

"Not exactly."

"You think I'll be persuaded to change my aims?" Farquar demanded angrily.

Opperly shrugged his helplessness. "No, I don't think you'll change your aims."

Clouds encroaching from the west blotted the parallelogram of sunlight between the two men.

As the slideway whisked him gently along the corridor toward his apartment Jorj Helmuth was thinking of his spaceship. For a moment the silver-winged vision crowded everything else out of his mind.

Just think, a spaceship with sails! He smiled a bit, marveling at the paradox.

Direct atomic power. Direct utilization of the force of the flying neutrons. No more ridiculous business of using a reactor to drive a steam engine, or boil off something for a jet exhaust—processes that were as primitive and wasteful as burning gunpowder to keep yourself warm.

Chemical jets would carry his spaceship above the atmosphere. Then would come the thrilling order, "Set sail for Mars!" The vast umbrella would unfold and open out around the stern, its rear or earthward side a gleaming expanse of radioactive ribbon perhaps only an atom thick and backed with a material that would reflect neutrons. Atoms in the ribbon would split, blasting neutrons astern at fantastic velocities. Reaction would send the spaceship hurtling forward.

In airless space, the expanse of sails would naturally not retard the ship. More radioactive ribbon, manufactured as needed in the ship itself, would feed out onto the sail as that already there became exhausted.

A spaceship with direct nuclear drive—and he, a Thinker, had conceived it completely except for the technical details! Having strengthened his mind by hard years of somno-learning, mind-casting, memory-straightening, and sensory training, he had assured himself of the executive power to control the technicians and direct their specialized abilities. Together they would build the true Mars rocket.

But that would only be a beginning. They would build the true Mind Bomb. They would build the true Selective Microbe Slayer. They would discover the true laws of ESP and the inner life. They would even—his imagination hesitated a moment, then strode boldly forward—build the true Maizie!

And then—then the Thinkers would be on even terms with the scientists. Rather, they'd be far ahead. No more deception.

He was so exalted by this thought that he almost let the slideway carry him past his door. He stepped inside and called, "Caddy!" He waited a moment, then walked through the apartment, but she wasn't there.

Confound the girl! he couldn't help thinking. This morning, when she should have made herself scarce, she'd sprawled about sleeping. Now, when he felt like seeing her, when her presence would have added a pleasant final touch to his glowing mood, she chose to be absent. He really should use his hypnotic control on her, he decided, and again there sprang into his mind the word—a pet form of her name—that would send her into obedient trance.

No, he told himself again, that was to be reserved for some moment of crisis or desperate danger, when he would need someone to strike suddenly and unquestioningly for himself and mankind. Caddy was merely a willful and rather silly girl, incapable at present of understanding the tremendous tensions under which he operated. When he had time for it, he would train her up to be a fitting companion without hypnosis.

Yet the fact of her absence had a subtly disquieting effect. It shook his perfect self-confidence just a fraction. He asked himself if he'd been wise in summoning the rocket physicists without consulting Tregarron.

But this mood, too, he conquered quickly. Tregarron wasn't his boss, but just the Thinkers' most clever salesman, an expert in the mumbo-jumbo so necessary for social control in this chaotic era. He himself, Jorj Helmuth, was the real leader in theoretics and over-all strategy, the mind behind the mind behind Maizie.

He stretched himself on the bed, almost instantly achieved maximum relaxation, turned on the somno-learner, and began the two-hour rest he knew would be desirable before the big conference.

Jan Tregarron had supplemented his shorts with pink coveralls, but he was still drinking beer. He emptied his glass and lifted it a lazy inch. The beautiful girl beside him refilled it without a word and went on stroking his forehead.

"Caddy," he said reflectively, without looking at her, "there's a little job I want you to do. You're the only one with the proper background. The point is: it will take you away from Jorj for some time."

"I'd welcome it," she said with decision. "I'm getting pretty sick of watching his push-ups and all his other mind and muscle stunts. And that damn somno-learner of his keeps me awake."

Tregarron smiled. "I'm afraid Thinkers make pretty sad sweethearts."

"Not all of them," she told him, returning his smile tenderly.

He chuckled. "It's about one of those rocket physicists in the list you brought me. A fellow named Willard Farquar."

Caddy didn't say anything, but she stopped stroking his forehead.

"What's the matter?" he asked. "You knew him once, didn't you?"

"Yes," she replied and then added, with surprising feeling, "The big, ugly ape!"

"Well, he's an ape whose services we happen to need. I want you to be our contact girl with him."

She took her hands away from his forehead. "Look, Jan," she said, "I wouldn't like this job."

"I thought he was very sweet on you once."

"Yes, as he never grew tired of trying to demonstrate to me. The clumsy, overgrown, bumbling baby! The man's disgusting, Jan. His approach to a woman is a child wanting candy and enraged because Mama won't produce it on the instant. I don't mind Jorj—he's just a pipsqueak and it amuses me to see how he frustrates himself. But Willard is—"

"—a bit frightening?" Tregarron finished for her.

"No!"

"Of course you're not afraid," Tregarron purred. "You're our beautiful, clever Caddy, who can do anything she wants with any man, and without whose—"

"Look, Jan, this is different—" she began agitatedly.

"—and without whose services we'd have got exactly nowhere. Clever, subtle Caddy, whose most charming attainment in the ever-appreciative eyes of Papa Jan is her ability to handle every man in the neatest way imaginable and without a trace of real feeling. Kitty Kaddy, who—"

"Very well," she said with a sigh. "I'll do it."

"Of course you will," Jan said, drawing her hands back to his forehead. "And you'll begin right away by getting into your nicest sugar-and-cream war clothes. You and I are going to be the welcoming committee when that ape arrives this afternoon."

"But what about Jorj? He'll want to see Willard."

"That'll be taken care of," Jan assured her.

"And what about the other dozen rocket physicists Jorj asked to come?"

"Don't worry about them."

The President looked inquiringly at his secretary across his littered desk in his home study at White House, Jr. "So Opperly didn't have any idea how that odd question about Maizie turned up in Section Five?"

His secretary settled his paunch and shook his head. "Or claimed not to. Perhaps he's just the absent-minded prof, perhaps, something else. The old feud of the physicists against the Thinkers may be getting hot again. There'll be further investigation."

The President nodded. He obviously had something uncomfortable on his mind. He said uneasily, "Do you think there's any possibility of it being true?"

"What?" asked the secretary guardedly.

"That peculiar hint about Maizie."

The secretary said nothing.

"Mind you, I don't think there is," the President went on hurriedly, his face assuming a sorrowful scowl. "I owe a lot to the Thinkers, both as a private person and as a public figure. Lord, a man has to lean on *something* these days. But just supposing it were true"—he hesitated, as before uttering blasphemy—"that there was a man inside Maizie, what could we do?"

The secretary said stolidly, "The Thinkers won our last election. They chased the Commies out of Iran. We brought them into the Inner Cabinet. We've showered them with public funds." He paused. "We couldn't do a damn thing."

The President nodded with equal conviction, and, not very happily, summed up: "So if anyone should go up against the Thinkers— and I'm afraid I wouldn't want to see that happen, whatever's true—it would have to be a scientist."

Willard Farquar felt his weight change the steps under his feet into an escalator. He cursed under his breath, but let them carry him, a defiant hulk, up to the tall and mystic blue portals, which silently parted when he was five meters away. The escalator changed to a slideway and carried him into a softly gleaming, high-domed room rather like the antechamber of a temple.

"Martian peace to you, Willard Farquar," an invisible voice intoned. "You have entered the Thinkers' Foundation. Please remain on the slideway."

"I want to see Jorj Helmuth," Willard growled loudly.

The slideway carried him into the mouth of a corridor and paused.

A dark opening dilated on the wall. "May we take your hat and coat!" a voice asked politely. After a moment the request was repeated, with the addition of, "Just pass them through."

Willard scowled, then fought his way out of his shapeless coat and passed it and his hat through in a lump. Instantly the opening contracted, imprisoning his wrists, and he felt his hands being washed on the other side of the wall.

He gave a great jerk which failed to free his hands from the snugly padded gyves. "Do not be alarmed," the voice advised him. "It is only an esthetic measure. As your hands are laved, invisible radiations are slaughtering all the germs in your body, while more delicate emanations are producing a benign rearrangement of your emotions."

The rather amateurish curses Willard was gritting between his teeth became more sulphurous. His sensations told him that a towel of some sort was being applied to his hands. He wondered if he would be subjected to a face-washing and even greater indignities. Then, just before his wrists were released, he felt—for a moment only, but unmistakably—the soft touch of a girl's hand.

That touch, like the mysterious sweet chink of a bell in darkness, brought him a sudden feeling of excitement, wonder.

Yet the feeling was as fleeting as that caused by a lurid advertisement, for as the slideway began to move again, carrying him past a series of depth pictures and inscriptions celebrating the Thinkers' achievements, his mood of bitter exasperation returned doubled. This place, he told himself, was a plague spot of the disease of magic in an enfeebled and easily infected world. He reminded himself that he was not without resources—the Thinkers must fear or need him, whether because of the Maelzel question or the necessity of producing a nuclear power spaceship. He felt his determination to smash them reaffirmed.

The slideway, having twice turned into an escalator, veered toward an opalescent door, which opened as silently as the one below. The slideway stopped at the threshold. Momentum carried him a couple of steps into the room. He stopped and looked around.

The place was a sybarite's modernistic dream. Sponge carpeting thick as a mattress and topped with down. Hassocks and couches that looked butter-soft. A domed ceiling of deep glossy blue mimicking the night sky, with the constellations tooled in silver. A wall of niches crammed with statuettes of languorous men, women, beasts. A self-service bar with a score of golden spigots. A depth TV screen simulating a great crystal ball. Here and there barbaric studs of hammered gold that might have been push buttons. A low table set for three with exquisite ware of crystal and gold. An ever-changing scent of resins and flowers.

A smiling fat man clad in pearl gray sports clothes came through one of the curtained archways. Willard recognized Jan Tregarron from his pictures, but did not at once offer to speak to him. Instead he let his gaze wander with an ostentatious contempt around the crammed walls, take in the bar and the set table with its many wineglasses, and finally return to his host.

"And where," he asked with harsh irony, "are the dancing girls?"

The fat man's eyebrows rose. "In there," he said innocently, indicating the second archway. The curtains parted.

"Oh, I *am* sorry," the fat man apologized. "There seems to be only one on duty. I hope that isn't too much at variance with your tastes."

She stood in the archway, demure and lovely in an off-the-bosom frock of pale skylon edged in mutated mink. She was smiling the first smile that Willard had ever had from her lips.

"Mr. Willard Farquar," the fat man murmured, "Miss Arkady Simms."

Jorj Helmuth turned from the conference table with its dozen empty chairs to the two mousily pretty secretaries.

"No word from the door yet, Master," one of them ventured to say.

Jorj twisted in his chair, though hardly uncomfortably, since it was a beautiful pneumatic job. His nervousness at having to face the twelve rocket physicists—a feeling which, he had to admit, had been unexpectedly great—was giving way to impatience.

"What's Willard Farquar's phone?" he asked sharply.

One of the secretaries ran through a clutch of desk tapes, then spent some seconds whispering into her throat-mike and listening to answers from the soft-speaker.

"He lives with Morton Opperly, who doesn't have one," she finally told Jorj in scandalized tones.

"Let me see the list," Jorj said. Then, after a bit, "Try Dr. Welcome's place."

This time there were results. Within a quarter of a minute he was handed a phone which he hung expertly on his shoulder.

"This is Dr. Asa Welcome," a reedy voice told him.

"This is Helmuth of the Thinkers' Foundation," Jorj said icily. "Did you get my communication?"

The reedy voice became anxious and placating. "Why yes, Mr. Helmuth, I did. Very glad to get it too. Sounded most interesting. Very eager to come. But—"

"Yes?"

"Well, I was just about to hop in my 'copter—my son's 'copter—when the other note came."

"What other note?"

"Why, the note calling the meeting off."

"I sent no other note!"

The other voice became acutely embarrassed. "But I considered it to be from you—or just about the same thing. I really think I had the right to assume that."

"How was it signed?" Jorj rapped.

"Mr. Jan Tregarron."

Jorj broke the connection. He didn't move until a low sound shattered his abstraction and he realized that one of the girls was whispering a call to the door. He handed back the phone and dismissed them. They went in a rustle of jackets and skirtlets, hesitating at the doorway but not quite daring to look back.

He sat motionless a minute longer. Then his hand crept fretfully onto the table and pushed a button. The room darkened and a long section of wall became transparent, revealing a dozen silvery models of spaceships, beautifully executed. He quickly touched another; the models faded and the opposite wall bloomed with an animated cartoon that portrayed with charming humor and detail the designing and construction of a neutron-drive spaceship. A third button, and a depth picture of deep star-speckled space opened behind the cartoon, showing a section of Earth's surface and in the far distance the tiny ruddy globe of Mars. Slowly a tiny rocket rose from the section of Earth and spread its silvery sails.

He switched off the pictures, keeping the room dark. By a faint table light he dejectedly examined his organizational charts for the neutron-drive project, the long list of books he had boned up on by somno-learning, the concealed table of physical constants and all sorts of other crucial details about rocket physics—a cleverly condensed encyclopedic "pony" to help out his memory on technical points that might have arisen in his discussion with the experts.

He switched out all the lights and slumped forward, blinking his eyes and trying to swallow the lump in his throat. In the dark his memory went seeping back, back, to the day when his math teacher had told him, very superciliously, that the marvelous fantasies he loved to read and hoarded by his bed weren't real science at all, but just a kind of lurid pretense. He had so wanted to be a scientist, and the teacher's contempt had cast a damper on his ambition.

And now that the conference was canceled, would he ever know that it wouldn't have turned out the same way today? That his somno-learning hadn't taken? That his "pony" wasn't good enough? That his ability to handle people extended only to credulous farmer Presidents and mousy girls in skirtlets? Only the test of meeting the experts would have answered those questions.

Tregarron was the one to blame! Tregarron with his sly tyrannical ways, Tregarron with his fear of losing the future to men who really understood theoretics and could handle experts. Tregarron, so used to working by deception that he couldn't see when it became a fault and a crime. Tregarron, who must now be shown the light—or, failing that, against whom certain steps must be taken.

For perhaps half an hour Jorj sat very still, thinking. Then he turned to the phone and, after some delay, got his party.

"What is it now, Jorj?" Caddy asked impatiently. "Please don't bother me with any of your moods, because I'm tired and my nerves are on edge."

He took a breath. When steps may have to be taken, he thought, one must hold an agent in readiness. "Caddums," he intoned hypnotically, vibrantly. "Caddums—"

The voice at the other end had instantly changed, become submissive, sleepy, suppliant.

"Yes, Master?"

Morton Opperly looked up from the sheet of neatly penned equations at Willard Farquar, who had somehow acquired a measure of poise. He neither lumbered restlessly nor grimaced. He removed his coat with a certain dignity and stood solidly before his mentor. He smiled. Granting that he was a bear, one might guess he had just been fed.

"You see?" he said. "They didn't hurt me."

"They didn't hurt you?" Opperly asked softly.

Willard slowly shook his head. His smile broadened.

Opperly put down his pen, folded his hands. "And you're as determined as ever to expose and smash the Thinkers?"

"Of course!" The menacing growl came back into the bear's voice, except that it was touched with a certain pleased luxuriousness. "Only from now on I won't be teasing the zoo animals, and I won't embarrass you by asking any more Maelzel questions. I have reached the objective at which those tactics were aimed. After this I shall bore from within."

"Bore from within," Opperly repeated, frowning. "Now where have I heard that phrase before?" His brow cleared. "Oh yes," he said listlessly. "Do I understand that you are becoming a Thinker, Willard?"

The other gave him a faintly pitying smile, stretched himself on the couch and gazed at the ceiling. All his movements were deliberate, easy.

"Certainly. That's the only realistic way to smash them. Rise high in their councils. Out-trick all their trickeries. Organize a fifth column. Then *strike!*"

"The end justifying the means, of course," Opperly said.

"Of course. As surely as the desire to stand up justifies your disturbing the air over your head. All action in this world is nothing but means."

Opperly nodded abstractedly. "I wonder if anyone else ever became a Thinker for those same reasons. I wonder if being a Thinker doesn't simply mean that you've decided you have to use lies and tricks as your chief method."

Willard shrugged. "Could be." There was no longer any doubt about the pitying quality of his smile.

Opperly stood up, squaring together his papers. "So you'll be working with Helmuth?"

"Not Helmuth. Tregarron." The bear's smile became cruel. "I'm afraid that Helmuth's career as a Thinker is going to have quite a setback."

"Helmuth," Opperly mused. "Morgenschein once told me a bit about him. A man of some idealism, despite his affiliations. Best of a bad lot. Incidentally, is he the one with whom—"

"—Miss Arkady Simms ran off?" Willard finished without any embarrassment. "Yes, that was Helmuth. But that's all going to be changed now."

Opperly nodded. "Good-by, Willard," he said.

Willard quickly heaved himself up on an elbow. Opperly looked at him for about five seconds, then, without a word, walked out of the room.

The only obvious furnishings in Jan Tregarron's office were a flat-topped desk and a few chairs. Tregarron sat behind the desk, the top of which was completely bare. He looked almost bored, except that his little eyes were smiling. Jorj Helmuth sat across the desk from him, a few feet back, erect and grim faced, while Caddy, shadowy in the muted light, stood against the wall behind Tregarron. She still wore the fur-trimmed skylon frock she'd put on that afternoon. She took no part in the conversation, seemed almost unaware of it.

"So you just went ahead and canceled the conference without consulting me?" Jorj was saying.

"You called it without consulting me." Tregarron playfully wagged a finger. "Shouldn't do that sort of thing, Jorj."

"But I tell you, I was completely prepared. I was absolutely sure of my ground."

"I know, I know," Tregarron said lightly. "But it's not the right time for it. I'm the best judge of that."

"When will be the right time?"

Tregarron shrugged. "Look here, Jorj," he said, "every man should stick to his trade, to his forte. Technology isn't ours."

Jorj's lips thinned. "But you know as well as I do that we are going to have to have a nuclear spaceship and actually go to Mars someday."

Tregarron lifted his eyebrows. "Are we?"

"Yes! Just as we're going to have to build a real Maizie. All the things we've done until now have been emergency measures."

"Really?"

Jorj stared at him. "Look here, Jan," he said, gripping his knees with his hands, "you and I are going to have to talk things through."

"Are you quite sure of that?" Jan's voice was very cool. "I have a feeling that it might be best if you said nothing and accepted things as they are."

"No!"

"Very well." Tregarron settled himself in his chair.

"I helped you organize the Thinkers," Jorj said, and waited. "At least, I was your first partner."

Tregarron barely nodded.

"Our basic idea was that the time had come to apply science to the life of man on a large scale, to live rationally and realistically. The only things holding the world back from this all-important step were the ignorance, superstition, and inertia of the average man, and the stuffiness and lack of enterprise of the academic scientists.

"Yet we knew that in their deepest hearts the average man and the professionals were both on our side. They wanted the new world visualized by science. They wanted the simplifications and conveniences, the glorious adventures of the human mind and body. They wanted the trips to Mars and into the depths of the human psyche, they wanted the robots and the thinking machines. All they lacked was the nerve to take the first big step—and that was what we supplied.

"It was no time for half measures, for slow and sober plodding. The world was racked by wars and neurosis, in danger of falling into the foulest hands. What was needed was a tremendous and thrilling appeal to the human imagination, an earth-shaking affirmation of the power of science for good.

"But the men who provided that appeal and affirmation couldn't afford to be cautious. They wouldn't check and double check. They couldn't wait for the grudging and jealous approval of the professionals. They had to use stunts, tricks, fakes—*anything to get over the big point*. Once that had been done, once mankind was headed down the new road, it would be easy enough to give the average man the necessary degree of insight to heal the breach with the professionals, to make good in actuality what had been made good only in pretense.

"Have I stated our position fairly?"

Tregarron's eyes were hooded. "You're the one who's telling it."

"On those general assumptions we established our hold on susceptible leaders and the mob," Jorj went on. "We built Maizie and the Mars rocket and the Mind Bomb. We discovered the wisdom of the Martians. We *sold* the people on the science that the professionals had been too high-toned to advertise or bring into the market place.

"But now that we've succeeded, now that we've made the big point, now that Maizie and Mars and science do rule the average human imagination, the time has come to take the second big step, to let accomplishment catch up with imagination, to implement fantasy with fact.

"Do you suppose I'd ever have gone into this with you if it hadn't been for the thought of that second big step? Why, I'd have felt dirty and cheap, a mere charlatan—except for the sure conviction that someday everything would be set right. I've devoted my whole life to that conviction, Jan. I've studied and disciplined myself, using every scientific means at my disposal, so that I wouldn't be found lacking when the day came to heal the breach between the Thinkers and the professionals. I've trained myself to be the perfect man for the job.

"Jan, the day's come and I'm the man. I know you've been concentrating on other aspects of our work; you haven't had time to keep up with my side of it. But I'm sure that as soon as you see how carefully I've prepared myself, how completely practical the neutron-drive rocket project is, you'll beg me to go ahead!"

Tregarron smiled at the ceiling for a moment. "Your general idea isn't so bad, Jorj, but your time scale is out of whack and your judgment is a joke. Oh yes. Every revolutionary wants to see the big change take place in his lifetime, Tch! It's as if he were watching evolutionary vaudeville and wanted the Ape-to-Man Act over in twenty minutes.

"Time for the second big step? Jorj, the average man's exactly what he was ten years ago, except that he's got a new god. More than ever he thinks of Mars as a Hollywood paradise, with wise men and yummy princesses. Maizie is Mama magnified a million times. As for professional scientists, they're more jealous and stuffy than ever. All they'd like to do is turn the clock back to a genteel dream world of quiet quadrangles and caps and gowns, where every commoner bows to the passing scholar.

"Maybe in ten thousand years we'll be ready for the second big step. Maybe. Meanwhile, as should be, the clever will rule the stupid for their own good. The realists will rule the dreamers. Those with free hands will rule those who have deliberately handcuffed themselves with taboos.

"Secondly, your judgment. Did you actually think you could have bossed those professionals, kept your mental footing in the intellectual melee? You, a nuclear physicist? A rocket scientist? Why, it's— Take it easy now, boy, and listen to me. They'd have torn you to pieces in twenty minutes and glad of the chance! You baffle me, Jorj. You know that Maizie and the Mars rocket and all that are fakes, yet you believe in your somno-learning and consciousness-expansion and optimism-pumping like the veriest yokel. I wouldn't be surprised to hear you'd taken up ESP and hypnotism. I think you should take stock of yourself and get a new slant. It's overdue."

He leaned back. Jorj's face had become a mask. His eyes did not flicker from Tregarron's, yet there was a subtle change in his expression. Behind Tregarron, Caddy swayed as if in a sudden gust of intangible wind and took a silent step forward from the wall.

"That's your honest opinion?" Jorj asked very quietly.

"It's more than that," Tregarron told him, just as unmelodramatically. "It's orders."

Jorj stood up purposefully. "Very well," he said. "In that case I have to tell you that—"

Casually, but with no waste motion, Tregarron slipped an ultrasonic pistol from under the desk and laid it on the empty top.

"No," he said, "let me tell you something. I was afraid this would happen and I made preparations. If you've studied your Nazi, Fascist, and Soviet history, you know what happens to old revolutionaries who don't move with the times. But I'm not going to be too harsh. I have a couple of boys waiting outside. They'll take you by 'copter to the field, then by jet to New Mex. Bright and early tomorrow morning, Jorj, you're leaving on a trip to Mars."

Jorj hardly reacted to the words. Caddy was two steps nearer Tregarron.

"I decided Mars would be the best place for you," the fat man continued. "The robot controls will be arranged so that your 'visit' to Mars lasts two years. Perhaps in that time you will have learned wisdom, such as realizing that the big liar must never fall for his own big lie.

"Meanwhile, there will have to be a replacement for you. I have in mind a person who may prove peculiarly worthy to occupy your position, with all its perquisites. A person who seems to understand that force and desire are the motive powers of life, and that anyone who believes the big lie proves himself strictly a jerk."

Caddy was standing behind Tregarron now, her half-closed, sleepy eyes fixed on Jorj's.

"His name is Willard Farquar. You see, I too believe in cooperating with the scientists, Jorj, but by subversion rather than conference. My idea is to offer the hand of friendship to a selected few of them—the hand of friendship with a nice big bribe in it." He smiled. "You were a good man, Jorj, for the early days, when we needed a publicist with catchy ideas about Mind Bombs, ray guns, plastic helmets, fancy sweaters, space brassières, and all that other corn. Now we can afford a solider sort of person."

Jorj moistened his lips.

"We'll have a neat explanation of what's happened to you. Callers will be informed that you've gone on an extended visit to imbibe the wisdom of the Martians."

Jorj whispered, "Caddums."

Caddy leaned forward. Her arms snaked down Tregarron's, as if to imprison his wrists. But instead she reached out and took the ultrasonic pistol and put it in Tregarron's right hand. Then she looked up at Jorj with eyes that were very bright.

She said very sweetly and sympathetically, "Poor Superman."

A Pail of Air

PA HAD sent me out to get an extra pail of air. I'd just about scooped it full and most of the warmth had leaked from my fingers when I saw the thing.

You know, at first I thought it was a young lady. Yes, a beautiful young lady's face all glowing in the dark and looking at me from the fifth floor of the opposite apartment, which hereabouts is the floor just above the white blanket of frozen air four storeys thick. I'd never seen a live young lady before, except in the old magazines—Sis is just a kid and Ma is pretty sick and miserable—and it gave me such a start that I dropped the pail. Who wouldn't, knowing everyone on Earth was dead except Pa and Ma and Sis and you?

Even at that, I don't suppose I should have been surprised. We all see things now and then. Ma sees some pretty bad ones, to judge from the way she bugs her eyes at nothing and just screams and screams and huddles back against the blankets hanging around the Nest. Pa says it is natural we should react like that sometimes.

When I'd recovered the pail and could look again at the opposite apartment, I got an idea of what Ma might be feeling at those times, for I saw it wasn't a young lady at all but simply a light—a tiny light that moved stealthily from window to window, just as if one of the cruel little stars had come down out of the airless sky to investigate why the Earth had gone away from the Sun, and maybe to hunt down something to torment or terrify, now that the Earth didn't have the Sun's protection.

I tell you, the thought of it gave me the creeps. I just stood there shaking, and almost froze my feet and did frost my helmet so solid on the inside that I couldn't have seen the light even if it had come out of one of the windows to get me. Then I had the wit to go back inside.

Pretty soon I was feeling my familiar way through the thirty or so blankets and rugs and rubbery sheets Pa has got hung and braced around to slow down the escape of air from the Nest, and I wasn't quite so scared. I began to hear the tick-ticking of the clocks in the Nest and knew I was getting back into air, because there's no sound outside in the vacuum, of course. But my mind was still crawly and uneasy as I pushed through the last blankets—Pa's got them faced with aluminium foil to hold in the heat—and came into the Nest.

Let me tell you about the Nest. It's low and snug, just room for the four of us and our things. The floor is covered with thick woolly rugs. Three of the sides are blankets, and the blankets roofing it touch Pa's head. He tells me it's inside a much bigger room, but I've never seen the real walls or ceiling.

Against one of the blanket-walls is a big set of shelves, with tools and books and other stuff, and on top of it a whole row of clocks. Pa's very fussy about keeping them wound. He says we must never forget time, and without a sun or moon, that would be easy to do.

The fourth wall has blankets all over except around the fireplace, in which there is a fire that must never go out. It keeps us from freezing and does a lot more besides. One of us must always watch it. Some of the clocks are alarm and we can use them to remind us. In the early days there was only Ma to take turns with Pa—I think of that when she gets difficult—but now there's me to help, and Sis too.

It's Pa who is the chief guardian of the fire, though. I always think of him that way: a tall man sitting crosslegged, frowning anxiously at the fire, his lined face golden in its light, and every so often carefully placing on it a piece of coal from the big heap beside it. Pa tells me there used to be guardians of the fire sometimes in the very old days—vestals, he calls them—although there was unfrozen air all around then and a sun too and you didn't really need a fire.

He was sitting just that way now, though he got up quick to take the pail from me and bawl me out for loitering—he'd spotted my frozen helmet right off. That roused Ma and she joined in picking on me. She's always trying to get the load off her feelings, Pa explains. He shut her up pretty fast. Sis let off a couple of silly squeals too.

Pa handled the pail of air in a twist of cloth. Now that it was inside the Nest, you could really feel its coldness. It just seemed to suck the heat out of everything. Even the flames cringed away from it as Pa put it down close by the fire.

Yet it's that glimmery blue-white stuff in the pail that keeps us alive. It slowly melts and vanishes and refreshes the Nest and feeds the fire. The blankets keep it from escaping too fast. Pa'd like to seal the whole place, but he can't—building's too earthquake-twisted, and besides he has to leave the chimney open for smoke. But the chimney has special things Pa calls baffles up inside it, to keep the air from getting out too quick that way. Sometimes Pa, making a joke, says it baffles him they keep on working, or work at all.

Pa says air is tiny molecules that fly away like a flash if there isn't something to stop them. We have to watch sharp not to let the air run low. Pa always keeps a big reserve supply of it in buckets behind the first blankets, along with extra coal and cans of food and bottles of vitamins and other things, such as pails of snow to melt for water. We have to go way down to the bottom floor for that stuff, which is a mean trip, and get it through a door to outside.

You see, when the Earth got cold, all the water in the air froze first and made a blanket ten feet thick or so everywhere, and then down on top of that dropped the crystals of frozen air, making another mostly white blanket sixty or seventy feet thick maybe.

Of course, all the parts of the air didn't freeze and snow down at the same time.

First to drop out was the carbon dioxide—when you're shovelling for water, you have to make sure you don't go too high and get any of that stuff mixed in, for it would put you to sleep, maybe for good, and make the fire go out. Next there's the nitrogen, which doesn't count one way or the other, though it's the biggest part of the blanket. On top of that and easy to get at, which is lucky for us, there's the oxygen that keeps us alive. It's pale blue, which helps you tell it from the nitrogen. It has to be colder for oxygen to freeze solid than nitrogen. That's why the oxygen snowed down last.

Pa says we live better than kings ever did, breathing pure oxygen, but we're used to it and don't notice.

Finally, at the very top, there's a slick of liquid helium, which is funny stuff.

All of these gases are in neat separate layers. Like a pussy caffay, Pa laughingly says, whatever that is.

I was busting to tell them all about what I'd seen, and so as soon as I'd ducked out of my helmet and while I was still climbing out of my suit, I cut loose. Right away Ma got nervous and began making eyes at the entry-slit in the blankets and wringing her hands together—the hand where she'd lost three fingers from frostbite inside the good one, as usual. I could tell that Pa was annoyed at me scaring her and wanted to explain it all away quickly, yet I knew he knew I wasn't fooling.

"And you watched this light for some time, son?" he asked when I finished.

I hadn't said anything about first thinking it was a young lady's face. Somehow that part embarrassed me.

"Long enough for it to pass five windows and go to the next floor."

"And it didn't look like stray electricity or crawling liquid or starlight focused by a growing crystal, or anything like that?"

He wasn't just making up those ideas. Odd things happen in a world that's about as cold as can be, and just when you think matter would be frozen dead, it takes on a strange new life. A slimy stuff comes crawling toward the Nest, just like an animal snuffing for heat —that's the liquid helium. And once, when I was little, a bolt of lightning—not even Pa could figure where it came from—hit the nearby steeple and crawled up and down it for weeks, until the glow finally died.

"Not like anything I ever saw," I told him.

He stood for a moment frowning. Then, "I'll go out with you, and you show it to me," he said.

Ma raised a howl at the idea of being left alone, and Sis joined in, too, but Pa quieted them. We started climbing into our outside clothes—mine had been warming by the fire. Pa made them. They have triple-pane plastic headpieces that were once big double-duty transparent food cans, but they keep heat and air in and can replace the air for a little while, long enough for our trips for water and coal and food and so on.

Ma started moaning again, "I've always known there was something outside there, waiting to get us. I've felt it for years—something that's part of the cold and hates all warmth and wants to destroy the Nest. It's been watching us all this time, and now it's coming after us. It'll get you and then come for me. Don't go, Harry!"

Pa had everything on but his helmet. He knelt by the fireplace and reached in and shook the long metal rod that goes up the chimney and knocks off the ice that keeps trying to clog it. Once a week he goes up on the roof to check if it's working all right. That's our worst trip and Pa won't let me make it alone.

"Sis," Pa said quietly, "come watch the fire. Keep an eye on the air, too. If it gets low or doesn't seem to be boiling fast enough, fetch another bucket from behind the blanket. But mind your hands. Use the cloth to pick up the bucket."

Sis quit helping Ma be frightened and came over and did as she was told. Ma quieted down pretty suddenly, though her eyes were still kind of wild as she watched Pa fix on his helmet tight and pick up a pail and the two of us go out.

Pa led the way and I took hold of his belt. It's a funny thing, I'm not afraid to go by myself, but when Pa's along I always want to hold on to him. Habit, I guess, and then there's no denying that this time I was a bit scared.

You see, it's this way. We know that everything is dead out there. Pa heard the last radio voices fade away years ago, and had seen some of the last folks die who weren't as lucky or well-protected as us. So we knew that if there was something groping around out there, it couldn't be anything human or friendly.

Besides that, there's a feeling that comes with it always being night, *cold* night. Pa says there used to be some of that feeling even in the old days, but then every morning the Sun would come and chase it away. I have to take his word for that, not ever remembering the Sun as being anything more than a big star. You see, I hadn't been born when the dark star snatched us away from the Sun, and by now it's dragged us out beyond the orbit of the planet Pluto, Pa says, and taking us farther out all the time.

We can see the dark star as it crosses the sky because it blots out stars, and especially when it's outlined by the Milky Way. It's pretty big, for we're closer to it than the planet Mercury was to the Sun, Pa says, but we don't care to look at it much and Pa won't set his clocks by it.

I found myself wondering whether there mightn't be something on the dark star that wanted us, and if that was why it had captured the Earth. Just then we came to the end of the corridor and I followed Pa out on the balcony.

I don't know what the city looked like in the old days, but now it's beautiful. The starlight lets you see it pretty well—there's quite a bit of light in those steady points speckling the blackness above. (Pa says the stars used to twinkle once, but that was because there was air.) We are on a hill and the shimmery plain drops away from us and then flattens out, cut up into neat squares by the troughs that used to be streets. I sometimes make my mashed potatoes look like it, before I pour on the gravy.

Some taller buildings push up out of the feathery plain, topped by rounded caps of air crystals, like the fur hood Ma wears, only whiter. On those buildings you can see the darker squares of windows, underlined by white dashes of air crystals. Some of them are on a slant, for many of the buildings are pretty badly twisted by the quakes and all the rest that happened when the dark star captured the Earth.

Here and there a few icicles hang, water icicles from the first days of the cold, other icicles of frozen air that melted on the roofs and dropped and froze again. Sometimes one of those icicles will catch the light of a star and send it to you so brightly you think the star has swooped into the city. That was one of the things Pa had been thinking of when I told him about the light, but I had thought of it myself first and known it wasn't so.

He touched his helmet to mine so we could talk easier and he asked me to point out the windows to him. But there wasn't any light moving around inside them now, or anywhere else. To my surprise, Pa didn't bawl me out and tell me I'd been seeing things. He looked all around quite a while after filling his pail, and just as we were going inside he whipped around without warning, as if to take some peeping thing off guard.

I could feel it, too. The old peace was gone. There was something lurking out there, watching, waiting, getting ready.

Inside, he said to me, touching helmets, "If you see something like that again, son, don't tell the others. Your Ma's sort of nervous these days and we owe her all the feeling of safety we can give her. Once —it was when your sister was born—I was ready to give up and die, but your Mother kept me trying. Another time she kept the fire going a whole week all by herself when I was sick. Nursed me and took care of two of you, too.

"You know that game we sometimes play, sitting in a square in the Nest, tossing a ball around? Courage is like a ball, son. A person can hold it only so long, and then he's got to toss it to someone else. When it's tossed your way, you've got to catch it and hold it tight— and hope there'll be someone else to toss it to when you get tired of being brave."

His talking to me that way made me feel grown-up and good. But it didn't wipe away the thing outside from the back of my mind— or the fact that Pa took it seriously.

It's hard to hide your feelings about such a thing. When we got back in the Nest and took off our outside clothes, Pa laughed about it all and told them it was nothing and kidded me for having such an imagination, but his words fell flat. He didn't convince Ma and Sis any more than he did me. It looked for a minute like we were all fumbling the courage-ball. Something had to be done, and almost before I knew what I was going to say, I heard myself asking Pa to tell us about the old days, and how it all happened.

He sometimes doesn't mind telling that story, and Sis and I sure like to listen to it, and he got my idea. So we were all settled around the fire in a wink, and Ma pushed up some cans to thaw for supper, and Pa began. Before he did, though, I noticed him casually get a hammer from the shelf and lay it down beside him.

It was the same old story as always—I think I could recite the main thread of it in my sleep—though Pa always puts in a new detail or two and keeps improving it in spots.

He told us how the Earth had been swinging around the Sun ever so steady and warm, and the people on it fixing to make money and wars and have a good time and get power and treat each other right or wrong, when without warning there comes charging out of space this dead star, this burned out sun, and upsets everything.

You know, I find it hard to believe in the way those people felt, any more than I can believe in the swarming number of them. Imagine people getting ready for the horrible sort of war they were cooking up. Wanting it even, or at least wishing it were over so as to end their nervousness. As if all folks didn't have to hang together and pool every bit of warmth just to keep alive. And how can they have hoped to end danger, any more than we can hope to end the cold?

Sometimes I think Pa exaggerates and makes things out too black. He's cross with us once in a while and was probably cross with all those folks. Still, some of the things I read in the old magazines sound pretty wild. He may be right.

The dark star, as Pa went on telling it, rushed in pretty fast and there wasn't much time to get ready. At the beginning they tried to keep it a secret from most people, but then the truth came out, what with the earthquakes and floods—imagine, oceans of *unfrozen* water!—and people seeing stars blotted out by something on a clear night. First off they thought it would hit the Sun, and then they thought it would hit the Earth. There was even the start of a rush to get to a place called China, because people thought the star would hit on the other side. Not that that would have helped them, they were just crazy with fear. But then they found it wasn't going to hit either side, but was going to come very close to the Earth.

Most of the other planets were on the other side of the Sun and didn't get involved. The Sun and the newcomer fought over the Earth for a little while—pulling it this way and that, in a twisty curve, like two dogs growling over a bone, Pa described it this time—and then the newcomer won and carried us off. The Sun got a consolation prize, though. At the last minute he managed to hold on to the Moon.

That was the time of the monster earthquakes and floods, twenty times worse than anything before. It was also the time of the Big Swoop, as Pa calls it, when the Earth speeded up, going into a close orbit around the dark star.

I've asked Pa, wasn't the Earth yanked then, just as he has done to me sometimes, grabbing me by the collar to do it, when I've been sitting too far from the fire. But Pa says no, gravity doesn't work that way. It was like a yank, but nobody felt it. I guess it was like being yanked in a dream.

You see, the dark star was going through space faster than the Sun, and in the opposite direction, and it had to speed up the world a lot in order to take it away.

The Big Swoop didn't last long. It was over as soon as the Earth was settled down in its new orbit around the dark star. But the earthquakes and floods were terrible while it lasted, twenty times worse than anything before. Pa says that all sorts of cliffs and buildings toppled, oceans slopped over, swamps and sandy deserts gave great sliding surges that buried nearby lands. Earth's blanket of air, still up in the sky then, was stretched out and got so thin in spots that people keeled over and fainted—though of course, at the same time, they were getting knocked down by the earthquakes that went with the Big Swoop and maybe their bones broke or skulls cracked.

We've often asked Pa how people acted during that time, whether they were scared or brave or crazy or stunned, or all four, but he's sort of leery of the subject, and he was again tonight. He says he was mostly too busy to notice.

You see, Pa and some scientist friends of his had figured out part of what was going to happen—they'd known we'd get captured and our air would freeze—and they'd been working like mad to fix up a place with airtight walls and doors, and insulation against the cold, and big supplies of food and fuel and water and bottled air. But the place got smashed in the last earthquakes and all Pa's friends were killed then and in the Big Swoop. So he had to start over and throw the Nest together quick without any advantages, just using any stuff he could lay his hands on.

I guess he's telling pretty much the truth when he says he didn't have any time to keep an eye on how other folks behaved, either then or in the Big Freeze that followed—followed very quick, you know, both because the dark star was pulling us away very fast and because Earth's rotation had been slowed by the tug-of-war and the tides, so that the nights were longer.

Still, I've got an idea of some of the things that happened from the frozen folk I've seen, a few of them in other rooms in our building, others clustered around the furnaces in the basements where we go for coal.

In one of the rooms, an old man sits stiff in a chair with an arm and a leg in splints. In another, a man and woman are huddled together in a bed with heaps of covers over them. You can just see their heads peeking out, close together. And in another a beautiful young lady is sitting with a pile of wraps huddled around her, looking hopefully toward the door, as if waiting for someone who never came back with warmth and food. They're all still and stiff as statues, of course, but just like life.

Pa showed them to me once in quick winks of his flashlight, when he still had a fair supply of batteries and could afford to waste a little light. They scared me pretty bad and made my heart pound, especially the young lady.

Now, with Pa telling his story for the umpteenth time to take our minds off another scare, I got to thinking of the frozen folk again. All of a sudden I got an idea that scared me worse than anything yet. You see, I'd just remembered the face I'd thought I'd seen in the window. I'd forgotten about that on account of trying to hide it from the others.

What, I asked myself, if the frozen folk were coming to life? What if they were like the liquid helium that got a new lease on life and started crawling toward the heat just when you thought its molecules ought to freeze solid for ever? Or like the electricity that moves endlessly when it's just about as cold as that? What if the ever-growing cold, with the temperature creeping down the last few degrees to the last zero, had mysteriously wakened the frozen folk to life—not warm-blooded life, but something icy and horrible?

That was a worse idea than the one about something coming down from the dark star to get us.

Or maybe, I thought, both ideas might be true. Something coming down from the dark star and making the frozen folk move, using them to do its work. That would fit with both things I'd seen—the beautiful young lady and the moving, starlight light.

The frozen folk with minds from the dark star behind their unwinking eyes, creeping, crawling, snuffing their way, following the heat to the Nest, maybe wanting the heat, but more likely hating it and wanting to chill it for ever, snuff out our fire.

I tell you, that thought gave me a very bad turn and I wanted very badly to tell the others my fears, but I remembered what Pa had said and clenched my teeth and didn't speak.

We were all sitting very still. Even the fire was burning silently. There was just the sound of Pa's voice and the clocks.

And then, from beyond the blankets, I thought I heard a tiny noise. My skin tightened all over me.

Pa was telling about the early years in the Nest and had come to the place where he philosophizes.

"So I asked myself then," he said, "what's the use of dragging it out for a few years? Why prolong a doomed existence of hard work and cold and loneliness? The human race is done. The Earth is done. Why not give up, I asked myself—and all of a sudden I got the answer."

Again I heard the noise, louder this time, a kind of uncertain, shuffling tread, coming closer. I couldn't breathe.

"Life's always been a business of working hard and fighting the cold," Pa was saying. "The Earth's always been a lonely place, millions of miles from the next planet. And no matter how long the human race might have lived, the end would have come some night. Those things don't matter. What matters is that life is good. It has a lovely texture, like some thick fur or the petals of flowers—you've never seen those, but you know our ice-flowers—or like the texture of flames, never twice the same. It makes everything else worth while. And that's as true for the last man as the first."

And still the steps kept shuffling closer. It seemed to me that the inmost blanket trembled and bulged a little. Just as if they were burned into my imagination, I kept seeing those peering, frozen eyes.

"So right then and there," Pa went on, and now I could tell that he heard the steps, too, and was talking loud so we maybe wouldn't hear them, "right then and there I told myself, that I was going on as if we had all eternity ahead of us. I'd have children and teach them all I could. I'd get them to read books. I'd plan for the future, try to enlarge and seal the Nest. I'd do what I could to keep everything beautiful and growing. I'd keep alive my feeling of wonder even at the cold and the dark and the distant stars."

But then the blanket actually did move and lift. And there was a bright light somewhere behind it. Pa's voice stopped and his eyes turned to the widening slit and his hand went out until it touched and gripped the handle of the hammer beside him.

In through the blanket stepped the beautiful young lady. She stood there looking at us in the strangest way, and she carried something bright and unwinking in her hand. And two other faces peered over her shoulders—men's faces, white and staring.

Well, my heart couldn't have been stopped for more than four or five beats before I realized she was wearing a suit and helmet like Pa's homemade ones, only fancier, and that the men were, too—and that the frozen folk certainly wouldn't be wearing those. Also, I noticed that the bright thing in her hand was just a kind of flashlight.

Sinking down very softly, Ma fainted.

The silence kept on while I swallowed hard a couple of times, and after that there was all sorts of jabbering and commotion.

They were simply people, you see. We hadn't been the only ones to survive; we'd just thought so, for natural enough reasons. These three people had survived, and quite a few others with them. And when we found out *how* they'd survived, Pa let out the biggest whoop of joy.

They were from Los Alamos and they were getting their heat and power from atomic energy. Just using the uranium and plutonium intended for bombs, they had enough to go on for thousands of years. They had a regular little airtight city, with airlocks and all. They even generated electric light and grew plants and animals by it. (At this Pa let out a second whoop, waking Ma from her faint.)

But if we were flabbergasted at them, they were double flabbergasted at us.

One of the men kept saying, "But it's impossible, I tell you. You can't maintain an air supply without hermetic sealing. It's simply impossible."

That was after he had got his helmet off and was using our air. Meanwhile, the young lady kept looking around at us as if we were saints, and telling us we'd done something amazing, and suddenly she broke down and cried.

They'd been scouting around for survivors, but they never expected to find any in a place like this. They had rocket ships at Los Alamos and plenty of chemical fuel. As for liquid oxygen, all you had to do was go out and shovel the air blanket at the top level. So after they'd got things going smoothly at Los Alamos, which had taken years, they'd decided to make some trips to likely places where there might be other survivors. No good trying longdistance radio signals, of course, since there was no atmosphere, no ionosphere, to carry them around the curve of the Earth. That was why all the radio signals had died out.

Well, they'd found other colonies at Argonne and Brookhaven and way around the world at Harwell and Tanna Tuva. And now they'd been giving our city a look, not really expecting to find anything. But they had an instrument that noticed the faintest heat waves and it had told them there was something warm down here, so they'd landed to investigate. Of course we hadn't heard them land, since there was no air to carry the sound, and they'd had to investigate around quite a while before finding us. Their instruments had given them a wrong steer and they'd wasted some time in the building across the street.

By now, all five adults were talking like sixty. Pa was demonstrating to the men how he worked the fire and got rid of the ice in the chimney and all that. Ma had perked up wonderfully and was showing the young lady her cooking and sewing stuff, and even asking about how the women dressed at Los Alamos. The strangers marvelled at everything and praised it to the skies. I could tell from the way they wrinkled their noses that they found the Nest a bit smelly, but they never mentioned that at all and just asked bushels of questions.

In fact, there was so much talking and excitement that Pa forgot about things, and it wasn't until they were all getting groggy that he looked and found the air had all boiled away in the pail. He got another bucket of air quick from behind the blankets. Of course that started them all laughing and jabbering again. The newcomers even got a little drunk. They weren't used to so much oxygen.

Funny thing, though—I didn't do much talking at all and Sis hung on to Ma all the time and hid her face when anybody looked at her. I felt pretty uncomfortable and disturbed myself, even about the young lady. Glimpsing her outside there, I'd had all sorts of mushy thoughts, but now I was just embarrassed and scared of her, even though she tried to be nice as anything to me.

I sort of wished they'd all quit crowding the Nest and let us be alone and get our feelings straightened out.

And when the newcomers began to talk about our all going to Los

Alamos, as if that were taken for granted, I could see that something of the same feeling struck Pa and Ma, too. Pa got very silent all of a sudden and Ma kept telling the young lady, "But I wouldn't know how to act there and I haven't any clothes."

The strangers were puzzled like anything at first, but then they got the idea. As Pa kept saying, "It just doesn't seem right to let this fire go out."

Well, the strangers are gone, but they're coming back. It hasn't been decided yet just what will happen. Maybe the Nest will be kept up as what one of the strangers called a "survival school." Or maybe we will join the pioneers who are going to try to establish a new colony at the uranium mines at Great Slave Lake or in the Congo.

Of course, now that the strangers are gone, I've been thinking a lot about Los Alamos and those other tremendous colonies. I have a hankering to see them for myself.

You ask me, Pa wants to see them, too. He's been getting pretty thoughtful, watching Ma and Sis perk up.

"It's different, now that we know others are alive," he explains to me. "Your mother doesn't feel so hopeless any more. Neither do I, for that matter, not having to carry the whole responsibility for keeping the human race going, so to speak. It scares a person."

I looked around at the blanket walls and the fire and the pails of air boiling away and Ma and Sis sleeping in the warmth and the flickering light.

"It's not going to be easy to leave the Nest," I said, wanting to cry, kind of. "It's so small and there's just the four of us. I get scared at the idea of big places and a lot of strangers."

He nodded and put another piece of coal on the fire. Then he looked at the little pile and grinned suddenly and put a couple of handfuls on, just as if it was one of our birthdays or Christmas.

"You'll quickly get over that feeling, son," he said. "The trouble with the world was that it kept getting smaller and smaller, till it ended with just the Nest. Now it'll be good to start building up to a real huge world again, the way it was in the beginning."

I guess he's right. You think the beautiful young lady will wait for me till I grow up? I asked her that and she smiled to thank me and then she told me she's got a daughter almost my age and that there are lots of children at the atomic places. Imagine that.

The Foxholes of Mars

EVER inward from the jagged horizon, the machines of death crept, edged, scurried, rocketed and tunneled towards him. It seemed as if all this purple-sunned creation had conspired to isolate and smash him. To the west—for all planets share a west, if nothing else—the nuclear bombs bloomed, meaningless giant fungi. While invisibly overhead the space ships roared as they dipped into the atmosphere —distant as gods, yet shaking the yellow sky. Even the soil was treacherous, nauseated by artificial earthquakes—nobody's mother, least of all an Earthman's.

"Why don't you cheer up?" the others said to him. "It's a mad planet." But he would not cheer up, for he knew what they said was literally true.

He ducked and compressed himself as objects many times shattered, spurted up and cascaded. Soon they would fall back and the enemy would retake the mangled thing they called an objective. Was it the sixth time? The seventh? And did the soldiers on the other side have six legs, or eight? The enemy was pretty haphazard as to what troops he used in this sector.

Worst was the noise. Meaningless, mechanical screeches tore at his skull, until thoughts rattled around in it like dry seeds in a dry pod. How could anyone ever love the various shock-transmitting mixtures of gases humorously called air? Even the vacuum of space was less hateful—it was silent and clean. He started to lift his hands to his ears, then checked the gesture, convulsed in soundless laughter and tearless weeping. There had been a galactic society—a galactic empire—once. He had played an unnoticed part on one of its nice quiet planets. But now? Galactic empire? Galactic horse-dung! Perhaps he had always hated his fellow men as much. But in the prewar days his hatred had been closely bound and meticulously repressed. It was still bound, tighter than ever, but it was no longer repressed from his thoughts.

The deadly engine he tended, silent for a moment, began again to chatter to those of the enemy, although its voice was mostly drowned by their booming ones, like a spiteful child in a crush of complacent adults.

It turned out they had been covering a withdrawal of Martian sappers and must now escape as best they might. The officer running beside him fell. He hesitated. The officer cursed a new, useless joint that had appeared in his leg. All the others—including the black-shelled Martians—were ahead. He glanced around fearfully and tormentedly, as if he were about to commit a hideous crime. Then he lifted the officer and staggered on, reeling like a top at the end of its spin. He was still grinning in a spasmic way when they reached the security of lesser danger; and even when the officer thanked him with curt sincerity he couldn't stop. Nevertheless, they gave him the Order of Planetary Merit for that.

He stared at the watery soup and meat shreds in his mess tin. The cellar was cool, and its seats—though built for creatures with four legs and two arms—were comfortable. The purple daylight was pleasantly muted. The noise had gone a little way off, playing cat and mouse. He was alone.

Of course life had never had any meaning, except for the chillingly sardonic one perceptible to the demons in the nuclear bombs and the silver giants in space who pushed the buttons; and he had no stomach to aspire to that. They'd had ten thousand years to fix things, those giants, and still all they could tell you was go dig yourself a hole.

It was just that in the old days the possibility of relaxation and petty self-indulgence, against the magnificent sham background of galactic empire, had permitted him to pretend life had a meaning.

Yet at a time like this, when such an illusion was needful, it ran out on you, jeered at you along with the lesser lies it had nurtured.

A three-legged creature skipped out of the shadows, halted at a distance, and subtly intimated it would like food. At first he thought it must be some Rigelian tripedal, but then he saw it was an Earth cat lacking a leg. Its movements were grotesque, but efficient, and not without a certain gracefulness. How it could have got to this planet, he found it hard to imagine.

"But you don't worry about that—or even about other cats, Three-legs," he thought bitterly. "You hunt alone. You mate with your own kind, when you can, but then only because it is most agreeable. You don't set up your own species as a corporate divinity and worship it, and yearn over the light-centuries of its empire, and eat out your heart because of it, and humbly spill your blood at its cosmic altar.

"Nor are you hoodwinked when the dogs bark about the greatness of humanity under a thousand different moons, or when the dumb cattle sigh from surfeit and gratefully chew their cuds under red, green and purple suns. You accept us as something sometimes help-ful. You walk into our space ships as you walked up to our fires. You use us. But when we're gone, you won't pine on our graves or starve in the pen. You'll manage, or try to."

The cat mewed and he tossed it a bit of meat which it caught in its teeth, shifting about cleverly on the two good hind legs. But as he watched it daintily nibble (though scrawny with famine), he sud-denly saw Kenneth's face, just as he had last seen it on Alpha Cen-tauri Duo. It seemed very real, projected against the maroon dark-ness towards the other end of the cellar. The full, tolerant lips lined at the corners, the veiledly appraising eyes, the space-sallow skin were all exactly as they had been when they roomed together at the Sign of the Burnt-Out Jet. But there was a richness and a zest about the face that he had missed before. He did not try to move toward the illusion, though he wanted to. Only looked. Then there came the sound of boots on the floor above, and the cat bounded away, hump-ing its hind quarters quite like a tripedal, and the vision quickly faded. For a long time he sat staring at the spot where it had been, feeling a strangely poignant unhappiness, as if the only worthwhile being in the world had died. Then he started to eat his food with the vague curiosity of a two-year-old, sometimes pausing with the spoon halfway to his mouth.

It was night and there was a ground mist through which the wine-colored moons showed like two sick eyes, and anything might have been moving in the shadows. He squinted and peered, but it was hard to make out the nature of any object, the landscape was so torn and distorted. Three men came out of the place of underground concealment to the left, joking together in hushed, hollow voices. One whom he knew well (a stocky soldier with big eyes and smirking lips and reddish stubble on his chin) greeted him with a friendly gibe about easy jobs. Then they wormed their way up and started to crawl toward where enemy scouts (six legs or eight?) were supposed to lie. He lost sight of them very quickly. He held his weapon ready, watching for the sight of the enemy.

Why did he hate the soldiers of the enemy so little? No more than a Martian hunting sand-dragons hates sand-dragons. His relationship with them was limited, almost abstract. How could he hate something so different from himself in form? He could only marvel that it too had intelligence. No, the enemy were merely, unfortunately, dangerous targets. Once he had seen one of them escape death, and it had made him feel happy, and he wanted to wave in a friendly way; even if it could only wriggle a tentacle in return. But as for the men who fought side by side with him, he hated them bitterly, loathed their faces, voices and physical mannerisms. The way this one chewed and that one spat. Their unchanging curses, clichés and jokes. All unendurably magnified, as if his nose were being rubbed in offal. For they were part of the same miserable, lying, self-worshipping galactic swarm as himself.

He wondered if he had hated the men at the office on Altair Una in the same way. Almost certainly. He recalled the long smoldering irritations over trifles that had seemed tremendous in the hours between the violin-moans of the time clock. But then there had been the safety valves and shock absorbers that make life tolerable, and also the illusion of purpose.

But now there was nothing, and everybody knew it.

They had no right to joke about it and continue the pretense.

He was shaking with anger. To kill indiscriminately would at least demonstrate his feelings. To focus death on the backs of men charging with inane hysteria. To toss a nuclear fizz-bomb into a dugout where men sought secret escape in dreams and repeated like prayers their rationalizations about galactic empires. Dying at his hand, they might for a moment understand their own vicious hypocrisy.

From out ahead, one of death's little mechanisms spoke concisely, rapidly. It seemed like a bugle call only he could hear.

Ruby moonlight slid suddenly across the grotesquely tortured ground. He raised his weapon and took aim. Its sound pleased him because it was like a soft groan of agony. Then he realized he had fired at the abruptly revealed shadow because it was that of the stocky soldier who had gibed and crawled away.

The moonlight blacked out as if a curtain had been drawn. His heart pounded. He ground his teeth and grinned. His feelings were fierce, but not yet determinate. He became aware of the smells of the ground and of the chemicals and metals: strong, sharp, interesting smells.

Then he found himself staring at a whitish patch that never got more than eight inches off the ground. Slowly it approached out of the darkness, like the inquisitive head of a huge ghost worm. It became a face with big eyes and smirking lips, fretted with red stubble. Mechanically he reached out a hand and helped the man down.

"Were you the one that winged him? That lousy spider would have gotten me for sure. I didn't see him until he fell on me. I'm all mucked up with his blue slime."

This then was the end. Hereafter he would give in to the mob, run with the hounds, die purposelessly like a lemming when the time came. He might even learn to nurse ideals, like dead dolls; dream in chaos. Never again would he aspire to the darker, icy insight that gave life a real, though horrible, meaning. He was a ridiculous little communal animal in a lemming horde racing across the galaxy and he would live like one.

He saw the small black object falling swiftly through the mist. The stocky soldier did not. There was a deafening blast that slapped the skin. Looking up he saw the stocky soldier still standing there. Without a head. As the body stumbled blindly forward, tripped and fell, he began to laugh in little hissing gusts through his teeth. His lips were drawn back, so that his jaw muscles twitched and pained him.

He felt contemptuous amusement at the blond soldier. The blond soldier had been to a third-rate nuclear technics school and believed it had been a serious mistake to put him in the infantry. Nevertheless the blond soldier was ambitious and took an unusual interest in the war.

They stood alone at the crest of a ridge thick with violet and yellow-spotted vines. In the valleys on either side, their units were pushing forward. Trails of dust and tracks of mashed vines extended as far as the eye could see. Various huge engines tromped forward, carrying men, and men ran fussily about, freeing engines that had met with some stop or hindrance, as if the two were inextricably united in an unimaginable symbiosis. Small machines bearing messengers went swiftly to and fro like centaurs, a superior type of individual. Other machines spied watchfully overhead. It was like some vast, clumsy monster feeling its way, cautiously putting out pseudopods, or horns like a snail's; withdrawing them puzzledly when they touched anything hurtful or strange; but always gathering itself for a new effort. It did not flow, but humped and hedged. Or scuttled. Like an army of Rigelian roaches. Or driver ants of Earth that were so like miniature Martians, with their black-weaponed soldiers, foragers, scouts, butchers, pack carriers.

And they were truly neither more nor less than ants. He was no more than an epidermal cell in a monster that was dueling with another monster, very careful of its inner organs but careless about its epidermis. There was something comfortingly abstract and impersonal about the idea of being united in such a way with many other men, not because of any shared purpose, but merely because they belonged to the same monster, a monster so large that it could readily do duty for fate and necessity. The fellowship of protoplasm.

The blond soldier murmured two or three words and for a moment he thought the whole army had spoken to him. Then he understood and made the necessary adjustment in the instrument they were setting up.

But those two or three words had plunged him with breath-taking abruptness into the worst sort of inner misery. What was abstract had become personal, and that was bad. To conceive a monster made of men was one thing; to feel the insensate, inescapable prod of a neighboring cell and realize the stifling, close-packed pressure of the whole was another. He lifted his hand to his collar. The very air seemed to convey to his skin the shoving and jostling of distant, invisible individuals. The nudge of the galactic horde.

They were at the end of the crest now, atop a little hillock, and he stared ahead to where the air was clearer. He felt as if he were suffocating. His new mood had come as utterly without warning as most of his moods now came, gushing up explosively from some wild, alien, ever expanding dimension within him.

Then, in the broad expanse of fantastically clouded sky ahead of him, he saw his friends' faces again, orderly and side by side but gigantic, like a pantheon of demigods. Just as he had in the cellar and several times since, only now altogether. The only faces that meant anything in the cosmos. Black George, with the wide grin that looked, but was not, stupid. Hollow-cheeked Loren, peering up with shy canniness, about to argue. Dark Helen, with her proud, subtle lips. Sallow Kenneth again, with his veiledly appraising eyes. And Albert, and Maurice, and Kate. And others whose features were blurred, heartbreakingly suggesting friends forgot. All transfigured and glowing with warmth and light. As meaningful as symbols, yet holding each within itself the quintessence of individuality.

He stood stock-still, beginning to tremble, feeling great guilt. How had he neglected and deserted them? His friends, the only ones deserving his loyalty, the only island for him in the cosmos-choking sea of humanity, the only ones with worth and meaning; compared to which race and creed and humanity were without significance. It was as self-evident and undeniable as a premise in mathematics. Heretofore he had seen only the masks of reality, the reflections, the countershadows. Now, at a bound, he stood beside the gods in darkness who pulled the wires.

The vision faded, became part of his mind. He turned, and it was as if he saw the blond soldier for the first time. How had he ever believed that he and the other soldier might have anything in common? The gulf between them was far, far greater than if they belonged to different species. Why had he ever given two thoughts to such a silly, squinty-eyed, bustling little organism? He never would again. It was all very clear.

"We'll get them this time," the other soldier said with conviction. "We've got the stuff now. We'll show the bugs. Come on."

It was wonderful, hysterical, insufferable. Yesterday spiders. To-day bugs. Tomorrow worms? The other soldier really believed it was important and noble. Could still pretend there was that kind of meaning and purpose to that sort of slaughter.

"Come on. Get the beta cycling," said the other soldier impatiently, nudging him.

It was all very clear. And he would never lose that clarity. By one action he would cut himself off from the galactic pack and cleave forever to the faces in the sky.

"Come on," ordered the other soldier, jerking at him.

He unsheathed his weapon, touched a button. Silently a dull black spot, not a hole, appeared in the back of the blond soldier's head. He hid the body, walked down the other side of the hill, and attached himself to another unit. By morning they were retreating again, the monster badly hurt and automatically resisting dissolution.

He was an officer now.

"I don't like him," said a soldier. "Of course, they all try to scare you, whether they know it or not. Part of the business. But with him it's different. I know he doesn't talk tough, or threaten or act grim. I know he's pleasant enough when he takes time to notice you. Even sympathetic. But there's something there I can't put my finger on. Something cold-blooded. Like he wasn't even alive—or as if we weren't. Even when he acts especially decent or thoughtful toward me, I know he doesn't give a damn. It's his eyes. I can read meaning in the eyes of a Fomalhautian blindworm. But I can't read anything in his."

The soaring city seemed alien though it had once been home. He liked it the better for that. Civilian clothes felt strange against his skin.

He whisked briskly along the slidewalk, taking the turns aimlessly when it split at the pedestrian cloverleafs. He looked at the passing faces with frank inquisitiveness, as if he were at a zoo. He just wanted to enjoy the feeling of anonymity for a little while. He knew what he was going to do afterwards. There were his friends, and there were the animals. And the fortunes of his friends were to be advanced.

Beside the next cloverleaf was a speaker, and a little crowd. There had been a good deal of that sort of stuff since the truce. Curiously he listened, recognized the weakness of the words. They were sloshed with ideals, tainted with unprofitable, poorly selected hatreds. The call to action was tinged by an undercurrent of bitterness that argued inaction would be better. They were civilized words and therefore useless to one who wanted to become an animal trainer on a galactic scale. What a zoo he'd have some day—and every single beast in it advertised as intelligent!

Other words and phrases began to ooze up into his mind. "Thinkers! Listen to me . . . cheated of what you deserve . . . misled by misled men . . . the galactic runaround . . . this engineered truce . . . the creatures who used the war to consolidate their power . . . The Cosmic Declaration of Servitude . . . life—to lose . . . liberty—to obey . . . and as for the pursuit of happiness—happiness is a light-millennium ahead of all of us . . . our universal rights. . . . We have thirty armored planetoids orbiting uselessly, three hundred star-ships, three thousand spaceships, and three million space veterans sweating in servile jobs in this system alone! Free Martia! Terra for All! Revenge . . ."

These unspoken words, he felt, were the harbingers of leadership. Alexander had done it. Hitler had done it. Smith had done it. Hrivlath had done it. The Neuron had done it. The Great Centaur had done it. All murderers—and only murderers won. He saw the brilliant light-years of his future stretch ahead, endlessly. He saw no details, but it was all of the same imperial color. Never again would he hesitate. Each moment would decide something. Each of his future actions would drop like a grain of sand from an ancient hour glass, inevitably.

Profound excitement seized him. The scene around him grew and grew until he seemed at the center of a vast, ominous spellbound crowd that filled the galaxy. The faces of his friends were close, eager and confident. And from a great distance, as if the stars themselves pricked out its pattern on the dark like a new constellation, he seemed to see his own face staring back at him, pale, skulleyed, and insatiably hungry.

The Big Holiday

THE WHISTLES blew. A thousand hands switched off pocket radios and wall-size television screens, right in the middle of the Martian newscast. Another 500 all around the town locked the motors of sky scooters and ground buggies. A dozen cash registers rang up lucky last sales and were silent, locked. Two thousand throats breathed a sigh of relief. Two thousand hearts began to warm.

The whistles blew. Mrs. Pullen slammed a last batch of cookies into the electronic oven, counted to ten, switched it off, wiped her face, and stood there beaming at the fragrant towers of her handi-work—a gray-haired princess in a cookie castle. Mrs. Goldfarb smiled at her brown and creamflecked woodpiles of blintzes. Mr. Gianelli, his eyes watering with heat and spices, admired his steaming log-jams of Italian sausage. Widowed Mr. Tomlinson was contemplating his bowls of hard-boiled eggs when a goddess shot him in the back with a silver arrow. He turned around and commented, "That tunic is a bit daring, pet." His daughter, new to grown-up life as a pussy willow, waved her plastic bow and said, "I'm going as Diana." Mr. Tomlinson mused, "Ah, the fleet-footed huntress."

The whistles blew. Mr. Jingles, so called by the children for the silver coins he always carried, emptied his pockets of them, added his green money, put it all away in the top drawer of his dresser. Everywhere else in the town billfolds and purses disappeared. Of-fices closed. Secretaries sprayed their noses with powder and flut-tered into their cloudlike electrosilk coats.

Mr. Debevois tore a May-something 2077 date-sheet off his desk calendar, made a paper dart of it, and shot it at his lagging stenographer, who was stooping to return a folder of microfilm to a bottom file drawer. Storekeepers took off their aprons and walked out, leaving doors unlocked. Plump Mr. Wilson pressed a button and a sign appeared on the movie-house marquee: NO SHOW TONIGHT. Beardy Mr. Goldfarb shrugged, smiled, put away a sheaf of teleflashed stock reports, unbuttoned a great big drawer and took out a great big parchment scroll. School children tore off across the soft sandy schoolyard and green lawns slippery with sunlight. Down at the little aluminum station the atomic train inched to a stop like a golden caterpillar and the engineer jumped out in his best clothes.

The whistles blew. Mr. Moriarty, the town mortician, with black-clad limbs thin as a spider's and hat tall as Abraham Lincoln's, looked around at the bare gleaming tables and rubbed his hands. He opened a big thick icebox door and looked into two coffins. "They'll keep," he said. He opened another and looked at the empty shelves and nodded. "In case anybody has the bad luck to die the next three days," he said. Then the spiderweb of wrinkles all over his face contracted in a smile. He said softly, "Or maybe that would be the nicest time of year to go."

The whistles stopped. From back of the firehouse, around the lovely new red-vaned fire-copter, twenty pairs of strong hands pushed an oldfashioned automobile, a convertible, black and fat as sin, armored with chromium and sprouting three antennae—for radio, phone, and television. They shoved it across the street with a shout and it jounced to rest in front of the courthouse, its antennae quivering.

While toward the courthouse square, down the leaf-bowered streets silent of traffic, 4,000 big and little feet came pounding.

In the empty schoolhouse, before the mirror in the girls' room, Miss Kidd decided that her inch-long eyelashes were securely attached. She painted herself sultry lips, then almost ruined them making anguished faces as she tugged at the girdle borrowed from the museum. Pausing to catch her breath, she leafed with morbid curiosity through the pile of themes her class had turned in. They were all titled "The Big Holiday." The first one began:

By some it is thot that the Big Holiday started with the merrimaking of the Pre-lentin festeval at Reo D. Janero . . .

She hastily turned to the next.

In the olden times of the 20th Century, people didnt injoy holidays very much. They worried too much about making money and buying and selling. They even tried to sell each other, like in the very faroff times of slavery . . .

(Beside this, Miss Kidd had red-penciled, "*Sell* a person *on* something. Old idiom. Means to persuade to buy, or convince of worth; has nothing to do with slavery.")

Resisting further temptation, Miss Kidd turned the themes face down and got back to work. She pinned together the plunging neckline of her antique cocktail dress, hesitated, then recklessly unpinned it. She put on a weird picture hat about three feet across, tossed a mink fur around her shoulders. "The fourth grade will have things to say about you," she told her reflection and hobbled out on unfamiliar French heels.

In the barber shop Mr. Felton, the town drunkard, lifted incredulous fingers to his fresh-shaven, lotioned cheeks. He watched the mirror with a beery wonder as they clad him in silk shirt, stiff collar, and a pin-striped suit. He gaped with delight as they draped a huge gold watch-chain across his paunch and speared his tie with a blinding diamond pin. Mr. Kantarian, the barber, stood back, walked around, and curtly nodded his approval.

Mr. Wilson stepped into a money bag with arms and legs, tightened the drawstring around his neck, and put on a golden crown. A thought struck him and he got out his pocketbook. "It isn't breaking a holiday rule," he reassured himself, "if I use the junk as a stage property." And he artistically stuffed twenty or thirty dollar bills into his neckband. Then he walked out of his movie house.

The square was already a-chatter and a-swirl with the town's two thousand. Mr. Wilson, conscious of the dignity of his role, ignored the attention he attracted. At the firehouse corner he was joined by Miss Kidd and Mr. Felton. The drunkard eyed the crowd, then stiffened his back. With ritualistic solemnity the three walked to the fat black convertible. There they were met by Mr. Moriarty, whose spider-webbed face was set in the gloomiest lines. He tipped his stovepipe hat and opened the rear door for Miss Kidd and Mr. Felton, then got in front beside Mr. Wilson, who had taken the wheel.

There was a shot and a puff of smoke. A figure in track pants and shirt emblazoned with golden bolts of lightning took off from across the square. He sped like the wind, the propeller of his beanie making a golden glory over his bent head. A goddess with a plastic bow gave an excited little yip. Mr. Tomlinson lifted a comprehending brow and remarked to her, "Jim Kelly, pet? So that's why you need to be fleet-footed."

"He's awfully shy too," she told him frankly.

Meanwhile the speedy topic of their conversation had sprung up on the back of the seat behind Mr. Wilson and begun pounding him on his money-green ruff and pointing frantically to the big old alarm clock strapped to his own wrist.

A dark man beat on a drum. Things got quiet. Mr. Goldfarb unrolled his parchment, cleared his throat, directed a severe stare at the occupants of the black car, and recited loudly, "Hear ye! Hear ye! Know all men here present that for the good of our hearts and minds and souls the following creatures are banished from town.

"First," he said, eyeing Mr. Wilson, "Money! Because he's a tyrant, a very Midas who turns the moon to two bits and the green grass to dingy green paper.

"Second," (Mr. Felton beamed as the stern gaze turned his way). "Success! Because he goes around with the wrong sort of people— I mean the gentleman I referred to first and the lady I'm referring to next." He looked at Miss Kidd. "Glamour! Because she's a huzzy who doesn't play fair. We like girls too much to let them be used to help sell soft drinks.

"And finally," he went on, turning to Jim Kelly and Mr. Moriarty, "Hurry and Worry! The one because while he's a good boy on a trip to Mars or the doctor, he's too hard on our hearts. The other— Worry—because he aids and abets all four aforementioned."

Mr. Jingles stepped up and began to tootle the funeral march, while dark Mr. Ambrose rumbled his drums ever so softly.

Mr. Goldfarb concluded, "These five are directed to leave town at once without pause or prayer. If they—or any of their equally guilty accomplices, such as Work, War, and Glory—should venture within the town limits during the next three days, we will violate the Constitution and visit upon them various cruel and unusual punishments."

He rolled up the parchment, folded his arms, stuck out his beard, and said, "Now, get!"

Mr. Wilson stamped on the starter. The exhaust puffed nose-wrinkling blue smoke. The fat black car moved forward ponderously. Ahead the bright-clad people lined up on either side, like rows of flowers.

"Goodby," they called.

They waved at Mr. Wilson. "Goodby, Money." He stared solemnly ahead, intent on steering.

"Goodby, Success," they called to Mr. Felton. Forgetting character, he waved happily back.

"Goodby, Glamour," they called to Miss Kidd. She smiled at them scornfully, threw back her shoulders, looked down her plunging neckline, gathered her courage and held her position.

"Goodby, Hurry. Goodby, Worry," they called to Jim Kelly and Mr. Moriarty. The latter creased his brow and shook his head doomfully. The sprinter wildly pleaded with Wilson for more speed.

The car passed between Mason's Hardware and the town's sole skyscraper, a ten-story glastic skylon. Buckets of black confetti filled the air, snowed on the car, peppered Miss Kidd with beauty spots. Black paper streamers unrolled lazily downward, snagged chromium grills, dragged behind like a black fringe.

Moving majestically always, the car reached the schoolyard with its new-gathered ranks of children. A line of third and fourth grade boys raised cap pistols and solemnly discharged them. "Goodby, Hurry. Goodby, Worry." A few fourth graders called, "Goodby, Miss Kidd," and some added, "Goodby, themes," but their voices were lost.

One boy, greatly daring, darted in front of the car, planted two suction cupped black plumes on the hood, and skipped away. They waved like black banderillas in the shoulders of a sluggish black bull.

"Goodby, Money. Goodby, Success. Goodby, Glamour.

"Goodby, goodby, goodby."

A half mile out of town, just beyond the flower-gay cemetery, Mr.

Wilson parked the fat black car. They all got out and took suitcases from the trunk compartment, changed to regular holiday clothes and strolled back to join the fun, half listening to a bibulous harangue by Mr. Felton on the pros and cons of the Big Holiday.

"Who's your girl friend this time?" Miss Kidd asked Jim Kelly with teacher-like camaraderie, but he blushed and sidled away without answering.

Two blocks off they could hear Mr. Pullen, the banker, sawing on his fiddle. Right in the dappling shade in front of the courthouse. Mr. Jingles was twittering his flute. Dark Mr. Ambrose was making his drums talk gay. The whole village band was turning its happiness to sound. Around, streams of women were piling tables high. Suddenly there was a rush to the west side of the square. Up Main Street, swept speckless for dancing, creaked a museum carriage, pulled like a rickshaw by half the eighth grade boys. Out of it jumped Mr. Ferguson, the butcher, dressed in a domino, face red with glee. He lifted down a girl dressed in white like a nymph or a bride. Seeing her in the insurance office, you'd never have guessed that Miss Wolzynski could look so pretty.

"Welcome, Friendship! Welcome, Love!"

Up from the back of the carriage, yawning and arm-stretching, rose tall Mr. Gutknecht, teacher and town historian, dressed like an oldtime farmer, with hay in his hair.

"Welcome, Laziness!"

Clang! Up popped a magnesium manhole cover and out shot Joe Turner, the town policeman, dressed in motley with a bladder on a stick.

"Welcome, Fun!"

Fun chased Mr. Ferguson, chased Miss Wolzynski, chased Mr. Gutknecht, who wouldn't be chased and only yawned as the bladder bounced off his back.

BZZ-bzz. A silver ambulance-copter droned over the square. Down snowed bushels of flowers. Down came a silken line. And down that, on a flower-decked parachute in a flower-decked dress, came Jenny, waitress at the Skylon Cafe. Her hair was so full of flowers you'd need to have seen her before to know it was corn-colored.

"Welcome, Joy!"

Mr. Goldfarb smiled at everything, wiped his forehead and his neck under his beard, and wrapped comradely fingers around a lapel of Mr. Wilson, who had just got back.

"Say," he said, "did you notice in the last flash that Amalgamated Planetoid shares have climbed to—"

Biff! Fun's bladder dented Mr. Goldfarb's fuzzy Homburg and Fun roared triumphantly, "Caught you talking news, Mr. Goldfarb! Next you'll be reading inch-thick newspapers, like the ancients did to pass away holidays. The forfeit is to wear your hat upside down for the next three days."

Mr. Goldfarb shrugged happily, upended the Homburg so he looked like an ancient bearded sailor, and headed for the food tables.

Things got livelier. Rotary, Baptist Church, Volunteer Fire Department, and Space Veterans put on acts and skits—just little stuff, the big shows were for tomorrow: the town's own live movies on real stages, the town's own lifesize TV shows without screens, ballets they danced themselves, games they played with their own hands, races they ran with their own feet, poetry they read with their own mouths—not to mention an original epic by Mr. Tomlinson entitled *Roosevelt's Farewell.*

People laughed, people talked, people milled, people mocked, people got it off their chests. It got dark. Small children were herded off to dormitories to be told wonderful stories by parents who babysat by turns. The square blossomed with bobbing lanterns. People ate quite a bit and drank quite a little. Space was cleared in the street and the dancing started.

Mr. Felton weaved up to Mr. Wilson, decided that this was the man he'd been arguing with in the dark for a long, long time. "Look," he said with brotherly aggressiveness, "I don't hold with those folk who say America never had any good holidays and parties until now. Why, America's the home of holidays." His aplomb became professorial and his tongue began to trip more lightly than any sober man's possibly could. "There's the clambake, the cocktail party, the Sunday school picnic, the convention, the moon-jaunt, the field day, the jam session, the ten-way telephone call, the treasure hunt, the week end, the round-the-world-in-a-day-and-a-half—" He gulped a huge breath and grabbed tight to Mr. Wilson, who showed signs of edging off. "—the pub crawl, the night-to-howl, the barbecue, the wiener roast, the Sunday copter soar, the Kentucky frolic, the county fair, the retreat, the psychodrama, the psychoanalysis, the space-scoot, the blanket party, bundling, the revival, the over-the-top-of-the-world, and the fishing trip!" He waved his arms wildly and proclaimed, "They had Christmas, New Year's, Labor Day, Mother's Day, Father's Day, Sweetest Day—oh, and all sorts of holidays a man might enjoy with pleasure and profit. Only—" (and he hiccuped wisely) "—they got just a little too profitable."

Miss Kidd, dressed like Cleopatra, glided in front of Mr. Wilson. He put his arms around her.

"I've always wanted to know what it was like to kiss a school-teacher," he said.

"Now you know," she told him three seconds later.

"Yes, I do," he agreed in awed tones, as Mr. Felton swayed off through the dancers.

It got real dark. New lights flamed and flared. The music got faster. Miss Kidd danced with Mr. Gutknecht. Mr. Felton swooped around with Mrs. Goldfarb. Mr. Kantarian danced with Mrs. Ferguson. Mr. Gianelli danced with Mrs. Lovesmith. Mr. Moriarty danced with Jenny and the wrinkles danced right off his face, maybe into his ears or under his collar. Octavia Tomlinson went to ask Jim Kelly to dance with her, but he saw her coming and ran away into the dark. So Diana strung a silver arrow to her plastic bow and went hunting.

Joy spun and flowers sprang from her dress, joined those under-foot. Friendship waltzed with Love, Fun cut didoes, while Laziness smiled and snoozed by turns. Dark shopfronts all around the square reflected a whirling rout of colors. But overhead there was nothing to turn back the happy hues and they shot upward, through air untroubled by radio waves or the roar of jets, to join those from a hundred thousand other towns on Earth and Mars, and flash a gay message to the twinkling, friendly stars.

The Night He Cried

I GLANCED down my neck secretly at the two snowy hillocks, ruby peaked, that were pushing out my blouse tautly without the aid of a brassière. I decided they'd more than do. So I turned away scornfully as his vast top-down convertible cruised past my street lamp. I struck my hip and a big match against the fluted column, and lit a cigarette. I was Lili Marlene to a T—or rather to a V-neckline. (I must tell you that my command of earth-idiom and allusion is remarkable, but if you'd had my training you wouldn't wonder.)

The convertible slowed down and backed up. I smiled. I'd been certain that my magnificently formed milk glands would turn the trick. I puffed on my cigarette languorously.

"Hi, Babe!"

Right from the first I'd known it was the man I was supposed to contact. Handsome hatchet face. Six or seven feet tall. Quite a creature. Male, as they say.

I hopped into his car, vaulting over the low door before he opened it. We zoomed off through New York's purple, smelly twilight.

"What's your name, Big Male?" I asked him.

Scorning to answer, he stripped me with his eyes. But I had confidence in my milk glands. Lord knows, I'd been hours perfecting them.

"Slickie Millane, isn't it?" I prompted recklessly.

"That's possible," he conceded, poker-faced.

"Well then, what are we waiting for?" I asked him, nudging him with the leftermost of my beautifully conical milk glands.

"Look here, Babe," he told me, just a bit coldly, "I'm the one who dispenses sex and justice in this area."

I snuggled submissively under his encircling right arm, still nudging him now and again with my left milk gland. The convertible sped. The skyscrapers shrank, exfoliated, became countryside. The convertible stopped.

As the hand of his encircling arm began to explore my prize possessions, I drew away a bit, not frustratingly, and informed him, "Slickie dear, I am from Galaxy Center . . ."

"What's that—a magazine publisher?" he demanded hotly, being somewhat inflamed by my cool milk glands.

". . . and we are interested in how sex and justice are dispensed in all areas," I went on, disregarding his interruption and his somewhat juvenile fondlings. "To be bold, we suspect that you may be somewhat misled about this business of sex."

Vertical, centimeter-deep furrows creased his brow. His head poised above mine like a hawk's. "What are you talking about, Babe?" he demanded with suspicious rage, even snatching his hands away.

"Briefly, Slickie," I said, "you do not seem to feel that sex is for the production of progeny or for the mutual solace of two creatures. You seem to think—"

His rage exploded into action. He grabbed a great big gun out of the glove compartment. I sprang to my two transmuted nether tentacles—most handsome gams if I, the artist, do say so. He jabbed the muzzle of the gun into my midriff.

"That's exactly what I mean, Slickie," I managed to say before my beautiful midriff, which I'd been at such pains to perfect, erupted into smoke and ghastly red splatter. I did a backward flipflop out of the car and lay still—a most fetching corpse with a rucked-up skirt. As the convertible snorted off triumphantly, I snagged hold of the rear bumper, briefly changing my hand back to a tentacle for better gripping. Before the pavement had abraded more than a few grams of my substance, I pulled myself up onto the bumper, where I proceeded to reconstitute my vanished midriff with material from the air, the rest of my body, and the paint on the trunk case. On this occasion the work went rapidly, with no artistic gropings, since I had the curves memorized from the first time I'd worked them out. Then I touched up my abrasions, stripped myself, whipped myself up a snazzy silver lamé evening frock out of chromium from the bumper, and put in time creating costume jewelry out of the tail light and the rest of the chrome.

The car stopped at a bar and Slickie slid out. For a moment his proud profile was silhouetted against the smoky glow. Then he was inside. I threw away the costume jewelry and climbed over the folded top and popped down on the leather-upholstered seat, scarcely a kilogram lighter than when I'd first sat there.

The minutes dragged. To pass them, I mentally reviewed the thousand-and-some basic types of mutual affection on the million-plus planets, not forgetting the one and only basic type of love.

There was a burst of juke-box jazz. Footsteps tracked from the bar toward the convertible. I leaned back comfortably with my silver-filmed milk glands dramatically highlighted.

"Hi, Slickie," I called, making my voice sweet and soft to cushion the shock.

Nevertheless it was a considerable one. For all of ten seconds he stood there, canted forward a little, like a wooden Indian that's just been nudged from behind and is about to topple.

Then with a naïve ingenuity that rather touched me, he asked huskily, "Hey, have you got a twin sister?"

"Could be," I said with a shrug that jogged my milk glands deliciously.

"Well, what are you doing in my car?"

"Waiting for you," I told him simply.

He considered that as he slowly and carefully walked around the car and got behind the wheel, never taking his eyes off me. I nudged him in my usual manner. He jerked away.

"What are you up to?" he inquired suspiciously.

"Why are you surprised, Slickie?" I countered innocently. "I've heard this sort of thing happens to you all the time."

"What sort of thing?"

"Girls turning up in your car, your bar, your bedroom—everywhere."

"Where'd you hear it?"

"I read it in your Spike Mallet books."

"Oh," he said, somewhat mollified. But then his suspicion came back. "But what are you really up to?" he demanded.

"Slickie," I assured him with complete sincerity, bugging my beautiful eyes, "I just love you."

This statement awakened in him an irritation so great that it overrode his uneasiness about me, for he cuffed me in the face—so suddenly that I almost forgot and changed it back to my top tentacle.

"I make the advances around here, Babe," he asserted harshly.

Completely under control again, I welled a tiny trickle of blood out of the left-hand corner of my gorgeous mouth. "Anything you say, Slickie, dear," I assented submissively and cuddled up against him in a prim, girlish way to which he could hardly take exception.

But I must have bothered or at least puzzled him, for he drove slowly, his dark-eaved eyes following an invisible tennis ball that bounded between me and the street ahead. Abruptly the eaves lifted and he smiled.

"Look, I just got an idea for a story," he said. "There's this girl from Galaxy Center—" and he whipped around to watch my reactions, but I didn't blink.

He continued, "I mean, she's sort of from the center of the galaxy, where everything's radioactive. Now there's this guy that's got her up in his attic." His face grew deeply thoughtful. "She's the most beautiful girl in the universe and he loves her like crazy, but she's all streaming with hard radiations and it'll kill him if he touches her."

"Yes, Slickie—and then?" I prompted after the car had dreamed its way for several blocks between high buildings.

He looked at me sharply. "That's all. Don't you get it?"

"Yes, Slickie," I assured him soothingly. My statement seemed to satisfy him, but he was still edgy.

He stopped the car in front of an apartment hotel that thrust toward the stars with a dark presumptuousness. He got out on the street side and walked around the rear end and suddenly stopped. I followed him. He was studying the gray bumper and the patch of raw sheet metal off which I'd used the paint. He looked around at me where I stood sprayed with silver lamé in the revealing lamp light.

"Wipe your chin," he said critically.

"Why not kiss the blood off it, Slickie?" I replied with an ingenuousness I hoped would take the curse off the suggestion.

"Aw nuts," he said nervously and stalked into the foyer so swiftly he might have been trying to get away from me. However, he made no move to stop me when I followed him into the tiny place and the even tinier elevator. In the latter cubicle I maneuvered so as to give him a series of breathtaking scenic views of the Grand Tetons that rose behind the plunging silver horizon of my neckline, and he unfroze considerably. By the time he opened the door of his apartment he had got so positively cordial that he urged me across the threshold with a casual spank.

It was just as I had visualized it—the tiger skins, the gun racks, the fireplace, the open bedroom door, the bar just beside it, the adventures of Spike Mallet in handsomely tooled leather bindings, the vast divan covered with zebra skin . . .

On the last was stretched a beautiful ice-faced blonde in a filmy negligee.

This was a complication for which I wasn't prepared. I stood rooted by the door while Slickie walked swiftly past me.

The blonde slithered to her feet. There was murder in her glacial eyes. "You two-timing rat!" she grated. Her hand darted under her negligee. Slickie's snaked under the lefthand side of his jacket.

Then it hit me what was going to happen. She would bring out a small but deadly silver-plated automatic, but before she could level it, Slickie's cannon would make a red ruin of her midriff.

There I was, standing twenty feet away from both of them—and this poor girl couldn't reconstitute herself!

Swifter than thought I changed my arms back to upper dorsal tentacles and jerked back both Slickie's and the girl's elbow. They turned around, considerably startled, and saw me standing twenty feet away. I'd turned my tentacles back to arms before they'd noticed them. Their astonishment increased.

But I knew I had won only a temporary respite. Unless something happened, Slickie's trigger-blissful rage would swiftly be refocused on this foolish fragile creature. To save her, I had to divert his ire to myself.

"Get that little tramp out of here," I ordered Slickie from the corner of my mouth as I walked past him to the bar.

"Easy, Babe," he warned me.

I poured myself a liter of scotch—I had to open a second bottle to complete the measure—and downed it. I really didn't need it, but the assorted molecules were congenial building blocks and I was rather eager to get back to normal weight.

"Haven't you got that tramp out of here yet?" I demanded, eyeing him scornfully over my insouciant silver-filmed shoulder.

"Easy, Babe," he repeated, the vertical furrows creasing his brow to a depth of at least a centimeter and a half.

"That's telling her, Slickie," the blonde applauded.

"You two-timing rat!" I plagiarized, whipping up my silver skirt as if to wisk a gun from my nonexistent girdle.

His cannon coughed. Always a good sportsman, I moved an inch so that the bullet, slightly mis-aimed, took me exactly in the right eye, messily blowing off the back of my head. I winked at Slickie with my left eye and fell back through the doorway into the bedroom darkness.

I knew I had no time to spare. When a man's shot one girl he begins to lose his natural restraint. Lying on the floor, I reconstituted my eye and did a quick patch-job on the back of my head in seventeen seconds flat.

As I emerged from the bedroom, they were entering into a clinch, each holding a gun lightly against the other's back.

"Slickie," I said, pouring myself a scant half liter of scotch, "I told you about that tramp."

The ice-blonde squawked, threw up her hands as if she'd had a shot of strychnine, and ran out the door. I fancied I could feel the building tilt as she leaned on the elevator button.

I downed the scotch and advanced, shattering the paralyzed space-time that Slickie seemed to be depending on as a defense.

"Slickie," I said, "let's get down to cases. I am indeed from Galaxy Center and we very definitely don't like your attitude. We don't care what your motives are, or whether they are derived from jumbled genes, a curdled childhood, or a sick society. We simply love you and we want you to reform." I grabbed him by a shivering shoulder that was now hardly higher than my waist, and dragged him into the bedroom, snatching up the rest of the scotch on the way. I switched on the light. The bedroom was a really lush lovenest. I drained the scotch—there was about a half liter left—and faced the cowering

Slickie. "Now do to me," I told him uncompromisingly, "the thing you're always going to do to those girls, except you have to shoot them."

He frothed like an epileptic, snatched out his cannon and emptied its magazine into various parts of my torso, but since he hit only two of my five brains, I wasn't bothered. I reeled back bloodily through the blue smoke and fell into the bathroom. I felt real crazy—maybe I shouldn't have taken that last half liter. I reconstituted my torso faster even than I had my head, but my silver lamé frock was a mess. Not wanting to waste time and reluctant to use any more reconstituting energy, I stripped it off and popped into the off-the-shoulders evening dress the blonde had left lying over the edge of the bathtub. The dress wasn't a bad fit. I went back into the bedroom. Slickie was sobbing softly at the foot of the bed and gently beating his head against it.

"Slickie," I said, perhaps a shade too curtly, "about this love business—"

He sprang for the ceiling but didn't quite burst through it. Falling back, by chance on his feet, he headed for the hall. Now it wasn't in my orders from Galaxy Center that he run away and excite this world—in fact, my superiors had strictly forbidden such a happening. I had to stop Slickie. But I was a bit confused—perhaps fuddled by that last half liter. I hesitated—then he was too far away, had too big a start. To stop him, I knew I'd have to use tentacles. Swifter than thought I changed them and shot them out.

"Slickie," I cried reassuringly, dragging him to me.

Then I realized that in my excitement, instead of using my upper dorsal tentacles, I'd used the upper ventral ones I kept transmuted into my beautiful milk glands. I do suppose they looked rather strange to Slickie as they came out of the bosom of my off-the-shoulders evening dress and drew him to me.

Frightening sounds came out of him. I let him go and tried to resume my gorgeous shape, but now I was really confused (that last half liter!) and lost control of my transmutations. When I found myself turning my topmost tentacle into a milk gland I gave up completely and—except for a lung and vocal cords—resumed my normal shape. It was quite a relief. After all, I had done what Galaxy Center had intended I should. From now on, the mere sight of a brassière in a show window would be enough to give Slickie the shakes.

Still, I was bothered about the guy. As I say, he'd touched me.

I caressed him tenderly with my tentacles. Over and over again I explained that I was just a heptapus and that Galaxy Center had selected me for the job simply because my seven tentacles would transmute nicely into the seven extremities of the human female.

Over and over again I told him how I loved him.

It didn't seem to help. Slickie Millane continued to weep hysterically.

The Big Trek

I DIDN'T KNOW if I'd got to this crazy place by rocket, space dodger, time twister—or maybe even on foot the way I felt so beat. My memory was gone. When I woke up there was just the desert all around me with the gray sky pressing down like the ceiling of an enormous room. The desert . . . and the big trek. And *that* was enough to make me stop grabbing for my memory and take a quick look at my pants to make sure I was human.

These, well, animals were shuffling along about four abreast in a straggly line that led from one end of nowhere to the other, right past my rocky hole. Wherever they were heading they seemed to have come from everywhere and maybe everywhen. There were big ones and little ones, some like children and some just small. A few went on two feet, but more on six or eight, and there were wrigglers, rollers, oozers, flutterers and hoppers; I couldn't decide whether the low-flying ones were pets or pals. Some had scales, others feathers, bright armor like beetles or fancy hides like zebras, and quite a few wore transparent suits holding air or other gases, or water or other liquids, though some of the suits were tailored for a dozen tentacles and some for no legs at all. And darn if their shuffle—to pick one word for all the kinds of movement—wasn't more like a dance than a lockstep.

They were too different from each other for an army, yet they weren't like refugees either, for refugees wouldn't dance and make music, even if on more feet than two or four and with voices and instruments so strange I couldn't tell which was which. Their higgledy-piggledy variety suggested a stampede from some awful disaster or a flight to some ark of survival, but I couldn't feel panic in them—or solemn purpose either, for that matter. They just shuffled happily along. And if they were a circus parade, as a person might think from their being animals and some of them dressed fancy, then who was bossing the show and where were the guards or the audience, except for me?

I should have been afraid of such a horde of monsters, but I wasn't, so I got up from behind the rock I'd been spying over and I took one last look around for footprints or blast-scar or time-twister whorls or some sign of how I'd got there, and then I shrugged my shoulders and walked down toward them.

They didn't stop and they didn't run, they didn't shoot and they didn't come out to capture or escort me; they kept on shuffling along without a break in the rhythm, but a thousand calm eyes were turned on me from the tops of weaving stalks or the depths of bony caverns, and as I got close a dusky roller like an escaped tire with green eyes in the unspinning hub speeded up a little and an opal octopus in a neat suit brimful of water held back, making room for me.

Next thing I knew I was restfully shuffling along myself, wondering how the roller kept from tipping and why the octopus moved his legs by threes, and how so many different ways of moving could be harmonized like instruments in a band. Around me was the murmuring rise and fall of languages I couldn't understand and the rainbow-changing of color patches that might be languages for the eye—the octopus dressed in water looked from time to time like a shaken up pousse-café.

I tried out on them what I seemed to remember as the lingoes of a dozen planets, but nobody said anything back at me directly—I almost tried Earth-talk on them, but something stopped me. A puffy bird-thing floating along under a gas-bag that was part of its body settled lightly on my shoulder and hummed gently in my ear and dropped some suspicious-looking black marbles and then bobbed off. A thing on two legs from somewhere ahead in the trek waltzed its way to my side and offered me a broken-edged chunk that was milky with light and crusty. The thing looked female, being jauntily built and having a

crest of violet feathers, but instead of nose and mouth her face
tapered to a rosy little ring and where breasts would be there was a
burst of pink petals. I gave my non-Earth lingoes another try. She
waited until I was quiet and then she lifted the crusty chunk to her
rosy ring, which she opened a little, and then she offered the chunk
to me again. I took it and tasted it and it was like brick cheese but
flaky and I ate it. I nodded and grinned and she puffed out her petals
and traced a circle with her head and turned to go. I almost said,
"Thanks, chick," because that seemed the right thing, but again something stopped me.

So the big trek had accepted me, I decided, but as the day wore
on (if they had days here, I reminded myself) the feeling of accept-
ance didn't give me any real security. It didn't satisfy me that I had
been given eats instead of being eaten and that I was part of a
harmony instead of a discord. I guess I was expecting too much. Or
maybe I was finding a strange part of myself and was frightened of
it. And after all it isn't reassuring to shuffle along with intelligent
animals you can't talk to, even if they act friendly and dance and sing
and now and then thrum strange strings. It didn't calm me to feel
that I was someplace that was homey and at the same time as lonely
as the stars. The monsters around me got to seem stranger and
stranger; I quit seeing their little tricks of personality and saw only
their outsides. I craned my neck trying to spot the chick with the
pink petals but she was gone. After a while I couldn't bear it any
longer. Some ruins looking like chopped-off skyscrapers had come in
sight earlier and we were just now passing them, not too close, so
although the flat sky was getting darker and pressing down lower and
although there were distant flashes of lightning and rumbles of thunder (I think that's what they were) I turned at a right angle and
walked away fast from the trek.

Nobody stopped me and pretty soon I was hidden in the ruins.
They were comforting at first, the little ruins, and I got the feeling
my ancestors had built them. But then I came to the bigger ones and
they *were* chopped-off skyscrapers and yet some of them were so
tall they scratched the dark flat sky and for a moment I thought I
heard a distant squeal like chalk on a giant blackboard that set my
teeth on edge. And then I got to wondering what had chopped off the

skyscrapers and what had happened to the people, and after that I began to see dark things loafing along after me close to the ruined walls. They were about as big as I was, but going on all fours. They began to follow me closer and closer, moving like clumsy wolves, the more notice I took of them. I saw that their faces were covered with hair like their bodies and that their jaws were working. I started to hurry and as soon as I did I began to hear the sounds they were making. The bad thing was that although the sounds were halfway between growls and barks, I could understand them.

"Hello, Joe."

"Whacha know, Joe?"

"That so, Joe?"

"Let's blow, Joe."

"C'mon Joe, let's go, go, go."

And then I realized the big mistake I'd made in coming to these ruins, and I turned around and started to run back the way I had come, and they came loping and lurching after me, trying to drag me down, and the worst thing was that I knew they didn't want to kill me, but just have me get down on all fours and run with them and bark and growl.

The ruins grew smaller, but it was very dark now and at first I was afraid that I had lost my way and next I was afraid that the end of the big trek had passed me by, but then the light brightened under the low sky like the afterglow of a sunset and it showed me the big trek in the distance and I ran toward it and the hairy things stopped skulking behind me.

I didn't hit the same section of the big trek, of course, but one that was enough like it to make me wonder. There was another dusky roller, but with blue eyes and smaller, so that it had to spin faster, and another many-legged creature dressed in water, and a jaunty chick with crimson crest and a burst of orange petals. But the difference didn't bother me.

The trek slowed down, the change in rhythm rippling back to me along the line. I looked ahead and there was a large round hole in the low sky and through it I could see the stars. And through it too the trek itself was swerving, each creature diving upward toward the winking points of light in the blackness.

I kept on shuffling happily forward, though more slowly now, and to either side of the trek I saw heaped on the desert floor space-suits tailored to fit every shape of creature I could imagine and fly him or her safely through the emptiness above. After a while it got to be my turn and I found a suit and climbed into it and zipped it snug and located the control buttons in the palms of the gloves and looked up. Then I felt more than control buttons in my fingers and I looked to either side of me and I was hand in hand with an octopus wearing an eight-legged spacesuit over his water-filled one and on the other side with a suited-up chick who sported a jet-black crest and pearl-gray petals.

She traced a circle with her head and I did the same, and the octopus traced a smaller circle with a free tentacle, and I knew that one of the reasons I hadn't used Earth-talk was that I was going to keep quiet until I learned or remembered *their* languages, and that another reason was that the hairy fourfooters back in the ruins had been men like me and I hated them but these creatures beside me were my kind, and that we had come to take one last look at the Earth that had destroyed itself and at the men who had stayed on Earth and not got away like me—to come back and lose my memory from the shock of being on my degraded ancestral planet.

Then we clasped hands tight, which pushed the buttons in our palms. Our jets blossomed out behind us and we were diving up together out of this world through the smoothly rounded doughnut hole toward the stars. I realized that space wasn't empty and that those points of light in the blackness weren't lonely at all.

Space-Time for Springers

GUMMITCH was a superkitten, as he knew very well, with an I. Q. of about 160. Of course, he didn't talk. But everybody knows that I. Q. tests based on language ability are very onesided. Besides, he would talk as soon as they started setting a place for him at table and pouring him coffee. Ashurbanipal and Cleopatra ate horsemeat from pans on the floor and they didn't talk. Baby dined in his crib on milk from a bottle and he didn't talk. Sissy sat at table but they didn't pour her coffee and she didn't talk—not one word. Father and Mother (whom Gummitch had nicknamed Old Horsemeat and Kitty-Come-Here) sat at table and poured each other coffee and they *did* talk. Q. E. D.

Meanwhile, he would get by very well on thought projection and intuitive understanding of all human speech—not even to mention cat patois, which almost any civilized animal could play by ear. The dramatic monologues and Socratic dialogues, the quiz and panel-show appearances, the felidological expedition to darkest Africa (where he would uncover the real truth behind lions and tigers), the exploration of the outer planets—all these could wait. The same went for the books for which he was ceaselessly accumulating material: *The Encyclopedia of Odors, Anthropofeline Psychology, Invisible Signs and Secret Wonders, Space-Time for Springers, Slit Eyes Look at Life,* et cetera. For the present it was enough to live existence to the hilt and soak up knowledge, missing no experience proper to his age level—to rush about with tail aflame.

So to all outward appearances Gummitch was just a vividly normal kitten, as shown by the succession of nicknames he bore along the magic path that led from blue-eyed infancy toward puberty: Little One, Squawker, Portly, Bumble (for purring not clumsiness), Old Starved-to-Death, Fierso, Loverboy (affection not sex), Spook and Catnik. Of these only the last perhaps requires further explanation: the Russians had just sent Muttnik up after Sputnik, so that when one evening Gummitch streaked three times across the firmament of the living room floor in the same direction, past the fixed stars of the humans and the comparatively slow-moving heavenly bodies of the two older cats, and Kitty-Come-Here quoted the line from Keats:

> Then felt I like some watcher of the skies
> When a new planet swims into his ken;

it was inevitable that Old Horsemeat would say, "Ah—Catnik!"

The new name lasted all of three days, to be replaced by Gummitch, which showed signs of becoming permanent.

The little cat was on the verge of truly growing up, at least so Gummitch overheard Old Horsemeat comment to Kitty-Come-Here. A few short weeks, Old Horsemeat said, and Gummitch's fiery flesh would harden, his slim neck thicken, the electricity vanish from everything but his fur, and all his delightful kittenish qualities rapidly give way to the earthbound singlemindedness of a tom. They'd be lucky, Old Horsemeat concluded, if he didn't turn completely surly like Ashurbanipal.

Gummitch listened to these predictions with gay unconcern and with secret amusement from his vantage point of superior knowledge, in the same spirit that he accepted so many phases of his outwardly conventional existence: the murderous sidelong looks he got from Ashurbanipal and Cleopatra as he devoured his own horsemeat from his own little tin pan, because they sometimes were given canned catfood but he never; the stark idiocy of Baby, who didn't know the difference between a live cat and a stuffed teddy bear and who tried to cover up his ignorance by making goo-goo noises and poking indiscriminately at all eyes; the far more serious—because cleverly hidden—maliciousness of Sissy, who had to be watched out for warily—

especially when you were alone—and whose retarded—even warped
—development, Gummitch knew, was Old Horsemeat and Kitty-
Come-Here's deepest, most secret, worry (more of Sissy and her evil
ways soon); the limited intellect of Kitty-Come-Here, who despite
the amounts of coffee she drank was quite as featherbrained as kittens are supposed to be and who firmly believed, for example, that
kittens operated in the same space-time as other beings—that to get
from *here* to *there* they had to cross the space *between*—and similar
fallacies; the mental stodginess of even Old Horsemeat, who although
he understood quite a bit of the secret doctrine and talked intelli-
gently to Gummitch when they were alone, nevertheless suffered from
the limitations of his status—a rather nice old god but a maddeningly
slow-witted one.

But Gummitch could easily forgive all this massed inadequacy
and downright brutishness in his felino-human household, because
he was aware that he alone knew the real truth about himself and
about other kittens and babies as well, the truth which was hidden
from weaker minds, the truth that was as intrinsically incredible as
the germ theory of disease or the origin of the whole great universe
in the explosion of a single atom.

As a baby kitten Gummitch had believed that Old Horsemeat's
two hands were hairless kittens permanently attached to the ends of
Old Horsemeat's arms but having an independent life of their own.
How he had hated and loved those two five-legged sallow monsters,
his first playmates, comforters and battle-opponents!

Well, even that fantastic discarded notion was but a trifling fancy
compared to the real truth about himself!

The forehead of Zeus split open to give birth to Minerva. Gummitch had been born from the waist-fold of a dirty old terrycloth
bathrobe, Old Horsemeat's basic garment. The kitten was intuitively
certain of it and had proved it to himself as well as any Descartes or
Aristotle. In a kitten-size tuck of that ancient bathrobe the atoms of
his body had gathered and quickened into life. His earliest memories
were of snoozing wrapped in terrycloth, warmed by Old Horsemeat's
heat. Old Horsemeat and Kitty-Come-Here were his true parents.
The other theory of his origin, the one he heard Old Horsemeat and
Kitty-Come-Here recount from time to time—that he had been the
only surviving kitten of a litter abandoned next door, that he had had

the shakes from vitamin deficiency and lost the tip of his tail and the hair on his paws and had to be nursed back to life and health with warm yellowish milk-and-vitamins fed from an eyedropper—that other theory was just one of those rationalizations with which mysterious nature cloaks the birth of heroes, perhaps wisely veiling the truth from minds unable to bear it, a rationalization as false as Kitty-Come-Here and Old Horsemeat's touching belief that Sissy and Baby were their children rather than the cubs of Ashurbanipal and Cleopatra.

The day that Gummitch had discovered by pure intuition the secret of his birth he had been filled with a wild instant excitement. He had only kept it from tearing him to pieces by rushing out to the kitchen and striking and devouring a fried scallop, torturing it fiendishly first for twenty minutes.

And the secret of his birth was only the beginning. His intellectual faculties aroused, Gummitch had two days later intuited a further and greater secret: since he was the child of humans he would, upon reaching this maturation date of which Old Horsemeat had spoken, turn not into a sullen tom but into a godlike human youth with reddish golden hair the color of his present fur. He would be poured coffee; and he would instantly be able to talk, probably in all languages. While Sissy (how clear it was now!) would at approximately the same time shrink and fur out into a sharp-clawed and vicious she-cat dark as her hair, sex and self-love her only concerns, fit harem-mate for Cleopatra, concubine to Ashurbanipal.

Exactly the same was true, Gummitch realized at once, for all kittens and babies, all humans and cats, wherever they might dwell. Metamorphosis was as much a part of the fabric of their lives as it was of the insects'. It was also the basic fact underlying all legends of werewolves, vampires and witches' familiars.

If you just rid your mind of preconceived notions, Gummitch told himself, it was all very logical. Babies were stupid, fumbling, vindictive creatures without reason or speech. What more natural than that they should grow up into mute sullen selfish beasts bent only on rapine and reproduction? While kittens were quick, sensitive, subtle, supremely alive. What other destiny were they possibly fitted for except to become the deft, word-speaking, book-writing, music-making, meat-getting-and-dispensing masters of the world? To dwell on the physical differences, to point out that kittens and men, babies and cats, are rather unlike in appearance and size, would be to miss the forest for the trees—very much as if an entomologist should proclaim metamorphosis a myth because his microscope failed to discover the wings of a butterfly in a caterpillar's slime or a golden beetle in a grub.

Nevertheless it was such a mind-staggering truth, Gummitch realized at the same time, that it was easy to understand why humans, cats, babies and perhaps most kittens were quite unaware of it. How to safely explain to a butterfly that he was once a hairy crawler, or to a dull larva that he will one day be a walking jewel? No, in such situations the delicate minds of man- and feline-kind are guarded by a merciful mass amnesia, such as Velikovsky has explained prevents us from recalling that in historical times the Earth was catastrophically bumped by the planet Venus operating in the manner of a comet before settling down (with a cosmic sigh of relief, surely!) into its present orbit.

This conclusion was confirmed when Gummitch in the first fever of illumination tried to communicate his great insight to others. He told it in cat patois, as well as that limited jargon permitted, to Ashurbanipal and Cleopatra and even, on the off chance, to Sissy and Baby. They showed no interest whatever, except that Sissy took advantage of his unguarded preoccupation to stab him with a fork.

Later, alone with Old Horsemeat, he projected the great new thoughts, staring with solemn yellow eyes at the old god, but the latter grew markedly nervous and even showed signs of real fear, so Gummitch desisted. ("You'd have sworn he was trying to put across something as deep as the Einstein theory or the doctrine of original sin," Old Horsemeat later told Kitty-Come-Here.)

But Gummitch was a man now in all but form, the kitten reminded himself after these failures, and it was part of his destiny to shoulder secrets alone when necessary. He wondered if the general amnesia would affect him when he metamorphosed. There was no sure answer to this question, but he hoped not—and sometimes felt that there was reason for his hopes. Perhaps he would be the first true kitten-man, speaking from a wisdom that had no locked doors in it.

Once he was tempted to speed up the process by the use of drugs. Left alone in the kitchen, he sprang onto the table and started to lap up the black puddle in the bottom of Old Horsemeat's coffee cup. It tasted foul and poisonous and he withdrew with a little snarl, frightened as well as revolted. The dark beverage would not work its tongue-loosening magic, he realized, except at the proper time and with the proper ceremonies. Incantations might be necessary as well. Certainly unlawful tasting was highly dangerous.

The futility of expecting coffee to work any wonders by itself was further demonstrated to Gummitch when Kitty-Come-Here, wordlessly badgered by Sissy, gave a few spoonfuls to the little girl, liberally lacing it first with milk and sugar. Of course Gummitch knew by now that Sissy was destined shortly to turn into a cat and that no amount of coffee would ever make her talk, but it was nevertheless instructive to see how she spat out the first mouthful, drooling a lot of saliva after it, and dashed the cup and its contents at the chest of Kitty-Come-Here.

Gummitch continued to feel a great deal of sympathy for his parents in their worries about Sissy and he longed for the day when he would metamorphose and be able as an acknowledged man-child truly to console them. It was heartbreaking to see how they each tried to coax the little girl to talk, always attempting it while the other was absent, how they seized on each accidentally wordlike note in the few sounds she uttered and repeated it back to her hopefully, how they were more and more possessed by fears not so much of her retarded (they thought) development as of her increasingly obvious maliciousness, which was directed chiefly at Baby . . . though the two cats and Gummitch bore their share. Once she had caught Baby alone in his crib and used the sharp corner of a block to dot Baby's large-domed lightly downed head with triangular red marks. Kitty-Come-Here had discovered her doing it, but the woman's first action had been to rub Baby's head to obliterate the marks so that Old Horsemeat wouldn't see them. That was the night Kitty-Come-Here hid the abnormal psychology books.

Gummitch understood very well that Kitty-Come-Here and Old Horsemeat, honestly believing themselves to be Sissy's parents, felt just as deeply about her as if they actually were and he did what little he could under the present circumstances to help them. He had recently come to feel a quite independent affection for Baby—the miserable little proto-cat was so completely stupid and defenseless—and so he unofficially constituted himself the creature's guardian, taking his naps behind the door of the nursery and dashing about noisily whenever Sissy showed up. In any case he realized that as a potentially adult member of a felino-human household he had his natural responsibilities.

Accepting responsibilities was as much a part of a kitten's life, Gummitch told himself, as shouldering unsharable intuitions and secrets, the number of which continued to grow from day to day.

There was, for instance, the Affair of the Squirrel Mirror.

Gummitch had early solved the mystery of ordinary mirrors and of the creatures that appeared in them. A little observation and sniffing and one attempt to get behind the heavy wall-job in the living room had convinced him that mirror beings were insubstantial or at least hermetically sealed into their other world, probably creatures of pure spirit, harmless imitative ghosts—including the silent Gummitch Double who touched paws with him so softly yet so coldly.

Just the same, Gummitch had let his imagination play with what would happen if one day, while looking into the mirror world, he should let loose his grip on his spirit and let it slip into the Gummitch Double while the other's spirit slipped into his body—if, in short, he should change places with the scentless ghost kitten. Being doomed to a life consisting wholly of imitation and completely lacking in opportunities to show initiative—except for the behind-the-scenes judgment and speed needed in rushing from one mirror to another to keep up with the real Gummitch—would be sickeningly dull, Gummitch decided, and he resolved to keep a tight hold on his spirit at all times in the vicinity of mirrors.

But that isn't telling about the Squirrel Mirror. One morning Gummitch was peering out the front bedroom window that overlooked the roof of the porch. Gummitch had already classified windows as semi-mirrors having two kinds of space on the other side: the mirror world and that harsh region filled with mysterious and dangerously organized-sounding noises called the outer world, into which grownup humans reluctantly ventured at intervals, donning special garments for the purpose and shouting loud farewells that were meant to be reassuring but achieved just the opposite effect. The coexistence of two kinds of space presented no paradox to the kitten who carried in his mind the 27-chapter outline of *Space-Time for Springers*—indeed, it constituted one of the minor themes of the book.

This morning the bedroom was dark and the outer world was dull and sunless, so the mirror world was unusually difficult to see. Gummitch was just lifting his face toward it, nose twitching, his front paws on the sill, when what should rear up on the other side, exactly in the space that the Gummitch Double normally occupied, but a dirty brown, narrow-visaged image with savagely low forehead, dark evil walleyes, and a huge jaw filled with shovel-like teeth.

Gummitch was enormously startled and hideously frightened. He felt his grip on his spirit go limp, and without volition he teleported himself three yards to the rear, making use of that faculty for cutting corners in space-time, traveling by space-warp in fact, which was one of his powers that Kitty-Come-Here refused to believe in and that even Old Horsemeat accepted only on faith.

Then, not losing a moment, he picked himself up by his furry seat, swung himself around, dashed downstairs at top speed, sprang to the top of the sofa, and stared for several seconds at the Gummitch Double in the wall-mirror—not relaxing a muscle strand until he was completely convinced that he was still himself and had not been transformed into the nasty brown apparition that had confronted him in the bedroom window.

"Now what do you suppose brought that on?" Old Horsemeat asked Kitty-Come-Here.

Later Gummitch learned that what he had seen had been a squirrel, a savage, nut-hunting being belonging wholly to the outer world (except for forays into attics) and not at all to the mirror one. Nevertheless he kept a vivid memory of his profound momentary conviction that the squirrel had taken the Gummitch Double's place and been about to take his own. He shuddered to think what would have happened if the squirrel had been actively interested in trading spirits with him. Apparently mirrors and mirror-situations, just as he had always feared, were highly conducive to spirit transfers. He filed the information away in the memory cabinet reserved for dangerous, exciting and possibly useful information, such as plans for climbing straight up glass (diamond-tipped claws!) and flying higher than the trees.

These days his thought cabinets were beginning to feel filled to bursting and he could hardly wait for the moment when the true rich taste of coffee, lawfully drunk, would permit him to speak.

He pictured the scene in detail: the family gathered in conclave at the kitchen table, Ashurbanipal and Cleopatra respectfully watching from floor level, himself sitting erect on chair with paws (or would they be hands?) lightly touching his cup of thin china, while Old Horsemeat poured the thin black steaming stream. He knew the Great Transformation must be close at hand.

At the same time he knew that the other critical situation in the household was worsening swiftly. Sissy, he realized now, was far older than Baby and should long ago have undergone her own somewhat less glamorous though equally necessary transformation (the first tin of raw horsemeat could hardly be as exciting as the first cup of coffee). Her time was long overdue. Gummitch found increasing horror in this mute vampirish being inhabiting the body of a rapidly growing girl, though inwardly equipped to be nothing but a most bloodthirsty she-cat. How dreadful to think of Old Horsemeat and Kitty-Come-Here having to care all their lives for such a monster! Gummitch told himself that if any opportunity for alleviating his parents' misery should ever present itself to him, he would not hesitate for an instant.

Then one night, when the sense of Change was so burstingly strong in him that he knew tomorrow must be the Day, but when the house was also exceptionally unquiet with boards creaking and snapping, taps adrip, and curtains mysteriously rustling at closed windows (so that it was clear that the many spirit worlds including the mirror one must be pressing very close), the opportunity came to Gummitch.

Kitty-Come-Here and Old Horsemeat had fallen into especially sound, drugged sleeps, the former with a bad cold, the latter with one unhappy highball too many (Gummitch knew he had been brooding about Sissy). Baby slept too, though with uneasy whimperings and joggings—moonlight shone full on his crib past a window shade which had whirringly rolled itself up without human or feline agency. Gummitch kept vigil under the crib, with eyes closed but with wildly excited mind pressing outward to every boundary of the house and even stretching here and there into the outer world. On this night of all nights sleep was unthinkable.

Then suddenly he became aware of footsteps, footsteps so soft they must, he thought, be Cleopatra's.

No, softer than that, so soft they might be those of the Gummitch Double escaped from the mirror world at last and padding up toward him through the darkened halls. A ribbon of fur rose along his spine.

Then into the nursery Sissy came prowling. She looked slim as an Egyptian princess in her long thin yellow nightgown and as sure of herself, but the cat was very strong in her tonight, from the flat intent eyes to the dainty canine teeth slightly bared—one look at her now would have sent Kitty-Come-Here running for the telephone number she kept hidden, the telephone number of the special doctor—and Gummitch realized he was witnessing a monstrous suspension of natural law in that this being should be able to exist for a moment without growing fur and changing round pupils for slit eyes.

He retreated to the darkest corner of the room, suppressing a snarl. Sissy approached the crib and leaned over Baby in the moonlight, keeping her shadow off him. For a while she gloated. Then she began softly to scratch his cheek with a long hatpin she carried, keeping away from his eye, but just barely. Baby awoke and saw her and Baby didn't cry. Sissy continued to scratch, always a little more deeply. The moonlight glittered on the jeweled end of the pin.

Gummitch knew he faced a horror that could not be countered by running about or even spitting and screeching. Only magic could fight so obviously supernatural a manifestation. And this was also no time to think of consequences, no matter how clearly and bitterly etched they might appear to a mind intensely awake.

He sprang up onto the other side of the crib, not uttering a sound, and fixed his golden eyes on Sissy's in the moonlight. Then he moved forward straight at her evil face, stepping slowly, not swiftly, using his extraordinary knowledge of the properties of space *to walk straight through her hand and arm as they flailed the hatpin at him*. When his nose-tip finally paused a fraction of an inch from hers his eyes had not blinked once, and she could not look away. Then he unhesitatingly flung his spirit into her like a fistful of flaming arrows and he worked the Mirror Magic.

Sissy's moonlit face, feline and terrified, was in a sense the last thing that Gummitch, the real Gummitch-kitten, ever saw in this world. For the next instant he felt himself enfolded by the foul black blinding cloud of Sissy's spirit, which his own had displaced. At the same time he heard the little girl scream, very loudly but even more distinctly, *"Mommy!"*

That cry might have brought Kitty-Come-Here out of her grave, let alone from sleep merely deep or drugged. Within seconds she was in the nursery, closely followed by Old Horsemeat, and she had caught up Sissy in her arms and the little girl was articulating the wonderful word again and again, and miraculously following it with the command—there could be no doubt, Old Horsemeat heard it too —"Hold me tight!"

Then Baby finally dared to cry. The scratches on his cheek came to attention and Gummitch, as he had known must happen, was banished to the basement amid cries of horror and loathing chiefly from Kitty-Come-Here.

The little cat did not mind. No basement would be one-tenth as dark as Sissy's spirit that now enshrouded him for always, hiding all the file drawers and the labels on all the folders, blotting out forever even the imagining of the scene of first coffee-drinking and first speech.

In a last intuition, before the animal blackness closed in utterly, Gummitch realized that the spirit, alas, is not the same thing as the consciousness and that one may lose—sacrifice—the first and still be burdened with the second.

Old Horsemeat had seen the hatpin (and hid it quickly from Kitty-Come-Here) and so he knew that the situation was not what it seemed and that Gummitch was at the very least being made into a sort of scapegoat. He was quite apologetic when he brought the tin pans of food to the basement during the period of the little cat's exile. It was a comfort to Gummitch, albeit a small one. Gummitch told himself, in his new black halting manner of thinking, that after all a cat's best friend is his man.

From that night Sissy never turned back in her development. Within two months she had made three years' progress in speaking. She became an outstandingly bright, light-footed, high-spirited little girl. Although she never told anyone this, the moonlit nursery and Gummitch's magnified face were her first memories. Everything before that was inky blackness. She was always very nice to Gummitch in a careful sort of way. She could never stand to play the game "Owl Eyes."

After a few weeks Kitty-Come-Here forgot her fears and Gummitch once again had the run of the house. But by then the transformation Old Horsemeat had always warned about had fully taken place. Gummitch was a kitten no longer but an almost burly tom. In him it took the psychological form not of sullenness or surliness but an extreme dignity. He seemed at times rather like an old pirate brooding on treasures he would never live to dig up, shores of adventure he would never reach. And sometimes when you looked into his yellow eyes you felt that he had in him all the materials for the book *Slit Eyes Look at Life*—three or four volumes at least—although he would never write it. And that was natural when you come to think of it, for as Gummitch knew very well, bitterly well indeed, his fate was to be the only kitten in the world that did not grow up to be a man.

Try and Change the Past

No, I WOULDN'T advise anyone to try to change the past, at least not his *personal* past, although changing the *general* past is my business, my fighting business. You see, I'm a Snake in the Change War. Don't back off—human beings, even Resurrected ones engaged in time-fighting, aren't built for outward wriggling and their poison is mostly psychological. "Snake" is slang for the soldiers on our side, like Hun or Reb or Ghibbelin. In the Change War we're trying to alter the past —and it's tricky, brutal work, believe me—at points all over the cosmos, anywhere and anywhen, so that history will be warped to make our side defeat the Spiders. But that's a much bigger story, the biggest in fact, and I'll leave it occupying several planets of microfilm and two asteroids of coded molecules in the files of the High Command.

Change one event in the past and you get a brand new future? Erase the conquests of Alexander by nudging a Neolithic pebble? Extirpate America by pulling up a shoot of Sumerian grain? Brother, that isn't the way it works at all! The space-time continuum's built of stubborn stuff and change is anything but a chain-reaction. Change the past and you start a wave of changes moving futurewards, but it damps out mighty fast. Haven't you ever heard of temporal reluctance, or of the Law of Conservation of Reality?

Here's a little story that will illustrate my point: This guy was fresh recruited, the Resurrection sweat still wet in his armpits, when he got the idea he'd use the time-traveling power to go back and make a couple of little changes in his past, so that his life would take a happier course and maybe, he thought, he wouldn't have to die and get mixed up with Snakes and Spiders at all. It was as if a new-enlisted feuding hillbilly soldier should light out with the high-power rifle they issued him to go back to his mountains and pick off his pet enemies.

Normally it couldn't ever have happened. Normally, to avoid just this sort of thing, he'd have been shipped straight off to some place a few thousand or million years distant from his point of enlistment and maybe a few light-years, too. But there was a local crisis in the Change War and a lot of routine operations got held up and one new recruit was simply forgotten.

Normally, too, he'd never have been left alone a moment in the Dispatching Room, never even have glimpsed the place except to be rushed through it on arrival and reshipment. But, as I say, there happened to be a crisis, the Snakes were shorthanded, and several soldiers were careless. Afterwards two N.C.'s were busted because of what happened and a First Looey not only lost his commission but was transferred outside the galaxy and the era. But during the crisis this recruit I'm telling you about had the opportunity and more to fool around with forbidden things and try out his schemes.

He also had all the details on the last part of his life back in the real world, on his death and its consequences, to mull over and be tempted to change. This wasn't anybody's carelessness. The Snakes give every candidate that information as part of the recruiting pitch. They spot a death coming and the Resurrection Men go back and recruit the person from a point a few minutes or at most a few hours earlier. They explain in uncomfortable detail what's going to happen and wouldn't he rather take the oath and put on scales? I never heard of anybody turning down that offer. Then they lift him from his lifeline in the form of a Doubleganger and from then on, brother, he's a Snake.

So this guy had a clearer picture of his death than of the day he bought his first car, and a masterpiece of morbid irony it was. He was living in a classy penthouse that had belonged to a crazy uncle of his —it even had a midget astronomical observatory, unused for years—

but he was stony broke, up to the top hair in debt and due to be dis-
possessed next day. He'd never had a real job, always lived off his
rich relatives and his wife's, but now he was getting a little too mature for his stern dedication to a life of sponging to be cute. His
charming personality, which had been his only asset, was deader
from overuse and abuse than he himself would be in a few hours.
His crazy uncle would not have anything to do with him any more.
His wife was responsible for a lot of the wear and tear on his social-
butterfly wings; she had hated him for years, had screamed at him
morning to night the way you can only get away with in a penthouse,
and was going batty herself. He'd been playing around with another
woman, who'd just given him the gate, though he knew his wife would
never believe that and would only add a scornful note to her screaming if she did.

It was a lousy evening, smack in the middle of an August heat
wave. The Giants were playing a night game with Brooklyn. Two
long-run musicals had closed. Wheat had hit a new high. There was a
brush fire in California and a war scare in Iran. And tonight a meteor
shower was due, according to an astronomical bulletin that had arrived in the morning mail addressed to his uncle—he generally
dumped such stuff in the fireplace unopened, but today he had looked
at it because he had nothing else to do, either more useful or more
interesting.

The phone rang. It was a lawyer. His crazy uncle was dead and in
the will there wasn't a word about an Asteroid Search Foundation.
Every penny of the fortune went to the no-good nephew.

This same character finally hung up the phone, fighting off a tend-
ency for his heart to spring giddily out of his chest and through the
ceiling. Just then his wife came screeching out of the bedroom. She'd
received a cute, commiserating, tell-all note from the other woman;
she had a gun and announced that she was going to finish him off.

The sweltering atmosphere provided a good background for sardonic catastrophe. The French doors to the roof were open behind
him but the air that drifted through was muggy as death. Unnoticed,
a couple of meteors streaked faintly across the night sky.

Figuring it would sure dissuade her, he told her about the inheritance. She screamed that he'd just use the money to buy more other
women—not an unreasonable prediction—and pulled the trigger.

The danger was minimal. She was at the other end of a big living room, her hand wasn't just shaking, she was waving the nickle-plated revolver as if it were a fan.

The bullet took him right between the eyes. He flopped down, deader than his hopes were before he got the phone call. He saw it happen because as a clincher the Resurrection Men brought him forward as a Doubleganger to witness it invisibly—also standard Snake procedure and not productive of time-complications, incidentally, since Doublegangers don't imprint on reality unless they want to.

They stuck around a bit. His wife looked at the body for a couple of seconds, went to her bedroom, blonded her graying hair by dousing it with two bottles of undiluted peroxide, put on a tarnished gold-lamé evening gown and a bucket of make-up, went back to the living room, sat down at the piano, played "Country Gardens" and then shot herself, too.

So that was the little skit, the little double blackout, he had to mull over outside the empty and unguarded Dispatching Room, quite forgotten by its twice-depleted skeleton crew while every available Snake in the sector was helping deal with the local crisis, which centered around the planet Alpha Centauri Four, two million years minus.

Naturally it didn't take him long to figure out that if he went back and gimmicked things so that the first blackout didn't occur, but the second still did, he would be sitting pretty back in the real world and able to devote his inheritance to fulfilling his wife's prediction and other pastimes. He didn't know much about Doublegangers yet and had it figured out that if he didn't die in the real world he'd have no trouble resuming his existence there—maybe it'd even happen automatically.

So this Snake—name kind of fits him, doesn't it?—crossed his fingers and slipped into the Dispatching Room. Dispatching is so simple a child could learn it in five minutes from studying the board. He went back to a point a couple of hours before the tragedy, carefully avoiding the spot where the Resurrection Men had lifted him from his lifeline. He found the revolver in a dresser drawer, unloaded it, checked to make sure there weren't any more cartridges around, and then went ahead a couple of hours, arriving just in time to see himself get the slug between the eyes same as before.

As soon as he got over his disappointment, he realized he'd learned something about Doublegangers he should have known all along, if his mind had been clicking. The bullets he'd lifted were Doublegangers, too; they had disappeared from the real world only at the point in space-time where he'd lifted them, and they had continued to exist, as real as ever, in the earlier and later sections of their lifelines—with the result that the gun was loaded again by the time his wife had grabbed it up.

So this time he set the board so he'd arrive just a few minutes before the tragedy. He lifted the gun, bullets and all, and waited around to make sure it stayed lifted. He figured—rightly—that if he left this space-time sector the gun would reappear in the dresser drawer, and he didn't want his wife getting hold of any gun, even one with a broken lifeline. Afterwards—after his own death was averted, that is—he figured he'd put the gun back in his wife's hand.

Two things reassured him a lot, although he'd been expecting the one and hoping for the other: his wife didn't notice his presence as a Doubleganger and when she went to grab the gun she acted as if it weren't gone and held her right hand as if there were a gun in it. If he'd studied philosophy, he'd have realized he was witnessing a proof of Leibnitz's Theory of Pre-established Harmony: that neither atoms nor human beings really affect each other, they just look as if they did.

But anyway he had no time for theories. Still holding the gun, he drifted out into the living room to get a box seat right next to Himself for the big act. Himself didn't notice him any more than his wife had.

His wife came out and spoke her piece same as ever. Himself cringed as if she still had the gun and started to babble about the inheritance, his wife sneered and made as if she were shooting Himself.

Sure enough, there was no shot this time, *and* no mysteriously appearing bullet hole—which was something he'd been afraid of. Himself just stood there dully while his wife made as if she were looking down at a dead body and went back to her bedroom.

He was pretty pleased: this time he actually *had* changed the past. Then Himself slowly glanced around at him, still with that dull look, and slowly came toward him. He was more pleased than ever because he figured now they'd melt together into one man and one lifeline again, and he'd be able to hurry out somewhere and establish an alibi, just to be on the safe side, while his wife suicided.

But it didn't quite happen that way. Himself's look changed from dull to desperate, he came up close . . . and suddenly grabbed the gun and quick as a wink put a thumb to the trigger and shot himself between the eyes. And flopped, same as ever.

Right there he was starting to learn a little—and it was an unpleasant shivery sort of learning—about the Law of Conservation of Reality. The four-dimensional space-time universe doesn't *like* to be changed, any more than it likes to lose or gain energy or matter. If it has to be changed, it'll adjust itself just enough to accept that change and no more. The Conservation of Reality is a sort of Law of Least Action, too. It doesn't matter how improbable the events involved in the adjustment are, just so long as they're possible at all and can be used to patch the established pattern. His death, at this point, was part of the established pattern. If he lived on instead of dying, billions of other compensatory changes would have to be made, covering many years, perhaps centuries, before the old pattern could be re-established, the snarled lifelines woven back into it—and the universe finally go on the same as if his wife had shot him on schedule.

This way the pattern was hardly effected at all. There were powder burns on his forehead that weren't there before, but there weren't any witnesses to the shooting in the first place, so the presence or absence of powder burns didn't matter. The gun was lying on the floor instead of being in his wife's hands, but he had the feeling that when the time came for her to die, she'd wake enough from the Pre-established Harmony trance to find it, just as Himself did.

So he'd learned a little about the Conservation of Reality. He also had learned a little about his own character, especially from Himself's last look and act. He'd got a hint that he had been trying to destroy himself for years by the way he'd lived, so that inherited fortune or accidental success couldn't save him, and if his wife hadn't shot him he'd have done it himself in any case. He'd got a hint that Himself hadn't merely been acting as an agent for a self-correcting universe when he grabbed the gun, he'd been acting on his own account, too —the universe, you know, operates by getting people to co-operate.

But although these ideas occurred to him, he didn't dwell on them, for he figured he'd had a partial success the second time. If he kept the gun away from Himself, if he dominated Himself, as it were, the melting-together would take place and everything else go forward as planned.

He had the dim realization that the universe, like a huge sleepy animal, knew what he was trying to do and was trying to thwart him. This feeling of opposition made him determined to outmaneuver the universe—not the first guy to yield to such a temptation, of course.

And up to a point his tactics worked. The third time he gimmicked the past, everything started to happen just as it did the second time. Himself dragged miserably over to him, looking for the gun, but he had it tucked away and was prepared to hold onto it. Encouragingly, Himself didn't grapple, the look of desperation changed to one of utter hopelessness, and Himself turned away from him and very slowly walked to the French doors and stood looking out into the sweating night. He figured Himself was just getting used to the idea of not dying. There wasn't a breath of air. A couple of meteors streaked across the sky. Then, mixed with the upseeping night sounds of the city, there was a low whirring whistle.

Himself shook a bit, as if he'd had a sudden chill. Then Himself turned around and slumped to the floor in one movement. Between his eyes was a black hole.

Then and there this Snake I'm telling you about decided never again to try and change the past, at least not his personal past. He'd had it, and he'd also acquired a healthy respect for a High Command able to change the past, albeit with difficulty. He scooted back to the Dispatching Room, where a sleepy and surprised Snake gave him a terrific chewing out and confined him to quarters. The chewing-out didn't bother him too much—he'd acquired a certain fatalism about things. A person's got to learn to accept reality as it is, you know—just as you'd best not be surprised at the way I disappear in a moment or two—I'm a Snake too, remember.

If a statistician is looking for an example of a highly improbable event, he can hardly pick a more vivid one than the chance of a man being hit by a meteorite. And, if he adds the condition that the meteorite hit him between the eyes so as to counterfeit the wound made by a 32-caliber bullet, the improbability becomes astronomical cubed. So how's a person going to outmaneuver a universe that finds it easier to drill a man through the head that way rather than postpone the date of his death?

A Deskful of Girls

YES, I SAID ghostgirls, sexy ones. Personally I never in my life saw any ghosts except the sexy kind, though I saw enough of those I'll tell you, but only for one evening, in the dark of course, with the assistance of an eminent (I should also say notorious) psychologist. It was an interesting experience, to put it mildly, and it introduced me to an unknown field of psycho-physiology, but under no circumstances would I want to repeat it.

But ghosts are supposed to be frightening? Well, who ever said that sex isn't? It is to the neophyte, female or male, and don't let any of the latter try to kid you. For one thing, sex opens up the unconscious mind, which isn't exactly a picnic area. Sex is a force and rite that is basic, primal; and the caveman or cavewoman in each of us is a truth bigger than the jokes and cartoons about it. Sex was behind the witchcraft religion, the sabbats were sexual orgies. The witch was a sexual creature. So is the ghost.

After all, what is a ghost, according to all traditional views, but the shell of a human being—an animated skin? And the skin is all sex—it's touch, the boundary, the mask of flesh.

I got that notion about skin from my eminent-notorious psychologist, Dr. Emil Slyker, the first and the last evening I met him, at the Countersign Club, though he wasn't talking about ghosts to begin with. He was pretty drunk and drawing signs in the puddle spilled from his triple martini.

He grinned at me and said, "Look here, What's-Your-Name—oh yes, Carr Mackay, Mister *Justine* himself. Well, look here, Carr, I got a deskful of girls at my office in this building and they're needing attention. Let's shoot up and have a look."

Right away my hopelessly naive imagination flashed me a vivid picture of a desk swarming inside with girls about five or six inches high. They weren't dressed—my imagination never dresses girls except for special effects after long thought—but these looked as if they had been modeled from the drawings of Heinrich Kley or Mahlon Blaine. Literal vest-pocket Venuses, saucy and active. Right now they were attempting a mass escape from the desk, using a couple of nail files for saws, and they'd already cut some trap doors between the drawers so they could circulate around. One group was improvising a blowtorch from an atomizer and lighter fluid. Another was trying to turn a key from the inside, using tweezers for a wrench. And they were tearing down and defacing small signs, big to them, which read YOU BELONG TO DR. EMIL SLYKER.

My mind, which looks down at my imagination and refuses to associate with it, was studying Dr. Slyker and also making sure that I behaved outwardly like a worshipful fan, a would-be Devil's apprentice. This approach, helped by the alcohol, seemed to be relaxing him into the frame of mind I wanted him to have—one of boastful condescension. Slyker was a plump gut of a man with a perpetually sucking mouth, in his early fifties, fair-complexioned, blond, balding, with the power-lines around his eyes and at the corners of the nostrils. Over it all he wore the ready-for-photographers mask that is a sure sign its wearer is on the Big Time. Eyes weak, as shown by the dark glasses, but forever peering for someone to strip or cow. His hearing bad too, for that matter, as he didn't catch the barman approaching and started a little when he saw the white rag reaching out toward the spill from his drink. Emil Slyker, "doctor" courtesy of some European universities and a crust like blued steel, movie columnist, pumper of the last ounce of prestige out of that ashcan word "psychologist," psychic researcher several mysterious rumored jumps ahead of Wilhelm Reich with his orgone and Rhine with his ESP, psychological consultant to starlets blazing into stars and other ladies in the bucks, and a particularly expert disher-out of that goulash of psychoanalysis, mysticism and magic that is the *chef-d'oeuvre* of our era. *And,* I was assuming, a particularly successful blackmailer. A stinker to be taken very seriously.

My real purpose in contacting Slyker, of which I hoped he hadn't got an inkling yet, was to offer him enough money to sink a small luxury liner in exchange for a sheaf of documents he was using to blackmail Evelyn Cordew, current pick-of-the-pantheon among our sex goddesses. I was working for another film star, Jeff Crain, Evelyn's ex-husband, but not "ex" when it came to the protective urge. Jeff said that Slyker refused to bite on the direct approach, that he was so paranoid in his suspiciousness as to be psychotic, and that I would have to make friends with him first. Friends with a paranoid!

So in pursuit of this doubtful and dangerous distinction, there I was at the Countersign Club, nodding respectfully happy acquiescence to the Master's suggestion and asking tentatively, "Girls needing attention?"

He gave me his whoremaster, keeper-of-the-keys grin and said, "Sure, women need attention whatever form they're in. They're like pearls in a vault, they grow dull and fade unless they have regular contact with warm human flesh. Drink up."

He gulped half of what was left of his martini—the puddle had been blotted up meantime and the black surface reburnished—and we made off without any fuss over checks or tabs; I had expected him to stick me with the former at least, but evidently I wasn't enough of an acolyte yet to be granted that honor.

It fitted that I had caught up with Emil Slyker at the Countersign Club. It is to a key club what the latter is to a top-crust bar. Strictly Big Time, set up to provide those in it with luxury, privacy and security. Especially security: I had heard that the Countersign Club bodyguarded even their sober patrons home late of an evening with or without their pickups, but I hadn't believed it until this well-dressed and doubtless well-heeled silent husky rode the elevator up the dead midnight office building with us and only turned back at Dr. Slyker's door. Of course I couldn't have got into the Countersign Club on my own—Jeff had provided me with my entree: an illustrated edition of the Marquis de Sade's *Justine,* its margins annotated by a world-famous recently-deceased psychoanalyst. I had sent it in to Slyker with a note full of flowery expression of "my admiration for your work in the psycho-physiology of sex."

The door to Slyker's office was something. No glass, just a dark expanse—teak or ironwood, I guessed—with EMIL SLYKER, CONSULTING PSYCHOLOGIST burnt into it. No Yale lock, but a large keyhole with a curious silver valve that the key pressed aside. Slyker showed me the key with a deprecating smile; the gleaming castellations of its web were the most complicated I'd ever seen, its stem depicted Pasiphaë and the bull. He certainly was willing to pay for atmosphere.

There were three sounds: first the soft grating of the turning key, then the solid snap of the bolts retracting, then a faint creak from the hinges.

Open, the door showed itself four inches thick, more like that of a safe or vault, with a whole cluster of bolts that the key controlled. Just before it closed, something very odd happened: a filmy plastic sheet whipped across the bolts from the outer edge of the doorway and conformed itself to them so perfectly that I suspected static electrical attraction of some sort. Once in place it barely clouded the silvery surface of the bolts and would have taken a close look to spot. It didn't interfere in any way with the door closing or the bolts snapping back into their channels.

The Doctor sensed or took for granted my interest in the door and explained over his shoulder in the dark, "My Siegfried Line. More than one ambitious crook or inspired murderer has tried to smash or think his or her way through that door. They've had no luck. They can't. At this moment there is literally no one in the world who could come through that door without using explosives—and they'd have to be well placed. Cozy."

I privately disagreed with the last remark. Not to make a thing of it, I would have preferred to feel in a bit closer touch with the silent corridors outside, even though they held nothing but the ghosts of unhappy stenographers and neurotic dames my imagination had raised on the way up.

"Is the plastic film part of an alarm system?" I asked. The Doctor didn't answer. His back was to me. I remembered that he'd shown himself a shade deaf. But I didn't get a chance to repeat my question for just then some indirect lighting came on, although Slyker wasn't near any switch ("Our talk triggers it," he said) and the office absorbed me.

Naturally the desk was the first thing I looked for, though I felt foolish doing it. It was a big deep job with a dark soft gleam that might have been that of fine-grained wood or metal. The drawers were file size, not the shallow ones my imagination had played with, and there were three tiers of them to the right of the kneehole—space enough for a couple of life-size girls if they were doubled up according to one of the formulas for the hidden operator of Maelzel's chess-playing automaton. My imagination, which never learns, listened hard for the patter of tiny bare feet and the clatter of little tools. There wasn't even the scurry of mice, which would have done something to my nerves, I'm sure.

The office was an L with the door at the end of this leg. The walls I could see were mostly lined with books, though a few line drawings had been hung—my imagination had been right about Heinrich Kley, though I didn't recognize these pen-and-ink originals, and there were some Fuselis you won't ever see reproduced in books handled over the counter.

The desk was in the corner of the L with the components of a hi fi spaced along the bookshelves this side of it. All I could see yet of the other leg of the L was a big surrealist armchair facing the desk but separated from it by a wide low bare table. I took a dislike to that armchair on first sight, though it looked extremely comfortable. Slyker had reached the desk now and had one hand on it as he turned back toward me, and I got the impression that the armchair had changed shape since I had entered the office—that it had been more like a couch to start with, although now the back was almost straight.

But the Doctor's left thumb indicated I was to sit in it and I couldn't see another chair in the place except the padded button on which he was now settling himself—one of those stenographer deals with a boxing-glove back placed to catch you low in the spine like the hand of a knowledgeable masseur. In the other leg of the L, besides the armchair, were more books, a heavy concertina blind sealing off the window, two narrow doors that I supposed were those of a closet and a lavatory, and what looked like a slightly scaled-down and windowless telephone booth until I guessed it must be an orgone box of the sort Reich had invented to restore the libido when the patient occupies it. I quickly settled myself in the chair, not to be gingerly about it. It was rather incredibly comfortable, almost as if it had adjusted its dimensions a bit at the last instant to conform to mine. The back was narrow at the base but widened and then curled in and over to almost a canopy around my head and shoulders. The seat too widened a lot toward the front, where the stubby legs were far apart. The bulky arms sprang unsupported from the back and took my own just right, though curving inwards with the barest suggestion of a hug. The leather or unfamiliar plastic was as firm and cool as young flesh and its texture as mat under my fingertips.

"An historic chair," the Doctor observed, "designed and built for me by von Helmholtz of the Bauhaus. It has been occupied by all my best mediums during their so-called trance states. It was in that chair that I established to my entire satisfaction the real existence of ectoplasm—that elaboration of the mucous membrane and occasionally the entire epidermis that is distantly analogous to the birth envelope and is the fact behind the persistent legends of the snake-shedding of filmy live skins by human beings, and which the spiritualist quacks are forever trying to fake with their fluorescent cheesecloth and doctored negatives. Orgone, the primal sexual energy?—Reich makes a persuasive case, still . . . But ectoplasm?— yes! Angna went into trance sitting just where you are, her entire body dusted with a special powder, the tracks and distant smudges of which later revealed the ectoplasm's movements and origin—chiefly in the genital area. The test was conclusive and led to further researches, very interesting and quite revolutionary, none of which I have published; my professional colleagues froth at the mouth, elaborating an opposite sort of foam, whenever I mix the psychic with psychoanalysis—they seem to forget that hypnotism gave Freud his start and that for a time the man was keen on cocaine. Yes indeed, an historic chair."

I naturally looked down at it and for a moment I thought I had vanished, because I couldn't see my legs. Then I realized that the upholstery had changed to a dark gray exactly matching my suit except for the ends of the arms, which merged by fine gradations into a sallow hue which blotted out my hands.

"I should have warned you that it's now upholstered in chameleon plastic," Slyker said with a grin. "It changes color to suit the sitter. The fabric was supplied me over a year ago by Henri Artois, the

French dilettante chemist. So the chair has been many shades: dead black when Mrs. Fairlee—you recall the case?—came to tell me she had just put on mourning and then shot her bandleader husband, a charming Florida tan during the later experiments with Angna. It helps my patients forget themselves when they're free-associating and it amuses some people."

I wasn't one of them, but I managed a smile I hoped wasn't too sour. I told myself to stick to business—Evelyn Cordew's and Jeff Crain's business. I must forget the chair and other incidentals, and concentrate on Dr. Emil Slyker and what he was saying—for I have by no means given all of his remarks, only the more important asides. He had turned out to be the sort of conversationalist who will talk for two hours solid, then when you have barely started your reply, give you a hurt look and say, "Excuse me, but if I can get a word in edge-wise—" and talk for two hours more. The liquor may have been helping, but I doubt it. When we had left the Countersign Club he had started to tell me the stories of three of his female clients—a surgeon's wife, an aging star scared by a comeback opportunity, and a college girl in trouble—and the presence of the bodyguard hadn't made him hold back on gory details.

Now, sitting at his desk and playing with the catch of a file drawer as if wondering whether to open it, he had got to the point where the surgeon's wife had arrived at the operating theater early one morning to publish her infidelities, the star had stabbed her press agent with the wardrobe mistress' scissors, and the college girl had fallen in love with her abortionist. He had the conversation-hogger's trick of keeping a half dozen topics in the air at once and weaving back and forth between them without finishing any.

And of course he was a male tantalizer. Now he whipped open the file drawer and scooped out some folders and then held them against his belly and watched me as if to ask himself, "Should I?"

After a maximum pause to build suspense he decided he should, and so I began to hear the story of Dr. Emil Slyker's girls, not the first three, of course—they had to stay frozen at their climaxes unless their folders turned up—but others.

I wouldn't be telling the truth if I didn't admit it was a let-down. Here I was expecting I don't know what from his desk and all I got was the usual glimpses into childhood's garden of father-fixation and sibling rivalry and the bed-changing *Sturm und Drang* of later adolescence. The folders seemed to hold nothing but conventional medico-psychiatric case histories, along with physical measurements and other details of appearance, unusually penetrating *précis* of each client's financial resources, occasional notes on possible psychic gifts and other extrasensory talents, and maybe some candid snapshots, judging from the way he'd sometimes pause to study appreciatively and then raise his eyebrows at me with a smile.

Yet after a while I couldn't help starting to be impressed, if only by the sheer numbers. Here was this stream, this freshet, this flood of females, young and not-so-young that all thinking of themselves as girls and wearing the girl's suede mask even if they didn't still have the girl's natural face, all converging on Dr. Slyker's office with money stolen from their parents or highjacked from their married lovers, or paid when they signed the six-year contract with semiannual options, or held out on their syndicate boyfriends, or received in a lump sum in lieu of alimony, or banked for dreary years every fortnight from paychecks and then withdrawn in one grand gesture, or thrown at them by their husbands that morning like so much confetti, or, so help me, advanced them on their half-written novels. Yes, there was something very impressive about this pink stream of womankind rippling with the silver and green of cash conveyed infallibly, as if all the corridors and streets outside were concrete-walled spillways, to Dr. Slyker's office, but not to work any dynamos there except financial ones, instead to be worked over by a one-man dynamo and go foaming madly or trickling depletedly away or else stagnate excitingly for months, their souls like black swamp water gleaming with mysterious lights.

Slyker stopped short with a harsh little laugh. "We ought to have music with this, don't you think?" he said. "I believe I've got the *Nutcracker Suite* on the spindle," and he touched one of an unobtrusive bank of buttons on his desk.

They came without the whisper of a turntable or the faintest preliminary susurrus of tape, those first evocative, rich, sensual, yet eery chords, but they weren't the opening of any section of the *Nutcracker* I knew—and yet, damn it, they sounded as if they should be. And then they were cut off as if the tape had been snipped and I looked at Slyker and he was white and one of his hands was just coming back

from the bank of buttons and the other was clutching the file folders as if they might somehow get away from him and both hands
were shaking and I felt a shiver crawling down my own neck.

"Excuse me, Carr," he said slowly, breathing heavily, "but that's
high-voltage music, psychically very dangerous, that I use only for
special purposes. It *is* part of the *Nutcracker,* incidentally—the 'Ghostgirls Pavan' which Tchaikovsky suppressed completely under orders
from Madam Sesostris, the Saint Petersburg clairvoyant. It was tape-
recorded for me by . . . no, I don't know you quite well enough to
tell you that. However, we will shift from tape to disk and listen to
the known sections of the suite, played by the same artists."

I don't know how much this recording or the circumstances added
to it, but I have never heard the "Danse Arabe" or the "Waltz of
the Flowers" or the "Dance of the Flutes" so voluptuous and ex-
quisitely menacing—those tinkling, superficially sugar-frosted bits of
music that class after class of little-girl ballerinas have minced and
teetered to *ad nauseam,* but underneath the glittering somber fancies
of a thorough-going eroticist. As Slyker, guessing my thoughts, ex-
pressed it: "Tchaikovsky shows off each instrument—the flute, the
throatier woodwinds, the silver chimes, the harp bubbling gold—as if
he were dressing beautiful women in jewels and feathers and furs
solely to arouse desire and envy in other men."

For of course we only listened to the music as background for
Dr. Slyker's zigzagging, fragmentary, cream-skimming reminiscences.
The stream of girls flowed on in their smart suits and flowered dresses
and bouffant blouses and toreador pants, their improbable loves and
unsuspected hates and incredible ambitions, the men who gave
them money, the men who gave them love, the men who took both,
the paralyzing trivial fears behind their wisely chic or corn-fed fresh
façades, their ravishing and infuriating mannerisms, the trick of eye
or lip or hair or wrist-curve or bosom-angle that was the focus of sex
in each.

For Slyker could bring his girls to life very vividly, I had to grant
that, as if he had more to jog his memory than case histories and
notes and even photographs, as if he had the essence of each girl
stoppered up in a little bottle, like perfume, and was opening them
one by one to give me a whiff. Gradually I became certain that there
were more than papers and pictures in the folders, though this revela-

tion, like the earlier one about the desk, at first involved a let-down. Why should I get excited if Dr. Slyker filed away mementos of his clients?—even if they were keepsakes of love: lace handkerchiefs and filmy scarves, faded flowers, ribbons and bows, 20-denier stockings, long locks of hair, gay little pins and combs, swatches of material that might have been torn from dresses, snippets of silk delicate as ghost dandelions—what difference did it make to me if he treasured this junk or it fed his sense of power or was part of his blackmail? Yet it did make a difference to me, for like the music, like the little fearful starts he'd kept giving ever since the business of the "Ghost-girls Pavan," it helped to make everything very real, as if in some more-than-ordinary sense he did have a deskful of girls. For now as he opened or closed the folders there'd often be a puff of powder, a pale little cloud as from a jogged compact, and the pieces of silk gave the impression of being larger than they could be, like a magician's colored handkerchiefs, only most of them were flesh-colored, and I began to get glimpses of what looked like X-ray photographs and artist's transparencies, maybe lifesize but cunningly folded, and other slack pale things that made me think of the ultra-fine rubber masks some aging actresses are rumored to wear, and all sorts of strange little flashes and glimmers of I don't know what, except there was that aura of femininity and I found myself remembering what he'd said about fluorescent cheesecloth and I did seem to get whiffs of very individual perfume with each new folder.

He had two file drawers open now, and I could just make out the word burnt into their fronts. The word certainly looked like PRESENT, and there were two of the closed file drawers labeled what looked like PAST and FUTURE. I didn't know what sort of hocus-pocus was supposed to be furthered by those words, but along with Slyker's darting, lingering monologue they did give me the feeling that I was afloat in a river of girls from all times and places, and the illusion that there somehow was a girl in each folder became so strong that I almost wanted to say, "Come on, Emil, trot 'em out, let me look at 'em."

He must have known exactly what feelings he was building up in me, for now he stopped in the middle of a saga of a starlet married to a Negro baseball player and looked at me with his eyes open a bit too wide and said, "All right, Carr, let's quit fooling around. Down at the Countersign I told you I had a deskful of girls and I wasn't kidding—although the truth behind that assertion would get me certified by all the little headshrinkers and Viennese windbags except it would scare the pants off them first. I mentioned ectoplasm earlier, and the proof of its reality. It's exuded by most properly stimulated women in deep trance, but it's not just some dimly fluorescent froth swirling around in a dark séance chamber. It takes the form of an envelope or limp balloon, closed toward the top but open toward the bottom, weighing less than a silk stocking but duplicating the person exactly down to features and hair, following the master-plan of the body's surface buried in the genetic material of the cells. It is a real shed skin but also dimly alive, a gossamer mannequin. A breath can crumple it, a breeze can whisk it away, but under some circumstances it becomes startlingly stable and resilient, a real apparition. It's invisible and almost impalpable by day, but by night, when your eyes are properly accommodated, you can just manage to see it. Despite its fragility it's almost indestructible, except by fire, and potentially immortal. Whether generated in sleep or under hypnosis, in spontaneous or induced trance, it remains connected to the source by a thin strand I call the 'umbilicus' and it returns to the source and is absorbed back into the individual again as the trance fades. But sometimes it becomes detached and then it lingers around as a shell, still dimly alive and occasionally glimpsed, forming the very real basis for the stories of hauntings we have from all centuries and cultures—in fact, I call such shells 'ghosts.' A strong emotional shock generally accounts for a ghost becoming detached from its owner, but it can also be detached artificially. Such a ghost is remarkably docile to one who understands how to handle and cherish it—for instance, it can be folded into an incredibly small compass and tucked away in an envelope, though by daylight you wouldn't notice anything in such an envelope if you looked inside. 'Detached artificially' I said, and that's what I do here in this office, and you know what I use to do it with, Carr?" He snatched up something long and daggerlike and gleaming and held it tight in his plump hand so that it pointed at the ceiling. "Silver shears, Carr, silver for the same reason you use a silver bullet to kill a werewolf, though those words would set the little headshrinkers howling. But would they be howling from outraged scientific attitude, Carr, or from professional jealousy or simply from fear? Just the same as it's unclear why they'd be howling, only certain they would be howling, if I told them that in every fourth or fifth folder in these files I have one or more ghostgirls."

He didn't need to mention fear—I was scared enough myself now, what with him spouting this ghost-guff, this spiritualism blather put far more precisely than any spiritualist would dare, this obviously firmly held and elaborately rationalized delusion, this perfect symbolization of a truly insane desire for power over women—filing them away in envelopes!—and then when he got bug-eyed and brandished those foot-long stiletto-shears . . . Jeff Crain had warned me Slyker was "nuts—brilliant, but completely nuts and definitely dangerous," and I hadn't believed it, hadn't really visualized myself frozen on the medium's throne, locked in ("no one without explosives") with the madman himself. It cost me a lot of effort to keep on the acolyte's mask and simper adoringly at the Master.

My attitude still seemed to be fooling him, though he was studying me in a funny way, for he went on, "All right, Carr, I'll show you the girls, or at least one, though we'll have to put out all the lights after a bit—that's why I keep the window shuttered so tightly—and wait for our eyes to accommodate. But which one should it be?—we have a large field of choice. I think since it's your first and probably your last, it should be someone out of the ordinary, don't you think, someone who's just a little bit special? Wait a second—I know." And his hand shot under the desk where it must have touched a hidden button, for a shallow drawer shot out from a place where there didn't seem to be room for one. He took from it a single fat file folder that had been stored flat and laid it on his knees.

Then he began to talk again in his reminiscing voice and damn if it wasn't so cool and knowing that it started to pull me back toward the river of girls and set me thinking that this man wasn't really crazy, only extremely eccentric, maybe the eccentricity of genius, maybe he actually had hit on a hitherto unknown phenomenon depending on the more obscure properties of mind and matter, describing it to me in whimsically florid jargon, maybe he really had discovered something in one of the blind spots of modern science-and-psychology's picture of the universe.

"Stars, Carr. Female stars. Movie queens. Royal princesses of the gray world, the ghostly chiaroscuro. Shadow empresses. They're realer

than people, Carr, realer than the great actresses or casting-couch
champions they start as, for they're symbols, Carr, symbols of our
deepest longings and—yes—most hidden fears and secretest dreams.
Each decade has several who achieve this more-than-life and less-
than-life existence, but there's generally one who's the chief symbol,
the top ghost, the dream who lures men along toward fulfillment and
destruction. In the Twenties it was Garbo, Garbo the Free Soul—
that's my name for the symbol she became; her romantic mask her-
alded the Great Depression. In the late Thirties and early Forties
it was Bergman the Brave Liberal; her dewiness and Swedish-
Modern smile helped us accept World War Two. And now it's"—he
touched the bulky folder on his knees—"now it's Evelyn Cordew the
Good-Hearted Bait, the gal who accepts her troublesome sexiness
with a resigned shrug and a foolish little laugh, and what general
catastrophe she foreshadows we don't know yet. But here she is, and
in five ghost versions. Pleased, Carr?"

I was so completely taken by surprise that I couldn't say anything
for a moment. Either Slyker had guessed my real purpose in contacting him, or I was faced with a sizable coincidence. I wet my lips and
then just nodded.

Slyker studied me and finally grinned. "Ah," he said, "takes you
aback a bit, doesn't it? I perceive that in spite of your moderate
sophistication you are one of the millions of males who have wistfully contemplated desert-islanding with Delectable Evvie. A complex cultural phenomenon, Eva-Lynn Korduplewski. The child of a
coal miner, educated solely in backstreet movie houses—shaped by
dreams, you see, into a master dream, an empress dream-figure. A
hysteric, Carr, in fact the most classic example I have ever encountered, with unequaled mediumistic capacities and also with a hyper-
trophied and utterly ruthless ambition. Riddled by hypochondrias,
but with more real drive than a million other avid school-girls tangled
and trapped in the labyrinth of film ambitions. Dumb as they come,
no rational mind at all, but with ten times Einstein's intuition—intuition enough, at least, to realize that the symbol our sex-exploiting
culture craved was a girl who accepted like a happy martyr the incan-
descent sexuality men and Nature forced on her—and with the patience and malleability to let the feathersoft beating of the black-
and-white light in a cheap cinema shape her into that symbol. I

sometimes think of her as a girl in a cheap dress standing on the shoulder of a big throughway, her eyes almost blinded by the lights of an approaching bus. The bus stops and she climbs on, dragging a pet goat and breathlessly giggling explanations at the driver. The bus is Civilization.

"Everybody knows her life story, which has been put out in a surprisingly accurate form up to a point: her burlesque-line days, the embarrassingly faithful cartoon-series *Girl in a Fix* for which she posed, her bit parts, the amazingly timed success of the movies *Hydrogen Blonde* and *The Jean Harlow Saga,* her broken marriage to Jeff Crain—What was that, Carr? Oh, I thought you'd started to say something—and her hunger for the real stage and intellectual distinction and power. You can't imagine how hungry for brains and power that girl became *after* she hit the top.

"I've been part of the story of that hunger, Carr, and I pride myself that I've done more to satisfy it than all the culture-johnnies she's had on her payroll. Evelyn Cordew has learned a lot about herself right where you're sitting, and also threaded her way past two psychotic crack-ups. The trouble is that when her third loomed up she didn't come to me, she decided to put her trust in wheat germ and yogurt instead, so now she hates my guts—and perhaps her own, on that diet. She's made two attempts on my life, Carr, and had me trailed by gangsters . . . and by other individuals. She's talked about me to Jeff Crain, whom she still sees from time to time, and Jerry Smyslov and Nick De Grazia, telling them I've got a file of information on her burlesque days and a few of her later escapades, including some interesting photostats and the real dope on her income and her tax returns, and that I'm using it to blackmail her white. What she actually wants is her five ghosts back, and I can't give them to her because they might kill her. Yes, kill her, Carr." He flourished the shears for emphasis. "She claims that the ghosts I've taken from her have made her lose weight permanently—'look like a skeleton' are her words—and given her fits of mental blackout, a sort of psychic fading—whereas actually the ghosts have bled off from her a lot of malignant thoughts and destructive emotions, which could literally kill her (or someone!) if reabsorbed—they're drenched with death-wish. Still, I hear she actually does look a little haggard, a trifle faded, in her last film, in spite of all Hollywood's medico-cosmetic lore, so maybe she has a sort of case against me. I haven't seen the film, I suppose you have. What do you think, Carr?"

I knew I'd been overworking the hesitation and the silent flattery, so I whipped out quickly, "I'd say it was due to her anemia. It seems to me that the anemia is quite enough to account for her loss of weight and her tired look."

"Ah! You've slipped, Carr," he lashed back, pointing at me triumphantly, except that instead of the outstretched finger there were those ridiculous, horrible shears. "Her anemia is one of the things that's been kept top-secret, known only to a very few of her intimates. Even in all the half-humorous releases about her hypochondrias that's one disease that has never been mentioned. I suspected you were from her when I got your note at the Countersign Club—the handwriting squirmed with tension and secrecy—but the *Justine* amused me—that was a fairly smart dodge—and your sorcerer's apprentice act amused me too, and I happened to feel like talking. But I've been studying you all along, especially your reactions to certain test-remarks I dropped in from time to time, and now you've really slipped." His voice was loud and clear, but he was shaking and giggling at the same time and his eyes showed white all the way around the irises. He drew back the shears a little, but clenched his fingers more tightly around them in a dagger grip, as he said with a chuckle, "Our dear little Evvie has sent all types up against me, to bargain for her ghosts or try to scare or assassinate me, but this is the first time she's sent an idealistic fool. Carr, why didn't you have the sense not to meddle?"

"Look here, Dr. Slyker," I countered before he started answering for me, "it's true I have a special purpose in contacting you. I never denied it. But I don't know anything about ghosts or gangsters. I'm here on a simple, businesslike assignment from the same guy who lent me the *Justine* and who has no purpose whatever beyond protecting Evelyn Cordew. I'm representing Jeff Crain."

That was supposed to calm him. Well, he did stop shaking and his eyes stopped wandering, but only because they were going over me like twin searchlights, and the giggle went out of his voice.

"Jeff Crain! Evvie just wants to murder me, but that cinematic Hemingway, that hulking guardian of hers, that human Saint Bernard tonguing the dry crumbs of their marriage—he wants to set the

T-men on me, and the boys in blue and the boys in white too. Evvie's agents I mostly kid along, even the gangsters, but for Jeff's agents I have only one answer."

The silver shears pointed straight at my chest and I could see his muscles tighten like a fat tiger's. I got ready for a spring of my own at the first movement this madman made toward me.

But the move he made was back across the desk with his free hand. I decided it was a good time to be on my feet in any case, but just as I sent my own muscles their orders I was hugged around the waist and clutched by the throat and grabbed by the wrists and ankles. By something soft but firm.

I looked down. Padded, broad, crescent-shaped clamps had sprung out of hidden traps in my chair and now held me as comfortably but firmly as a gang of competent orderlies. Even my hands were held by wide, velvet-soft cuffs that had snapped out of the bulbous arms. They were all a nondescript gray but even as I looked they began to change color to match my suit or skin, whichever they happened to border.

I wasn't scared. I was merely frightened half to death.

"Surprised, Carr? You shouldn't be." Slyker was sitting back like an amiable schoolteacher and gently wagging the shears as if they were a ruler. "Streamlined unobtrusiveness and remote control are the essence of our times, especially in medical furniture. The buttons on my desk can do more than that. Hypos might slip out—hardly hygienic, but then germs are overrated. Or electrodes for shock. You see, restraints are necessary in my business. Deep mediumistic trance can occasionally produce convulsions as violent as those of electroshock, especially when a ghost is cut. And I sometimes administer electroshock too, like any garden-variety headshrinker. Also, to be suddenly and firmly grabbed is a profound stimulus to the unconscious and often elicits closely-guarded facts from difficult patients. So a means of making my patients hold still is absolutely necessary—something swift, sure, tasteful and preferably without warning. You'd be surprised, Carr, at the situations in which I've been forced to activate those restraints. This time I prodded you to see just how dangerous you were. Rather to my surprise you showed yourself ready to take physical action against me. So I pushed the button. Now we'll be able to deal comfortably with Jeff Crain's problem . . . and yours. But first I've a promise to keep to you. I said I would show you one of Evelyn Cordew's ghosts. It will take a little time and after a bit it will be necessary to turn out the lights."

"Dr. Slyker," I said as evenly as I could, "I—"

"Quiet! Activating a ghost for viewing involves certain risks. Silence is essential, though it will be necessary to use—very briefly— the suppressed Tchaikovsky music which I turned off so quickly earlier this evening." He busied himself with the hi fi for a few moments. "But partly because of that it will be necessary to put away all the other folders and the four ghosts of Evvie we aren't using, and lock the file drawers. Otherwise there might be complications."

I decided to try once more. "Before you go any further, Dr. Slyker," I began, "I would really like to explain—"

He didn't say another word, merely reached back across the desk again. My eyes caught something coming over my shoulder fast and the next instant it clapped down over my mouth and nose, not quite covering my eyes, but lapping up to them—something soft and dry and clinging and faintly crinkled feeling. I gasped and I could feel the gag sucking in, but not a bit of air came through it. That scared me seven-eighths of the rest of the way to oblivion, of course, and I froze. Then I tried a very cautious inhalation and a little air did seep through. It was wonderfully cool coming into the furnace of my lungs, that little suck of air—I felt I hadn't breathed for a week.

Slyker looked at me with a little smile. "I never say 'Quiet' twice, Carr. The foam plastic of that gag is another of Henri Artois' inventions. It consists of millions of tiny valves. As long as you breathe softly—very, very softly, Carr—they permit ample air to pass, but if you gasp or try to shout through it, they'll close up tight. A wonderfully soothing device. Compose yourself, Carr; your life depends on it."

I have never experienced such utter helplessness. I found that the slightest muscular tension, even crooking a finger, made my breathing irregular enough so that the valves started to close and I was in the fringes of suffocation. I could see and hear what was going on, but I dared not react, I hardly dared think. I had to pretend that most of my body wasn't there (the chameleon plastic helped!), only a pair of lungs working constantly but with infinite caution.

Slyker had just set the Cordew folder back in its drawer, without closing it, and started to gather up the other scattered folders, when he touched the desk again and the lights went out. I have mentioned that the place was completely sealed against light. The darkness was complete.

"Don't be alarmed, Carr," Slyker's voice came chuckling through it. "In fact, as I am sure you realize, you had better not be. I can tidy up just as handily—working by touch is one of my major skills, my sight and hearing being rather worse than appears—and even your eyes must be fully accommodated if you're to see anything at all. I repeat, don't be alarmed, Carr, least of all by ghosts."

I would never have expected it, but in spite of the spot I was in (which actually did seem to have its soothing effects), I still got a little kick—a very little one—out of thinking I was going to see some sort of secret vision of Evelyn Cordew, real in some sense or faked by a master faker. Yet at the same time, and I think beyond all my fear for myself, I felt a dispassionate disgust at the way Slyker reduced all human drives and desires to a lust for power, of which the chair imprisoning me, the "Siegfried Line" door, and the files of ghosts, real or imagined, were perfect symbols.

Among immediate worries, although I did a pretty good job of suppressing all of them, the one that nagged at me the most was that Slyker had admitted to me the inadequacy of his two major senses. I didn't think he would make that admission to someone who was going to live very long.

The black minutes dragged on. I heard from time to time the rustle of folders, but only one soft thud of a file drawer closing, so I knew he wasn't finished yet with the putting-away and locking-up job.

I concentrated the free corner of my mind—the tiny part I dared spare from breathing—on trying to hear something else, but I couldn't even catch the background noise of the city. I decided the office must be soundproofed as well as light-sealed. Not that it mattered, since I couldn't get a signal out anyway.

Then a noise did come—a solid snap that I'd heard just once before, but knew instantly. It was the sound of the bolts in the office door retracting. There was something funny about it that took me a moment to figure out: there had been no preliminary grating of the key.

For a moment too I thought Slyker had crept noiselessly to the door, but then I realized that the rustling of folders at the desk had kept up all the time.

And the rustling of folders continued. I guessed Slyker had not noticed the door. He hadn't been exaggerating about his bad hearing.

There was the faint creaking of the hinges, once, twice—as if the door were being opened and closed—then again the solid snap of the bolts. That puzzled me, for there should have been a big flash of light from the corridor—unless the lights were all out.

I couldn't hear any sound after that, except the continued rustling of the file folders, though I listened as hard as the job of breathing let me—and in a crazy kind of way the job of cautious breathing helped my hearing, because it made me hold absolutely still yet without daring to tense up. I knew that someone was in the office with us and that Slyker didn't know it. The black moments seemed to stretch out forever, as if an edge of eternity had got hooked into our time-stream.

All of a sudden there was a *swish,* like that of a sheet being whipped through the air very fast, and a grunt of surprise from Slyker that started toward a screech and then was cut off as sharp as if he'd been gagged nose-and-mouth like me. Then there came the scuff of feet and the squeal of the castors of a chair, the sound of a struggle, not of two people struggling, but of a man struggling against restraints of some sort, a frantic confined heaving and panting. I wondered if Slyker's little lump of chair had sprouted restraints like mine, but that hardly made sense.

Then abruptly there was the whistle of breath, as if his nostrils had been uncovered, but not his mouth. He was panting through his nose. I got a mental picture of Slyker tied to his chair some way and eying the darkness just as I was doing.

Finally out of the darkness came a voice I knew very well because I'd heard it often enough in movie houses and from Jeff Crain's tape-recorder. It had the old familiar caress mixed with the old familiar giggle, the naïveté and the knowingness, the warm sympathy and cool-headedness, the high-school charmer and the sybil. It was Evelyn Cordew's voice, all right.

"Oh for goodness sake stop threshing around, Emmy. It won't help you shake off that sheet and it makes you look so funny. Yes, I said 'look,' Emmy—you'd be surprised at how losing five ghosts improves your eyesight, like having veils taken away from in front of them; you get more sensitive all over.

"And don't try to appeal to me by pretending to suffocate. I tucked the sheet under your nose even if I did keep your mouth covered. Couldn't bear you talking now. The sheet's called wraparound plastic —I've got my chemical friend too, though he's not Parisian. It'll be next year's number-one packaging material, he tells me. Filmy, harder to see than cellophane, but very tough. An electronic plastic, no less, positive one side, negative the other. Just touch it to something and it wraps around, touches itself, and clings like anything. Like I just had to touch it to you. To make it unwrap fast you can just shoot some electrons into it from a handy static battery—my friend's advertising copy, Emmy—and it flattens out *whang*. Give it enough electrons and it's stronger than steel.

"We used another bit of it that last way, Emmy, to get through your door. Fitted it outside, so it'd wrap itself against the bolts when your door opened. Then just now, after blacking out the corridor, we pumped electrons into it and it flattened out, pushing back all the bolts. Excuse me, dear, but you know how you love to lecture about your valved plastics and all your other little restraints, so you mustn't mind me giving a little talk about mine. And boasting about my friends too. I've got some you don't know about, Emmy. Ever heard the name Smyslov, or the Arain? Some of them cut ghosts themselves and weren't pleased to hear about you, especially the past-future angle."

There was a protesting little squeal of castors, as if Slyker were trying to move his chair.

"Don't go away, Emmy. I'm sure you know why I'm here. Yes, dear, I'm taking them all back as of now. All five. And I don't care how much death-wish they got, because I've got some ideas for that. So now 'scuse me, Emmy, while I get ready to slip into my ghosts."

There wasn't any noise then except Emil Slyker's wheezy breathing and the occasional rustle of silk and the whir of a zipper, followed by soft feathery falls.

"There we are, Emmy, all clear. Next step, my five lost sisters. Why, your little old secret drawer is open—you didn't think I knew about that, Emmy, did you? Let's see now, I don't think we'll need music for this—they know my touch; it should make them stand up and shine."

She stopped talking. After a bit I got the barest hint of light over by the desk, very uncertain at first, like a star at the limit of vision, where it keeps winking back and forth from utter absence to the barest dim existence, or like a lonely lake lit only by starlight and glimpsed through a thick forest, or as if those dancing points of light that persist even in absolute darkness and indicate only a restless retina and optic nerve had fooled me for a moment into thinking they represented something real.

But then the hint of light took definite form, though staying at the dim limit of vision and crawling back and forth as I focused on it because my eyes had no other point of reference to steady it by.

It was a dim angular band making up three edges of a rectangle, the top edge longer than the two vertical edges, while the bottom edge wasn't there. As I watched it and it became a little clearer, I saw that the bands of light were brightest toward the inside—that is, toward the rectangle they partly enclosed, where they were bordered by stark blackness—while toward the outside they faded gradually away. Then as I continued to watch I saw that the two corners were rounded while up from the top edge there projected a narrow, lesser rectangle—a small tab.

The tab made me realize that I was looking at a file folder silhouetted by something dimly glowing inside it.

Then the top band darkened toward the center, as would happen if a hand were dipping into the folder, and then lightened again as if the hand were being withdrawn. Then up out of the folder, as if the invisible hand were guiding or coaxing it, swam something no brighter than the bands of light.

It was the shape of a woman, but distorted and constantly flowing, the head and arms and upper torso maintaining more of an approximation to human proportions than the lower torso and legs, which were like churning, trailing draperies or a long gauzy skirt. It was extremely dim, so I had to keep blinking my eyes, and it didn't get brighter.

It was like the figure of a woman phosphorescently painted on a long-skirted slip of the filmiest silk that had silk-stocking-like sheaths for arms and head attached—yes, and topped by some illusion of dim silver hair. And yet it was more than that. Although it looped up gracefully through the air as such a slip might when shaken out by a woman preparing to put it on, it also had a writhing life of its own.

But in spite of all the distortions, as it flowed in an arc toward the ceiling and dove downward, it was seductively beautiful and the face was recognizably that of Evvie Cordew.

It checked its dive and reversed the direction of its flow, so that for a moment it floated upright high in the air, like a filmy nightgown a woman swishes above her head before she slips into it.

Then it began to settle toward the floor and I saw that there really was a woman standing under it and pulling it down over her head, though I could see her body only very dimly by the reflected glow of the ghost she was drawing down around her.

The woman on the floor shot up her hands close to her body and gave a quick wriggle and twist and ducked her head and then threw it back, as a woman does when she's getting into a tight dress, and the flowing glowing thing lost its distortions as it fitted itself around her.

Then for a moment the glow brightened a trifle as the woman and her ghost merged and I saw Evvie Cordew with her flesh gleaming by its own light—the long slim ankles, the vase-curve of hips and waist, the impudent breasts almost as you'd guess them from the bikini shots, but with larger aureoles—saw it for an instant before the ghostlight winked out like white sparks dying, and there was utter darkness again.

Utter darkness and a voice that crooned, "Oh that was like silk, Emmy, pure silk stocking all over. Do you remember when you cut it, Emmy? I'd just got my first screen credit and I'd signed the seven-year contract and I knew I was going to have the world by the tail and I felt wonderful and I suddenly got terribly dizzy for no reason and I came to you. And you straightened me out for then by coaxing out and cutting away my happiness. You told me it would be a little like giving blood, and it was. That was my first ghost, Emmy, but only the first."

My eyes, recovering swiftly from the brighter glow of the ghost returning to its sources, again made out the three glowing sides of the file folder. And again there swam up out of it a crazily churning phosphorescent woman trailing gauzy streamers. The face was recognizably Evvie's, but constantly distorting, now one eye big as an orange then small as a pea, the lips twisting in impossible smiles and grimaces, the brow shrinking to that of a pinhead or swelling to that of a mongolian idiot, like a face reflected from a plate-glass window running with water. As it came down over the real Evelyn's face there was a moment when the two were together but didn't merge, like the faces of twins in such a flooded window. Then, as if a squeegee had been wiped down it, the single face came bright and clear, and just as the darkness returned she caressed her lips with her tongue.

And I heard her say, "That one was like hot velvet, Emmy, smooth but with a burn in it. You took it two days after the sneak preview of *Hydrogen Blonde,* when we had the little party to celebrate after the big party, and the current Miss America was there and I showed her what a really valuable body looked like. That was when I realized that I'd hit the top and it hadn't changed me into a goddess or anything. I still had the same ignorances as before and the same awkwardnesses for the cameramen and cutters to hide—only they were worse because I was in the center of the show window—and I was going to have to fight for the rest of my life to keep my body like it was and then I was going to start to die, wrinkle by wrinkle, lose my juice cell by cell, like anybody else."

The third ghost arched toward the ceiling and down, waves of phosphorescence flickering it all the time. The slender arms undulated like pale serpents and the hands, the finger- and thumb-tips gently pressed together, were like the inquisitive heads of serpents—until the fingers spread so the hands resembled five-tongued creeping puddles of phosphorescent ink. Then into them as if into shoulder-length ivory silk gloves came the solid fingers and arms. For a bit the hands, first part to be merged, were brightest of the whole figure and I watched them help fit each other on and then sweep symmetrically down brow and cheeks and chin, fitting the face, with a little sidewise dip of the ring fingers as they smoothed in the eyes. Then they swept up and back and raked through both heads of hair, mixing them. This ghost's hair was very dark and, mingling, it toned down Evelyn's blonde a little.

"That one felt slimy, Emmy, like the top crawled off of a swamp.

Remember, I'd just teased the boys into fighting over me at the Troc. Jeff hurt Lester worse than they let out and even old Sammy got a black eye. I'd just discovered that when you get to the top you have all the ordinary pleasures the boobs yearn for all their lives, and they don't mean anything, and you have to work and scheme every minute to get the pleasures beyond pleasure that you've got to have to keep your life from going dry."

The fourth ghost rose toward the ceiling like a diver paddling up from the depths. Then, as if the whole room were filled with its kind of water, it seemed to surface at the ceiling and jackknife there and plunge down again with a little swoop and then reverse direction again and hover for a moment over the real Evelyn's head and then sink slowly down around her like a diver drowning. This time I watched the bright hands cupping the ghost's breasts around her own as if she were putting on a luminescent net brassiere. Then the ghost's filminess shrank suddenly to tighten over her torso like a cheap cotton dress in a cloudburst.

As the glow died to darkness a fourth time, Evelyn said softly, "Ah but that was cool, Emmy. I'm shivering. I'd just come back from my first location work in Europe and was sick to get at Broadway, and before you cut it you made me relive the yacht party where I overheard Ricco and the author laughing at how I'd messed up my first legitimate play reading, and we swam in the moonlight and Monica almost drowned. That was when I realized that nobody, even the bottom boobs in the audience, really respected you because you were their sex queen. They respected the little female boob in the seat beside them more than they did you. Because you were just something on the screen that they could handle as they pleased inside their minds. With the top folk, the Big Timers, it wasn't any better. To them you were just a challenge, a prize, something to show off to other men to drive them nuts, but never something to love. Well, that's four, Emmy, and four and one makes all."

The last ghost rose whirling and billowing like a silk robe in the wind, like a crazy photomontage, like a surrealist painting done in a barely visible wash of pale flesh tones on a black canvas, or rather like an endless series of such surrealist paintings, each distortion melting into the next—trailing behind it a gauzy wake of draperies which I realized was the way ghosts were always pictured and described. I watched the draperies bunch as Evelyn pulled them down around her, and then they suddenly whipped tight against her thighs, like a skirt in a strong wind or like nylon clinging in the cold. The final glow was a little stronger, as if there were more life in the shining woman than there had been at first.

"Ah that was like the brush of wings, Emmy, like feathers in the wind. You cut it after the party in Sammy's plane to celebrate me being the top money star in the industry. I bothered the pilot because I wanted him to smash us in a dive. That was when I realized I was just property—something for men to make money out of (and me to make money, too, out of me) from the star who married me to prop his box-office rating to the sticks theater owner who hoped I'd sell a few extra tickets. I found that my deepest love—it was once for you, Emmy—was just something for a man to capitalize on. That any man, no matter how sweet or strong, could in the end never be anything but a pimp. Like you, Emmy."

Just darkness for a while then, darkness and silence, broken only by the faint rustling of clothing.

Finally her voice again: "So now I got my pictures back, Emmy. All the original negatives, you might say, for you can't make prints of them or second negatives—I don't think. Or is there a way of making prints of them, Emmy—duplicate women? It's not worth letting you answer—you'd be bound to say yes to scare me.

"What do we do with you now, Emmy? I know what you'd do to me if you had the chance, for you've done it already. You've kept parts of me—no, five real *me's*—tucked away in envelopes for a long time, something to take out and look at or run through your hand or twist around a finger or crumple in a ball, whenever you felt bored on a long afternoon or an endless night. Or maybe show off to special friends or even give other girls to wear—you didn't think I knew about that trick, did you, Emmy?—I hope I poisoned them, I hope I made them burn! Remember, Emmy, I'm full of death-wish now, five ghosts of it. Yes, Emmy, what do we do with you now?"

Then, for the first time since the ghosts had shown, I heard the sound of Dr. Slyker's breath whistling through his nose and the muffled grunts and creakings as he lurched against the clinging sheet.

"Makes you think, doesn't it, Emmy? I wish I'd asked my ghosts what to do with you when I had the chance—I wish I'd known how to ask them. They'd have been the ones to decide. Now they're too mixed in.

"We'll let the other girls decide—the other ghosts. How many dozen are there, Emmy? How many hundred? I'll trust their judgment. Do your ghosts love you, Emmy?"

I heard the click of her heels followed by soft rushes ending in thuds—the file drawers being yanked open. Slyker got noisier.

"You don't think they love you, Emmy? Or they do but their way of showing affection won't be exactly comfortable, or safe? We'll see."

The heels clicked again for a few steps.

"And now, music. The fourth button, Emmy?"

There came again those sensual, spectral chords that opened the "Ghostgirls Pavan," and this time they led gradually into a music that seemed to twirl and spin, very slowly and with a lazy grace, the music of space, the music of free fall. It made easier the slow breathing that meant life to me.

I became aware of dim fountains. Each file drawer was outlined by a phosphorescent glow shooting upward.

Over the edge of one drawer a pale hand flowed. It slipped back, but there was another, and another.

The music strengthened, though spinning still more lazily, and out of the phosphorescence-edged parallelogram of the file drawers there began to pour, swiftly now, pale streams of womankind. Ever-changing faces that were gossamer masks of madness, drunkenness, desire and hate; arms like a flood of serpents; bodies that writhed, convulsed, yet flowed like milk by moonlight.

They swirled out in a circle like slender clouds in a ring, a spinning circle that dipped close to me, inquisitively, a hundred strangely slitted eyes seeming to peer.

The spinning forms brightened. By their light I began to see Dr. Slyker, the lower part of his face tight with the transparent plastic, only the nostrils flaring and the bulging eyes switching their gaze about, his arms tight to his sides.

The first spiral of the ring speeded up and began to tighten around his head and neck. He was beginning to twirl slowly on his tiny chair, as if he were a fly caught in the middle of a web and being spun in a cocoon by the spider. His face was alternately obscured and illuminated by the bright smoky forms swinging past it. It looked as if he was being strangled by his own cigarette smoke in a film run backwards.

His face began to darken as the glowing circle tightened against him.

Once more there was utter darkness.

Then a whirring click and a tiny shower of sparks, three times repeated, then a tiny blue flame. It moved and stopped and moved, leaving behind it more silent tiny flames, yellow ones. They grew. Evelyn was systematically setting fire to the files.

I knew it might be curtains for me, but I shouted—it came out as a kind of hiccup—and my breath was instantly cut off as the valves in the gag closed.

But Evelyn turned. She had been bending close over Emil's chest and the light from the growing flames highlighted her smile. Through the dark red mist that was closing in on my vision I saw the flames begin to leap from one drawer after another. There was a sudden low roar, like film or acetate shavings burning.

Suddenly Evelyn reached across the desk and touched a button. As I started to red out, I realized that the gag was off, the clamps were loose.

I floundered to my feet, pain stabbing my numbed muscles. The room was full of flickering brightness under a dirty cloud bulging from the ceiling. Evelyn had jerked the transparent sheet off Slyker and was crumpling it up. He started to fall forward, very slowly. Looking at me she said, "Tell Jeff he's dead." But before Slyker hit the floor, she was out the door. I took a step toward Slyker, felt the stinging heat of the flames. My legs were like shaky stilts as I made for the door. As I steadied myself on the jamb I took a last look back, then lurched on.

There wasn't a light in the corridor. The glow of the flames behind me helped a little.

The top of the elevator was dropping out of sight as I reached the shaft. I took the stairs. It was a painful descent. As I trotted out of the building—it was the best speed I could manage—I heard sirens coming. Evelyn must have put in a call—or one of her "friends," though not even Jeff Crain was able to tell me more about them: who her chemist was and who were the Arain—it's an old word for spider,

but that leads nowhere. I don't even know how she knew I was working for Jeff; Evelyn Cordew is harder than ever to see and I haven't
tried. I don't believe even Jeff's seen her; though I've sometimes
wondered if I wasn't used as a cat's paw.

I'm keeping out of it—just as I left it to the firemen to discover
Dr. Emil Slyker "suffocated by smoke" from a fire in his "weird"
private office, a fire which it was reported did little more than char
the furniture and burn the contents of his files and the tapes of his
hi fi.

I think a little more was burned. When I looked back the last time
I saw the Doctor lying in a strait jacket of pale flames. It may have
been scattered papers or the electronic plastic. I think it was ghostgirls burning.

Rump-Titty-Titty-Tum-Tah-Tee

ONCE UPON a time, when just for an instant all the molecules in the world and in the collective unconscious mind got very slippery, so that just for an instant something could pop through from the past or the future or other places, six very important intellectual people were gathered together in the studio of Simon Grue, the accidental painter.

There was Tally B. Washington, the jazz drummer. He was beating softly on a gray hollow African log and thinking of a composition he would entitle "Duet for Water Hammer and Whistling Faucet."

There were Lafcadio Smits, the interior decorator, and Lester Phlegius, the industrial designer. They were talking very intellectually together, but underneath they were wishing very hard that they had, respectively, a really catchy design for modernistic wallpaper and a really new motif for industrial advertising.

There were Gorius James McIntosh, the clinical psychologist, and Norman Saylor, the cultural anthropologist. Gorius James McIntosh was drinking whisky and wishing there were a psychological test that would open up patients a lot wider than the Rorschach or the TAT, while Norman Saylor was smoking a pipe but not thinking or drinking anything especially.

It was a very long, very wide, very tall studio. It had to be, so there would be room on the floor to spread flat one of Simon Grue's canvases, which were always big enough to dominate any exhibition with yards to spare, and room under the ceiling for a very tall, very strong scaffold.

The present canvas hadn't a bit of paint on it, not a spot or a smudge or a smear, except for the bone-white ground. On top of the scaffold were Simon Grue and twenty-seven big pots of paint and nine clean brushes, each eight inches wide. Simon Grue was about to have a new accident—a semi-controlled accident, if you please. Any minute now he'd plunge a brush in one of the cans of paint and raise it over his right shoulder and bring it forward and down with a great loose-wristed snap, as if he were cracking a bullwhip, and a great fissioning gob of paint would go *splaaAAT* on the canvas in a random, chance, arbitrary, spontaneous and therefore quintuply accidental pattern which would constitute the core of the composition and determine the form and rhythm for many, many subsequent splatters and maybe even a few contact brush strokes and impulsive smearings.

As the rhythm of Simon Grue's bouncy footsteps quickened, Norman Saylor glanced up, though not apprehensively. True, Simon had been known to splatter his friends as well as his canvases, but in anticipation of this Norman was wearing a faded shirt, old sneakers and the frayed tweed suit he'd sported as assistant instructor, while his fishing hat was within easy reach. He and his armchair were crowded close to a wall, as were the other four intellectuals. This canvas was an especially large one, even for Simon.

As for Simon, pacing back and forth atop his scaffold, he was experiencing the glorious intoxication and expansion of vision known only to an accidental painter in the great tradition of Wassily Kandinsky, Robert Motherwell and Jackson Pollock, when he is springily based a good twenty feet above a spotless, perfectly prepared canvas. At moments like this Simon was especially grateful for these weekly gatherings. Having his five especial friends on hand helped create the right intellectual milieu. He listened happily to the hollow rhythmic thrum of Tally's drumming, the multisyllabic rippling of Lester's and Lafcadio's conversation, the gurgle of Gorius' whisky bottle, and happily watched the mystic curls of Norman's pipe smoke. His entire being, emotions as well as mind, was a blank tablet, ready for the kiss of the universe.

Meanwhile the instant was coming closer and closer when all the molecules in the world and in the collective unconscious mind would get very slippery.

Tally B. Washington, beating on his African log, had a feeling of oppression and anticipation, almost (but not quite) a feeling of apprehension. One of Tally's ancestors, seven generations back, had been a Dahomey witch doctor, which is the African equivalent of an intellectual with artistic and psychiatric leanings. According to a very private family tradition, half joking, half serious, this five-greats-grandfather of Tally had discovered a Jumbo Magic which could "lay holt" of the whole world and bring it under its spell, but he had perished before he could try the magic or transmit it to his sons. Tally himself was altogether skeptical about the Jumbo Magic, but he couldn't help wondering about it wistfully from time to time, especially when he was beating on his African log and hunting for a new rhythm. The wistful feeling came to him right now, building on the feeling of oppression and anticipation, and his mind became a tablet blank as Simon's.

The slippery instant arrived.

Simon seized a brush and plunged it deep in the pot of black paint. Usually he used black for a final splatter if he used it at all, but this time he had the impulse to reverse himself.

Of a sudden Tally's wrists lifted high, hands dangling loosely, almost like a marionette's. There was a dramatic pause. Then his hands came down and beat out a phrase on the log, loudly and with great authority.

*Rump-titty-titty-tum-*TAH-*tee!*

Simon's wrist snapped and the middle air was full of free-falling paint which hit the canvas in a fast series of *splaaAAT's* which was an exact copy of Tally's phrase.

*Rump-titty-titty-tum-*TAH-*tee!*

Intrigued by the identity of the two sounds, and with their back hairs lifting a little for the same reason, the five intellectuals around the wall rose and stared, while Simon looked down from his scaffold like God after the first stroke of creation.

The big black splatter on the bone-white ground was itself an exact copy of Tally's phrase, sound made sight, music transposed into visual pattern. First there was a big roundish blot—that was the *rump*. Then two rather delicate, many-tongued splatters—those were the *titties*. Next a small *rump*, which was the *tum*. Following that a big blot like a bent spearhead, not so big as the *rump* but even more emphatic—the TAH. Last of all an indescribably curled and broken little splatter which somehow seemed exactly right for the *tee*.

The whole big splatter was as like the drummed phrase as an identical twin reared in a different environment and as fascinating as a primeval symbol found next to bison paintings in a Cro-Magnon cave. The six intellectuals could hardly stop looking at it and when they did, it was to do things in connection with it, while their minds were happily a-twitter with all sorts of exciting new projects.

There was no thought of Simon doing any more splattering on the new painting until this first amazing accidental achievement had been digested and pondered.

Simon's wide-angle camera was brought into play on the scaffold and negatives were immediately developed and prints made in the darkroom adjoining the studio. Each of Simon's friends carried at least one print when he left. They smiled at each other like men who share a mysterious but powerful secret. More than one of them drew his print from under his coat on the way home and hungrily studied it.

At the gathering next week there was much to tell. Tally had introduced the phrase at a private jam session and on his live jazz broadcast. The jam session had improvised on and developed the phrase for two solid hours and the musicians had squeaked with delight when Tally finally showed them the photograph of what they had been playing, while the response from the broadcast had won Tally a new sponsor with a fat pocketbook.

Gorius McIntosh had got phenomenal results from using the splatter as a Rorschach inkblot. His star patient had seen her imagined incestuous baby in it and spilled more in one session than in the previous hundred and forty. Stubborn blocks in two other analyses had been gloriously broken, while three catatonics at the state mental hospital had got up and danced.

Lester Phlegius rather hesitantly described how he was using "something like the splatter, really not too similar" (he said) as an attention-getter in a forthcoming series of Industrial-Design-for-Living advertisements.

Lafcadio Smits, who had an even longer and more flagrant history of stealing designs from Simon, brazenly announced that he had reproduced the splatter as a silk-screen pattern on linen. The pattern was already selling like hotcakes at five arty gift shops, while at this very moment three girls were sweating in Lafcadio's loft turning out more. He braced himself for a blast from Simon, mentally rehearsing the attractive deal he was prepared to offer, one depending on percentages of percentages, but the accidental painter was strangely abstracted. He seemed to have something weighing on his mind.

The new painting hadn't progressed any further than the first splatter.

Norman Saylor quizzed him about it semi-privately.

"I've developed a sort of artist's block," Simon confessed to him with relief. "Whenever I pick up a brush I get afraid of spoiling that first tremendous effect and I don't go on." He paused. "Another thing—I put down papers and tried some small test-splatters. They all looked almost exactly like the big one. Seems my wrist won't give out with anything else." He laughed nervously. "How are you cashing in on the thing, Norm?"

The anthropologist shook his head. "Just studying it, trying to place it in the continuum of primitive signs and universal dream symbols. It goes very deep. But about this block and this . . . er . . . fancied limitation of yours—I'd just climb up there tomorrow morning and splatter away. The big one's been photographed, you can't lose that."

Simon nodded doubtfully and then looked down at his wrist and quickly grabbed it with his other hand, to still it. It had been twitching in a familiar rhythm.

If the tone of the gathering after the first week was enthusiastic, that after the second was euphoric. Tally's new drummed theme had given rise to a musical fad christened Drum 'n' Drag which promised to rival Rock 'n' Roll, while the drummer himself was in two days to appear as a guest artist on a network TV program. The only worry was that no new themes had appeared. All the Drum 'n' Drag pieces were based on duplications or at most developments of the original drummed phrase. Tally also mentioned with an odd reluctance that a few rabid cats had taken to greeting each other with a four-handed patty-cake that beat out *rump-titty-titty-tum*-TAH-*tee*.

Gorius McIntosh was causing a stir in psychiatric circles with his amazing successes in opening up recalcitrant cases, many of them hitherto thought fit for nothing but eventual lobotomy. Colleagues with M.D.s quit emphasizing the lowly "Mister" in his name, while several spontaneously addressed him as "Doctor" as they begged him for copies of the McSPAT (McIntosh's Splatter Pattern Apperception Test). His name had been mentioned in connection with the assistant directorship of the clinic where he was a humble psychologist. He also told how some of the state patients had taken to pommelling each other playfully while happily spouting some gibberish variant of the original phrase, such as *"Bump-biddy-biddy-bum-*BAH-*bee!"* The resemblance in behavior to Tally's hepcats was noted and remarked on by the six intellectuals.

The first of Lester Phlegius' attention-getters (identical with the splatter, of course) had appeared and attracted the most favorable notice, meaning chiefly that his customer's front office had received at least a dozen curious phone calls from the directors and presidents of cognate firms. Lafcadio Smits reported that he had rented a second loft, was branching out into dress materials, silk neckties, lampshades and wallpaper, and was deep in royalty deals with several big manufacturers. Once again Simon Grue surprised him by not screaming robbery and demanding details and large simple percentages. The accidental painter seemed even more unhappily abstracted than the week before.

When he ushered them from his living quarters into the studio they understood why.

It was as if the original big splatter had whelped. Surrounding and overlaying it were scores of smaller splatters. They were all colors of a well-chosen artist's-spectrum, blending with each other and pointing each other up superbly. But each and every one of them was a perfect copy, reduced to one half or less, of the original big splatter.

Lafcadio Smits wouldn't believe at first that Simon had done them free-wrist from the scaffold. Even when Simon showed him details proving they couldn't have been stencilled, Lafcadio was still unwilling to believe, for he was deeply versed in methods of mass-producing the appearance of handwork and spontaneity.

But when Simon wearily climbed the scaffold and, hardly looking at what he was doing, flipped down a few splatters exactly like the rest, even Lafcadio had to admit that something miraculous and frightening had happened to Simon's wrist.

Gorius James McIntosh shook his head and muttered a remark

about "stereotyped compulsive behavior at the artistic-creative level. Never heard of it getting *that* stereotyped, though."

Later during the gathering, Norman Saylor again consulted with Simon and also had a long confidential talk with Tally B. Washington, during which he coaxed out of the drummer the whole story of his five-greats-grandfather. When questioned about his own researches, the cultural anthropologist would merely say that they were "progressing." He did, however, have one piece of concrete advice, which he delivered to all the five others just before the gathering broke up.

"This splatter does have an obsessive quality, just as Gory said. It has that maddening feeling of incompleteness which cries for repetition. It would be a good thing if each of us, whenever he feels the thing getting too strong a hold on him, would instantly shift to some engrossing activity which has as little as possible to do with arbitrarily ordered sight and sound. Play chess or smell perfumes or eat candy or look at the moon through a telescope, or stare at a point of light in the dark and try to blank out your mind—something like that. Try to set up a countercompulsion. One of us might even hit on a counterformula—a specific antidote—like quinine for malaria."

If the ominous note of warning in Norman's statement didn't register on all of them just then, it did at some time during the next seven days, for the frame of mind in which the six intellectuals came to the gathering after the third week was one of paranoid grandeur and hysterical desperation.

Tally's TV appearance had been a huge success. He'd taken to the TV station a copy of the big splatter and although he hadn't intended to (he said) he'd found himself showing it to the M.C. and the unseen audience after his drum solo. The immediate response by phone, telegram and letter had been overwhelming but rather frightening, including a letter from a woman in Smallhills, Arkansas, thanking Tally for showing her "the wondrous picture of God."

Drum 'n' Drag had become a national and even international craze. The patty-cake greeting had become general among Tally's rapidly-growing horde of fans and it now included a staggering slap on the shoulder to mark the TAH. (Here Gorius McIntosh took a drink from his bottle and interrupted to tell of a spontaneous, rhythmic, lock-stepping procession at the state hospital with an even more violent

TAH-blow. The mad march had been forcibly broken up by attendants and two of the patients treated at the infirmary for contusions.) *The New York Times* ran a dispatch from South Africa describing how police had dispersed a disorderly mob of University of Capetown students who had been chanting, *"Shlump Shliddy Shliddy Shlump* SHLAH *Shlee!"*—which the correspondents had been told was an anti-apartheid cry phrased in pig-Afrikaans.

For both the drummed phrase and the big splatter had become a part of the news, either directly or by inferences that made Simon and his friends alternately cackle and shudder. An Indiana town was fighting a juvenile phenomenon called Drum Saturday. A radio-TV columnist noted that Blotto Cards were the latest rage among studio personnel; carried in handbag or breast pocket, whence they could be quickly whipped out and stared at, the cards were claimed to be an infallible remedy against boredom or sudden attacks of anger and the blues. Reports of a penthouse burglary included among the objects listed as missing "a recently-purchased spotted linen wall-hanging"; the woman said she did not care about the other objects, but pleaded for the hanging's return, "as it was of great psychological comfort to my husband." Splatter-marked raincoats were a high-school fad, the splattering being done ceremoniously at Drum 'n' Drag parties. An English prelate had preached a sermon inveighing against "this deafening new American craze with its pantherine overtones of mayhem." At a press interview Salvador Dali had refused to say anything to newsmen except the cryptic sentence, "The time has come."

In a halting, hiccupy voice Gorius McIntosh reported that things were pretty hot at the clinic. Twice during the past week he had been fired and triumphantly reinstated. Rather similarly at the state hospital Bump Parties had been alternately forbidden and then encouraged, mostly on the pleas of enthusiastic psychiatric aides. Copies of the McSPAT had come into the hands of general practitioners who, ignoring its original purpose, were using it as a substitute for electroshock treatment and tranquilizing drugs. A group of progressive psychiatrists calling themselves the Young Turks were circulating a statement that the McSPAT constituted the worst threat to classical Freudian psychoanalysis since Alfred Adler, adding a grim scholarly reference to the Dancing Mania of the Middle Ages. Gorius finished his report by staring around almost frightenedly at his five friends and clutching the whisky bottle to his bosom.

Lafcadio Smits seemed equally shaken, even when telling about the profits of his pyramiding enterprises. One of his four lofts had been burglarized and another invaded at high noon by a red-bearded Greenwich Village Satanist protesting that the splatter was an illicitly procured Taoist magic symbol of direst power. Lafcadio was also receiving anonymous threatening letters which he believed to be from a criminal drug syndicate that looked upon Blotto Cards as his creation and as competitive to heroin and lesser forms of dope. He shuddered visibly when Tally volunteered the information that his fans had taken to wearing Lafcadio's splatter-patterned ties and shirts.

Lester Phlegius said that further copies of the issue of the costly and staid industrial journal carrying his attention-getter were unprocurable and that many had vanished from private offices and wealthy homes or, more often, simply had the crucial page ripped out.

Norman Saylor's two photographs of the big splatter had been pilfered from his locked third-floor office at the university, and a huge copy of the splatter, painted in a waterproof black substance, had appeared on the bottom of the swimming pool in the girls' gymnasium.

As they continued to share their experiences, it turned out that the six intellectuals were even more disturbed at the hold the drummed phrase and the big splatter had got on them individually and at their failure to cope with the obsession by following Norman's suggestions. Playing at a Sunday-afternoon bar concert, Tally had got snagged on the phrase for fully ten minutes, like a phonograph needle caught in one groove, before he could let go. What bothered him especially was that no one in the audience had seemed to notice and he had the conviction that if something hadn't stopped him (the drum skin ruptured) they would have sat frozen there until, wrists flailing, he died of exhaustion.

Norman himself, seeking escape in chess, had checkmated his opponent in a blitz game (where each player must move without hesitation) by banging down his pieces in the *rump-titty* rhythm—and his subconscious mind had timed it, he said, so that the last move came right on the *tee;* it was a little pawn-move after a big queen-check on the TAH. Lafcadio, turning to cooking, had found himself mixing salad with a *rump-titty* flourish. (". . . and a madman to mix it, as the old Spanish recipe says," he finished with a despairing giggle.) Lester Phlegius, seeking release from the obsession in the companionship of a lady spiritualist with whom he had been carrying on a strictly Platonic love affair for ten years, found himself enlivening with the *rump-titty* rhythm the one chaste embrace they permitted themselves to each meeting. Phoebe had torn herself away and slapped him full-arm across the face. What had horrified Lester was that the impact had coincided precisely with the TAH.

Simon Grue himself, who hadn't stirred out of his apartment all week but wandered shivering from window to window in a dirty old bathrobe, had dozed in a broken armchair and had a terrifying vision. He had imagined himself in the ruins of Manhattan, chained to the broken stones (before dozing off he had wound both wrists heavily with scarves and cloths to cushion the twitching), while across the dusty jagged landscape all humanity tramped in an endless horde screeching the accursed phrase and every so often came a group of them carrying a two-story-high poster (". . . like those Soviet parades," he said) with the big splatter staring blackly down from it. His nightmare had gone on to picture the dreadful infection spreading from the Earth by spaceship to planets revolving around other stars.

As Simon finished speaking Gorius McIntosh rose slowly from his chair, groping ahead of himself with his whisky bottle.

"That's it!" he said from between bared clenched teeth, grinning horribly. "That's what's happening to all of us. Can't get it out of our minds. Can't get it out of our muscles. Psychosomatic bondage!" He stumbled slowly across the circle of intellectuals toward Lester, who was sitting opposite him. "It's happening to me. A patient sits down across the desk and says with his eyes dripping tears, 'Help me, Doctor McIntosh,' and I see his problems clearly and I know just how to help him and I get up and I go around the desk to him"—he was standing right over Lester now, bottle raised high above the industrial designer's shoulder—"and I lean down so that my face is close to his and then I shout RUMP-TITTY-TITTY-TUM-TAH-TEE!"

At this point Norman Saylor decided to take over, leaving to Tally and Lafcadio the restraining of Gorius, who indeed seemed quite docile and more dazed than anything else now that his seizure was spent, at least temporarily. The cultural anthropologist strode to the center of the circle, looking very reassuring with his darkly billowing pipe and his strong jaw and his smoky tweeds, though he kept his hands clasped tightly together behind him, after snatching his pipe with one of them.

"Men," he said sharply, "my research on this thing isn't finished by a long shot, but I've carried it far enough to know that we are dealing with what may be called an ultimate symbol, a symbol that is the summation of all symbols. It has everything in it—birth, death, mating, murder, divine and demonic possession, all of life, the whole lot—to such a degree that after you've looked at it, or listened to it, or *made* it, for a time, you simply don't *need* life any more."

The studio was very quiet. The five other intellectuals looked at him. Norman rocked on his heels like any normal college professor, but his arms grew perceptibly more rigid as he clasped his hands even more tightly behind his back, fighting an exquisite compulsion.

"As I say, my studies aren't finished, but there's clearly no time to carry them further—we must act on such conclusions as I have drawn from the evidence assembled to date. Here's briefly how it shapes up: We must assume that mankind possesses an actual collective unconscious mind stretching thousands of years into the past and, for all I know, into the future. This collective unconscious mind may be pictured as a great dark space across which radio messages can sometimes pass with difficulty. We must also assume that the drummed phrase and with it the big splatter came to us by this inner radio from an individual living over a century in the past. We have good reason to believe that this individual is, or was, a direct male ancestor, in the seventh generation back, of Tally here. He was a witch doctor. He was acutely hungry for power. In fact, he spent his life seeking an incantation that would put a spell on the whole world. It appears that he found the incantation at the end, but died too soon to be able to use it—without ever being able to embody it in sound or sign. Think of his frustration!"

"Norm's right," Tally said, nodding somberly. "He was a mighty mean man, I'm told, and mighty persistent."

Norman's nod was quicker and also a plea for undivided attention. Beads of sweat were dripping down his forehead. "The thing came

to us when it did—came to Tally specifically and through him to Simon
—because our six minds, reinforcing each other powerfully, were momentarily open to receive transmissions through the collective unconscious, and because there is—was—this sender at the other end
long desirous of getting his message through to one of his descend-
ants. We cannot say precisely where this sender is—a scientifically
oriented person might say that he is in a shadowed portion of the
space-time continuum while a religiously oriented person might aver
that he is in Heaven or Hell."

"I'd plump for the last-mentioned," Tally volunteered. "He was
that kind of man."

"Please, Tally," Norman said. "Wherever he is, we must operate
on the hope that there is a counter formula or negative symbol—
yang to this yin—which he wants, or wanted, to transmit too—something that will stop this flood of madness we have loosed on the
world."

"That's where I must differ with you, Norm," Tally broke in, shaking his head more somberly than he had nodded it, "if Old Five-
Greats ever managed to start something bad, he'd never want to stop
it, especially if he knew how. I tell you he was mighty mighty mean
and—"

"Please, Tally! Your ancestor's character may have changed with
his new environment, there may be greater forces at work on him—in
any case, our only hope is that he possesses and will transmit to us the
counter formula. To achieve that, we must try to recreate, by artificial
means, the conditions that obtained in this studio at the time of the
first transmission."

A look of acute pain crossed his face. He unclasped his hands
and brought them in front of him. His pipe fell to the floor. He looked
at the large blister the hot bowl had raised in one palm. Then clasping his hands together in front of him, palm to palm, with a twisting
motion that made Lafcadio wince, he continued rapping out the
words.

"Men, we must act at once, using only such materials as can be
rapidly assembled. Each of you must trust me implicitly. Tally, I
know you don't use it any more, but can you still get weed, the genuine crushed leaf? Good, we may need enough for two or three dozen
sticks. Gory, I want you to fetch the self-hypnotism rigmarole that's

so effective—no, I don't trust your memory and we may need copies. Lester, if you're quite through satisfying yourself that Gory didn't break your collarbone with his bottle, you go with Gory and see that he drinks lots of coffee. On your way back buy several bunches of garlic, a couple of rolls of dimes, and a dozen red railway flares. Oh yes, and call up your mediumistic lady and do your damnedest to get her to join us here—her talents may prove invaluable. Laf, tear off to your home loft and get the luminous paint and the black velvet hangings you and your red-bearded ex-friend used—yes, I know about that association!—when you and he were dabbling with black magic. Simon and I will hold down the studio. All right, then—" A spasm crossed his face and the veins in his forehead and cords in his neck bulged and his arms were jerking with the struggle he was waging against the compulsion that threatened to overpower him. "All right, then—*Rump-titty-titty-tum*-GET-MOVING!"

An hour later the studio smelt like a fire in a eucalyptus grove. Such light from outside as got past the cabalistically figured hangings covering windows and skylight revealed the shadowy forms of Simon, atop the scaffold, and the other five intellectuals, crouched against the wall, all puffing their reefers, sipping the sour smoke industriously. Their marijuana-blanked minds were still reverberating to the last compelling words of Gory's rigmarole, read by Lester Phlegius in a sonorous bass.

Phoebe Saltonstall, who had refused reefers with a simple, "No thank you, I always carry my own peyote," had one wall all to herself. Eyes closed, she was lying along it on three small cushions, her pleated Grecian robe white as a winding sheet.

Round all four walls waist-high went a dimly luminous line with six obtuse angles in it besides the four corners; Norman said that made it the topological equivalent of a magician's pentalpha or pentagram. Barely visible were the bunches of garlic nailed to each door and the tiny silver discs scattered in front of them.

Norman flicked his lighter and the little blue flame added itself to the six glowing red points of the reefers. In a cracked voice he cried, "The time approaches!" and he shambled about rapidly setting fire to the twelve railway flares spiked into the floor through the big canvas.

In the hellish red glow they looked to each other like so many devils. Phoebe moaned and tossed. Simon coughed once as the dense clouds of smoke billowed up around the scaffold and filled the ceiling.

Norman Saylor cried, *"This is it!"*

Phoebe screamed thinly and arched her back as if in electroshock.

A look of sudden agonized amazement came into the face of Taliaferro Booker Washington, as if he'd been jabbed from below with a pin or hot poker. He lifted his hands with great authority and beat out a short phrase on his gray African log.

A hand holding a brightly-freighted eight-inch brush whipped out of the hellish smoke clouds above and sent down a great fissioning gout of paint that landed on the canvas with a sound that was an exact visual copy of Tally's short drummed phrase.

Immediately the studio became a hive of purposeful activity. Heavily-gloved hands jerked out the railway flares and plunged them into strategically located buckets of water. The hangings were ripped down and the windows thrown open. Two electric fans were turned on. Simon, half-fainting, slipped down the last feet of the ladder, was rushed to a window and lay across it gasping. Somewhat more carefully Phoebe Saltonstall was carried to a second window and laid in front of it. Gory checked her pulse and gave a reassuring nod.

Then the five intellectuals gathered around the big canvas and stared. After a while Simon joined them.

The new splatter, in Chinese red, was entirely different from the many ones under it and it was an identical twin of the new drummed phrase.

After a while the six intellectuals went about the business of photographing it. They worked systematically but rather listlessly. When their eyes chanced to move to the canvas they didn't even seem to see what was there. Nor did they bother to glance at the black-on-white prints (with the background of the last splatter touched out) as they shoved them under their coats.

Just then there was a rustle of draperies by one of the open windows. Phoebe Saltonstall, long forgotten, was sitting up. She looked around her with some distaste.

"Take me home, Lester," she said faintly but precisely.

Tally, half-way through the door, stopped. "You know," he said puzzledly, "I still can't believe that Old Five-Greats had the public spirit to do what he did. I wonder if she found out what it was that made him—"

Norman put his hand on Tally's arm and laid a finger of the other on his own lips. They went out together, followed by Lafcadio, Gorius, Lester and Phoebe. Like Simon, all five men had the look of drunkards in a benign convalescent stupor, and probably dosed with paraldehyde, after a bout of DTs.

The same effect was apparent as the new splatter and drummed phrase branched out across the world, chasing and eventually overtaking the first one. Any person who saw or heard it proceeded to repeat it once (make it, show it, wear it, if it were that sort of thing, in any case pass it on) and then forget it—and at the same time forget the first drummed phrase and splatter. All sense of compulsion or obsession vanished utterly.

Drum 'n' Drag died a-borning. Blotto Cards vanished from handbags and pockets, the McSPATS I and II from doctor's offices and psychiatric clinics. Bump Parties no longer plagued and enlivened mental hospitals. Catatonics froze again. The Young Turks went back to denouncing tranquilizing drugs. A fad of green-and-purple barberpole stripes covered up splattermarks on raincoats. Satanists and drug syndicates presumably continued their activities unhampered except by God and the Treasury Department. Capetown had such peace as it deserved. Spotted shirts, neckties, dresses, lampshades, wallpaper, and linen wall hangings all became intensely passé. Drum Saturday was never heard of again. Lester Phlegius' second attention-getter got none.

Simon's big painting was eventually hung at one exhibition, but it got little attention even from critics, except for a few heavy sentences along the lines of "Simon Grue's latest elephantine effort fell with a thud as dull as those of the gobs of paint that in falling composed it." Visitors to the gallery seemed able only to give it one dazed look and then pass it by, as is not infrequently the case with modern paintings.

The reason for this was clear. On top of all the other identical splatters it carried one in Chinese red that was a negation of all symbols, a symbol that had nothing in it—the new splatter that was the identical twin of the new drummed phrase that was the negation and completion of the first, the phrase that had vibrated out from

Tally's log through the red glare and come slapping down out of Simon's smoke cloud, the phrase that stilled and ended everything (and which obviously can only be stated here once): "Tah-*titty-titty-tee*-toe!"

The six intellectual people continued their weekly meetings almost as if nothing had happened, except that Simon substituted for splatter-work a method of applying the paint by handfuls with the eyes closed, later treading it in by foot. He sometimes asked his friends to join him in these impromptu marches, providing wooden shoes imported from Holland for the purpose.

One afternoon, several months later, Lester Phlegius brought a guest with him—Phoebe Saltonstall.

"Miss Saltonstall has been on a round-the-world cruise," he explained. "Her psyche was dangerously depleted by her experience in this apartment, she tells me, and a complete change was indicated. Happily now she's entirely recovered."

"Indeed I am," she said, answering their solicitous inquiries with a bright smile.

"By the way," Norman said, "at the time your psyche was depleted here, did you receive any message from Tally's ancestor?"

"Indeed I did," she said.

"Well, what did Old Five-Greats have to say?" Tally asked eagerly. "Whatever it was, I bet he was pretty crude about it!"

"Indeed he was," she said, blushing prettily. "So crude, in fact, that I wouldn't dare attempt to convey that aspect of his message. For that matter, I am sure that it was the utter fiendishness of his anger and the unspeakable visions in which his anger was clothed that so reduced my psyche." She paused.

"I don't know where he was sending from," she said thoughtfully. "I had the impression of a warm place, an intensely warm place, though of course I may have been reacting to the railway flares." Her frown cleared. "The actual message was short and simple enough:

" 'Dear Descendant, They *made* me stop it. It was beginning to catch on *down here*.' "

Little Old Miss Macbeth

THE SPHERE of dim light from the electric candle on the orange crate was enough to show the cot, a little bare wall behind it and concrete floor beneath it, a shrouded birdcage on the other side of the cot, and nothing more. Spent batteries and their empty boxes overflowed the top of the orange crate and made a little mound. Three fresh batteries remained in a box by the candle.

The little old woman turned and tossed in her sleep under the blankets. Her face was troubled and her mouth pursed in a thin line that turned downward at the corners—a tragic mask scaled down for a little old lady. At times, without waking, she'd creep her hands up from under the blanket and touch her ears, as though they were assaulted by noise—though the silence was profound.

At last, as if she could bear it no longer, she slowly sat up. Her eyes opened, though she did not wake, staring out with the fixity of unconscious seeing. She put her feet into snug felt slippers with a hole in the left toe. She took a woolly bathrobe from the foot of the cot and pulled it around her. Without looking, still sitting on the edge of the cot, she reached for the electric candle. Then she got up and crossed the floor to a door, carrying the candle, which made on the ceiling a circle of light that followed her. At no time was the full size of the room revealed. Her face was still a prim little tragic mask, eyes open, fast asleep.

Outside the door she went down one flight of an iron stairway, which sounded from its faint deep ringing under her light tread as if there were many more flights above. She went through another door, a heavy, softly moaning one like the stage door of a theater, and closed it behind her and stood still.

If you'd been there outside, you'd have seen her holding the electric candle, and a small semicircle of brick wall and iron door behind her and another semicircle of sidewalk under her feet, and nothing more, no other side to the street, no nothing—the feeble light went no further. Then after a while you'd have noticed a ribbon of faint stars overhead—a narrow ribbon, too narrow to show constellations, as if the unseen buildings here were very high. And if you'd have looked up a second time, you'd have wondered if a few of the stars hadn't moved or changed color, or if there weren't extra stars now or missing ones, and it would have worried you.

The little old lady didn't wait long. She started down the street in the dim globe of light from her electric candle, keeping close to the curb, so that even the wall on her side of the street was almost lost in darkness. Her felt slippers scuffed softly. Otherwise the city, for that was what it seemed to be, was absolutely quiet. Except that after a couple of blocks a very faint angry buzzing became audible. And the corner at the next cross street was outlined now by an extremely faint red glow, the exact color of neon signs.

The old lady turned the corner into a block that was crawling with luminous worms, about forty or fifty of them, as thick as your thumb and long as your arm, though some were shorter. They weren't bright enough to show anything but themselves. They were all colors, but neon red was commonest. They moved like caterpillars but a little faster. They looked like old neon tubes come alive and crawled down out of signs, but blackened and dimmed by ages of ions. They crawled in sine curves on the sidewalks and street, a few of them on ledges a little way up the walls, and one or two along what must have been wires hanging overhead. As they moved they buzzed and the wires sang.

They seemed to be aware of the little old lady, for two or three came and circled her, keeping outside her dim globe of light. When she turned at the next corner a mercury-violet one followed her a little way, lifting its head to buzz and crackle angrily, exactly like a defective neon sign.

This block was black again with just the ribbon of elusive stars. But although the little old lady still kept close to the curb, the sidewalk was narrower and the electric candle showed wrecked display windows with jagged edges and occasional stretches of almost unbroken, thick glass. The old lady's eyes, seeing in her sleep, didn't waver to either side, but if you'd have been there you'd have dimly seen dummies behind the broken windows, the men in zoot suits and wide-brimmed hats, the women in tight skirts and glimmering blouses, and although they stood very stiff you'd have wondered if their eyes didn't follow the little old lady as she passed, and there'd have been no way for you to know, as soon as her globe of light was gone, that they didn't step out carefully between the glass razors and follow.

In the next block a ghost light swirled across a flatness that began about a story up in the dark. It seemed to be something moving through the ten thousand bulbs of an old theater marquee, barely quickening for an instant their brittle old filaments—a patchy, restless shimmer. Across the street, but rather higher, there appeared, on the very threshold of vision, a number of large rectangular signs, their murky colors irregularly revealed and concealed—giant bats crawling across almost completely faded luminescent billboards would have given the effect. While at least twenty stories up, at the edge of the dubious starlight, one small window spilled yellow light.

Halfway down the next block the little old lady turned in from the curb to a fence of iron pickets. She leaned against a gate, giving a querulous little moan, the only sound she'd uttered, and it swung in, crunching against the gravel.

She pressed it shut behind her and walked ahead, her slippers crushing dead leaves, her thin nostrils wrinkling mindlessly at the smell of weeds and dust. Directly overhead a small square of stars projected from the ribbon. She went up wooden steps and across a porch and through a six-paneled door that creaked as she opened and shut it.

The halls of the house were bare and its stairs uncarpeted and its woodwork tritely ornate. When she reached the third floor with her dim globe of light there was the faintest crunch from below and a little later a creaking. She took hold of a rope that hung from above and added some of her weight to it, swaying a little, and a ladder swung out of the ceiling and bumped against the floor.

She mounted the ladder, stooping, breathing just a little heavily, into a low attic. Her candle showed trunks and boxes, piles of folded draperies, a metal-ribbed dressmaker's dummy and the horn of an old phonograph.

Then you would have heard it: *pling!*—four seconds, six, seven— another *pling!*—another seven seconds—*pling!* again—*pling!*— *pling!*——*pling!*

The torment in her sleeping face deepened. She crossed between the piles to a sink against the wall. On the lip of the single verdigrised faucet a drop slowly formed as she approached and just as she got there it fell—*pling!*—and a quick spasm crossed her face.

She put down the electric candle on the drainboard and took the handle of the faucet in both hands and leaned against it, not looking at it. There was one more *pling!* but then no more. She touched the lip of the faucet with a finger and it came away barely wet. She waited but no new drop formed.

Then her face smoothed out into a small mask of dispassion, the mouth thin and straight, and she took up her candle and started back. On the ladder and stairs and out on the walk and the street she was no longer alone. Presences thronged around her, angry and menacing, just beyond the candle's glow, and leaves crackled under other feet than her own. The light from the high window by the stars pulsed poisonously green, the winged shapes crawled more restlessly across the spent luminescence of the billboards, and all the witch-light in the theater marquee drained down into the lowest bulbs, the ones nearest her as she passed.

The wrecked display windows in the Block of the Babes and Zoot-Suiters were all empty.

In the Street of the Neon Worms the colored crawlers all came swiftly toward her, buzzing loudly and angrily, more cracklingly than bees, swarming close to her feet in ribbons of rainbow fire and following her around the corner for half a block.

But none of these things, nor the perceptible dimming of her electric candle, ruffled for one instant her expression of calm security.

She mounted the iron stairs, crossed the boundless room, sat down on the cot and put the electric candle on the orange crate among the heaped dead batteries.

One of them rolled off and hit the floor with a little *tump!* She started, quivered her head and blinked her eyes. Wakefulness had at last come into them. She sat motionless for a while, remembering. She sighed once and smiled a little smile, then she sat up straighter and her thin silvery eyebrows drew together in a frown of determination. She found a fountain pen and a small pad of onionskin paper among the batteries. She tucked a scrap of carbon paper under the top sheet and wrote rapidly for a minute. She tore off the top sheet, folded it and rolled it up tightly, then tucked it into an aluminum cylinder hardly bigger than a paper match.

She got up and went around the cot. She took the cover off the birdcage, opened the small door, and took out a black pigeon. Moaning to it affectionately, she wired the cylinder to one foot. Then she kissed its beak and threw it into the darkness. There was a flapping which grew steadily fainter, then suddenly broke off, as if the bird had winged through a window.

The dim globe of light had shrunk to half its original size, but it was still enough to show the little old lady's face as she got into bed and pulled up the blankets. Her eyes were closed now. She sighed once more and the corners of her lips lifted in another little smile. She became still, the blankets rising and falling almost imperceptibly over her chest, and the smile stayed.

The light was also enough to show the carbon of her note, which read:

Dear Evangeline,

I was overjoyed to receive your note and discover that you too at last have a city of your own and of course your own things. How is Louisville since the Destruction? Quiet, I trust. Pittsburgh is so noisy. I am thinking of moving to Cincinnati. Do you know if it has a tenant?

Yours very truly,
Miss Macbeth

Mariana

MARIANA HAD been living in the big villa and hating the tall pine trees around it for what seemed like an eternity when she found the secret panel in the master control panel of the house.

The secret panel was simply a narrow blank of aluminum—she'd thought of it as room for more switches if they ever needed any, perish the thought!—between the air-conditioning controls and the gravity controls. Above the switches for the three-dimensional TV but below those for the robot butler and maids.

Jonathan had told her not to fool with the master control panel while he was in the city, because she would wreck anything electrical, so when the secret panel came loose under her aimlessly questing fingers and fell to the solid rock floor of the patio with a musical *twing* her first reaction was fear.

Then she saw it was only a small blank oblong of sheet aluminum that had fallen and that in the space it had covered was a column of six little switches. Only the top one was identified. Tiny glowing letters beside it spelled TREES and it was on.

When Jonathan got home from the city that evening she gathered her courage and told him about it. He was neither particularly angry nor impressed.

"Of course there's a switch for the trees," he informed her deflatingly, motioning the robot butler to cut his steak. "Didn't you know they were radio trees? I didn't want to wait twenty-five years for them and they couldn't grow in this rock anyway. A station in the city broadcasts a master pine tree and sets like ours pick it up and project it around homes. It's vulgar but convenient."

After a bit she asked timidly, "Jonathan, are the radio pine trees ghostly as you drive through them?"

"Of course not! They're solid as this house and the rock under it—to the eye and to the touch too. A person could even climb them. If you ever stirred outside you'd know these things. The city station transmits pulses of alternating matter at sixty cycles a second. The science of it is over your head."

She ventured one more question: "Why did they have the tree switch covered up?"

"So you wouldn't monkey with it—same as the fine controls on the TV. And so you wouldn't get ideas and start changing the trees. It would unsettle *me,* let me tell you, to come home to oaks one day and birches the next. I like consistency and I like pines." He looked at them out of the dining-room picture window and grunted with satisfaction.

She had been meaning to tell him about hating the pines, but that discouraged her and she dropped the topic.

About noon the next day, however, she went to the secret panel and switched off the pine trees and quickly turned around to watch them.

At first nothing happened and she was beginning to think that Jonathan was wrong again, as he so often was though would never admit, but then they began to waver and specks of pale green light churned across them and then they faded and were gone, leaving behind only an intolerably bright single point of light—just as when the TV is switched off. The star hovered motionless for what seemed a long time, then backed away and raced off toward the horizon.

Now that the pine trees were out of the way Mariana could see the real landscape. It was flat grey rock, endless miles of it, exactly the same as the rock on which the house was set and which formed the floor of the patio. It was the same in every direction. One black two-lane road drove straight across it—nothing more.

She disliked the view almost at once—it was dreadfully lonely and depressing. She switched the gravity to moon-normal and danced about dreamily, floating over the middle-of-the-room bookshelves and the grand piano and even having the robot maids dance with her, but it did not cheer her. About two o'clock she went to switch on the pine trees again, as she had intended to do in any case before Jonathan came home and was furious.

However, she found there had been changes in the column of six little switches. The TREES switch no longer had its glowing name. She remembered that it had been the top one, but the top one would not turn on again. She tried to force it from "off" to "on" but it would not move.

All the rest of the afternoon she sat on the steps outside the front door watching the black two-lane road. Never a car or a person came into view until Jonathan's tan roadster appeared, seeming at first to hang motionless in the distance and then to move only like a microscopic snail although she knew he always drove at top speed—it was one of the reasons she would never get in the car with him.

Jonathan was not as furious as she had feared. "Your own damn fault for meddling with it," he said curtly. "Now we'll have to get a man out here. Dammit, I hate to eat supper looking at nothing but those rocks! Bad enough driving through them twice a day."

She asked him haltingly about the barrenness of the landscape and the absence of neighbors.

"Well, you wanted to live *way out*," he told her. "You wouldn't ever have known about it if you hadn't turned off the trees."

"There's one other thing I've got to bother you with, Jonathan," she said. "Now the second switch—the one next below—has got a name that glows. It just says HOUSE. It's turned on—I haven't touched it! Do you suppose . . ."

"I want to look at this," he said, bounding up from the couch and slamming his martini-on-the-rocks tumbler down on the tray of the robot maid so that she rattled. "I bought this house as solid, but there are swindles. Ordinarily I'd spot a broadcast style in a flash, but they just might have slipped me a job relayed from some other planet or solar system. Fine thing if me and fifty other multi-megabuck men were spotted around in identical houses, each thinking his was unique."

"But if the house is based on rock like it is . . ."

"That would just make it easier for them to pull the trick, you dumb bunny!"

They reached the master control panel. "There it is," she said helpfully, jabbing out a finger . . . and hit the HOUSE switch.

For a moment nothing happened, then a white churning ran across the ceiling, the walls and furniture started to swell and bubble like cold lava, and then they were alone on a rock table big as three tennis courts. Even the master control panel was gone. The only thing that was left was a slender rod coming out of the grey stone at their feet and bearing at the top, like some mechanistic fruit, a small block with the six switches—that and an intolerably bright star hanging in the air where the master bedroom had been.

Mariana pushed frantically at the HOUSE switch, but it was unlabelled now and locked in the "off" position, although she threw her weight at it stiff-armed.

The upstairs star sped off like an incendiary bullet, but its last flashbulb glare showed her Jonathan's face set in lines of fury. He lifted his hands like talons.

"You little idiot!" he screamed, coming at her.

"No Jonathan, no!" she wailed, backing off, but he kept coming.

She realized that the block of switches had broken off in her hands. The third switch had a glowing name now: JONATHAN. She flipped it.

As his fingers dug into her bare shoulders they seemed to turn to foam rubber, then to air. His face and grey flannel suit seethed iridescently, like a leprous ghost's, then melted and ran. His star, smaller than that of the house but much closer, seared her eyes. When she opened them again there was nothing at all left of the star or Jonathan but a dancing dark after-image like a black tennis ball.

She was alone on an infinite flat rock plain under the cloudless, star-specked sky.

The fourth switch had its glowing name now: STARS.

It was almost dawn by her radium-dialled wristwatch and she was thoroughly chilled, when she finally decided to switch off the stars. She did not want to do it—in their slow wheeling across the sky they were the last sign of orderly reality—but it seemed the only move she could make.

She wondered what the fifth switch would say. ROCKS? AIR? Or even . . . ?

She switched off the stars.

The Milky Way, arching in all its unalterable glory, began to churn, its component stars darting about like midges. Soon only one remained, brighter even than Sirius or Venus—until it jerked back, fading, and darted to infinity.

The fifth switch said DOCTOR and it was not on but off.

An inexplicable terror welled up in Mariana. She did not even want to touch the fifth switch. She set the block of switches down on the rock and backed away from it.

But she dared not go far in the starless dark. She huddled down and waited for dawn. From time to time she looked at her watch dial and at the night-light glow of the switch-label a dozen yards away.

It seemed to be growing much colder.

She read her watch dial. It was two hours past sunrise. She remembered they had taught her in third grade that the sun was just one more star.

She went back and sat down beside the block of switches and picked it up with a shudder and flipped the fifth switch.

The rock grew soft and crisply fragrant under her and lapped up over her legs and then slowly turned white.

She was sitting in a hospital bed in a small blue room with a white pin-stripe.

A sweet, mechanical voice came out of the wall, saying, "You have interrupted the wish-fulfilment therapy by your own decision. If you now recognize your sick depression and are willing to accept help, the doctor will come to you. If not, you are at liberty to return to the wish-fulfilment therapy and pursue it to its ultimate conclusion."

Mariana looked down. She still had the block of switches in her hands and the fifth switch still read DOCTOR.

The wall said, "I assume from your silence that you will accept treatment. The doctor will be with you immediately."

The inexplicable terror returned to Mariana with compulsive intensity.

She switched off the doctor.

She was back in the starless dark. The rocks had grown very much colder. She could feel icy feathers falling on her face—snow.

She lifted the block of switches and saw, to her unutterable relief, that the sixth and last switch now read, in tiny glowing letters: MARIANA.

The Man Who Made Friends With Electricity

WHEN MR. SCOTT showed Peak House to Mr. Leverett, he hoped he wouldn't notice the high-tension pole outside the bedroom window, because it had twice before queered promising rentals—so many elderly people were foolishly nervous about electricity. There was nothing to be done about the pole except try to draw prospective tenants' attention away from it—electricity follows the hilltops and these lines supplied more than half the juice used in Pacific Knolls.

But Mr. Scott's prayers and suave misdirections were in vain—Mr. Leverett's sharp eyes lit on the "negative feature" the instant they stepped out on the patio. The old New Englander studied the short thick wooden column, the 18-inch ridged glass insulators, the black transformer box that stepped down voltage for this house and a few others lower on the slope. His gaze next followed the heavy wires swinging off rhythmically four abreast across the empty grey-green hills. Then he cocked his head as his ears caught the low but steady frying sound, varying from a crackle to a buzz of electrons leaking off the wires through the air.

"Listen to that!" Mr. Leverett said, his dry voice betraying excitement for the first time in the tour. "Fifty thousand volts if there's five! A power of power!"

"Must be unusual atmospheric conditions today—normally you

can't hear a thing," Mr. Scott responded lightly, twisting the truth
a little.

"You don't say?" Mr. Leverett commented, his voice dry again,
but Mr. Scott knew better than to encourage conversation about a
negative feature. "I want you to notice this lawn," he launched out
heartily. "When the Pacific Knolls Golf Course was subdivided, the
original owner of Peak House bought the entire eighteenth green
and—"

For the rest of the tour Mr. Scott did his state-certified real estate
broker's best, which in Southern California is no mean performance,
but Mr. Leverett seemed a shade perfunctory in the attention he
accorded it. Inwardly Mr. Scott chalked up another defeat by the
damn pole.

On the quick retrace, however, Mr. Leverett insisted on their
lingering on the patio. "Still holding out," he remarked about the
buzz with an odd satisfaction. "You know, Mr. Scott, that's a restful
sound to me. Like wind or a brook or the sea. I hate the clatter of
machinery—that's the *other* reason I left New England—but this is
like a sound of nature. Downright soothing. But you say it comes
seldom?"

Mr. Scott was flexible—it was one of his great virtues as a salesman.

"Mr. Leverett," he confessed simply, "I've never stood on this
patio when I didn't hear that sound. Sometimes it's softer, sometimes louder, but it's always there. I play it down, though, because
most people don't care for it."

"Don't blame you," Mr. Leverett said. "Most people are a pack
of fools or worse. Mr. Scott, are any of the people in the neighboring
houses Communists to your knowledge?"

"No, sir!" Mr. Scott responded without an instant's hesitation.
"There's not a Communist in Pacific Knolls. And that's something,
believe me, I'd never shade the truth on."

"Believe you," Mr. Leverett said. "The east's packed with Communists. Seem scarcer out here. Mr. Scott, you've made yourself a
deal. I'm taking a year's lease on Peak House as furnished and
at the figure we last mentioned."

"Shake on it!" Mr. Scott boomed. "Mr. Leverett, you're the kind
of person Pacific Knolls wants."

They shook. Mr. Leverett rocked on his heels, smiling up at the softly crackling wires with a satisfaction that was already a shade possessive.

"Fascinating thing, electricity," he said. "No end to the tricks it can do or you can do with it. For instance, if a man wanted to take off for elsewhere in an elegant flash, he'd only have to wet down the lawn good and take twenty-five foot of heavy copper wire in his two bare hands and whip the other end of it over those lines. Whang! Every bit as good as Sing Sing and a lot more satisfying to a man's inner needs."

Mr. Scott experienced a severe though momentary sinking of heart and even for one wildly frivolous moment considered welshing on the verbal agreement he'd just made. He remembered the red-haired lady who'd rented an apartment from him solely to have a quiet place in which to take an overdose of barbiturates. Then he reminded himself that Southern California is, according to a wise old saw, the home (actual or aimed-at) of the peach, the nut and the prune; and while he'd had few dealings with real or would-be starlets, he'd had enough of crackpots and retired grouches. Even if you piled fanciful death wishes and a passion for electricity atop rabid anti-communist and anti-machine manias, Mr. Leverett's personality was no more than par for the S. Cal. course.

Mr. Leverett said shrewdly, "You're worrying now, aren't you, I might be a suicider? Don't. Just like to think my thoughts. Speak them out too, however peculiar."

Mr. Scott's last fears melted and he became once more his pushingly congenial self as he invited Mr. Leverett down to the office to sign the papers.

Three days later he dropped by to see how the new tenant was making out and found him in the patio ensconced under the buzzing pole in an old rocker.

"Take a chair and sit," Mr. Leverett said, indicating one of the tubular modern pieces. "Mr. Scott, I want to tell you I'm finding Peak House every bit as restful as I hoped. I listen to the electricity and let my thoughts roam. Sometimes I hear voices in the electricity—the wires talking, as they say. You've heard of people who hear voices in the wind?"

"Yes, I have," Mr. Scott admitted a bit uncomfortably and then, recalling that Mr. Leverett's check for the first quarter's rent was safely cleared, was emboldened to speak his own thoughts. "But wind is a sound that varies a lot. That buzz is pretty monotonous to hear voices in."

"Pshaw," Mr. Leverett said with a little grin that made it impossible to tell how seriously he meant to be taken. "Bees are highly intelligent insects, entomologists say they even have a language, yet they do nothing but buzz. I hear voices in the electricity."

He rocked silently for a while after that and Mr. Scott sat.

"Yep, I hear voices in the electricity," Mr. Leverett said dreamily. "Electricity tells me how it roams the forty-eight states—even the forty-ninth by way of Canadian power lines. Electricity goes everywhere today—into our homes, every room of them, into our offices, into government buildings and military posts. And what it doesn't learn that way it overhears by the trace of it that trickles through our phone lines and over our air waves. Phone electricity's the little sister of power electricity, you might say, and little pitchers have big ears. Yep, electricity knows everything about us, our every last secret. Only it wouldn't think of telling most people what it knows, because they believe electricity is a cold mechanical force. It isn't—it's warm and pulsing and sensitive and friendly underneath, like any other live thing."

Mr. Scott, feeling a bit dreamy himself now, thought what good advertising copy that would make—imaginative stuff, folksy but poetic.

"*And* electricity's got a mite of viciousness too," Mr. Leverett continued. "You got to tame it. Know its ways, speak it fair, show no fear, make friends with it. Well now, Mr. Scott," he said in a brisker voice, standing up, "I know you've come here to check up on how I'm caring for Peak House. So let me give *you* the tour."

And in spite of Mr. Scott's protests that he had no such inquisitive intention, Mr. Leverett did just that.

Once he paused for an explanation: "I've put away the electric blanket and the toaster. Don't feel right about using electricity for menial jobs."

As far as Mr. Scott could see, he had added nothing to the furnishings of Peak House beyond the rocking chair and a large collection of Indian arrow heads.

Mr. Scott must have talked about the latter when he got home, for a week later his nine-year-old son said to him, "Hey, Dad, you know that old guy you unloaded Peak House onto?"

"Rented is the only proper expression, Bobby."

"Well, I went up to see his arrow heads. Dad, it turns out he's a snake-charmer!"

Dear God, thought Mr. Scott, *I knew there was going to be something really impossible about Leverett. Probably like hilltops because they draw snakes in hot weather.*

"He didn't charm a real snake, though, Dad, just an old extension cord. He squatted down on the floor—this was after he showed me those crumby arrow heads—and waved his hands back and forth over it and pretty soon the end with the little box on it started to move around on the floor and all of a sudden it lifted up, like a cobra out of a basket. It was real spooky!"

"I've seen that sort of trick," Mr. Scott told Bobby. "There's a fine thread attached to the end of the wire pulling it up."

"I'd have seen a thread, Dad."

"Not if it were the same color as the background," Mr. Scott explained. Then he had a thought. "By the way Bobby, was the other end of the cord plugged in?"

"Oh it was, Dad! He said he couldn't work the trick unless there was electricity in the cord. Because you see, Dad, he's really an electricity-charmer. I just said snake-charmer to make it more exciting. Afterwards we went outside and he charmed electricity down out of the wires and made it crawl all over his body. You could see it crawl from part to part."

"But how could you see that?" Mr. Scott demanded, struggling to keep his voice casual. He had a vision of Mr. Leverett standing dry and sedate, entwined by glimmering blue serpents with flashing diamond eyes and fangs that sparked.

"By the way it would make his hair stand on end, Dad. First on one side of his head, then on the other. Then he said, 'Electricity, crawl down my chest,' and a silk handkerchief hanging out of his top pocket stood out stiff and sharp. Dad, it was almost as good as the Museum of Science and Industry!"

Next day Mr. Scott dropped by Peak House, but he got no chance to ask his carefully thought-out questions, for Mr. Leverett greeted him with, "Reckon your boy told you about the little magic show I put on for him yesterday. I like children, Mr. Scott. Good Republican children like yours, that is."

"Why yes, he did," Mr. Scott admitted, disarmed and a bit flustered by the other's openness.

"I only showed him the simplest tricks, of course. Kid stuff."

"Of course," Mr. Scott echoed. "I guessed you must have used a fine thread to make the extension cord dance."

"Reckon you know all the answers, Mr. Scott," the other said, his eyes flashing. "But come across to the patio and sit for a while."

The buzzing was quite loud that day, yet after a bit Mr. Scott had to admit to himself that it *was* a restful sound. And it had more variety than he'd realized—mounting crackles, fading sizzles, hisses, hums, clicks, sighs: If you listened to it long enough, you probably would begin to hear voices.

Mr. Leverett, silently rocking, said, "Electricity tells me about all the work it does and all the fun it has—dances, singing, big crackling band concerts, trips to the stars, foot races that make rockets seem like snails. Worries, too. You know that electric breakdown they had in New York? Electricity told me why. Some of its folks went crazy—overwork, I guess—and just froze. It was a while before they could send others in from outside New York and heal the crazy ones and start them moving again through the big copper web. Electricity tells me it's fearful the same thing's going to happen in Chicago and San Francisco. Too much pressure.

"Electricity doesn't *mind* working for us. It's generous-hearted and it loves its job. But it would be grateful for a little more consideration—a little more recognition of its special problems.

"It's got its savage brothers to contend with, you see—the wild electricity that rages in storms and haunts the mountaintops and comes down to hunt and kill. Not civilized like the electricity in the wires, though it will be some day.

"For civilized electricity's a great teacher. Shows us how to live clean and in unity and brother-love. Power fails one place, electricity's rushing in from everywhere to fill the gap. Serves Georgia same as Vermont, Los Angeles same as Boston. Patriotic too—only revealed its greatest secrets to true-blue Americans like Edison and Franklin. Did you know it killed a Swede when he tried that kite trick? Yep, electricity's the greatest power for good in all the U.S.A."

Mr. Scott thought sleepily of what a neat little electricity cult Mr. Leverett could set up, every bit as good as Science of Mind or Krishna Venta or the Rosicrucians. He could imagine the patio full of earnest seekers while Krishna Leverett—or maybe High Electro Leverett—dispensed wisdom from his rocker, interpreting the words of the humming wires. Better not suggest it, though—in Southern California such things had a way of coming true.

Mr. Scott felt quite easy at heart as he went down the hill, though he did make a point of telling Bobby not to bother Mr. Leverett any more.

But the prohibition didn't apply to himself. During the next months Mr. Scott made a point of dropping in at Peak House from time to time for a dose of "electric wisdom." He came to look forward to these restful, amusingly screwy breaks in the hectic round. Mr. Leverett appeared to do nothing whatever except sit in his rocker on the patio, yet stayed happy and serene. There was a lesson for anybody in that, if you thought about it.

Occasionally Mr. Scott spotted amusing side effects of Mr. Leverett's eccentricity. For instance, although he sometimes let the gas and water bills go, he always paid up phone and electricity on the dot.

And the newspapers eventually did report short but severe electric breakdowns in Chicago and San Francisco. Smiling a little frowningly at the coincidences, Mr. Scott decided he could add fortune-telling to the electricity cult he'd imagined for Mr. Leverett. "Your life's story foretold in the wires!"—more novel, anyway, than crystal balls or Talking with God.

Only once did the touch of the gruesome, that had troubled Mr. Scott in his first conversation with Mr. Leverett, come briefly back, when the old man chuckled and observed, "Recall what I told you about whipping a copper wire up there? I've thought of a simpler way, just squirt the hose at those H-T lines in a hard stream, gripping the metal nozzle. Might be best to use the hot water and throw a box of salt in the heater first." When Mr. Scott heard that he was glad that he'd warned Bobby against coming around.

But for the most part Mr. Leverett maintained his mood of happy serenity.

When the break in that mood came, it did so suddenly, though afterwards Mr. Scott realized there had been one warning note sounded when Mr. Leverett had added onto a rambling discourse, "By the way, I've learned that power electricity goes all over the world, just like the ghost electricity in radios and phones. It travels to foreign shores in batteries and condensers. Roams the lines in Europe and Asia. Some of it even slips over into Soviet territory. Wants to keep tabs on the Communists, I guess. Electric freedom-fighters."

On his next visit Mr. Scott found a great change. Mr. Leverett had deserted his rocking chair to pace the patio on the side away from the pole, though every now and then he would give a quick funny look up over his shoulder at the dark muttering wires.

"Glad to see you, Mr. Scott. I'm real shook up. Reckon I better tell someone about it so if something happens to me they'll be able to tell the FBI. Though I don't know what *they*'ll be able to do.

"Electricity just told me this morning it's got a world government —it had the nerve to call it that—and that it doesn't care a snap for either us *or* the Soviets and that there's Russian electricity in our wires and American electricity in theirs—it shifts back and forth with never a quiver of shame.

"When I heard that you could have knocked me down with a paper dart.

"What's more, electricity's determined to stop any big war that may come, no matter how rightful that war be or how much in defense of America. If the buttons are pushed for the atomic missiles, electricity's going to freeze and refuse to budge. And it'll flash out and kill anybody who tries to set them off another way.

"I pleaded with electricity, I told it I'd always thought of it as American and true—reminded it of Franklin and Edison—finally I commanded it to change its ways and behave decent, but it just chuckled at me with never a spark of love or loyalty.

"Then it threatened me back! It told me if I tried to stop it, if I revealed its plans it would summon down its savage brothers from the mountains and with their help it would seek me out and kill me! Mr. Scott, I'm all alone up here with electricity on my window sill. What am I going to do?"

Mr. Scott had considerable difficulty soothing Mr. Leverett enough to make his escape. In the end he had to promise to come back in the morning bright and early—silently vowing to himself that he'd be damned if he would.

His task was not made easier when the electricity overhead, which had been especially noisy this day, rose in a growl and Mr. Leverett turned and said harshly, "Yes, I hear!"

That night the Los Angeles area had one of its very rare thunderstorms, accompanied by gales of wind and torrents of rain. Palms and pines and eucalyptus were torn down, earth cliffs crumbled and sloshed, and the great square concrete spillways ran brimful from the hills to the sea.

The lightning was especially fierce. Several score Angelinos, to whom such a display was a novelty, phoned civil defense numbers to report or inquire fearfully about atomic attack.

Numerous freak accidents occurred. To the scene of one of these Mr. Scott was summoned next morning bright and early by the police —because it had occurred on a property he rented and because he was the only person known to be acquainted with the deceased.

The previous night Mr. Scott had awakened at the height of the storm when the lightning had been blinding as a photoflash and the thunder had cracked like a mile-long whip just above the roof. At that time he had remembered vividly what Mr. Leverett had said about electricity threatening to summon its wild giant brothers from the hills. But now, in the bright morning, he decided not to tell the police about that or say anything to them at all about Mr. Leverett's electricity mania—it would only complicate things to no purpose and perhaps make the fear at his heart more crazily real.

Mr. Scott saw the scene of the freak accident before anything was moved, even the body—except there was now, of course, no power in the heavy corroded wire wrapped tight as a bullwhip around the skinny shanks with only the browned and blackened fabric of cotton pyjamas between.

The police and the power-and-light men reconstructed the accident this way: At the height of the storm one of the high-tension lines had snapped a hundred feet away from the house and the end, whipped by the wind and its own tension, had struck back freakishly through the open bedroom window of Peak House and curled once around the legs of Mr. Leverett, who had likely been on his feet at the time, killing him instantly.

One had to strain that reconstruction, though, to explain the additional freakish elements in the accident—the facts that the high-tension wire had struck not only through the bedroom window, but then through the bedroom door to catch the old man in the hall, and that the black shiny cord of the phone was wrapped like a vine twice around the old man's right arm, as if to hold him back from escaping until the big wire had struck.

The Good New Days

"THEY DON'T BUILD slums like they used to," Whitey Edwards told me, reaching up for a loose corner of the flexo and pulling it down to prove his point. It domed springily over our dreg-bottomed coffee cups, revealing in the hidden space behind it the limp multicolored spaghetti of the utilities piping: gas, water, metered syntho-milk, sewage, coaxed TV, med-mist, Musik, robo-talk, robo-juice, tele, vele, elec, gelec, and such. Few of them running fat with their peculiar contributions to the good life, I judged.

"That may be so," I answered, slapping aside the dodderer's hands and thumbing the blue elastic panel back in place with a fast rub along its adhesive edge. Again it decently covered the flaccid tangle of what looked like rainbow-hued sheep's gut and rubber unmentionables. "But they built Ma like a bull and she'll gore and trample you if she finds you tearing down her kitchen. It's bad enough what the giant centipedes are doing."

The jumbo TV, jammed between sink and fridge, flickered weak and ghostly. A gaggle of five-job wives and eight-job men were having a closed-end discussion of everything in creation on the executive patio edge of a swimming pool big enough to hide a space-to-seabottom cruiser. Their sweet eldritch cackle was unintelligible, but their state of undress was a slight counter-irritant to boredom.

Whitey Edwards sighed, not looking at these suburban goddesses, but squinting his rheumy eyes against the Monday sun coming up like doom over the dusty flats between Beatsville and the Henleys' happy if fragile little family castle. Earth's spotted, spitting, seething star shot its angry rays under the great awning rigged in front of our windows and door.

"Once," the old boy said, shaking the head-topping that gave him his name, "they built slums solid with steel beams and heavy lath and great bloody pipes of iron and tile and lead that made 'em think twice before they tore 'em down. But now . . ." He sighed his wheezy grief. Whitey'd used to be a con-and-destruction worker decades back, before the robots took that over, before I was born.

The TV zoomered in on a taut little job in bolero jacket and loin-cloth. The sound cleared for her fast, happy words ". . . caring for this pool put my husband and I in the pool-counselor raquette . . ." and died.

I started to tell Whitey I had even more current job sorrows than his. Since Thursday I'd been terminated from my street-smiler's job for competing with the psychiatrists, robot and human, and for all I know with the giant centipedes. Just then my brother Dick erupted from the bed-closets, throwing clothes over his sallow nakedness like a Gypsy escaping from a Nazi gas chamber—or as if he were a sprint-in-the-gutter one-jobber. And with that job only since Friday night after being three weeks on probationary relief.

I called sweetly at him, "Are you scared a customer will put a gush of quarters into one of your metal bandits with her own little pinkies if you're a minute late?"

Dick scowled, gyrating around a stubborn trouser leg. "Don't you worry, Dickie," I kept on. "All the women I illicitly psyched were as nervous of machinery as sex; they wanted a man to do it for them."

Society, graciously, used to let people work vending and other coin-operated machines, like laundromats. But now, like laundro-mats too, you have to pay an attendant to do it for you—because machines are temperamental and individual enterprise is almost as holy as money and anyway, there aren't enough jobs to go around more than two or three times.

Dick groggled something at me and got the door open, all set for a spring-heel takeoff. But there in his way was a tiny man, dressed like a respectable beetle, with dimpled fist raised to knock. He had glasses with zoomer lenses; silver antennae quivered out of his gray hat; a flat black belly-box was his ventral carapace. He looked around, especially at the cluttered floor, as if we were a touch unsavory, but he held his ground.

As Dick paused at this coleopterous apparition, Ma came charging out of the bed-closets, red in the face and black was the rest of her. She grappled Dick around the elbows and roared, "Stop! No son of mine is going out to give battle to the 21st Century on an empty stomach." Grabbing a quarter orange she shoved it between his teeth like a boxer's mouthpiece and then snatching this way and that she slammed a sandwich in his one hand and a cup in the other and on the next time around poured it steaming full.

No one can deny that Ma stands squarely in back of her four sons, like the manager of a quartet of fistic champions, conscious of our genius and determined that it get recognition in the form of seven- or eight-job careers. Though at the moment Dick was the only one of us with any job at all, except for Tom, who lives away with his wife and two kids. But obstructions and setbacks never daunt Ma. It's not the money she's after, mostly, it's the glory of the House of Henley pitted against the whole bloody world.

Pricked by tender filial warmth, I eyed her—a murderous son-punishing behemoth but my blessed mother—while Whitey gave her an unseen wave. He's an old admirer she tolerates ever since Pa recognized her superior nuclear power and died.

Dick bit out and swallowed the meat of the orange and tongued aside the peel so as to yell that the coffee was burning his hand and what would it do to his throat? Ma ripped the fridge open against the pull of the great spring I'd fixed outside to keep it shut since the latch broke. She whisked out an ice-cube and tucked it in Dick's cup. The fridge door thudded shut and the spring whirred like a rattlesnake about to jump loose and strike, but it didn't.

Then Dick gulped his coffee while Ma held him and screeched in his ear about using lunch hour to scout for a second job and not stalk girls. When he'd finished his drink, she gagged him with his sandwich and let him go.

The beetle-man dodged aside. Dick took off with a straight-line velocity that would have broken his neck and scattered his bones if we'd still been living on the twentieth floor and not in this ground-level flat they tricked us into exchanging for.

The TV blinked and—presto—there was a soldierly file of eight-job men (tabbed for that by the digit on their left shoulder) single-footing with pleasant monotony past the golden plastic statue of a twelve-jobber. Each as he reached screen-center turned head and shouted an inaudible but optimistic something at me and bared all his perfectly tended teeth in a dazzling grin.

I breathed a happy sigh and got set for a spell of quiet—at least until the centipedes decided to start scuttling—but just then the beetle-man poked his head in and piped politely at Ma. "Good morning. Mrs. Henley, I'm your area med statistician, come to take your blood-pressure and photo-snap your insides and all for posterity, like we arranged for a week ago."

Ma slowly turned her head and glared at him like a bull that spots the matador, or, more likely, a peanut-vendor strolling across the ring. The red in her face went purple and she slowly reached for the bubbling coffee flask and slowly lifted it. The beetle-man innocently watched the lethal globe ascend with its tip-tilting seething brown hemicore, as if all this were a job-indoctrination demonstration in astrophysics.

Whitey started up, but I pushed him back in his chair, saying rapidly, "Not you. Even being an old friend of the family wouldn't save you from the horns at this moment."

Then I rasped loud as ambulance-brakes at Ma, "Hold your hand, you murdering old frump!"

She turned at once, as I'd known she would. I cited her and she charged me with the coffee flask high, very much like a small Miura, but armed in a fashion to have made Manolete himself turn pale. But I slipped her with a half veronica and as she went past I kissed her low on the back of the neck, just at the spot where the matador's sword goes in. I whisked my arms around her beloved thick waist, and the next instant she and Whitey and I were as happy as tin larks together flitting through a sparkling star cluster, and she was pouring fresh coffee for us.

But the beetle-man, never dreaming the deadly peril he'd been in, advanced another step into the kitchen and called, "Mrs. Henley, it's very needful you have your medical inspection. You're distorting area med statistics and there are drastic penalties for evading med census. No need for you to undress, just hold still now—"

I pushed the coffee flask back against the wall and I stroked Ma as I held her tight, so she didn't go quite as purple as she howled at him, "You filthy med-spy!—do you think I'll submit to your peepings and be stuff for your filthy pictures when I'm not granted decent human med service if I do sicken? Here I have four grand sons, supermen all—Meaghan here, who's a master mind doctor, and Harry who's still in bed, the greatest poet in the world, and Dick the Prince of Personalities, whom you saw speeding to work and I need not comment on, and Tom, who's a bloody wonder—and the filthy world takes so little note of them that if I go to the clinic it's only robot doctors who'll see me and never a flesh-and-blood physician!"

Whatever the topic of her rant, Ma always gets in a commercial for her boys.

The beetle-man quivered back a little at all that, but not very far, and piped soothingly, "Mrs. Henley, there's nothing vulgar or inferior about robo-med. The Secretary of Mental Health himself prefers—" He started to take another step into the room.

"That old sham!" Ma roared, palpitating in my grasp and purpling dark. "He's the same one whose minions are forever sentencing my genius son Harry to the clutches of the remedial psychiatrists."

"But Mrs. Henley," the little fellow went on with rash courage, "I can see with my own eyes you're not in the best of health. An immediate med-check—"

That gave me my opening and I shoved Ma into Whitey's arms and advanced on the beetle-man quickly, waving my finger like a sword between his bug eyes. "You watch yourself, lad," I cried, "or they'll be terminating you for making diagnoses who are only census-taker. That's what the licensed psychers did to me for adding only a few words of insight and wisdom to my street-smiling."

At that very moment a ghostly pattering began and swiftly grew louder. It seemed to come from everywhere.

"What's that?" the little chap asked wonderingly.

"The giant centipedes," I told him.

He paled and his zoomered eyes searched the shadows under table and sink as he scuttled backwards, and just at that moment, perhaps from the floor being swayed by our movements, the great spring on the fridge came loose and went klishing across the floor very close to his feet—a twenty-inch coil of gray wire. He leaped for the lintel of the doorway to hoist himself out of reach of the venomous monster of his imagination, but he missed and fell and went leaping off as if old Fu Manchu's whole blessed menagerie were at his heels. In pure pity I followed him under the great awning, polka-dotted now by the shadows showing through of the stuff pattering down on it, and caught up with him just beyond the mounting flake-drift.

"Don't be frightened," I told him, grappling him gently and forcing him to lift his zoomers to the ragged-topped wall behind, now only four to six stories high instead of the thirty it had been a week ago. Along its roller coaster margin two sinuous many-legged great silver beasties scampered, chomping great bites out of it and raining the digested fragments down from their rear ends in concrete cornflakes.

"Those are the giant centipedes," I explained. "Demolishment robots, only."

I was thinking of how Harry might make a shuddery poem of them —glittery cosmic crawlers nibbling the gray rim of infinity, eating their way in toward us from the ends of the universe—when at that instant a weightier chunk, rejected by one of the creature's delicate digestive apparatus, no doubt, came thunking down like a meteor not four feet from us, denting the hard ground and raising a geyser of dust. The beetle-man darted off a dozen more steps while I ducked back under the awning, calling to him, "Now be off with you, little official, and trouble Ma no more. She's too much for you, but let that not cast you down. Look on her as a revenant from a hardier, crueler age— a duchess out of place."

I'd no sooner got back in the kitchen, where Ma and Whitey were chatting over their coffee, than Ellie, Dick's wife, came out of the bed-closets full-dressed with bright suitcases in her hands and a dirty dark look in her eyes. She was saying, "Listen all of you, for I'll not tell it twice: I'm leaving that one-job no-good and going back to my last husband, who's still got the three jobs I left him with when I thought to better myself by entering this house of mad pride and sloth and poets snoring," and she brushed past me, the silver spring twinging again as she chanced to kick it.

"Meaghan, let her go, who can't appreciate the Prince of Personalities," Ma said to me loftily, her color down to ladylike bright pink again, but I still would have followed and argued with Ellie—Dick didn't deserve to be deserted when he'd just got a toe on the bottom rung of the ladder, which of course was why she was leaving him though she didn't know it, a jealous no-job little wifey—except that just then who should appear in the doorway but my eldest brother, Tom, filling it with his big grin and his great shoulders and his aura of three-job success—or would it be four now?—and saying, "Hi, Ma. Ellie leaving Dick again? Who's the tiny one hanging around outside? Housing official come to coax you once more from this death trap? Hello, Whitey. No, no coffee, Ma, I want to talk to Meaghan here. I've got something for the lad!"

I knew what that meant, of course, and I was already hunched on my hands and knees, starting to fix the spring to the fridge again—a job that might easily take the rest of the day, I decided—when I felt Ma's kindly talons on my shoulder, lifting me up, and she saying, "Whitey'll fix that, Meaghan," and then her beloved claws were propelling me to a seat at the table flush against the blue flexo, with my cup in front of me and beyond that Tom's great face as full of a smile of eager elder-brother benignity as my cup was of steaming coffee —Ma having poured again and dropped in a pinch of dexy (I saw her) to give me spirit.

All the while I was thinking chiefly, *What job's he found now that's so bad he won't take it himself but offer it to me?* It'd have to be pretty bad, for at last count Tom's three jobs were grinding mirrors for leisure-time astronomers who hadn't time to grind their own —that's one—and selling retailers a brand of all-cornsilk cancer-free cigarets with the genuine coal-tar taste and the nicotine life—that's two—and answering for a robot answering service whenever the decibel-rating of the caller's voice began to indicate extreme rage. He still had the third job, at any rate, by the phone-rig hanging around his neck.

"Meaghan," he beamed, "next to an all-girl squad of revivalist angels, there's naught so wondrous as brother-love. I got something great for you. By the by, I have Number Four myself now—I travel in ladies' glow-in-the-dark underthings."

As Ma raised a cheer at that, I looked around for escape, but Whitey was squatting at the fridge and blocking the door to the outer world, as happy with his tinkering as a great-grandfather cockroach (one of which was walking up his leg) while Ma, cheering still but with a policeman's eye on me, was taking a cup of coffee big and smoking as a volcano into the bed-closets—to fire Harry's poetic genius, no doubt, or in lieu of that toss him on his lazy feet.

"Meaghan—" Tom began, but just then his neck phone rang and he twitched it on and I could hear a voice like angry wasps. Tom listened and his face grew pink—he takes after Ma in that—and he said, "Certainly, madam. However—" and then his face grew purple and he began to bubble his mouth like a fish.

I leaned across the table and put my lips to the mouthpiece and shouted, "I love you dearly, unknown, indeed I do. I love you dearly, madam, brood upon that," and I twitched the thing off.

"That won't satisfy her," Tom said when he got his right color back and his breath.

"It will for twenty minutes," I told him, "and what in this world is good for any longer?" And then I added, reckless in my light-heartedness, "You were saying . . . ?"

"Meaghan," Tom began again, "I know you had this trifling street-smiler's job—"

"Not so trifling or little," I defended, though I hadn't intended to. "The sociologists decided people looked too tense and glum going back and forth to work and shopping and so on, so they hired folk like myself to mingle among 'em and strike up talk, casual-like, to cheer 'em up. Not quite the worst idea in the world, either."

"Yes, but you went too far," Tom reminded me. "You pried into people's minds to find their real troubles and set 'em straight. That's psychers' work, my lad, and you can't blame that august profession for resenting your competition and having you terminated."

"I helped the people I talked to," I countered stubbornly. "I couldn't have talked to them at all, Tom, if I hadn't something solid to say."

"I love you dearly, madam, brood upon that," Tom said. "Solid!"

"I don't worry 'em or push any of their desperation buttons, though I glimpsed banks of those," I protested on. "I just encouraged 'em to widen their minds and feelings a little and get some of the comic side-wash of others' troubles and cheer up naturally."

"There you've hit the nub of it," Tom asserted, wagging a finger in my face. "You tried to deliver more than your job called for, instead of learning to do it with a minimum of effort and finding another job to go with it, to swell your income—and then another after that."

He gave a quick look around—to make sure Ma hadn't come back, I soon realized—and then, leaning forward, said with a confidential hush, "Oh, Meaghan, my boy, I've learned so much of the world since I got away from here and Ma's no longer firing me with resentments and wild ambitions. The world's a very tidy comfortable place if only you'll remember there are three billion other lunatic climbers in it—and do no more than you're told and watch the smiles and frowns of your superiors and keep your eyes open and your nostrils flared for flicker or scent of another chance to make money. Step fast, keep adding one little job to the next like beads on a necklace, and forget Ma and her wild dreams. Oh, and did I tell you my Katie's got two jobs herself now too?—and never a one she'd have had with Ma around to hold her down."

"Ma's all right," I told him sharply. "She's got more courage and determination and vision than the four of us'll ever have together. And such a fierce self-punishing drive I wonder she's still alive. How would you ever have got out of here to a place of your own without Ma booting you?"

"True, true," he agreed. "Nevertheless, Ma's a hopeless romantic. She wants her four sons to be Dukes of the World, lording it over all."

I couldn't help chuckling at that. "When I was still street-smiling," I confided, "a little man, who thought he was a great romantic, opened his mind to me wanting only to escape from the prison of his life and aim a flashing sword at other men and capture with love their women—and corral all the single girls going around loose, too. After we both looked at this stirring picture a while, we realized that what he really wanted was to have all women mother him and puff him up and lead him through life like a great bobbing red balloon."

"That's the way with all romantics, including Ma," Tom said, taking advantage of me straightway. "She wants her sons to be princes and kings, or board chairmen at all events, not realizing there's a billion others starting up the success ladder with them—and not one with a genuine ion drive. Not realizing that the competition's too stiff for any man to dream of being more than an eight-job statistic with his peers. Or ten at most."

The TV now was sailing over a great pile of gently crumpled bed-clothes, which struck me as most pleasant and unlikely. Then I realized it was orbiting the Earth high above the clouds and there low in the foreground were the backs of beautifully barbered heads and now a sign flashing across the clouds: "Vacation Jaunts through Space for Nine-Job Heroes of Democracy."

"You're right about the competition," I agreed quickly with Tom. "I'm no enemy of democracy, I'm one of its darlingest friends, but there's no question it's upped the competition more than ever it was in Earth's history. We've got more machines, more health, more freedom of movement, more education, more leisure, more time for making money in our spare time, more almost equal people, *and* more incentives, more quick showy rewards for the quickly successful—with the result that the competition burns us out fast enough to equalize all the longevity created by medical advance."

"It doesn't seem to be burning you out," Tom observed.

"Now listen here, Tom my boy," I continued, warming to my subject. "Isn't there something altogether crazy about a world that wants to turn everyone into merchants no matter what their natural psychological class—a world that's turned even scientists and poets and adventurers and soldiers and priests into merchants busy selling themselves—a world that's feared so much that the machine would take away all jobs that it's gone ape creating jobs and financial ventures by the billions. With each reduction in working hours paralleled by an equal or greater increase in time spent on a part-time and sideline jobs—a world that's so money-conscious that a man who takes his eyes off the dollar for a month or a day or even ten seconds—"

"Your eyes don't look red with squinting at silver," Tom observed like a lemon. "Besides, you're deafening me."

Just then Ma came lumbering daintily in again and asked Tom, "What's this wondrous job you've got for Meaghan? I can't wait any longer to hear." Just as if she hadn't been hearing every word and writhing at my negativisms.

I groaned as if on the verge of defeat. Tom laughed and said, "I was forgetting about that. What with Mea talking of billions of jobs, my one got lost in the stampede. Well, it seems that the repair robots are getting unpredictable everywhere, spending too much time on some jobs and not enough on others, and passing up still others altogether. One repaired a leak so well it built an armor wall six feet thick around the leak and himself— Fortunata, they called that one. Another found a leak and did nothing but start making identical leaks in all the pipes he followed—until thousands of them were squirting behind him. A demolition robot started shooting rocks at a new-risen glastic building. Yet the circuits of these robots are in perfect order and they always behave properly under factory tests. So what must be done is to have a man follow each metal trouble-shooter and note every move he makes, watch his behavior day after day—taking weeks if necessary so the robot will get used to his presence and not vary his behavior to please or confuse or harm the watcher. Oh, it's a fine sort of job—no work at all—sort of like what they called Sidewalk Inspecting back in the depths of history."

I said, "I suppose the robots they're having the most trouble with are the ones that repair heat-tunnels and sewers and other delightful underground conduits."

"How did you know that?" Tom asked me very quickly. "Old sunken spillways and aqueducts and chimneys too, though—some of the last poking thousands of feet high into the clear heady air. A most healthful job, my boyo—a regular mountain-climbing and spelunking vacation."

I said softly, "I think I'd rather drown parboiled in this coffee cup than play psychiatric aide to a manic genius robot with a breakneck wander-urge who's waiting for his metal consciousness to brighten with its first jeweled unhuman pictures and electricity-loving impulses. The machines are coming awake, did you know that, Tom? All the machines—"

"No, it's but one machine," a softer dreamier voice, mournful as a breeze through dead leaves, cut in on me. The adolescent wraith with hair like blond spiderweb, who was Ma's poet genius and my youngest brother Harry, came drifting in from the bed-closets as if blown rather than walking. I could tell from the light-year look in his blue eyes that he'd conned his remedial psycher out of some pills.

He went on, "The whole Earth is one great metal machine, a dull steel marble amongst the aggies and glassies of the other planets. If anyone ever went out there with earth-eyes and not a spaceman's, he'd see it rolling along, over and over, like a great silver shop-made tumblebug spotted with cities and wet here and there with oceans, blinking the eyes of its ice-caps and smoking its volcanos and folding and unfolding its harrow-footed space-crazy legs in time with the phases of the moon. And if you looked real close you'd see millions of fleas jumpin' off it and beginning the long fall to the nadir."

At that moment the TV jumped to a 24-hour satellite starward of Terra and showed us the whole moonlit Earth backed by the Milky Way, as if snared by a diamond-dewy spiderweb. Ma squeaked a proud sigh at Harry's words thus coming out illustrated.

"Will you take the job?" Tom rasped at me.

"Tomorrow I will for sure," I told him. "And that's all the answer you'll ever get from me—tomorrow or any other day."

Ma tapped her hoof and flashed a rageful eye at me. "Tom," she said to him, "if Meaghan scorns it, how about Harry? Think of it, Harry, you always claim you want to be alone. Roaming those cool tunnels and sewers all by yourself except for some witless machine you'll catch onto in ten minutes. You'll have all the time and quiet in the world to create your poetry. Why, underground your poetry will sprout like roots, I'm sure, and run fast as crabgrass."

"Ma," Harry said, "sooner than take that job I'd head for Beatsville today rather than tomorrow."

"You wouldn't do that, Harry," Ma wailed menacingly. "Tell me you wouldn't." Ma's always prided herself that no matter how slumlike we live and close to Beatsville, we'd never get there. In Beatsville they pretend even worse than in the suburbs, pretend to be supermen and pretend to be animals, and creep each night to the electrified boundary to pick up the food and drink left for them.

But Harry nodded again and then Ma began yelling at Tom that he was trying to break up what was left of her family, having splintered himself off first. Whitey came alive and flapped his hands at her cautiously, like a torero ready to jump the fence. I slitted my eyes as if I were falling asleep. Tom got red as Ma and said the hell with us, he was going for good. So Ma stamped this way and that, now roaring at Harry and me for our sloth, now bellowing at Tom for his disloyalty. Then she lifted her arms to heaven and froze.

At that instant the beetle-man popped into the doorway and pointed his antennae at her. No one saw him but me.

Tom's face grew redder and he gave a snort and turned on his heel toward the door just as the beetle-man ducked out of sight. Tom had no sooner stamped out than the beetle-man popped in again behind him, waving a gray-black transparency he'd whipped from his black belly-box.

"Mrs. Henley," he piped rapidly, "I got a perfect shot of all your insides, but that's all that's perfect about it. You must come to the clinic right away with me. Your heart's like a watermelon and your aorta and pulmonary like summer squash." He waggled a finger at me. "Diagnosis by a medspector is permissible in dire emergencies."

Ma's face went purple. At that instant I felt the building quiver from the top down and a heartbeat later something burst through the awning and struck Tom as if he were a very thick spike and it a hammer driving him into the ground.

Ma screamed a great single scream and took a step forward and then stiffened and fell back, and I caught her in my arms and lowered her to the floor and pillowed her head. Outside I could hear the beetle-man buzzing into his neckphone for an ambulance like the fool he was—for Tom's head was smashed to the neck. Then I was wondering how Tom's blood could have got on Ma, for there was blood on her chest and then more and more of it, like a bull fallen from the final thrust and pumping his heart out, and then I realized it was Ma's blood from her lungs, gurgling with her Cheyne-Stokes breathing.

Whitey came fluttering down at her other side.

Harry was standing looking at us and he was trembling, and then we heard the siren far off, and then another, and then the two of them coming closer fast, and as they came closer and their angry wailing grew louder, Harry began to tremble more, and as their sound burst into the open of the razed blocks, he cried, "I'm off to Beatsville," and he was sprinting by the time he went through the door.

I knew what was coming, although there was nothing I could do but hold Ma. Then I knew that what was coming had come, for there was a shout and a great squealing of brakes and a scream and a thud and the brakes still squealing.

Then Ma stopped breathing, but she still looked angry.

It was a long time before anyone came in. I went on holding Ma and wiping her face clean, though it stayed red for all that. I heard one ambulance leave and then the other. Finally a doctor came in, and the beetle-man too, and the doctor looked at Ma and shook his head and said that if only she'd been med-checked regularly it need never have happened, but I told him, "You didn't know Ma." And the beetle-man buzzed into his neckphone for an ambulance back.

I said chokily, "She died brave, charging the muleta dead on, and I'm damned if I'll award society a single hoof of her, let alone the horns or the tail." No one got it. The beetle-man eyed me and took a surreptitious note.

Then for a while I was signing papers and listening to this and that, but finally they were all gone, the living and dead, and I was alone with Whitey and I remembered we ought to tell Dick.

The TV was showing a great musical review with hundreds of highly talented actors and actresses, all of them seven-job folk and this the eighth job for all of them. Flights of smiles were going back and forth across the screen, like seagulls wheeling at sunset.

The concrete cornflakes were still pattering on the awning. I marched us straight under the hole the rock had made that killed Tom, and they pelted on our hair and shoulders and necks like feathery hail.

We climbed the flake-drift and I paused and turned around. The giant centipedes were busily crawling back and forth, the one swinging aside most cleverly to let the other pass. They'd chewed their way here and there down to the second floor.

I looked down to our shadowed doorway with the faintest flicker of TV still coming out of it, and I thought I'd like to drive a nail a mile long down through the center of that room, pinning it there forever, and engrave in the head of the nail, in letters a foot deep, "A Family Lived Here."

But that was a little beyond the scope of my engineering, so, pushing Whitey ahead of me, off I went to tell Dick, laughing and crying.

America The Beautiful

I AM RETURNING to England. I am shorthanding this, July 5, 2000, aboard the Dallas-London rocket as it arches silently out of the diffused violet daylight of the stratosphere into the eternally star-spangled purpling night of the ionosphere.

I have refused the semester instructorship in poetry at UTD, which would have munificently padded my honorarium for delivering the Lanier Lectures and made me for four months second only to the Poet in Residence.

And I am almost certain that I have lost Emily, although we plan to meet in London in a fortnight if she can wangle the stopover on her way to take up her Peace Corps command in Niger.

I am not leaving America because of the threat of a big war. I believe that this new threat, like all the rest, is only another move, even if a long and menacing queen's move, in the game of world politics, while the little wars go endlessly on in Chad, Czechoslovakia, Sumatra, Siam, Baluchistan, and Bolivia as America and the Communist League firm their power boundaries.

And I am certainly not leaving America because of any harassment as a satellitic neutral and possible spy. There may have been surveillance of my actions and lectures, but if so it was as impalpable as the checks they must have made on me in England before granting me visiting clearance. The U.S. intelligence agencies have become almost incredibly deft in handling such things. And I was entertained in America more than royally—I was made to feel at home by a family with a great talent for just that.

No, I am leaving because of the shadows. The shadows everywhere in America, but which I saw most clearly in Professor Grissim's serene and lovely home. The shadows which would irresistibly have gathered behind my instructor's lectern, precisely as I was learning to dress with an even trimmer and darker reserve while I was a guest at the Grissims' and even to shower more frequently. The shadows which revealed themselves to me deepest of all around Emily Grissim, and which I could do nothing to dispel.

I think that you, or at least I, can see the shadows in America more readily these days because of the very clean air there. Judging only from what I saw with my own eyes in Texas, the Americans have completely licked their smog problem. Their gently curving freeways purr with fast electric cars, like sleek and disciplined silver cats. Almost half the nation's power comes from atomic reactors, while the remaining coal-burning plants loose back into the air at most a slight shimmer of heat. Even the streams and rivers run blue and unsmirched again, while marine life is returning to the eastern Great Lakes. In brief, America is beautiful, for with the cleanliness, now greater than that of the Dutch, has come a refinement in taste, so that all buildings are gracefully shaped and disposed, while advertisements, though molding minds more surely than ever, are restrained and almost finically inoffensive.

The purity of the atmosphere was strikingly brought to my notice when I debarked at Dallas rocketport and found the Grissims waiting for me outdoors, downwind of the landing area. They made a striking group, all of them tall, as they stood poised yet familiarly together: the professor with his grizzled hair still close-trimmed in military fashion, for he had served almost as long as a line officer and in space services as he had now as a university physicist; his slim, white-haired wife; Emily, like her mother in the classic high-waisted, long-skirted Directoire style currently fashionable; and her brother Jack, in his dress pale grays with sergeant's stripes, on furlough from Siam.

Their subdued dress and easy attitudes reminded me of a patrician Roman's toga dropping in precise though seemingly accidental folds.

The outworn cliché about America being Rome to England's Greece came irritatingly to my mind.

Introductions were made by the professor, who had met my father at Oxford and later seen much of him during the occupation of Britain throughout the Three Years' Alert. I was surprised to find their diction almost the same as my own. We strolled to their electric station wagon, the doors of which opened silently at our approach.

I should have been pleased by the simple beauty of the Grissims, as by that of the suburban landscape through which we now sped, especially since my poetry is that of the Romantic Revival, which looks back to Keats and Shelley more even than to Shakespeare. Instead, it rubbed me the wrong way. I became uneasy and within ten minutes found myself beginning to talk bawdy and make nasty little digs at America.

They accepted my rudeness in such an unshocked, urbane fashion, demonstrating that they understood though did not always agree with me, and they went to such trouble to assure me that not all America was like this, there were still many ugly stretches, that I soon felt myself a fool and shut up. It was I who was the crass Roman, I told myself, or even barbarian.

Thereafter Emily and her mother kept the conversation going easily and soon coaxed me back into it, with the effect of smoothing the grumbling and owlish young British poet's ruffled feathers.

The modest one storey, shaded by slow-shedding silvery eucalyptus and mutated chaparral, which was all that showed of the Grissim home, opened to receive our fumeless vehicle. I was accompanied to my bedroom-and-study, served refreshments, and left there to polish up my first lecture. The scene in the view window was so faithfully transmitted from the pickup above, the air fresher if possible than that outdoors, that I found it hard to keep in mind I was well underground.

It was at dinner that evening, when my hosts made such a nicely concerted effort to soothe my nervousness over my initial lecture, and largely succeeded, that I first began truly to like and even respect the Grissims.

It was at the same instant, in that pearly dining room, that I first became aware of the shadows around them.

Physical shadows? Hardly, though at times they really seemed that.

I recall thinking, my mind still chiefly on my lecture, something like, *These good people are so wedded to the way of war, the perpetual little wars and the threat of the big one, and have been so successful in masking the signs of its strains in themselves, that they have almost forgotten that those strains are there. And they love their home and country, and the security of their taut way of life, so deeply that they have become unaware of the depth of that devotion.*

My lecture went off well that night. The audience was large, respectful, and seemingly even attentive. The number of African and Mexican faces gave the lie to what I'd been told about integration being a sham in America. I should have been pleased, and I temporarily was, at the long, mutedly drumming applause I was given and at the many intelligent, flattering comments I received afterward. And I should have stopped seeing the shadows then, but I didn't.

Next morning Emily toured me around city and countryside on a long silvery scooter, I riding pillion behind her. I remember the easy though faintly formal way in which she drew my arms around her waist and laid her hand for a moment on one of mine, meanwhile smiling cryptically over-shoulder. Besides that smile, I remember a charming Spanish-American graveyard in pastel stucco, the towering Kennedy shrine, the bubbling, iridescent tubes of algae farming converging toward the horizon, and rockets taking off in the distance with their bright, smokeless exhausts. Emily was almost as unaffected as a British girl and infinitely more competent, in a grand style. That one day the shadows vanished altogether.

They returned at evening when after dinner we gathered in the living room for our first wholly unhurried and relaxed conversation, my lectures being spaced out in a leisurely—to Americans, not to me—one day in two schedule.

We sat in a comfortable arc before the wide fireplace, where resinous woods burned yellow and orange. Occasionally Jack would put on another log. From time to time, a light shower of soot dropped back from the precipitron in the chimney, the tiny particles as they fell flaring into brief white points of light, like stars.

A little to my surprise, the Grissims drank as heavily as the English, though they carried their liquor very well. Emily was the exception to this family pattern, contenting herself with a little sherry and three long, slim reefers, which she drew from an elegant foil package covered with gold script and Lissajous curves, and which she inhaled sippingly, her lips rapidly shuddering with a very faint, low, trilling sound.

Professor Grissim set the pattern by deprecating the reasons for America's domestic achievements, which I had led off by admitting were far greater than I'd expected. They weren't due to any peculiar American drive, he said, and certainly not to any superior moral fiber, but simply to technology and computerized civilization given their full head and unstinting support. The powerful sweep of those two almost mathematical forces had automatically solved such problems as overpopulation, by effortless and aesthetic contraception, and stagnant or warped brain potential, by unlimited semiautomated education and psychiatry—just as on a smaller scale the drug problem had largely been resolved by the legalization of marijuana and peyote, following the simple principle of restricting only the sale of quickly addictive chemicals and those provably damaging to nervous tissue— "Control the poisons, but let each person learn to control his intoxicants, especially now that we have metabolic rectifiers for the congenitally alcoholic."

I was also told that American extremism, both of the right and left, which had seemed such a big thing in mid-century, had largely withered away or at least been muted by the great surge of the same forces which were making America ever more beautiful and prosperous. Cities were no longer warrens of discontent. Peace marches and Minutemen rallies alike, culminating in the late sixties, had thereafter steadily declined.

While impressed, I did not fall into line, but tried to point out some black holes in this glowing picture. Indeed, feeling at home with the Grissims now and having learned that nothing I could say would shock them into anger and confusion, I was able to be myself fully and to reveal frankly my anti-American ideas, though of course more politely and, I hoped, more tellingly than yesterday—it seemed an age ago—driving from the rocketport.

In particular, I argued that many or most Americans were motivated by a subtle, even sophisticated puritanism, which made them feel that the world was not safe unless they were its moral arbiters, and that this puritanism was ultimately based on the same swollen concern about property and money—industry, in its moral sense—

that one found in the Swiss and Scottish Presbyterians and most of the early Protestants.

"You're puritans with a great deal of style and restraint and wide vision," I said. "Yet you're puritans just the same, even though your puritanism is light years away from that of the Massachusetts theocrats and the harsh rule Calvin tried to impose on Geneva. In fact," I added uncautiously, "your puritanism is not so much North European as Roman."

Smiles crinkled briefly at that and I kicked myself for having myself introduced into the conversation that hackneyed comparison.

At this point Emily animatedly yet coolly took up the argument for America, pointing out the nation's growing tolerance and aestheticism, historically distinguishing Puritanism from Calvinism, and also reminding me that the Chinese and Russians were far more puritanical than any other peoples on the globe—and not in a sophisticated or subtle way either.

I fought back, as by citing the different impression I'd got of the Russians during my visits in the Soviet Union and by relaying the reports of close colleagues who had spent time in China. But on the whole Emily had the best of me. And this was only partly due to the fact that the longer I sparred with her verbally, the less concerned I became to win my argument, and the more to break her calm and elicit some sharp emotional reaction from her, to see that pale skin flush, to make those reefer-serene eyes blaze with anger. But I wasn't successful there either.

At one point Jack came to her aid, mildly demonstrating for American broad-mindedness by describing to us some of the pleasure cities of southern Asia he'd visited on R.&R.

"Bangkok's a dismal place now, of course," he began by admitting, "with the Com-g'rillas raiding up to and even into it, and full of fenced-off bombed and booby-trapped areas. Very much like the old descriptions of Saigon in the sixties. As you walk down the potholed streets, you listen for the insect hum of a wandering antipersonnel missile seeking human heat, or the faint flap-flap of an infiltrator coming down on a whirligig parachute. You brace your thoughts against the psychedelic strike of a mind-bomb. Out of the black alley ahead there may charge a fifty-foot steel centipede, the remote-controlled sort we use for jungle fighting, captured by the enemy and jiggered to renegade.

"But most of old Bangkok's attractive features—and the entrepreneurs and girls and other entertainers that go with them—have been transferred en masse to Kandy and Trincomalee in Ceylon." And he went on to describe the gaily orgiastic lounges and bars, the fresh pastel colors, the spicy foods and subtly potent drinks, the clean little laughing harlots supporting their families well during the ten years of their working life between fifteen and twenty-five, the gilded temples, the slim dancers with movements stylized as their black eyebrows, the priests robed in orange and yellow.

I tried to fault him in my mind for being patronizing, but without much success.

"Buddhism's an attractive way of life," he finished, "except that it doesn't know how to wage war. But if you're looking only for nirvana, I guess you don't need to know that." For an instant his tough face grew bleak, as if he could do with a spot of nirvana himself, and the shadows gathered around him and the others more thickly.

During the following off-lecture evenings we kept up our fireplace talks and Emily and I returned more than once to our debate over puritanism, while the rest listened to us with faint, benevolent smiles, that at times seemed almost knowing. She regularly defeated me.

Then on the sixth night she delivered her crowning argument, or celebrated her victory, or perhaps merely followed an impulse. I had just settled myself in bed when the indirect lightning of my "doorbell" flooded the room with brief flashes, coming at three-second intervals, of a rather ghastly white light. Blinking, I fumbled on the bedside table for the remote control of the room's appliances, including tri-V and door, and thumbed the button for the latter.

The door moved aside and there, silhouetted against the faint glow of the hall, was the dark figure of Emily, like a living shadow. She kept her finger, however, on the button long enough for two more silent flashes to illuminate her briefly. She was wearing a narrow kimono—Jack's newest gift, she later told me—and her platinum hair, combed straight down like an unrippling waterfall, almost exactly matched the silvery, pale gray silk. Without quite overdoing it, she had made up her face somewhat like a temple dancer's—pale powder, almost white; narrow slanting brows, almost black; green eye-shadow with a pinch of silvery glitter; and the not-quite-jarring sensual note of crimson lips.

She did not come into my room, but after a pause during which I sat up jerkily and she became again a shadow, she beckoned to me.

I snatched up my dressing gown and followed her as she moved noiselessly down the hall. My throat was dry and constricted, my heart was pounding a little, with apprehension as well as excitement. I realized that despite my near week with the Grissims, a part of my mind was still thinking of the professor and his wife as a strait-laced colonel and his lady from a century ago, when so many retired army officers lived in villas around San Antonio, as they do now too around the Dallas-Ft. Worth metropolitan area.

Emily's bedroom was not the austere silver cell or self-shrine I had sometimes imagined, especially when she was scoring a point against me, but an almost cluttered museum-workshop of present interests and personal memorabilia. She'd even kept her kindergarten study-machine, her first CO_2 pistol, and a hockey stick, along with mementos from her college days and her Peace Corps tours.

But those I noticed much later. Now pale golden light from a rising full moon, coming through the great view window, brimmed the room. I had just enough of my wits left to recall that the real moon was new, so that this must be a tape of some past night. I never even thought of the Communist and American forts up there, with their bombs earmarked for Earth. Then, standing straight and tall and looking me full in the eyes, like some Amazonian athlete, or Phryne before her judges, Emily let her kimono glide down from her shoulders.

In the act of love she was energetic, but tender. No, the word is courteous, I think. I very happily shed a week of tensions and uncertainties and self-inflicted humiliations.

"You still think I'm a puritan, don't you?" she softly asked me afterward, smiling at me sideways with the smeared remains of her crimson mouth, her gray eyes enigmatic blurs of shadow.

"Yes, I do," I told her forthrightly. "The puritan playing the hetaera, but still the puritan."

She answered lazily, "I think you like to play the Hun raping the vestal virgin."

That made me talk dirty to her. She listened attentively—almost famishedly, I thought, for a bit—but her final comment was "You do that very well, dear," just before using her lips to stop mine, which would otherwise have sulphurously cursed her insufferable poise.

Next morning I started to write a poem about her but got lost in analysis and speculation. Tried too soon, I thought.

Although they were as gracious and friendly as ever, I got the impression that the other Grissims had quickly become aware of the change in Emily's and my relationship. Perhaps it was that they showed a slight extra fondness toward me. I don't know how they guessed—Emily was as cool as always in front of them, while I kept trying to play myself, as before. Perhaps it was that the argument about puritanism was never resumed.

Two evenings afterward the talk came around to Jack's and Emily's elder brother Jeff, who had fallen during the Great Retreat from Jammu and Kashmir to Baluchistan. It was mentioned that during his last furlough they had been putting up an exchange instructor from Yugoslavia, a highly talented young sculptress. I gathered that she and Jeff had been quite close.

"I'm glad Jeff knew her love," Emily's mother said calmly, a tear behind her voice, though not on her cheeks. "I'm very glad he had that." The professor unobtrusively put his hand on hers.

I fancied that this remark was directed at me and was her way of giving her blessing to Emily's and my affair. I was touched and at the same time irritated—and also irritated at myself for feeling irritated. Her remark had brought back the sahdows, which darkened further when Jack said a touch grimly and for once with a soldier's callousness, though grinning at me to remove any possible offense, "Remember not to board any more lady artists or professors, mother, at least when I'm on leave. Bad luck."

By now I was distinctly bothered by my poetry block. The last lectures were going swimmingly and I ought to have been feeling creative, but I wasn't. Or rather, I was feeling creative but I couldn't create. I had also begun to notice the way I was fitting myself to the Grissim family—muting myself, despite all the easiness among us. I couldn't help wondering if there weren't a connection between the two things. I had received the instructorship offer, but was delaying my final answer.

After we made love together that night—under a sinking crescent moon, the real night this time, repeated from above—I told Emily about my first trouble only. She pressed my hand. "Never stop writing poetry, dear," she said. "America needs poetry. This family—"

That broken sentence was as close as we ever got to talking about marriage. Emily immediately recovered herself with an uncharacteristically ribald "Cheer up. I don't even charge a poem for admission."

Instead of responding to that cue, I worried my subject. "I should be able to write poetry here," I said. "America is beautiful, the great golden apple of the Hesperides, hanging in the west like the setting sun. But there's a worm in the core of that apple, a great scaly black dragon."

When Emily didn't ask a question, I went on, "I remember an advertisement. 'Join all your little debts into one big debt.' Of course, they didn't put it so baldly, they made it sound wonderful. But you Americans are like that. You've collected all your angers into one big anger. You've removed your angers from things at home—where you seem to have solved your problems very well, I must admit— and directed those angers at the Communist League. Or instead of angers, I could say fears. Same thing."

Emily still didn't comment, so I continued, "Take the basic neurotic. He sets up a program of perfection for himself—a thousand obligations, a thousand ambitions. As long as he works his program, fulfilling those obligations and ambitions, he does very well. In fact, he's apt to seem like a genius of achievement to those around him, as America does to me. But there's one big problem he always keeps out of his program and buries deep in his unconscious—the question of who he really is and what he really wants—and in the end it always throws him."

Then at last Emily said, speaking softly at first, "There's something I should tell you, dear. Although I talk a lot of it from the top of my mind, deep down I loathe discussing politics and international relations. As my old colonel used to tell me, 'It doesn't matter much which side you fight on, Emily, so long as you have the courage to stand up and be counted. You pledge your life, your fortune, and your sacred honor, and you live up to that pledge!' And now, dear, I want to sleep."

Crouching on the edge of her bed before returning to my room, and listening to her breathing regularize itself, I thought, "Yes, you're looking for nirvana too. Like Jack." But I didn't wake her to say it, or any of the other things that were boiling up in my brain.

Yet the things I left unsaid must have stayed and worked in my mind, for at our next fireside talk—four pleasant Americans, one Englishman with only one more lecture to go—I found myself launched into a rather long account of the academic Russian family I stayed with while delivering the Pushkin Lectures in Leningrad, where the smog and the minorities problems have been licked too. I stressed the Rosanovs' gentility, their friendliness, the tolerance and sophistication which had replaced the old rigid insistence on *kulturny* behavior, and also the faint melancholy underlying and somehow vitiating all they said. In short, I did everything I knew to underline their similarity to the Grissims. I ended by saying "Professor Grissim, the first night we talked, you said America's achievement had been due almost entirely to the sweep of science, technology, and computerized civilization. The people of the Communist League believe that too—in fact, they made their declaration of faith earlier than America."

"It's very strange," he mused, nodding. "So like, yet so unlike. Almost as if the chemical atoms of the East were subtly different from those of the West. The very electrons—"

"Professor, you don't actually think—"

"Of course not. A metaphor only."

But whatever he thought, I don't believe he felt it only as a metaphor.

Emily said sharply to me, "You left out one more similarity, the most important. That they hate the Enemy with all their hearts and will never trust or understand him."

I couldn't find an honest and complete answer to that, though I tried.

The next day I made one more attempt to turn my feelings into poetry, dark poetry, and I failed. I made my refusal of the instructorship final, confirmed my reservation on the Dallas-London rocket for day after tomorrow, and delivered the last of the Lanier Lectures.

The Fourth of July was a quiet day. Emily took me on a repeat of our first scooter jaunt, but although I relished the wind on my face and our conversation was passably jolly and tender, the magic was gone. I could hardly see America's beauty for the shadows my mind projected on it.

Our fireside conversation that night was as brightly banal. Midway we all went outside to watch the fireworks. It was a starry night, very clear of course, and the fireworks seemed vastly remote—transitory extra starfields of pink and green and amber. Their faint cracks and booms sounded infinitely distant, and needless to say, there was not a ribbon or whiff of chemical smoke. I was reminded of my last night in Leningrad with the Rosanovs after the Pushkin Lectures. We'd all strolled down the Kirovskiy Prospekt to the Bolshaya Neva, and across its glimmering waters watched the Vladivostok mail rocket take off from the Field of Mars up its ringed electric catapult taller far than the Eiffel Tower. That had been on a May Day.

Later that night I went for the first time by myself to Emily's door and pressed its light-button. I was afraid she wouldn't stop by for me and I needed her. She was in a taut and high-strung mood, unwilling to talk in much more than monosyllables, yet unable to keep still, pacing like a restless feline. She wanted to play in the view window the tape of a real battle in Bolivia with the original sounds too, muted down. I vetoed that and we settled for an authentic forest fire recorded in Alaska.

Sex and catastrophe fit. With the wild red light pulsing and flaring in the bedroom, casting huge wild shadows, and with the fire's muted roar and hurricane crackle and explosions filling our ears, we made love with a fierce and desperate urgency that seemed almost—I am eternally grateful for the memory—as if it would last forever. Sex and a psychedelic trip also have their meeting point.

Afterward I slept like a sated tiger. Emily waited until dawn to wake me and shoo me back to my bedroom.

Next day all the Grissims saw me off. As we strolled from the silver station wagon to the landing area, Emily and I dropped a little behind. She stopped, hooked her arms around me, and kissed me with a devouring ferocity. The others walked on, too well bred ever to look back. The next moment she was her cool self again, sipping a reefer.

Now the rocketship is arching down. The stars are paling. There is a faint whistling as the air molecules of the stratosphere begin to carom off the titanium skin. We had only one flap, midway of freefall section of the trip, when we briefly accelerated and then decelerated to match, perhaps in order to miss a spy satellite or one of the atomic-headed watchdog rockets eternally circling the globe. The direction comes, "Secure seat harnesses."

I just don't know. Maybe I should have gone to America drunk as Dylan Thomas, but purposefully, bellowing my beliefs like the word or the thunderbolts of God. Maybe then I could have fought the shadows. No. . . .

I hope Emily makes it to London. Perhaps there, against a very different background, with shadows of a different sort . . .

In a few more seconds the great jet will begin to brake, thrusting its hygienic, aseptic exhaust of helium down into the filthy cancerous London smog, and I will be home.

Afterword

All I ever try to write is a good story with a good measure of strangeness in it. The supreme goddess of the universe is Mystery, and being well entertained is the highest joy.

I write my stories against backgrounds of science, history and fantasy worlds of swords and sorcery. I write about the intensely strange everyday human mind and the weird and occult—about which I am a skeptic yet which interest me vastly. I always try to be meticulously accurate in handling these backgrounds, to be sure of my facts no matter what fantastic stories I build from them.

The tales in this volume are predominantly science fantasy. They are arranged in the order in which they were first published, all except "Gonna Roll the Bones." It seemed best to lead off with a story that displayed to advantage all my talents, such as they are. It was actually written next to the last of the twenty-two stories in this book.

I'm sure you'll agree that authors' remarks are egotistical effusions at best, so I'll devote this space to telling a bit of the history of the stories—and to effusing egotistically.

"Gonna Roll the Bones" was written to a dull anticlimax and set aside for six months. After this fortuitous opportunity for subconscious growth, it was rewritten under pressure to meet the deadline of Harlan Ellison's monumental anthology *Dangerous Visions*. The story luckily won the Hugo and Nebula novelette awards for 1967. Theodore Sturgeon said of it in a review, "Fritz Leiber is at his cadenced, ringing best in a completely successful blend of science fiction and myth, adventure and horror."

"Sanity" and "Wanted—An Enemy" were done for *Astounding Stories* (now *Analog*) and its master editor John W. Campbell, Jr., who taught me more about plotting and motivation than any other individual. These two stories reflect my wry worries about war, pacifism, and world government.

"The Man Who Never Grew Young" seemed to write itself (Ray Bradbury told me he wished he'd written it. Do all *his* stories write themselves? I doubt it) for my first hardcover book, published by Arkham House and the ever-helpful August Derleth.

"The Ship Sails at Midnight" is the romantic tale of a love that was unconventional, at least then. The goddess Mystery makes an appearance, perhaps. I picked it as my best single story for a Derleth anthology.

"The Enchanted Forest" was another story for Campbell—and for another Derleth anthology—done after a dry period of some five years.

"Coming Attraction," which Judith Merril calls "satire at its most terrifyingly prophetic," was denounced by a minority of its first readers as Unamerican (I don't know why—it's Unrussian too) and praised by quite a few fellow writers. Isaac Asimov said, "Can times become even more neurotic than they are now? Well, read 'Coming Attraction' by Fritz Leiber on our neurotic future." It and the novelette "Poor Superman" mirror the intense concern of 1950 with McCarthyism, computerization and, above all, the bomb. Damon Knight said about the novelette, "Fritz Leiber is at his brilliant best when sticking pins into some prominent member of the American Paranoids' Association—e.g., Mickey Spillane in "The Night He Cried," or, in the present case, our old friend Alfred van Vogt." (Wrong on the second count, Damon. In "Poor Superman" I had in mind L. Ron Hubbard and Campbell himself, the latter a very helpful but very well-intentioned innocent bystander at the monstrous birth of dianetics, mother of scientology.) "A Pail of Air" pictures a struggle against another sort of world doom. All three stories were published in Horace Gold's then new (1950), stimulatingly modern magazine, *Galaxy*.

"The Big Holiday" was my second sale (1953) to the other new, stimulatingly modern—and highly literate—magazine, *Fantasy and Science Fiction.* Its editor, the brilliant Anthony Boucher, helped me more than any other person—but perhaps for H. P. Lovecraft and Harry Fischer—to give my stories style and literary polish. Boucher called my story "the finest conception we have yet of the *fun* of the future—a Breughel-like canvas of merriment."

As Damon Knight noted, I wrote "The Night He Cried" because I was distantly angry at Mickey Spillane for the self-satisfied violence and loveless sex and anti-feminism he was introducing into detective fiction *and* because he had the temerity to publish a couple of stories in the fantasy field, about which I have a parental concern. My rage seems remote now, yet the point was valid.

"The Big Trek" got me a gorgeous magazine-cover illustration by Emsh. Like "Foxholes," it was first written with a modern setting and sold only when I gave it a colorful futurian one.

"Space-Time for Springers" was my first story about the self-sufficient and subtle aristocrats of the animal world. Frederik Pohl wrote of it extravagantly, "Fritz Leiber was not born with a caul—believe it if you can! For his greatest gift is the knack of second sight, the talent that sees beneath the outer garments of flesh and blood into the heart of things, and people—and of cats."

"Try and Change the Past" was my first short story in the Change-War or Big-Time series. The novel *The Big Time,* published simultaneously, went on to win me my first Hugo.

The novelette "A Deskful of Girls" got me another colorful magazine cover, this one by Kelly Freas. The story is about the sexual hangups and love goddesses of the 1950s, written for fun and chills.

"Rump-Titty-Titty-Tum-Tah-Tee" takes a humorous look at arty intellectuals and advertisers. Anthony Boucher remarked of it, "An editor finds himself fascinated and a little frightened when he publishes a story which evokes such disproportionately intense response as to make it obvious that the author has unconsciously hit upon some basic and deeply communicative symbol."

"Little Old Miss Macbeth" caused Robert P. Mills, then editor of *Fantasy and Science Fiction,* to observe, "Surely Fritz Leiber is the most vividly *visual* of all science-fantasy writers." This seems extreme, yet for me vision *is* "worth all the rest" of the senses, as Macbeth put it. It may be due to my youth as an actor and the child of actors. I visualize most of my stories and set many of them on an imaginary stage. Some, like *The Big Time,* have only one set.

"Mariana" was another story that seemed to write itself—a gift from the goddesses *after* I had unremittingly toiled word by word through four tales for the all-Leiber issue of the magazine *Fantastic,* the last one of which hung me up so that the only way I could finish it was to write it *backwards* from the end to the middle, scene by laborious scene. "Mariana" was selected by Judith Merril for *The Year's Best SF.*

So was "The Man Who Made Friends With Electricity," a supernatural horror story stemming from the California environment of my last decade and a half. Before that, Chicago was my place.

"The Good New Days" looks at the Beat Generation and our slum planet, but aims at entertainment first.

"America the Beautiful" might be thought of as "Coming Attraction" revisited. Another Britisher encounters a different, but equally disturbing future America. Low-key and heavy on the atmosphere, but as always I've tried to make the story the thing.

So there you have them, the best of my science-fantasy stories, in my estimation. Three from the 1940s, no less than fourteen from the 1950s, four from the 1960s, one from the 1970s. 1958 was my peak year by this numerical and egocentric criterion, with five stories. 1950 was second, with three, while 1951 and 1952 had two apiece. I seem to have had four chief bursts of creativity, triggered off by the Second World War, the nuclear bomb, the sputniks, and the war in Vietnam. I'm glad I've been able to react to those dreadful stimuli with laughter as well as fears. Edmund Cooper wrote in *The Sunday Times* of London, "Fritz Leiber has a wicked imagination. Wicked enough to make us laugh at an impossible future containing nightmarish aspects of our own times."

So, as I say, there you have them, the best of my science-fantasy stories. But I hope to write better ones. I'll never stop writing. It's one occupation in which being crazy, even senile, *might* help.

—FRITZ LEIBER